DEAD
TIDE

Fiona McIntosh is an internationally bestselling author of novels for adults and children. She co-founded an award-winning travel magazine with her husband, which they ran for fifteen years while raising their twin sons before she became a full-time author. Fiona roams the world researching and drawing inspiration for her novels, and runs a series of highly respected fiction masterclasses. She calls South Australia home.

FIONA McINTOSH

DEAD TIDE

MICHAEL JOSEPH
an imprint of
PENGUIN BOOKS

MICHAEL JOSEPH

UK | USA | Canada | Ireland | Australia
India | New Zealand | South Africa | China

Michael Joseph is part of the Penguin Random House group of companies
whose addresses can be found at global.penguinrandomhouse.com.

Penguin
Random House
Australia

First published by Michael Joseph, 2023

Cover photography/illustrations: beach by Fiona McIntosh; figure and birds
© Silas Manhood/Trevillion Images
Cover design by Louisa Maggio Design
Typeset in Bembo by Midland Typesetters, Australia

Printed and bound in Australia by Griffin Press, an accredited
ISO AS/NZS 14001 Environmental Management Systems printer

A catalogue record for this
book is available from the
National Library of Australia

ISBN 978 1 76104 647 6

penguin.com.au

We at Penguin Random House Australia acknowledge that Aboriginal and Torres Strait Islander
peoples are the Traditional Custodians and the first storytellers of the lands on which we live
and work. We honour Aboriginal and Torres Strait Islander peoples' continuous connection
to Country, waters, skies and communities. We celebrate Aboriginal and Torres Strait Islander
stories, traditions and living cultures; and we pay our respects to Elders past and present.

For the three McIntosh boys, reunited in Adelaide.
Great to have you home, Will, Jack and Jason.

1

When would it stop? They'd said nothing about lingering pain, but these cramps forced her to hold her breath and count through them when they came; they were like something too big trying to squeeze through a small hole. Agonising while they lasted . . . and they were lasting increasingly longer, becoming more frequent.

Had they left something behind? Had they torn something?

The cramps were invisible. But the bloating . . . Amelia hoped she could somehow wing an excuse for wearing her raincoat indoors. She pretended to fuss inside her satchel, feigning distraction with files and notebooks so Mads wouldn't ask what was wrong, but she knew it was futile. Mads missed nothing and the bright toothpaste white of her spanking new A-line waterproof rain jacket was like a beacon, demanding the question be asked.

The lecturer cast a glance out across his small class, who were studying crime and its definitions this semester. 'Ah, Miss Peters. I see you've decided to rejoin us.' From any of the other lecturers, the words may have cut deep enough to wound. But coming from Detective Superintendent Jack Hawksworth, with his warm tone and ghosting smile, it felt like a welcome. He followed it up – 'Feeling better?' – confirming to Amelia why he was her favourite tutor . . . probably everyone's favourite this semester. Pity he wasn't here permanently.

She blushed. 'Bit of a sniffle,' she lied. 'I didn't want to pass it around.'

'For which we're all grateful to you,' Jack Hawksworth said, pulling files from a briefcase and placing them on the desk in a short stack. His grin widened. 'You're back just in time for the gruesome stuff. So I promised you all a summary of what a day in the life of a detective attending a post-mortem feels like.'

This won some murmured cheers of approval.

Her friend Madeleine – Mads – slid her an approving look, murmuring, 'I like your raincoat.'

'Not too clinical?' Amelia replied quickly, hoping to joke her way through the oddity of still being dressed for outdoors.

Mads grinned. 'No. It's rather spectacular, actually. I'd like one in every colour.'

'You can afford to,' Amelia quipped.

'Aren't you warm?'

Amelia feigned a shiver as she felt the low but reaching tendrils of another cramp warning her of its impending arrival. 'No. I think I've caught something.'

'I thought you'd call,' Mads whispered as Hawksworth turned his back to write something on the whiteboard.

'I only got back yesterday morning,' Amelia said under her breath, looking away from the handsome lecturer's back.

'And?'

'Fine,' she murmured, lying again. 'Well, I am feeling a bit yuck, but that's to be expected, apparently. I didn't dare take any more time away from lectures, especially not *his*,' she said, returning her gaze to the very senior detective, who had taken a sabbatical to teach this short course for university students.

'In the UK we call this forensic pathology a post-mortem, while in America it's known as an autopsy. It's an identical process. The pathologist is establishing what exactly killed the person who is lying on their table, but out of that study will come a host of other valuable information that can add enormous assistance to the investigating team if the death is suspicious.'

Hawksworth wrote some bullet points on the whiteboard, his felt marker squeaking on the plastic surface.

'Let me give you a good example of how a death that appeared rather straightforward turned out to be a lot more complicated and resulted in a conviction of murder . . .'

Mads persisted. 'So when are you going to tell me how it all went down? Or is it still a big secret?'

'No.' Amelia frowned. 'After class we can—'

'Er, Miss Rundle?'

Both their gazes snapped to Hawksworth as he turned from the board to look directly at Mads. 'Call me a narcissist, but I hate competing for attention. Both you and Miss Peters might benefit from tuning in to this if you plan to pass this semester.'

They murmured apologies in unified embarrassment.

Something about his amused expression told Amelia that in another setting, Hawksworth might have winked. He didn't. Instead, he returned to his anecdote about a day when he was still a young detective constable and had attended his first 'PM', as he called it, and passed out in the city mortuary, banging his chin on one of the tables and requiring stitches. That soon had the whole class, including the two girls, smiling.

'It's true, and the least auspicious start I could have made, being sneered at by Dr Blood, as we knew him – one of the most senior and least empathetic pathologists that Scotland Yard had dealings with. The first day we all filed in, he slid a drawer from the mortuary fridge, removed a partially eaten sandwich, took a bite and put it back.'

The class gasped, some chuckling, and Hawksworth continued, with everyone now seemingly hanging on his words.

'Then he slid out another drawer, this time with a corpse inside to reinforce the need for the tag on the toe, et cetera. He explained in great detail why we had to count the bodies in when we arrived and out when we left, and enter that figure into the book. And then he, casual as you please, began making an incision into a body from neck to navel. "Get that out of the way," I think his words were, referring to me, pale and leaning against his fridge,' Hawksworth said, bringing more laughter.

Amelia and Madeleine forgot their private conversation and focused on the lecture. Hawksworth went on to describe what initially appeared to be a clear-cut case of rape and murder but became far more complex as the pathologist discovered a sinister illness within the victim that was likely the cause of death, even though she'd been physically abused during a break-in.

Later, in the café, huddled in a corner to stay warm on the chilly spring day, Mads winkled the story out of Amelia about what was really going on with her.

'To tell you the truth, there's not really much to say. It was like a mini break,' she explained on the tail end of a mighty cramp that caused her to ball her fists beneath the table as she tried not to show too much in her expression. 'There were three of us. One was from Birmingham, another from a place called Hassocks . . . and me.' She found a smile.

'All from universities?'

'Two of us were. The girl from Hassocks was a barmaid, a bit older than us but not by that much. We all needed money.' Amelia shrugged.

'So, carry on. You went to the airport. Then what?'

'They drove me to London City Airport and escorted me to the gate and onto a JAT Airways flight to Vilnius.'

'Oh, posh. Now, where's that again?'

'Blimey, Mads, did you do any geography at school?' The pain had passed again. She could be herself.

Her friend laughed. 'Hated it.'

'It's the capital of Lithuania. The old quarter, as they call it, is lovely in its own way. Some parts of the city are a bit Cold War, but we weren't in that section. It was very modern where we were taken.' She sipped her coffee, remembering the excellent hot chocolates she had enjoyed at the old-style chocolate salons in the cobbled streets of Vilnius, while she waited for her body to do what it knew how to do. 'The hotel was like any hotel,' she remarked.

'Oh, like you stay in them all the time, Millie,' Mads sneered, but with mirth.

'It was nothing special, but nothing bad about it. A room key, a bed, a bathroom, room service. It was a tiny modern apartment, like that one we stayed in at York when we visited.'

'Oh, well, that's disappointing. I was hoping you were going to come back with stories of something more Slavic.'

'It's not Slavic, you oaf. It's a Baltic country.'

'Russian, whatever.'

'Old USSR,' Amelia corrected. 'The clinic . . .' Her words trailed off and she gave a grimace, unable to hide it this time. The pain was unbearable again. She held her head against the palm of her hand.

'What's wrong?'

Amelia shook her head. 'I really don't feel that well.' She knew she'd been ailing in a shallow way for days. Now it felt like she was sinking much deeper into whatever it was her body was fighting. She could feel her belly swelling, tightening against the elastic of her trackpants.

'What sort of not well?'

'I think I'm going to throw up.'

'Come on, let's get some air.'

Amelia allowed herself to be helped up from the table. Suddenly, even the sound of the coffee being ground was like a hammer in her mind. She leaned against the wall, trying to look inconspicuous while Mads paid.

Her friend returned. 'Any better?'

'No, worse, I think. Something's wrong, Mads. My head feels like it's going to explode, but so does my tummy.'

Mads supported her as they left the café, ostensibly cradling her shoulders but in all truth holding her up, Amelia realised.

Mads tried to reassure her. 'It's different food, different water. You only got back yesterday, so you're jetlagged . . . and all those drugs you mentioned – they've got to be having some side effects,' she rationalised. 'Either that or you've got food poisoning.' She tipped her friend a sympathetic grin.

Amelia wanted to believe it, but her instincts were saying otherwise. She let Mads lead her to a taxi rank.

'Don't make a fuss,' Mads said. 'It's on me. You know how Dad insists on sending money each month.'

'I'll pay you back.'

'Don't be daft. Make me a chocolate cake or something. You know I can't bake.'

The taxi ride back to the share house in Putney took an age. When they finally arrived, neither of Amelia's flatmates were around. She struggled to get her key out of her bag.

'Bloody hell, you're useless. Let me,' Mads said cheerfully. She pushed open the door and sighed. 'I'm glad it's the ground floor, Millie, 'cause I doubt I'd be able to carry you any further.' She was trying to brighten her up; Amelia could hear it. 'Sofa or bed?'

'Bed,' she said, with a groan.

Mads helped her to undress and change into a T-shirt and pyjama bottoms. 'Do you mind me mentioning that your tummy looks swollen?'

'I don't know what's happening,' Amelia said, now struggling to speak because it hurt so much. 'Painkillers.' She pointed in the direction of her dressing table, the one she'd bought at a boot sale and painted a pistachio colour in the shabby chic style.

'These are ibuprofen,' Mads said, looking at the box. 'I don't think you should take any more of those until you see a doctor, which I'm going to organise next – and Mum, as she'll bring a car over. Let me make some tea for you.' She headed into the kitchen, where Amelia could hear her clanking about with a kettle and teapot.

She let herself sink deeper into her pillow. What was happening? They had warned that the drugs and all the stimulation they produced in her body could make her belly swell. So perhaps she was a textbook case in that regard. But the clinic had said nothing about pain. She needed relief. It was becoming too hard to wince through, as the sharp waves of each cramp crashed to shore. On the rim of her mind, she was aware of Mads calling for an ambulance, and then she phoned Amelia's mum and her own.

All arrived too late. Amelia was dead by midnight.

2

DUBAI

As an ambulance was hurtling towards Putney, and two startled mothers were dropping what they were doing and climbing into taxis, a man in his thirties had just taken his seat in Row 54 of an aircraft about to leave Dubai International Airport.

He was on the aisle, his preferred position, but hadn't yet buckled in to seat 54C, presuming there would be other passengers needing to squeeze past. Like everyone in his situation, he began to daydream that they never arrived and he miraculously had the whole row to himself. His company really should be paying for business class, he thought. His role deserved it, but the company said economy made him less conspicuous and they couldn't justify charging the client more.

Yeah, yeah. He hated being the grunt, with all the risk and no privilege. He snuck a peek down the aisle, hoping that the couple with the hideous matching tracksuits and excessive gold jewellery were not about to look over his head and say, 'This is us.'

He could smell the woman's perfume already, and the man's backwards-facing cap, deliberately unshaven face and exaggerated strut told him plenty about this couple. Her name was going to be something like Sharlet or Shardae, and he would call her Shar or Shardy. His name would be Nicky or Nico.

He shook his head slightly. When did he get to be so mean? He liked his job, if he was honest with himself; he certainly loved the travel, enjoying the absence from home and the downtime in new cities. But with each subsequent journey he could feel the craving for more status. The pay was okay, but he was the one at the coalface, taking the risks, exposing himself to scrutiny. All he wanted was the chance to sit in the fancy airline lounges, drinking sparkling water from chilled glass bottles or ordering a glass of wine, and not have to mix with the herd.

The A380 had a lot more space than the triple sevens, and he was relieved it was the flight to Sydney and not the direct to Adelaide this time, which had been a regular route for the past three journeys. He far preferred this aircraft, which didn't service South Australia. Even though he had to transfer to Adelaide first, it was easier and quicker to get out of Adelaide Airport; there were fewer passengers and now, with e-passports, he and the other wily passengers from the lower deck could rush past the gang of rich boomers on their way back from Europe. Achy joints and dithering minds would give them cause to deliberate whether to pause in the Duty Free or just keep going, juggling passports, searching for the spectacles they'd already taken the precaution of putting on their heads or tucking into pockets.

His mother regularly waggled a finger at him when he made these amusing observations. 'One day, Greg, you'll be our age and your children will give you that not-very-well disguised sneer when you are taking longer than them to do something. And you'll remember this moment that will come back to haunt you.'

She'd said it playfully and they'd laughed, but he still felt far too young to be caught dead wondering where his glasses were or which queue to join.

He made an effort to appear unassuming in his job, remaining as unmemorable as possible, as the company requested. He was neatly but casually dressed in a soft grey hoodie and long-sleeved T-shirt over worn-in jeans and leather sneakers. Only the sneakers shouted their brand – everything else he wore noted its brand only with modest, tiny logos.

As a middle-aged couple arrived for the two spare seats beside him, he politely moved to the aisle and did not show his disappointment at not having the row to himself. Instead, he smiled at them, even helping to store their hand luggage, fussing to get it to fit alongside his rather large backpack.

'Thank you,' the woman said. 'Now, I've got everything out that I think I might need,' she added unnecessarily, and he didn't break his smile as she got settled next to the window, pushing her things into the seat pocket.

The man who accompanied her remained standing, aware others were coming behind. He had a sharper tone in his voice as he spoke. 'Be sure, love, because we don't want to be pests.' He glanced at their neighbour. 'Hi, I'm Pete, and this is my wife, Sue,' he said, slipping into the row next to his wife.

'Greg,' he replied, pressing himself up against the seats so a family carrying a young child with red and watery eyes could move through.

The men's eyes met. 'Let's hope he sleeps,' Pete said, sounding wearied already.

'I hope I won't need to bother you, Greg,' Sue said, peeping around her husband standing in front of the middle seat. She was holding her iPad, touching the glasses that were held on a shiny rope around her neck and checking again that a toiletries bag was at her feet. Two passports and a pen were tucked into the seat pocket in case they were needed, as well as her husband's paperback.

'Charger?' Greg offered. 'It's a long flight between here and Sydney.'

'Charger!' she exclaimed. 'Thank you.' And they had to get down her hand luggage once again, Pete rolling his eyes. 'I'll scream if I run out of power for my iPad,' she explained.

'Sorry about this, mate,' Pete said.

Greg shook his head kindly as if it really was trifling, despite inwardly screaming at the tedium of it all.

'Right, settled?' Pete said, eyeing Sue. He took his seat in the middle.

'All sorted,' his wife said.

'Don't worry, just let me know if you need anything,' Greg said, taking the bag and replacing it overhead, checking once again that his backpack was flush against the side of the luggage compartment and had not been disturbed. He finally sat.

Across the aisle, a much younger man with gingery blond dreadlocks, joshing with his mate who was seated and chewing gum, heaved a bag carelessly into the same compartment.

'Hey, be careful,' Greg said, his tone changing for the first time. He stood up again.

'Sorry, mate. You've got loads of room in there.'

'Fine, but don't fling stuff around.'

'I didn't *fling*,' the dreadlocked fellow said, sounding indignant.

Greg could see the green gum at the corner of the younger man's mouth. A waft of peppermint sat between them.

'Can I help?' the flight attendant asked, his cologne swirling towards them before he did as he sensed a problem and arrived into the tension. The cologne mixed with peppermint created a strange aroma that was sickening at two o'clock in the morning.

'Nah, all good,' Greg said. 'Just sorting out space.'

'Is that fragile?' The attendant, who was Filipino, Greg thought, wore a badge that denoted him as Benjie. He nodded towards Greg's backpack. He wore a bright, white smile that he'd obviously practised a lot.

Greg gave a shrug. 'Well, not fragile, but I don't really want other stuff thrown against it.' He knew he sounded petulant, and he watched the dreadlocked man from 54E roll his eyes. Benjie, meanwhile, schooled his features to neutral, but Greg could tell that behind his even expression he wanted to do the same.

Pete and Sue were watching him too, Sue casting him a reassuring nod of sympathy, as though she agreed that people had lost their manners in modern air travel. He half expected her to say to anyone who might listen, 'Gone are the days of dressing for travel. This tracksuit laziness shouldn't be allowed!' but she didn't; instead, she began fiddling with the articulated folds of her iPad's leather cover and keyboard, which seemed to baffle her momentarily.

'There's plenty of room,' Benjie confirmed, pointing to yawning bins elsewhere that had little in them. 'It's not a full flight tonight.' His look suggested that Dreadlocks could make the standoff disappear if he would only move his gear. Another flight attendant excused herself as she pushed past them all and whispered something. Benjie gave the air a kiss in her direction to make her laugh.

'S'okay, mate. I can use that one,' Dreadlocks said, bringing everyone relief.

'Thanks,' Greg said calmly, inwardly relieved.

'No worries,' Dreadlocks breezed and he winked at his mate in 54D, who grinned back, mouthing something cheeky.

Greg finally settled himself back into seat 54C but his mind was churning. He could lipread and had just caught what the man in the seat opposite had said: *Let's hope it's not a bomb in that backpack!*

★

On the other side of the world, in metropolitan South Australia, a woman in her early thirties accepted the encouraging smile of her husband and felt the squeeze of his hand while they waited.

'We did the right thing,' Simon said, as if able to listen in and answer the question that had been bouncing around her mind for months.

She nodded. They'd talked it over so many times. Her nerves felt stretched so tight they were like cling film over a vessel; she was convinced her mind would make a drumming sound if it were tapped. Her treacherous eyes began to leak helpless tears.

'Anna, you do want this, right?'

'Of course,' she ground out through the emotion choking her throat. 'I want this more than anything but . . .'

'But what? We can still pull—'

'No, no, that's not what I mean. I just wish they were mine . . . ours. From both of us.'

His expression crumpled. Simon wasn't prone to tears but his eyes became moist as he nodded. 'In a perfect world,' he murmured. 'But this is the only way, Anna.'

She squeezed his hand back to get his full attention. 'I'm just feeling nervous and it's making me go over old ground. We've talked this over and over and we wouldn't be here right now if we both didn't believe this was the way – something we both want.' She sniffed, starting to get on top of the crush of anxiety. 'I love that we at least have you in all of this. I feel jealous that we don't have me, that's all.'

'We do though,' he pressed, his tone earnest and full of reason. 'After today it's all about you. You alone can make this happen.' He bent closer to ensure she understood. 'I love you, Anna. Today we start our family.'

'What if it doesn't—?'

'Shhh.' He covered her lips with his fingertips. 'It will.'

The door opened and the gynaecologist bustled in. Anna could tell he was smiling behind his mask. 'Ready, Anna? Simon?' he asked, sounding bright, full of optimism. They'd met so many times, had him commiserate so often, that they greeted each other like friends. He seated himself on a stool between Anna's bent legs. Her feet were in stirrups, and he now pushed her gown halfway up her thighs. He too was fully gowned, his thatch of blond hair, which Anna had previously noted was just beginning to show silvery flecks at the temple, caught up in a hat that looked like an old-fashioned shower cap. His eyes smiled at her behind the lenses of his clear glasses. 'Feeling powerful, Anna?'

'I'm ready,' she said, her voice almost cracking on the surge of anticipation she was sure they were all feeling.

'*Believe*, okay?' He waited for her nod. 'Right, now relax all your muscles for me.'

So easy for a bloke to say that. It wasn't his vagina. He didn't even have one to know how wretched the process felt. She felt the cool of the speculum enter her body and curve up before she heard the horrible ratcheting noise of the screw being turned to open the walls of her vagina. She was used to it. Didn't stop her hating it, of course, just like every other woman on the planet who had experienced a pelvic examination or pap smear. For Anna, though, it was just another uncomfortable, sometimes painful, hurdle to get over that took her closer to the finish line.

'Inserting the tube now. Relax for me, Anna,' he said again, sounding more commanding. 'I know that's counterintuitive but everything now is about you losing all the tension in your body. Be ready to greet your embryos. Make it feel welcoming, not hard and hostile.'

'Trying,' she panted, wanting to add, *you bastard*. But he was simply doing his best by her, she knew that.

'I know, I know. All my patients wish I could be a woman for just one day and have this done to me.'

At least he understood that much. She tried to smile but only managed to nod through tears, then watched him reach towards the hatch in the wall where a masked clinician – she couldn't tell whether it was a man or woman – also fully robed, reached through to hand the doctor a tiny syringe. *My future*, she thought. *Please, babies. Please . . . one of you hang on for me.*

'Thanks,' the doctor said and quickly inserted the syringe into the thin, flexible tube already in place in the opening of her cervix. 'Here we go, Anna and Simon. We are putting in two beautiful embryos that you've created.'

It was kind of him to say it that way. Both she and Simon knew the magic had happened in a laboratory. It was Simon's sperm, but not her egg. They'd chosen the donor from a catalogue and although she'd tried to put it out of her mind and she'd certainly not aired the notion, it had felt like shopping. At first it had been fun, and she'd felt full of excitement as she stared deep into the faces of the women who were prepared to donate their eggs.

They were all young in the section that Anna and Simon had chosen from. All fertile twenty-somethings and, in this group, all Caucasian. Anna was blonde and Simon was dark-haired, so a child with their genes would likely be dark too; she felt lucky that any of the donors would be suitable in this respect. She and Simon were both blue-eyed, so that cut down the choices to the donors with blue, green or grey eyes. Anna didn't want to think of herself as shallow enough to be drawn to the women whose features sat together in a way she considered pretty; it seemed ludicrous that in her situation of being so desperate to have a baby she would let the looks of the donor be important . . . and still they were. Somewhere in her desperation of not being able to use her own genetic material, she wanted the child to possess some of her physical attributes. They wouldn't have her personality or character traits but she could live with that, as the child would share some of Simon's, and he was the loveliest man next to her father who walked the earth, she was sure. She adored Simon, so she would adore his child, assuming she could carry it to full term. But it still grated that these women were fulfilling her role, that it was eggs from one of their ovaries that would make her baby. If the child's looks echoed her own somehow, it would help make sure she was never tempted to think of her child as anything but hers.

They'd whittled the catalogue of potentials down to two donors. No names or addresses were shown. The two they'd chosen were 'A from UK' or 'C from Denmark'. Both were blonde, blue-eyed. One was pretty in a girl-next-door sort of way. The other was more classically pretty with elfin features and a dreamy expression. Simon liked the Dane. But Anna felt herself drawn to the British girl. She looked normal, down to earth, and while none of the photos showed the girls smiling – they were all like passport photos – the UK donor looked like she was suppressing a smile.

Anna liked that because she knew at one time, before babies became the single topic on which her thoughts turned, she'd been like that, full of secret smiles about everything from the man she was falling in love with to her career as a children's book illustrator. It suggested the donor was giving her eggs with joy . . . a gift of pleasure. Sure, she was being paid for her DNA material, not that the catalogue mentioned the ugly business of money. Instead, it emphasised how much these young women wanted to help others to have children. It wasn't that she didn't believe it. But somewhere over the course of her years of trying for a baby, with the miscarriages and failed IVF cycles, she had fallen into a state of cynicism. For a start, A from UK didn't look old enough to be in the years of motherhood, so her supposed desire to help others experience the joy of being a parent felt insincere. But Anna didn't care. She was glad to have access to A from UK for the gift of her healthy young eggs. She already knew A's eggs had accepted Simon's sperm – a fact that somehow, ridiculously, made her feel a pang of jealousy, but deeply grateful at the same time.

'Watch the screen, you two . . .' The gynaecologist paused dramatically. 'And a flash . . .' he said. 'Did you see it?'

They both murmured into the silence that they had. Anna felt Simon squeeze her shoulder.

'That was both embryos going in. And we're done,' he said, sounding triumphant. 'Now you take over, Anna. You and Mother Nature are going to work this out.'

She felt the withdrawal of the equipment from her body and the slight soreness left behind; she was probably bleeding slightly. It meant stinging when she urinated for a day or so, and there would definitely be no sex. All that counted now was the two embryos that had begun to divide and show their potential, to make themselves comfy within. She just prayed that they kept dividing, kept growing.

3

LONDON

Jack looked out into the class as his students got settled. It was the penultimate tutorial he would hold before returning to his old life as a detective, and as much as he knew it was time to get back into the saddle, he wondered if he was ready. Maybe he should accept the offer of another semester at the university. It was tempting, and would please the Dean.

Lecturing was certainly a change in pace and perspective from life working an op. And after the last one, which had involved so much death and despair – not to mention a hospital bed – he had welcomed the absorbing distraction of working alongside seemingly carefree university students. Officially he was still convalescing, but soon he'd have to notify his boss about returning to work. He'd already decided it was going to be a desk job for a while.

He was still seeing Lauren Starling, but he had sensibly kept this lovely woman at a distance. Not so far as to be insulting but just enough so that neither of them got carried away with notions of permanency. He suspected Lauren's ambition would take care of that soon anyway, and for now it was a comfortable and affectionate romance. There had been honesty from before the first kiss; he'd warned her not to get in too deep, although he'd said it as much for himself because Lauren was the type of woman one could fall over the cliff for and never want to land. She had it all going on. She was a catch. She was a joy. She was texting.

Jack glanced at his phone, on silent, and clicked the message.

News! Tell you tonight. That could only mean one thing: the promotion to editor of the New York weekend magazine. Well, good, he supposed. She would now be moving to a new city and that meant the decision had been made for them. They'd become the best of friends, who just happened to have dated.

He looked up from his phone, waved it and spoke to the class. 'Everyone in?' He scanned the room. 'How about phones onto silent, everyone?'

The class obeyed, although he heard one text message ping its arrival somewhere, and as they busied themselves with sorting out their phones, he felt a private pang of regret regarding Lauren, which he knew was of no use to either of them.

'You always ask so nicely,' one of the female students remarked as she slung her phone back into her bag.

Jack grinned, put his phone into his pocket and let the thought of losing Lauren go. It had always been the plan. 'Well, in my day they used to throw chalk at us to get our attention. And Mr Lovejoy, who regularly defied his name, used to throw the wooden blackboard cleaners at us. Those hurt. I'm afraid that's not allowed any more. I figure good manners work, right?'

The student smiled back at him. There was promise in that smile and he held his breath momentarily, taken aback by the raw sexuality on display in some of these youngsters. He felt old and looked away deliberately to let her know there was absolutely no chance of that, then scanned the room again.

'Miss Rundle? Where is your friend, Miss Peters? Surely not sick again.'

The student's face crumpled and she began to cry. Others noticed and Jack's expression fell to mortified as he stepped around his desk and moved towards the teary student. More than a dozen gazes followed him; he sensed they knew something, if his instincts were serving him. 'Madeleine, isn't it?'

She nodded. 'Maddie.'

Jack cleared his throat. 'Okay, everyone, go over Chapter Six, will you? You need to know that procedure off by heart. We'll tackle that next lesson and you've all still got your papers due by tomorrow, so why not take some time in class to finesse those.'

A collective groan sounded, though it had no heat, but Jack was already looking back at his tearful charge.

'Come with me, Maddie, please.'

While the class began flicking through their books to find the chapter, Jack escorted Maddie outside the classroom and closed the door, frowning. He dug into his pocket for a handkerchief. 'Here.'

She took it, sniffing, and dabbed at her eyes. 'Smells of you.'

'Does it?' He drew away slightly. These girls were all so direct. 'What's happened to your friend, er, Amelia? That is her name, isn't it?'

'She preferred Millie, always called me Mads,' she said, opening up the handkerchief to its full square and covering her face with it momentarily. 'I'm sorry, I shouldn't have come into class – I just didn't know what to do when you asked about her. I thought . . . I thought you knew.'

'Don't be sorry. Hang on – what should I know?' he asked.

Maddie's expression folded in on itself again. 'That she died. Her funeral is tomorrow,' she said, and her bluntness felt like he'd been clubbed; it made him hold his breath. 'Her brother just sent me a text message about it as you asked us to put our phones on silent.'

Jack's mind instantly reverberated with a sound similar to the steady, single tone of the test card he remembered on the BBC before twenty-four-hour television existed. Its piercing tone, akin to tinnitus he was sure, drowned out thought for a few heartbeats as he stood there, mouth slightly ajar, trying to make sense of what Maddie had just uttered. He hated to be so predictable and obvious when words finally arrived. 'Funeral? Madeleine, how did she die?'

Maddie shrugged, looking lost. 'After our last lesson with you she started to feel dizzy and sick. I helped her to get home but she became really ill, sicker by the moment, and we got her into an ambulance but she'd lost consciousness and was hospitalised. Her parents believed she was probably dehydrated or had caught a virus on her holiday, and we all just presumed in a couple of days with the right care, she'd be . . .' Maddie dissolved into tears again.

The college likely knew but hadn't yet advised him as he wasn't in daily. 'Listen, Maddie. Um, let me just sort the class out and I'll organise to get you home with someone, okay?'

She looked up at him. 'Thanks. I don't think I can face going back in.'

He nodded. 'Give me a couple of minutes, okay?' He led her to a bench outside the building. 'Stay here and take a few breaths. I'll be back.'

He was as good as his word, moving out of earshot from Maddie and ringing the university admin to explain what had transpired, fielding their apology for being tardy with relevant information and answering questions as best he could. 'I don't have any detail but yes someone from the college should go. Apparently she found out via a text message from Amelia's brother just a minute or two ago. I guess we'll discover more in due course.' No one, it seemed, was available to accompany Maddie home. 'Well, I'm not sending her off alone,' Jack said in answer to the excuses that came down the phone. He moved back to Maddie, offered an arm, and began to walk her out of the campus to the main entrance. 'And while it's not preferred protocol, I am still a Detective Superintendent and she's clearly and understandably upset, so I'll take her. And can someone please let my class know they've got an early mark but they'd better know Chapter Six backwards for next time.' He listened and then answered, 'No, they'll understand.'

In a blink he'd hailed a taxi and was bundling Maddie in while he continued his conversation with the college office. 'No, can you ring Madeleine's parents, please? I don't want them having a nasty surprise.' He paused. 'Er, yes, Kathy, I do mean right now – we're already on our way. We should make sure someone's at home so I don't have to leave her alone,' he urged. 'No, the class is fine but you may need to contact the college counsellors. Okay, thanks.'

Jack slipped the phone back into his pocket and got into the car. 'What's your address?' Maddie murmured it. He directed the driver, then sat back and turned to Maddie. 'Where did you say she'd been?'

'Um . . . Lithuania. The old part of Vilnius, she said.'

'On her own?' He noted Maddie's lips pursing and leapt to the logical next question. 'Boyfriend?'

She shook her head. 'She's getting over Tim. Hasn't seen anyone properly since their break-up about six months ago. It's why she's in a share house now . . . or was.' She began tearing up again.

'Okay.' Jack frowned, considering what Maddie wasn't telling him. 'Was it a holiday?'

'Just a mini break.' Maddie sniffed. 'Three days.'

'In the middle of term?' He frowned.

Maddie shrugged. 'She's smart. She always catches up.' She covered her mouth again as fresh tears arrived. '*Caught up*. Millie was a good student.'

'Yes, she was,' he agreed. 'Why Lithuania?'

She swallowed. 'I can't. It's a secret.'

'Right.' He didn't let her hear the sigh, kept it to himself.

'And I'm sorry about your hanky,' she said, noting some mascara had stained it.

'Don't be. Keep it.'

'She'd be so jealous of me.'

'Millie would?'

'Here in a taxi with you holding my hand, using your hanky . . . She was so fond of you. We all are. You're the favourite lecturer in the college.'

He smiled to hide how awkward that suddenly made him feel. 'And you're my favourite class,' he said carefully, wishing he could extricate his hand from the twenty-year-old's grip. What had felt avuncular, protective, suddenly felt vaguely uncomfortable following her admission.

'It's just around this corner and then second left,' Maddie said, sitting forward to direct the driver.

Jack took his chance to remove his hand. 'Maddie, this secret visit to Lithuania. Could it have hurt Amelia? Was it the reason she might have become so ill?'

She surprised him by nodding; he had presumed she'd deny it immediately. Instead, she seemed glad he'd persisted, eager to unburden herself. 'She needed the money. They all did.'

He blinked as the taxi began to slow. 'All?' The detective in him kicked in and his tone remained neutral.

'A barmaid from Hassocks and another girl from uni.'

'Here we go,' the driver said, flicking off the meter.

'Can you wait, please? I'll be heading back.'

'Sure, guv.' The driver began fiddling with his phone.

Before Jack could re-focus on Maddie, a woman had emerged from the front door and was crunching onto the gravel drive. It was an impressive three-storey Victorian house in Battersea that spoke of wealth and comfort.

'Darling?' The woman, presumably Maddie's mother, looked worried. She hugged her child but looked at Jack as he stepped out of the car.

'Mrs Rundle?' The woman nodded and her sharply cut bob, a perfect auburn that reflected the sun, swung with the gesture. 'I'm Detective Superintendent Jack Hawksworth, on sabbatical from the normal role. I'm one of Madeleine's lecturers. She was in my class when she got the news about Amelia's funeral.'

She held out a hand to shake his. Despite being in body-hugging training gear and sneakers that looked new, she wore a tasteful set of sparkling rings and a tennis bracelet that shimmered its row of diamonds. Hardly activewear, Jack thought, but he could see from whom Maddie derived her attractiveness.

'Yes, the college just contacted me . . . I didn't think it was such a good idea but Maddie was determined to go in today.'

Maddie looked at him from her mother's embrace. 'You can leave a message for me at the college if you need help or want to say any more about Millie's trip,' he encouraged.

Maddie shook her head. 'Thanks for bringing me home.'

'Yes, thank you, Mr Hawksworth, that's very decent of you. Maddie's mentioned how much she enjoys your class.'

He smiled. 'Bye, Maddie.'

On the journey back he wondered why it was that Amelia and two other women had gone to Lithuania . . . it had to be over four hours in flight time. That was a long way to go to earn some money. Three days, Maddie said. A long way for a short stay, too. In what way had Amelia been earning that money?

4

ADELAIDE

Greg's journey had been mercifully seamless: no hold-ups in Sydney, clearing customs and immigration with ease before he loped to the domestic terminal and took a Qantas flight that met its departure time. He was in desperate need of a shower and was holding off the other major ablution until he reached private facilities.

It had been twenty hours since he'd left his hotel in Dubai. With his constant travel, he'd learned how to limit his food intake before and during flights to stave off jetlag and reduce trips to the toilets, often skipping breakfast when everyone else was woken by the sulphurous smell of eggs, usually presented as rubbery omelettes in economy. Despite eating only hours before, those around him seemed to eagerly greet the distraction of another tray of plastic-covered food to fiddle with, sad fruit and stale croissants, but Greg could forego it all to give his bowel a fighting chance of making it back to his unit in Adelaide, where he'd have his own bathroom and could take his time. 'Always make time for your bowel, Greg,' his grandmother used to say.

It made him smile to think of her. He wished he could hug his grandparents again, both gone now but living large in his memory. They were proud of him, had said it often enough, both impressed that he dashed across the world the way he did.

'I'm really just a courier,' he'd assured them. 'But I like the travel and I often get a few days off in an interesting city to explore.'

His father was not so impressed. 'When are you going to use that degree you're still paying off?'

Greg didn't want to be an accountant. Never had. He'd only completed the undergraduate course to please a father who could never be pleased. 'Soon, Dad. Just seeing the world first.'

He dutifully lined up for a taxi at Adelaide Airport, where the attendant was far more cheerful and polite than the ones in Sydney usually were, and as much as he yearned to give the address of his own unit, he gave the address for where he was required to make his delivery. The driver was listening to what Greg thought was Hindi music; it was on low. And his conversation, definitely in Hindi, via a mobile headphone speaker that he pulled close to his mouth, was also being murmured as he navigated the traffic speeding away from the airport.

Greg wondered how the person on the other end could hear. None of his business. He put his head back against the headrest and watched the familiar landscape of Sir Donald Bradman Drive whiz past. They weren't catching any lights either; he was going to make good time to the lab and arrive well within the prescribed time parameters.

On the other side of the world, Jack's tall frame paused at security and he flashed his warrant.

'Going to the Sharpe retirement bash, sir?' the guard asked in a thick Australian accent as he took the warrant to scrutinise it properly.

It made Jack smile. He'd heard his sister's accent begin to change slightly, apparently without her knowing. She'd laughed it off when he mentioned it, but it had been years now that she'd lived and loved life in Sydney. Why wouldn't Australia rub a bit of that posh grammar school edge off her English accent and replace it with a twang of its own to claim her properly? She'd begun to end sentences with an upward intonation to make them sound like questions – not all the time, but it was creeping into their phone calls and he thought it was fun.

His niece and nephew were going to be Aussies through and through, no doubt enjoying that strange football code and becoming cricket-mad, sun-loving, surfing kids. It might seem like a cliché but they were living it; both of them were sporty, bronzed and certainly not the types to fear school camp or spiders. He'd caught sight of a huntsman only once in his sister's home and it had been more than enough to make him hold his breath in shock at its leg span. He'd not had to exaggerate its size either when re-telling the experience to his colleagues over work drinks to christen a new building, enjoying watching Kate Carter, a DCI since their last operation together, give a shudder. He'd be seeing her again tonight.

'What's an Aussie doing in downtown Broadway London?' he asked the guard, grinning.

'Blame the wife. She's a doctor finishing some medical training over here. Me, I'm just happy to get some shifts for the time being. I'm an insurance investigator in my other life. But we haven't been here long enough for me to establish myself.'

'Good luck to you both,' Jack said, accepting the return of his warrant.

The security guard tipped him a salute. 'Fifth floor.'

Jack nodded and headed to the lifts in the tower block that faced Broadway's underground station. He suspected the event would be a tame affair and not at all like on *Prime Suspect*; the TV series would have people believe that retirement parties were full of drunks and strippers. He was joined by several senior people he knew vaguely, but the last person to scurry into the lift on a pair of scarlet heels was the wonderful Joan Field, who greeted the others like friends but saved her most enthusiastic welcome for him.

'Jack! You're back!'

She leaned in and he kissed her with genuine affection on both cheeks. 'I am. Another scar to add to my battle wounds,' he said with another grin. 'I know it's a while ago, but thanks again for visiting at the hospital.'

'Oh, I couldn't miss the opportunity to see you in a hospital gown. I wanted to make you a casserole and bring it over but frankly I don't know where you live these days,' she admonished him.

'Sometimes neither do I,' he quipped. 'I will settle in somewhere soon, but I'm spending a couple of months helping Lauren out by taking a sub-lease on her flat.'

Joan obviously knew they were no longer together from the way her eyes shadowed momentarily. Was there nothing in his life that Joan didn't know about? Instead of pursuing the obvious she made a clicking sound with her tongue. 'And I can imagine that's no slum.'

He chuckled but didn't give an inch. 'Is this a sad day?' he whispered instead, leaning close to her ear.

'Probably, but we mustn't let him know we think so,' she murmured in reply. 'It's a changing of the guard, isn't it?'

He nodded. 'Always wise to leave on a high.'

'That's what I told him when he began to make the inevitable groaning sounds about retirement. He didn't want this get-together either. But tonight's actually for Mary and the boys to appreciate just what a brilliant career the grumpy old man has enjoyed.'

As the bell dinged to signal their arrival, the men in front parted to let Joan walk through the open door first and she neatly eased past them on her stilettos. Jack was always impressed by the effortless, old-style glamour she brought to the corridors around New Scotland Yard. Stepping out, he heard the cheerful babble emanating from the restaurant that acted as a carvery during weekdays for the officers. Tonight the adjacent canteen had been opened up as a function room to take the one hundred or so attendees there to thank Martin Sharpe and celebrate his stellar career, which had left no cases out in the cold. All the brass inside would be in civvies because drinking in uniform, even politely, should never happen.

Jack glanced at his watch: twenty to seven. Drinks were in full swing, but he'd timed his arrival well. By seven, the master of ceremonies would call the happy group to order and speeches would follow. Jack escorted Joan in on his arm but they parted as they were greeted by others. He saw only relief on the face of Kate.

'I thought you'd never arrive,' she said, giving him a snake-eyed glare.

He kissed her on each cheek, inhaling her perfume, recognising the familiar warm floral heart as Shalimar, which he knew would have filled the immediate surrounds with a chilly citrus vapour upon its first spray. This scent suited Kate because, like her, it ran cold and hot.

'Fashionably late, I think Joan would say,' he replied. 'You smell lovely.'

She smiled at the compliment. 'How does she always manage to look so amazing?'

'Well, you look pretty amazing yourself.'

She lightly slapped his chest with the back of her hand. 'Don't flirt, Jack. It's confusing.'

'I'm not,' he said, offering her first choice from the tray of drinks that had suddenly arrived in front of them, courtesy of a young waitress. She took a flute of sparkling wine and he followed suit. 'Just being honest. So how's life in Vice?'

She tipped her head one way and then back. 'Interesting. What about you? You're lecturing at the moment?'

'Yes, that's right. And enjoying myself.'

'Really? I heard about . . .'

'About Lauren and me?'

She nodded. 'Yeah, I'm sorry. I figured you two were a match.'

He smiled. 'No. We talked about it. My career is not conducive to settling down and hers was set to take off again. We had no intention of getting in each other's way.'

'That sounds so mature.'

He laughed. 'It is.'

'I can't imagine either of you were happy to say farewell.' It seemed Kate could see through the sensible excuse.

Jack nodded; he knew he should be honest with his friend and colleague. 'It was hard, Kate. I liked her a lot and it wouldn't have taken much to make her knock back New York, but that would have been a whole load of guilt and I carry enough of that around.'

'Is she doing okay?'

'Do you worry about her?' He grinned, trying to lighten the awkwardness.

'All night long,' she admitted in a dry tone. 'So long as you're fine.'

He squeezed her wrist. 'I am.'

Her smile all but said 'on the market again?' but he let it pass. They would always have this thing between them, he knew.

'So, a college lecturer now. Phew, all those young heartstrings being stretched,' she teased.

He shook his head with dismay. 'Bloody hell, they are young. And so forward.'

She laughed. '*To Sir, with Love*? Be careful, Jack.'

'I am . . . very.'

'What's next for you? Surely you're not going to stay at the uni full time?'

'No, in fact I'll finish up this semester.'

'And?'

He shrugged. 'Desk job. I want the quiet life for a while. No operation, no thrill-seeking at all.'

She nodded, more serious now. 'How *are* you?'

Jack sighed. He could always be honest with Kate. 'Still aches a bit.' He touched the site of the stab wound, almost without realising he had.

'Your heart or your wound?' She was not jesting.

'Both. I can't shake the sadness that our old foe went the way she did, and I've arrived at the conclusion that I'll never shake the sensation of that knife going in.'

Kate shuddered. 'Can't blame you. But perhaps Anne McEvoy's in a better place.'

He nodded, thinking of the promise he'd made. He'd discovered her child was living in Yorkshire, with a couple who worshipped her. They'd adopted a son before her and so now she had a solid, loving family to grow up within. Her new mother was generous, happy to privately keep in touch with Jack. He asked nothing more. 'We'll call you Uncle Jack, an old friend from schooldays, okay?' she'd said after sharing a coffee one bright afternoon in Leeds.

'Pay attention, children,' Joan said, sidling up to them both and re-focusing Jack on the proceedings.

Someone had rigged up a microphone and was calling everyone
to order. Jack tuned out until one of Sharpe's oldest colleagues
took the microphone and settled down the cheers, wolf whistles
and clapping. Jack smiled as the old policeman began to recount
some prime cases that he and Sharpe had been involved with.
He began to reference Martin's idiosyncrasies, including his fiery
temper, which brought smiles all round, and then shared some
amusing anecdotes before he became more serious and mentioned
two bravery awards and Sharpe's outstanding service.

Then it was Sharpe's turn to step up to the microphone and
Jack grinned at how uncomfortable he looked receiving all this
attention. He was predictably humble in his response as he gave
thanks to his colleagues, leaving out no one he had worked with
over the years. '. . . standing over there, trying to be modest.'

Kate nudged Jack as they watched Sharpe give a thumbs up.

'To you, Jack. Thanks for being one of my most reliable
colleagues . . .' Jack looked down while the praise came thick and
fast from the man he respected most in his work and indeed his
life. Sharpe had been mentor and friend, sometimes father. He
was relieved when the speech was over and a special gift of an
engraved crystal decanter was presented with flowers for the long-
suffering Mary. Jack was more than aware of how difficult it likely
was being married to any dedicated member of the police force,
but particularly one as senior and committed as Sharpe.

It was nearing eight-thirty and although everyone would start
dispersing by nine, Jack was keen to be gone and strolled up to
make his farewells. He apologised for interrupting Martin, who
was chatting amiably to someone who could only be a few years
younger. 'Thanks for the thanks,' Jack said and didn't feel embarrassed to hug his old friend.

'Bloody hell, I hate speeches and couldn't believe how choked
up I got.'

'I don't think you left anyone out, sir,' Jack said, falling back on old habits of gentle ribbing. 'Not even your heart surgeon.'

Even Sharpe had to laugh. 'Mary insisted I included everyone down to the ruddy postman. It's just Martin now, by the way,' he said, waggling a finger. 'Now, Jack, let me introduce you to Bill Davies. Bill and I go back a long way. He's one of the top guys in the Australian police, based in Sydney.'

Jack shook hands with a man who was built square like a shed. He wore a roomy double-breasted suit with braces, and Jack noted he was drinking a mineral water, which seemed to fly in the face of the idea of a typical Aussie bloke. 'Pleasure to meet you, sir,' Jack said. 'I have a sister who lives in Sydney.'

'Lucky girl,' Bill said with a wink. 'Visit much?'

Jack nodded. 'Often. Last year in fact, and I've got a hankering to get back, maybe the end of this year or early next. I've got a niece and nephew growing up on the other side of the world and they're my only family.'

Davies nodded. 'Why don't you come and do a stint?'

'Work, you mean?'

Davies shrugged. 'Why not? A working holiday . . . Kill two birds and all that.'

'Tempting.' Jack chuckled. 'I . . . er, I'm taking a bit of a break right now, actually.'

The Australian nodded. 'Martin mentioned.'

Jack slid his old boss a glance and Sharpe held a hand up in surrender. 'Just talk, Jack. Everyone's impressed with your last op and how quickly you brought it to a close.'

'At a high cost, sir.'

Sharpe nodded. 'But it doesn't hurt to broaden your networks.'

Davies agreed. 'Reach me via Australia House. I'm staying in London for a few months on long service leave, doing the family rounds. I've been promising my wife a holiday for so long that our children have grown up, married and are having children of their own, so we're about to get trapped in grandparenting duties.'

'Now or never?' Jack asked.

'Exactly.' Davies dipped into the inside pocket of his jacket and withdrew a card. 'Call me. I think the more we share specialties the better.'

'Thanks,' Jack said and shook hands with him again. He gave Martin a soft smile just as Mary arrived.

'Leaving already, Jack?'

He gave an apologetic shrug. 'Thank you for inviting me this evening.'

'Well, come and visit soon. Martin can take you out on the little sailboat our family has given him for his retirement.'

Jack glanced at Martin. 'So the deck shoes came in handy, sir?'

Martin grimaced. 'I know you can sail, Jack. We'll go out and chew the cud.'

Jack smiled. 'That's a promise.'

'I was sorry to hear about you and Lauren,' Mary said, giving a moue of maternal despair. 'No lovely woman on the horizon?'

'Taking a break from romance, Mary,' he said and kissed her cheek. 'I promise to visit and keep the old rogue entertained.'

'Keep that promise,' she warned.

Jack headed for the door but hadn't escaped Kate's notice, it seemed. She caught up with him.

'Are you leaving me here alone, you treacherous sod?'

He laughed. 'Walk me down?'

She gave him a gentle backslap against his arm. 'Sure.'

He pressed the button for the lift, which was mercifully already at their floor and the doors opened. Inside, descending, he cut her a look. 'Anyone in your life right now?'

'I am seeing someone. It's new. He's . . . well, he's nice.' She laughed. 'He's a schoolteacher.'

Jack's smile was all warmth. 'Brilliant.'

She nodded, looking oddly shy. 'Never saw myself with someone so . . .' He waited for her to find the right words. 'Well, so everyday. He cooks for me. He likes to go for walks or drives in the countryside. At the weekend and especially if I'm working, he's an English Heritage guide.' She gave a sound of soft but not displeasurable despair. 'He's tame, quiet, makes me feel safe.'

Jack leant in and kissed her cheek. 'I am very happy for you.'

'I have no idea where it's going or what it is, other than comfy.'

'Comfy's good.' He smiled. 'Our working life needs that to come home to.'

The lift door opened. 'Yes. I choose to stay at Dan's rather than the other way around because when I get in there are always lights on, heating on, something delicious on the simmer, a glass of wine being poured. I'm really enjoying being looked after.'

'What does he teach?'

'History of art. He paints too – he's quite good. The students love him.'

Talk of Dan the teacher jogged his memory. 'Kate, can I ask a favour?'

'Shoot,' she said, both of them nodding at the security guard as they left the building.

'Something's been bothering me about one of my students.'

'Okay,' she said, folding her arms against the evening chill.

'She went to Lithuania for three days, got sick . . . and died.'

'Died?' Kate repeated, frowning. 'From what?'

He shrugged. 'Her closest friend wouldn't explain. Said the trip was a secret.'

'So, how can I help?'

'Can you just have a rummage,' he said, emphasising the final word with a small grin, 'and see if there are any flags up?'

He watched her mind leap to where his had already been. 'You mean girls . . . trafficking?'

He nodded. 'Escort services – high end. Pretty English girls, although why they'd need ours I don't know. Russian girls are beautiful.'

'And you're qualified to make that call no doubt,' she joked. At his look she put her hand up. 'Okay, okay. I'll look. I haven't heard anything recently. How long ago did this happen?'

'About two weeks.'

'Right. Give me her name.'

'Amelia Peters. She's twenty . . . was.'

'Did you get details from the coroner?'

He shook his head. 'I didn't interfere because the parents were obviously in disbelieving grief. Her pal said it was probably food poisoning, but she was the one who made a comment about the trip being a secret – needing to make money – and I can't let it go in my mind. Oh, and there were two others girls, apparently.'

Kate leaned in and kissed him on both cheeks. 'I'll have a rummage,' she promised. 'Don't leave it so long next time, Jack.'

'Let's have a drink. Bring Dan, I'll bring, er . . . someone. We can be normal couples for a moment.'

She laughed. 'I don't think so,' she said, but blew him another kiss and they turned in different directions.

5

ADELAIDE

Greg arrived at a nondescript building on Greenhill Road in Eastwood. The best he could describe it, if asked, would be to say that it had been modern in its moment during the 1990s, when panoramic stretches of dark plate glass were the height of architectural design in the area. It was low rise; just two storeys with an underground car park. All the buildings in this sweep looked much the same.

'Want me to wait, mate?' the driver asked.

Greg shook his head at the taxi driver. 'No, I'll be fine.'

'You'll struggle finding one down here on a Sunday evening,' the man tried, turning down the music that had accompanied them from the airport.

'It's okay, thanks. I don't live far away. How much?'

The man switched off the meter and pointed, suddenly no longer interested in Greg or his fare, turning the music back up. Greg paid him with the cash he had been given before he'd left

Australia and asked for a receipt, which the now-bored driver took his time in handing over. Greg got out without bothering to thank the driver, who was already glancing at his side mirror, indicator flashing to nip back into the lean traffic. This same road on a weekday could crush one's soul, especially if one was running late, because the traffic could hastily bank up on the arterial road that led all the way to the hills and, if you happened to live in the prized eastern suburbs, was the pathway down to Anzac Highway and the seaside town of Glenelg.

Greg skipped up the stairs and pressed the intercom button. He waited, imagining the woman inside standing from her stool and stretching her lean limbs. He'd already sent a text that he was en route so his arrival was no surprise, not that it would be anyway – he was scheduled for drop-off this evening.

'Greg?' came Nikki Lawson's smokey tone from the speaker.

'Yep,' he answered.

'Down in a sec,' she said, and the intercom went dead.

He lifted a hand and waved as Nikki emerged from the lift doors, which allowed light to flood the shadows of the otherwise deserted reception. He'd always had a thing for Nikki, with her bubbly mop of hair that she bleached, her pale make-up and always bright red lips . . . it did something for him. Sadly, she was not interested in him romantically, invested only in the platonic partnership that they'd crafted these past three years. But as tired as he was, he felt a zing of interest as she cast him one of her sunny smiles from that full mouth of hers.

Nikki used a key to unlock a small side door that was normally shut when the automatic sliding doors were engaged during business hours. 'Hello, you. Tired?' she said, sounding like she cared.

He knew she did, just not how he would like. He let it go. 'I'm all right. Used to it.'

She locked the door behind them. 'No problems?'

'None. Not even a delay.'

'I know, great timing. How many are you carrying?'

'Twenty.'

'Excellent.' She grinned as they walked to the lift and hit the button for the second level. 'I should use the stairs but it means switching on all the lights and I don't want to draw attention.'

'I worked it out,' he said, grinning back. 'How's everything?'

'Ever busy. Tomorrow's going to be murder. Lots of women in for their transfers.'

'Isn't it usually like that?'

'Busy, yes. But when we've got as many nervous couples in reception as tomorrow, their anxiety levels become exhausting.'

He followed her into the lab. It was familiar. They'd done this several times before. Greg unzipped his backpack and took out a metal box.

'These always remind me of miniature band boxes . . . You're like a roadie for a pack of elves,' Nikki remarked and Greg laughed as he flipped the locks and the metal casing was removed to reveal a dewar flask. 'All looks good,' she said.

'When things go so smoothly, it feels like all our precautions are unnecessary.'

'Until the day they're not,' she said in a wry tone, as if he should know better than to make the comment. She used a sharp tool to snip through the zip ties that feigned security, signalling that the pewter-coloured dewar had not been tampered with. Except it had. 'Right. Let me just make sure the tank is ready before we open up.' She pulled on a thick pair of blue gloves that they used in labs when handling corrosive chemicals.

Greg waited and watched while Nikki moved over to a large tank, where the clinic – called MultiplyMed – collected and protected their product in liquid nitrogen to keep the precious eggs and especially the embryos frozen.

'Okay, good to go,' she said, and Greg used the handle that looped and locked either side of the blue lid to shift the dewar closer. At her nod, he removed it.

Chilled vapours lifted on release like wraiths on the hunt. Nikki waited for them to subside slightly as the liquid nitrogen's work was now done; it had kept the dewar's contents safely at below freezing point from before Greg left for the airport in Dubai . . . in fact from its originating point in Europe. It had been topped up in more ways than one in the Emirates city. Nikki used specially tooled wire hooks to lift the steel cup inside the dewar. Sitting innocently within that cup were twenty-five narrow metal goblets, each containing several plastic straws. The straws always reminded Greg of the inside of a Bic biro. Except these didn't contain ink.

'So, let me just quickly check ours off,' Nikki said, picking up a clipboard and handing it to Greg. 'You read and I'll find them.'

He began slowly reading off names and numbers while Nikki removed the goblet bearing the corresponding label on its seal. She then placed it in a groove on a strip of foam poking out of a much larger chemical tank; the foam was soaked with liquid nitrogen. They repeated this until twenty corresponding goblets were all neatly in place and she sealed the tank.

'Leaves us with five?' Greg asked.

'Yep. You'd better get them away. They're waiting.'

'All spoken for?'

'Every last one I imagine. Business is good,' she quipped, helping him to re-seal the dewar. 'When's the next drop? Next week?'

'Er,' he began, then frowned, flicking through a mental diary. 'Yes, I'm off again next Monday to Europe. I start the journey back on Friday,' he added.

'That sounds right. I think we're already scheduled for a Sunday pick-up in Dubai,' she replied.

He met her gaze. 'No change to the plan?'

She shook her head. 'You overnight in Dubai and the delivery will come to your hotel.'

'Much easier if I flew business, Nikki. A lot less risk and jostling.'

Nikki sighed audibly through her nostrils. 'You stand to make five thousand dollars from this trip alone.'

'So do you, with little of the fatigue or responsibility. I need something to make the risk a little sweeter.'

She glared at him through narrowing eyelids. 'Greg, you know there's little to no risk. You're carrying legitimate product with all the legit documentation.'

'But what if they checked?'

'You mean what if they clipped open fragile, precious human material accompanied by all the right paperwork to discover a few extra straws?' She didn't hide the derision in her tone or the sarcastic query on her face.

'Well, I'm the one carrying it.'

'It's never happened.'

'Always a first time, Nikki.'

'Leave it, Greg.'

'No!' he snapped, wishing he hadn't, but committing to sharing his frustration now. '*You* don't have to squeeze in next to the fatties, or smellies, or chatties, or put up with the sneezes, coughs and the endless trips to the toilet by others.'

'And what, they don't sneeze or cough or use the loo in business?'

'Apparently not! They look smug, well fed, well rested and they have so much more room.'

'Get over it, Greg. Don't shit in the nest. You've got a good thing going.'

'I am doing something illegal.'

'And you get paid handsomely for it. Besides, I don't see anyone begging you to do it. Are you forgetting I could lose my job, my reputation, my future if I'm found out to be part of this?' She didn't wait for an answer. 'And I get half what you get paid for doing my bit. I feel I have more to lose than you, if I'm honest, but do you hear me complaining?'

'You know what I mean. I get that you're taking chances too but I'm not asking for more money in my pocket, only for a comfier, less stressful journey. Everything will become easier as a result, and it won't be long before I start amassing the points that will cover a couple of the journeys. I'm happy to plough the points back into the *business arrangement*,' he said, making inverted comma signs in the air. 'Listen, I know too much. I'm like an old timer, a pro. I think they'll say yes because they won't want to lose me or risk—'

'Risk what, Greg?' She was alert now, her tone pointed. 'Be careful.'

'Hey, hey,' he said, hands up to ward off her hostility. 'I didn't mean anything by that. I just want a chance to say my piece. I've got ideas.'

'It sounded like a threat.'

'No,' he soothed her, shrugging. 'We're all in this together, but why have someone who's unhappy when it costs so little to fix the issue?'

She looked suddenly tired of the conversation. 'I'll talk to them. You'd better get going. Come on, I'll just top up the liquid nitro in that dewar before I let you out.'

He thought about suggesting they go for a drink later, just to chat it through, but Nikki didn't look as though she was in the mood for small talk with anyone.

★

In London, Jack was foaming the milk for his coffee when his mobile phone buzzed on the kitchen bench. He cursed the timing – preparing coffee was his favourite task – but he put down the small jug and answered the call.

'Hello?'

'Jack?' The voice sounded intrigued that he had answered his phone.

'Kate?' She laughed at how he mimicked her questioning tone. 'Who did you expect to answer my phone?'

'Oh, I don't know, some bedroom-eyed wench with tousled hair.'

'You're getting me so wrong, you know.' He leaned against the bench and rolled his eyes, hoping she could hear it in his voice.

'I don't think so. Anyway, listen. I've done a little digging about your student.'

Jack straightened. 'And?'

'The coroner's report says she died of sepsis.' At his long pause, Kate added, 'Have I lost you?'

'No, no, I'm here. Sepsis?' He was incredulous.

'Yeah. It seems she had some sort of minor procedure while she was away and whatever they did, they nicked her bowel.'

Jack closed his eyes in frustration for Amelia, who'd had a bright future ahead. 'Any idea about what they were up to?'

'Well, could be any number of surgical procedures. They went in via a laparoscopy.'

He cursed beneath his breath.

'There is one little glimmer of interest though.'

'Go on,' Jack encouraged her, trying not to sound overly eager; he sensed more disappointment might follow.

'Well, she had been ovulating.'

'So?'

'How much do you know about ovulating women, Jack?'

'That they become unreasonable?' He said it deliberately to bait her and won the response he was after.

'I shall hurt you for that when I next see you. You can choose — hedge clippers or a hammer?'

He laughed. 'I'm sorry, I don't know enough, if that's what you're asking.'

'Let me enlighten you,' she said in a droll tone. 'A woman ovulates each month and if, when that egg is released from one of her ovaries, it travels through the fallopian tubes without being fertilised, then it is washed away with the detritus in her womb that prepared for the potential growing of an embryo. Are you with me?'

'Yes,' he said, sounding deliberately bored. 'I do know that much.'

'Good. It's called menstruation.' She had adopted a tone of condescension now. 'It's that time when—'

He laughed and cut her off. 'I'm not a complete Neanderthal.'

'No? Anyway, it happens that occasionally two eggs might be released in the same period.'

'And if both successfully fertilise, we get twins. Yes, I did biology at school too, Kate.'

'Okay.' She chuckled. 'I'll get to the point. Amelia had been ovulating big time. And by that, I mean both her ovaries were incredibly swollen and the pathologist could see something in the order of seventeen eruptions where eggs had burst from their vault, so to speak.'

'That doesn't sound normal.'

'I can assure you it's not. The pathologist has confirmed it is mystifying. A woman's body knows exactly what it's doing and how to do it, and there's nothing to be gained by releasing that many precious eggs. She's born with a lifetime supply but the body uses discretion. So releasing seventeen at once is unusual, if not highly unlikely in the natural process. You only need one.'

'And given there are millions of sperm on the hunt . . .'

'Exactly. An egg is huge by comparison, so they can hardly miss it unless they're dumb sperm.'

They both laughed at that, and Jack imagined she was probably thinking much the same as him about all the dim-witted male crims they'd met over their careers.

'But even sperm from a tremendous idiot knows what it's looking for,' Kate finished.

'Did the pathologist offer the coroner's court any reason?'

'He did. He suggested that ovulation-stimulating drugs were likely the culprit.'

'But why? She was so young . . .'

'Well, I doubt it was in order to get pregnant, Jack. I think young Amelia might have been in Lithuania on a money-making exercise, selling her eggs.'

Dawn broke in his mind with a heavenly chorus to match. Suddenly Amelia's secret trip made sense.

'Okay, very grateful to you, Kate.'

'Yep, you owe me,' she joked and rang off.

Jack picked up the jug of half-foamed milk and threw it down the sink, hoping it would take his frustration at Amelia dying for a few extra pounds with it.

Greg had made his way to the second delivery address on foot. It really wasn't that far away, the goods were safely re-packed – 're-nitroed', as he liked to think of it – and it felt good to stretch his legs after the long flight. Tomorrow he might go for a run around the parklands of the old racing track and the next day he would aim to do the Mount Lofty ascent, though it would mean getting up very early. These days it was like spaghetti junction up there, with all the yummy mummies getting back into shape, the boomers seeing if they still could, even firemen training in all their gear. It was suddenly de rigueur to be testing oneself on the Waterfall Gully to Mount Lofty trail.

He passed the factory outlet of Haigh's Chocolates and was reminded that he hadn't visited in a while. The smell alone made one buy; it felt all too easy to get sucked into the 'seconds' shelves where a myriad of delicious, ever so slightly wonky treats were on offer at reduced prices, not that he'd noticed any wonkiness. And then of course it was equally tempting to walk the aisles inhaling the rich smells of caramelised sugar and of irresistible cocoa wafting around instead of heading straight to the counter to pay. Plus, and this was important, you were always offered a sample taste of something. Easter was his favourite, when the staff would break up Easter eggs for customers to try and all it took was a little taste to convince them to buy a few.

Greg had learned about giving away product to increase sales when he was in his early teens and working for Wendy's Supa Sundaes. His father attended the same golf club as one of the owners; a little chat on the sixteenth with Phil Rogers and he'd put them in touch with his local franchisee. Greg was soon behind the counter learning how to twist the perfect soft serve and decorate it as a witch for Halloween or Rudolf for Christmas or a clown during non-festive times. Here he'd learned about what the company amusingly called the 'Bogof' – the Buy One Get One Free voucher. When a cone was ordered and paid for, the assistant would often hand over one of these bogofs and it enticed the customer to return and redeem it, considering it a freebie, when in fact they'd had to buy two cones to get that third one for free. Greg remembered how his manager had railed against the idea initially, fretting at handing out free product. Mr Rogers had visited the store to explain it fully.

'You're giving away nothing, Les,' he'd assured him, explaining in the simplest of terms the logic, which included the minuscule outlay of the ingredients of a free cone as compared to the full price of the cones they'd had to buy to trigger the free one. It had finally made sense to Les, although Greg had grasped the concept just looking at the hot pink voucher. It worked, too, creating loyalty and excitement in their customers.

Greg had begun to think the clinic he moonlighted for should employ a similar principle. Reproductive medicine did not come cheap, particularly on the black market. He'd heard rumours that a world egg bank or something along those lines was to be set up, with promises of reproductive products being more affordable and accessible. Surely, if the black marketeers offered a buy-two-get-one-free system, then desperate women might try another round. BTGOF wasn't quite as catchy, of course, but he wouldn't suggest they sold it that way. More that the clinic was taking a caring attitude to the wellbeing and mental health of its patrons. Yes, 'wellbeing' – that was the new in-word in marketing speak. Perhaps he could suggest to Nikki that he meet the boss, or at least speak to him on the phone and share some of his ideas. He had some regarding transport as well as this one for giving the business longevity. Nikki called him Mr Gucci, though Greg knew that was just a nickname – probably because of his designer clothes, but he really didn't know why the top mind in the enterprise was referred to in this way. He was desperate to find out more about the elusive figure who had masterminded the whole operation and called the shots; Nikki acted like she knew him, but Greg wasn't convinced she'd actually met him.

'Going back to the well,' he murmured, imagining saying that to Mr Gucci as he explained that the patient could trigger the use of that free egg, sperm or embryo transfer whenever they wanted. 'They'd hardly put just one egg or embryo back in.' He pictured himself giving a small shrug while seated in a café across from Gucci. 'More likely they'll use their free transfer and add a couple more, so it actually drives more business through.' That wording sounded clumsy, though. He'd need to finesse it.

Greg smiled. He was full of new ideas, and he felt he could actually make a difference to this underground operation if he could just get close enough to earn Mr Gucci's trust.

Feeling chuffed with his notion to help couples over the line, he decided that yes, he would treat himself to a visit to Haigh's tomorrow but only after he'd earned the calories running. He cut across Greenhill Road, entering the parklands and, using the path, wound his way back towards the city and East Terrace. After a fifteen-minute steady clip on long legs, Greg was ringing the bell on a small but tastefully renovated double-fronted, single-storey cottage behind the glamorous East Terrace sprawl that housed clinic after clinic in leafy, quiet streets. This was medical territory, sandwiched between St Andrew's Hospital and Wakefield Hospital with all their respective off-shoot services from pathology to X-rays.

He stared into the security screen and soon enough the door opened to reveal a lab technician.

'You're a bit late,' he said, impolitely speaking through a yawn.

'I'm not actually,' Greg replied, feeling unhelpfully more awake than he wished. 'I've made great time from Dubai.'

'Whatever,' came the unimpressed response. 'Come on, I want to get home.'

Don't we all, Greg thought. This grumpy guy was the regular lab technician here, not nearly as qualified as Nikki, who was a highly experienced embryologist with a degree and Honours in her related subjects and actually made decisions based on her knowledge. This guy was a grunt – a bit like Greg himself was at present, he had to admit, but at least his own job had the sparkle of faraway places and soon, he hoped, would offer the edge of a better class of travel. Grinch, as Greg decided to name him, had only these four walls and some chemical tanks to look at rather than the icons of Europe that Greg was regularly treated to.

'Five straws, right?' Grinch said, yawning again.

'Right.'

'Okay, let's get them loaded. They're all being transferred in the next day or so.'

Greg couldn't wait to be rid of the dewar and its small group of human eggs that he'd taken care of since Dubai. His role was finished in this job run. 'See you later,' he said to the technician, who was now unloading the goblets and their goodies into a tank of liquid nitrogen.

'Next time,' he said over his shoulder, before adding, 'Lock the door on the way out.'

Greg wanted to flip the bird at the security screen, but he knew it was childish, plus he had just persuaded Nikki to talk to Mr Gucci about him. That wasn't worth risking and he began to daydream about the fabulous lounge in Dubai that he might be able to use on his next trip. Tall bottles of sparkling water on demand, good coffee, food aplenty, comfy seats . . . Not to mention free wi-fi and a separate check-in from the herd, giving him the opportunity to adopt that 'I'm a bit important' air. A business class hotel stopover near the airport would be the norm. Given he spent a lot of his life in airports waiting for connections, standing in queues and worrying about delays, the idea of upmarket travel provided an overload of happy thoughts as Greg made his way back across the parklands, dragging his small suitcase, this time in the direction of his modest unit at Dulwich on the edge of the city.

In his upbeat mood he decided to follow through on another life goal: to run in the London Marathon. Next year, he'd do it. That gave him a full twelve months to train, which he'd begin this weekend running up Mount Lofty. *Who knows, Greg,* he thought, as he visualised himself crossing the finish line to huge applause, *you might make the front pages yet.*

6

The family that lived in Palm Street looked like any other well-heeled family of Medindie, South Australia. The posh neighbourhood was characterised by quiet, wide, leafy streets, the thwack of tennis balls on Saturday afternoons and a boisterous, wine-fuelled atmosphere on summer evenings. Children playing in their sandstone-rimmed, inground pools with water features and expensive tiling from Europe knew nothing of their privilege despite the private schools they attended – Wilderness if they were girls, and St Peter's College if they were boys. Occasionally the more liberal-minded decided their children needed a mixed-gender education, with a more eclectic gathering from all over the state that included some battlers who wanted a top education for their children. If the family was of that ilk they'd choose Pembroke School.

As was murmured, 'old money' lived in these tightly held postcodes. Most of these families kept moving in a tight circle week to week; the wives drove SUVs up to school gates, Pilates and to lunch, while the husbands drove an assortment of

Mercedes, BMWs, Audis and, of course, Porsches, to work and their weekend sport. Dogs were pedigree, increasingly a mix of popular, reliable breeds that didn't shed, and shown off around the incredible choice of parkland that not only embraced the city but was dotted all over the well-to-do suburbs.

Holiday homes were kept at a few select spots – Victor Harbor for family money, while for newer money it was Port Willunga, known affectionately as Port Willy, and Encounter Bay. Middleton Beach was gaining in popularity, too, and then, of course, the jewel, Kangaroo Island – referred to as KI – which gave ultimate bragging rights. These folk would likely take off for the whole school summer break so their children could play with buckets and spades on safe, deserted beaches for weeks on end. In winter some families headed to the ski fields, though Europe was always on the menu for the parents seeking a more grown-up escape.

Jem Maddox was one of these mothers. Her name was Jemima but she was rarely called that by anyone. She had attended Wilderness, where her two daughters, Isabelle and Holly, were now students, except she had boarded. Her parents based themselves in the Barossa Valley for much of the week; the family owned a prestigious wine label and vineyards across all the wine country of South Australia. Jem had studied art but hadn't gone on with it in any professional capacity, having met Mark, the man she wanted to marry, at Adelaide University. He too came from money and his parents lived in Springfield, another salubrious suburb on the other side of town, with sprawling homes that were more eclectic than the sombrely elegant, traditional bluestones of North Adelaide where her family had its city base.

She'd married her uni sweetheart, who at twenty-five was hitting his stride, and given up her casual graphic design work to travel with him, first to London, then to Scotland and to another lucrative post in Singapore, before returning to South Australia as their firstborn, a son, began to get close to school age.

The family expanded, adding the two pretty golden-headed sisters to dark-haired Hugh, who'd done prep at 'Saints'. He was one of those cheerful students who avoided negative attention by staying in the slipstream of average achievement across all his academic subjects but winning a lot of cheers on the field for his cricket and footy. Mark had begun to dream of his son being drafted into the AFL or playing cricket for Australia's top XI. Jem hoped he'd choose the latter because the collisions of those boys on the footy oval were too frightening.

The girls were thriving at 'Wildy', and they'd now got a weekday routine going where Mark dropped off Hugh while she and the girls lingered over breakfast and then, after slipping into her training gear, in which she still cut a great figure in her late thirties, she walked them to school in Hawkers Road.

This morning was no different. As the girls yelled their goodbyes and ran in to meet their friends, Jem lifted her hand in a wave to her daughters and then in a wider arc to a cluster of mothers she knew. She noted that the scintillatingly wealthy Alannah Petras, whom everyone seemed to orbit, was not in their midst. Their husbands played golf together, but so far the eighteen official holes and perhaps the nineteenth at the club house had been their only social meets. Mark was pressing to have the power couple to their home for a meal.

Normally she preferred to bring the dog and take her post drop-off exercise in the quieter foothills but today she decided to jog along the River Torrens trail, known locally as the linear track. It began somewhere in Athelstone and swooped thirty kilometres following the river, connecting through bridges all the way to the river's mouth at the edge of Adelaide's CBD, passing through glorious parkland, past the Adelaide Zoo, the

University, the rowing sheds and moving in a line that echoed the great North Terrace, behind the Adelaide Festival Centre to the Torrens Weir that dated back to 1881.

Jem's grandparents had been there as children when the sluice gates were first opened in the late 1920s. 'Turned what was just a pile of muddy waterholes into this splendid lake in the middle of the city,' her grandfather had told her. So now she always thought of him whenever she made it as far as the weir.

The majority of the track was under bitumen and conveniently ran both sides of the river. It used to be a favourite route of hers but she'd become miffed by the presence of more and more cyclists, some of whom hit dangerous speeds as they used the track to commute into the city without having to negotiate a single car.

Jem parked her SUV behind the Hackney Hotel and skipped across the road to one of the small but many entrances into the linear track. Immediately a bike came hurtling along, its rider urgently ringing the bell. She mentally waved a fist at the speedster; he looked like a student and was probably running late for a tutorial. *Hope you fail*, she thought churlishly and then told herself she hadn't meant it, she just needed her morning coffee. She could grab one if she went all the way to the weir and back – a seven-kilometre walk, but why not? She was feeling good and had no one but the cleaner to return home to. Best she took her time anyway, or the cleaner liked to stop and chat.

She found her rhythm, usually just over six kilometres per hour – that's what her treadmill told her at home anyway – and got lost in her thoughts. First the children, and then the widening distance between her and Mark. He was looking a bit haggard recently, not his usual crisp, starched self. When she'd asked, he'd fobbed her off: 'Just work. The usual.'

Work was demanding for all the gynaecologists in Adelaide; everyone knew South Australia was a good state for raising children. People left, of course, perhaps for tertiary study, certainly for work, but they also often returned because they felt it in their DNA that South Australia was an easy place to live. Good schools abounded and traffic was nothing like what they would have encountered in the eastern states.

She gave a wry inward smile that South Australia also seemed to yield bizarre and ugly crimes, from child porn syndicates to the infamous 'bodies in the barrel' murders. Oh yes, crime flourished but thankfully it didn't touch her in the rarefied air of her cloistered existence.

Jem arrived at the weir faster than she'd anticipated and paused to watch the water rushing past beneath her. She looked back at the long curve of the linear track, not even out of breath and feeling suddenly very fortunate for her blessed life where nothing seemed to go wrong. 'Touch wood,' she murmured, bending down to touch the boards on the bridge and pretending to re-tie her sneaker laces. She was about to set off when a voice stopped her.

'Hey, Jem!'

It was Belinda Maynard, a busybody mother. 'Oh, hi, Bel. How are you?'

'Good, good. This is Kara – she's new. Her son's in our year at Saints.'

'Welcome, Kara. New to the school or new to Adelaide?'

'Both,' the woman said. 'It's quiet,' she said, slightly pointedly.

'You'll get used to it,' Bel assured her. 'You won't want to go back to the hellhole of Sydney, I promise. Now, Jem, I think I saw Mark just now in a café.'

Jem frowned. 'My husband, Mark?' It felt stupid to ask that. Why else would one of the snoopiest members of the mothers' fraternity even mention the guy?

'Yes, *your* Mark. How many do you know?'

'Sorry. Mark's at his rooms though.'

Bel shrugged. 'Well, it was the dashing Dr Maddox I just saw drinking coffee over the bridge in the sun.'

'With a woman?' Jem immediately regretted that question too.

Bel raised her eyebrows, quick to jump on the subtext. 'Did I say with a woman? Gosh, suspicious mind, Jem! Yes, but don't worry, it all looked above board. She was in walking gear. I'd kill for her hot pink trainers. Haven't seen those around our shores – must be an overseas buy,' she pondered vacantly. But Jem wasn't fooled; Bel was prodding.

'Probably work.' Jem dismissed it.

'You'll catch him if you hurry. See you, Jem. Don't forget the fundraiser later this week. We need everyone there.' Bel kissed the air somewhere near Jem's cheek and then prodded Kara in the direction they were heading.

Jem set off at a jog as though that was always her intention. Turning her back on the loud rush of waters, she made her way across the bridge to the other bank. At the café Bel had mentioned, she paused, bending again to tighten the laces on her sneakers that didn't need tightening. Under the brim of her peaked cap she stole a glance around at all the café patrons. No Mark.

Busybody Bel had obviously been mistaken. Jem straightened, jogged on until she was just past the café's walls and then dropped back to her normal walking stride to dial Mark. Voicemail. She dialled again and this time he picked up.

'Hi, it's me,' she said.

'I gather,' he replied. 'Clinic's on. Anything wrong?'

'Nothing . . . er, I was out on a jog.'

'And?'

She frowned. 'Where are you?'

'I just told you,' he said, sounding ever so slightly indignant. 'Why?'

'I can hear traffic.'

'I've just seen a client out to her car.'

'Oh . . . a bit odd,' she said, giving a short laugh that sounded fake even to her.

'If you'd told her what I just had to, you might also have escorted a weeping woman into the car park. Look, Jem, my next patient is waiting, so if this isn't imp—'

'Sorry, it's not. Um, you won't forget to pick up—'

'No, I don't forget, you know that.'

'Yes. Sorry. You get on and I'll get home.'

'See you tonight. I'll be home around seven. You've remembered the barbecue with the Petrases on Sunday?' he said. 'Make sure you get the very best cut of lamb, please. Go to that special butcher in Norwood.'

She didn't want to, had thought she'd just nip into the Coles at St Peters or check out the butcher in that small, easy-to-park shopping centre, but she said, 'Of course.' The truth was that the meat, though outrageously pricey, would be better from the butcher he mentioned. 'See you later, then.'

He didn't reply. He simply rang off.

That's how they were now; no longer much to say to one another other than the daily grind stuff of family life. If they were discussing the children then, yes, both could be animated and even share some smiles, but sometime over the last few years, they'd drifted. She hadn't seen it coming. She hadn't even realised it was happening. But try as she might, she couldn't seem to spark his interest again. It was like living with an entirely new version of Mark Maddox – and now she was checking up on him.

Jem grimaced, admonishing herself for being suspicious. Marriage had changed their relationship, of course. Children, work, life . . . rubbing away against the surface of their original love, layered with lust, to change its shape like sandstone. She could remember their time in London, when he'd come home from a night shift in the ER and wake her up, still damp from a shower, kissing her shoulder and nuzzling at her ear. They were mad for each other back then. Their lovely Victorian flat in Battersea was their haven – their sex cave, Mark called it – and afterwards they'd sleep tangled in each other. But it hadn't been like that for years, and the physical contact had dropped away dramatically over the last two years to almost non-existent in the past six months.

She justified it to herself, knowing they were often both too tired to do much more than wish one another hello and goodbye. There was increasingly more demand on their limited time together as Mark's work intensified and so did family life.

Mark loved their trio every bit as fiercely as she did, she knew that. There was nothing he wouldn't do for his children and, while his relationship with her may have receded to politeness, the bond he shared with each of them had only grown.

They still travelled whenever they could and those were times to reconnect. He could still make her laugh and he liked to spend money on her, although increasingly she suspected that was more about his ego rather than spoiling her. She could still turn him on if the moment was right and she knew how to manage his moods, but lately, where had his desire for her gone? If she had only one word to describe them as a couple she'd say they were reliable; they no longer had the little secret smiles she used to love. Romance had disappeared and yet it was romance she craved – just a tiny bit to feel that rush of helpless desire again. Now, their conversation revolved about the practicality of their wealthy life-style. Did they go to the beach house this summer or take the kids to Disneyland? Did they upgrade the cars this year or wait for when the new models were available? Those days of daydreaming together, when they owned nothing and everything felt far away, were well and truly over. Now there was no daydreaming. *You want it, get it. You don't like something, change it.*

Jem would swap the new conservatory they were talking about building for a weekend picnicking in bed like they used to. *Let it go*, she told herself. Mark worked his arse off to provide and when the children became more independent, they would rediscover each other. 'Your father and I did,' her mother had counselled only recently when Jem had shared her concern that they were drifting apart.

Jem shook off her thoughts, feeling even more guilty now for even bothering to look in the café when she knew he was at work in his busy clinic.

Stupid Bel. Too nosy for her own good and such a stirrer.

7

LONDON

Jack was ushered into the office of the new Chief Superintendent of Homicide and Serious Crime branch, where he hovered in the doorway.

'Ma'am,' he said, nodding, tempering his desire to beam her a bright smile. Carol Rowland's track record suggested she was suspicious of overt charm from colleagues. As he regarded the tightly scraped-back hair, which couldn't hold back what gravity and years had wreaked, the loose, plump skin around her jaw, he remembered his old boss's advice: 'She's a top police officer but old school. Be warned, she'll eat your balls for breakfast, Jack. Don't expect touchy-feely. You've been warned.'

'Ah, good morning, Detective Superintendent Hawksworth.'

He couldn't pinpoint where she was from, but was there a northern lilt hiding in that voice somewhere?

He allowed a modest smile to ghost and disappear. 'Please call me Jack.'

'All right. Come in. Can I offer you anything? I'll be having a coffee myself.'

'Er, no, thank you, ma'am. I've just had one actually,' he lied. There was no way he was drinking instant coffee from the Yard.

'And how are you, Jack?' She didn't wait for his answer, gesturing to the chair in front of her large desk in the spacious office. 'Fully healed?'

'Bit achey in places but otherwise fine, thank you,' he said, undoing his jacket and seating himself.

'I've been reading your enviable track record for catching your man – or woman, even.' She slid her gaze up from his file and there was something reptilian and knowing about the look; his instincts knew this was an agile mind forged from experience. Carol Rowland had joined as a cadet in her teens and was now in her mid-fifties. Her resumé read impressively, her rise meteoric, even considering that the Metropolitan Police Department had taken up the challenge to promote women in the Force.

'I like to finish what I begin,' he replied, wishing he didn't sound glib.

There was a knock at the door and her assistant stepped in quietly, placing a cup of coffee on Rowland's desk.

'Thanks, Jan,' Rowland said with the briefest of polite smiles and Jan disappeared as swiftly as she'd arrived.

Jack watched the steam rise from what looked like watered-down mud, but then he was biased when it came to anything but Italian-style espresso.

'Well, Jack,' she said, taking a sip.

He could hear from her more business-like tone that the pleasantries – such that they were – were now over. He welcomed it.

'My impression is that the former Acting Chief of this division gave you plenty of rope?' She formed the statement as a question, cornering him into responding.

'Martin Sharpe and I had a good understanding.' His expression dropped; that had come out all wrong. 'What I mean, ma'am, is that he understood how I work and allowed me to run my ops with some freedom.'

'Martin and I are from different generations.'

Jack gave a slight shrug of appreciation for this fact, unsure of what she wanted from him.

'I make my team more accountable, Jack. Are you prepared to be more accountable?'

He frowned. 'In what way?'

'In every way,' she replied.

Jack had expected as much. 'Well, if I'm leading an op then I like to choose my own people.'

'I don't see a problem with that, but I'm long enough in the tooth to know that when your private life steps across the invisible boundary into your working life, problems occur.'

Jack frowned more deeply. 'I know things got complicated—'

'Not getting it? Let me spell it out for you, Jack. A prisoner is dead because of you disregarding protocol. She had no business being involved in Operation Mirror.'

He dipped his gaze. That much was true.

'And then let's consider your previous op,' she began airily.

He knew what was coming.

'Another of your lovely women is dead . . . because of you.'

Jack's belly felt as though it was squirming with worms. He did not need to be reminded of a very dark time of his life.

'Now, let's bring ourselves up to date with an ambitious journalist whose life was put at risk during your most recent op.'

'To be fair, she was already involved – she approached me about the story—'

'Yes, but you brought her firmly into the killer's sights and if not for some heroism on your part, she too might be cooling in a grave. Now, this is a pattern, Jack. Three women involved in your cases, and three women involved with you. What is your problem? Are you a serial killer of hearts or what?'

'I . . .' He shook his head. 'I do not deliberately solicit attention from women who are linked to my work.'

She gave him a slow blink, considering his answer. 'I take a dim view of golden boys in the Force. It's my experience that they lose perspective, feel they're bigger than their positions, superior to the protocols . . . that they can be rebels without repercussion.'

'I don't like that title and I don't consider myself as such.'

'But, you see, so many others do. You really are a poster boy for New Scotland Yard. TV loves you. When you're on screen you can captivate the audience.' She regarded him with a vaguely bemused expression.

He shook his head, perplexed. 'What do you want me to say?'

'Nothing just yet. I want you to listen.' She paused, waiting for him.

He felt like saying, 'Yes, mother,' but resisted, simply raising his gaze to meet hers, anticipating some sort of axe that was about to fall.

'You're an enigma, Jack. Everything I can discover suggests that you have earned your reputation as one of our finest detectives. The people who work with you, including the receptionists, canteen staff and security guards, have nothing but praise. You have some sort of superpower, being enormously liked by all despite your popularity with women and your blokey friendliness with men. You're a chameleon.'

'I thought I was an enigma.' It slipped out and he was immediately chastened by her held breath and pursed lips.

'Be careful, Jack. Praise from me is rare.'

'Ma'am. This does not feel like praise. It feels like a dressing down.'

'Does it?' she asked, not sounding surprised. 'I'm simply setting some boundaries for our working relationship going forward.'

'By criticising me?'

'By offering up an observer's view of how vulnerable you seem to be to a needy woman. And by needy, I don't mean helpless. I mean in need of friendship or, more to the point, romance. You seem to readily oblige and it bleeds into the cases, both metaphorically and literally.'

'I do not seek this attention. They are not prey. I am not a predator.'

'No, and I want to be clear that I am not accusing you of using your position to influence these women. But I suspect, Jack, that you are as vulnerable as the women who fall for you.'

He frowned at her. 'What do you mean?'

'You show an antiquated chivalry that is admirable but also dangerous in your work. Can I cite the police psychologist? You were sent to her for counselling and yet I've been assured you both enjoyed a period of . . . shall we say, passion?'

'Let's,' he said, unable to hide his despair.

'All right. I won't go on, Jack, but I'm hoping you take my point that you work in a slipstream of danger and anyone who shares your life, especially if they are somehow linked to your work, might face some of that danger too.'

'Ma'am, I'll say again that I don't go looking for these relationships; somehow they find me.'

Her look of feigned pity made him sigh.

'I'm keen for us to agree that you will, from hereon, be more aware of who you develop romantic . . . entanglements with. I would be grateful if they were not people involved in a case that you may be investigating. Let's keep the lanes clean and clearly outlined. It means I don't have to front the gutter press, read the lascivious headlines or field questions that take the focus away from an operation and onto your sex life.'

He winced as Martin's remark – *Be warned, she'll eat your balls for breakfast* – haunted him.

Rowland's stern expression shifted to interested. 'Now, I've read your report but I'd like to hear your rationale for wanting to head off to Australia from you directly.'

He suspected that he hadn't hidden well enough the surprise that had surely flickered across his face; after this humiliating conversation he hadn't expected to be talking about his hunch regarding a new organised crime syndicate. Jack cleared his throat, ignored the warmth that had developed at his collar and began the story with Amelia's untimely death, feeling relieved that the more he talked about the potential lead in the black market of human fertility, the further he left behind his burning shame.

His tone became less pointed as he felt himself relax into the facts of his discovery. 'It was purely coincidence, ma'am. And I suppose I could have let it go but she was a bright girl, a good student and popular, with plenty of potential, and I resented that her life had been given so cheaply. Just a bit of digging has yielded some more and ominously similar cases.'

Rowland flicked a page in Jack's report and nodded for him to continue. 'The deaths have occurred up and down the country. The ages and demographics of the women who died are wildly different – from a twenty-year-old from London to a 36-year-old in Birmingham, a 32-year-old in Bristol and a 26-year-old in Norwich. And only one or two resembled another, so it's easy to understand how no flags were immediately raised.'

'Until you joined the dots of their backstories.'

'Yes.' He waited but she looked back at him, clearly anticipating more. 'Er, while deaths ranged from sepsis – as in Amelia's case – to rapid internal bleeding, pelvic infections, abscesses, et cetera, all of these women, despite being of different ages, backgrounds and ethnicities, had some commonalities.'

'Walk me through them, Jack,' Rowland said, reaching for her cup again, and he watched her full, unpainted lips blow on the hot liquid before wrinkling into a pout over the rim of the cup to sip again. He swore he could taste the bitter, burnt flavour of the instant coffee she was drinking.

Jack leaned forward in his seat. 'All of these deaths occurred directly following a short trip into Eastern Europe. I have narrowed down the destinations to Vilnius in Lithuania and Belgrade in Serbia. Each of the women were of child-bearing age, still ovulating, still menstruating.' He hoped he didn't sound awkward, but she seemed distracted, listening carefully.

'Still fertile,' she murmured, nodding.

'Exactly. Each was found to have traces of clomiphene citrate, which is a drug prescribed to stimulate ovulation, and human chorionic gonadotropin was found too, which triggers egg release from the ovary.'

'Are these drugs available in Britain on the NHS?'

'Absolutely. Our National Health Service provides for couples needing precisely this sort of fertility treatment. Saint Mary's Hospital in Manchester was the first to be a fully NHS-funded IVF unit in the UK – that was back in 1982. The procedure for egg stimulation and collection is standard, done daily all over the country.'

'So . . .' She fixed him with an intense stare. She wore no make-up, her features fresh and honest with her eyes being the most startling; they were the colour of freshly cured concrete and just as hard. 'No reason for these women to be heading abroad, whether they live in Cardiff, Glasgow or Canterbury.'

He looked away from the stare that had pinned him. 'None whatsoever if they were seeking treatment. Top clinics abound here. However, if they were selling their eggs, then there was every reason to head abroad.'

'Do you believe there are no clinics providing illegal funds for human material in the United Kingdom, Jack?' She sounded dubious.

Now he did grin; it arrived helplessly. 'No, ma'am. I'm sure there are, but we don't have any proof of these . . . not yet anyway. What we do know is that there is clandestine activity of this type underway in Vilnius and Belgrade – because I have the bodies to prove just how wrong things have gone. I know that these groups send in marketers to prey on common rooms in sixth-form colleges and canteens in unis, training schools. Perhaps they even leave flyers on women's cars outside supermarkets. Amelia Peters was keeping it a tight secret from her family but her closest friend was able to tell me more. Presumably Amelia had signed something or certainly been cautioned, perhaps even frightened into keeping her activities confidential.'

'And all were paid?'

'Yes, that's another commonality. For most of these women we have evidence – mostly circumstantial, I'll admit – that each was suddenly flush.' For the first time he took out a small notebook and flipped through a few pages. 'Er, Mary from Bristol suddenly purchased a new boiler and fixed the leaky roof of a house she shares with partner, Ken; they've been together for more than ten years. Ken says he knew of no money to do this and the need for repairs had created a lot of angst in an otherwise happy relationship.'

Rowland nodded for him to continue.

'Sally from Norwich, who worked as a part-time cleaner, part-time carer, was able to take herself and her kids for a holiday in Spain, which baffled her parents, who had only the previous month lent her money to pay for her mortgage. Sally had been to Belgrade for a weekend, claiming it was a training course in a new direct marketing campaign for cleaning products.'

'Hmm, that's creative,' his boss murmured.

'This family also said the children had never been on a proper holiday and Sally had taken out an injunction against her ex because of his violence. I gather the trip was an escape after yet another horrible beating.' He took a breath. 'Amelia, the student in my class, paid one month's rent that was in arrears and two additional months in advance, in cash. Her flatmates said she had always been behind but they liked her because she was clean and quiet, so they cut her some slack. She also paid for a season ticket on the Underground, replaced her coat and settled some other, smaller overdue bills, all in the same week. Meanwhile, Jenny from Birmingham paid a substantial amount towards a new car for her son who had just been offered a job that needed him to provide his own wheels. This woman was a school librarian, a single mother of one, who her friends say was constantly fretting about money and especially that she wanted to help her son win his new job.'

The Chief Superintendent rolled her eyes and sighed. 'It's so shitty to hear this. Seems no one's doing it to buy diamonds, eh?'

'No. In each case it was a sort of desperate measure to either cover bills or do something special for others.' He shrugged. 'I could go on but they all read much the same.'

'So you believe they're selling their eggs for good money but the surgery has gone wrong.'

'Precisely. I imagine dozens proceed without any hassle and no one is any the wiser. In these instances, where it's gone wrong, all is well at first; they come home and then there are complications. I suspect for every complication there could be two dozen successful procedures, but I have no handle on this yet.'

'Right. So, why Australia?'

Jack nodded. 'Amelia's mother was very helpful in working through her daughter's movements before her death. She found a couple of taxi receipts that showed the same destination in Vilnius. I thought it would be a hotel but it turns out it is a clinic. With the help of a couple of mates from SOCA I have been able to establish that the clinic is involved in reproductive medicine, amongst other obstetric and gynaecological disciplines.'

'Okay. And is the Serious Organised Crime Agency involved in this as a formal investigation?'

'No. It was a favour to me.'

She frowned. As he couldn't fully read her consternation and was worried a reprimand might be coming for leaning on mates, he skipped forward.

'I've looked into who owns the clinic in Vilnius and amongst the directors is someone who goes by the name of John Smith.'

Her gaze snapped to his and her expression was one of light incredulity.

Jack lifted a shoulder in a shrug. 'Set off my internal alarm too. A little more digging with some help of some others'—he cleared his throat—'and it turns out this person is based in Australia.'

'How many other directors?'

'Plenty in the clinic, which offers everything from recon-structive surgery to straightforward obstetrics, if it ever is straightforward,' he commented, giving her a glance. 'But there are only two directors in the division known as Veistis. That's Lithuanian for "breed" or "propagate".'

'Catchy,' she remarked, making him smile inwardly and have his first inkling that this woman may have some humour she kept hidden.

'Indeed, ma'am,' he said, risking a grin. 'Once I had the name, I used up some credit I had with Interpol and we were able to hunt down John Smith as a director of a similar clinic in Belgrade.'

'While I feel a strong desire to tackle you about your use of other divisions and services, I can't help but feel intrigued. I find myself saying, "Very good, Jack." I'm impressed.'

'It's a start.'

'And you want me to sign off on a joint op?'

'In a perfect world, yes, although I'm figuring from your tone that isn't likely.'

'The Australians will respond positively, I'm sure.' She sighed. 'We're talking how many deaths here? Six?'

He shook his head. 'Of those I feel confident attributing to the clinics in Eastern Europe, it's eight English women in the space of around two years. I imagine the true figure could be more.'

'Eight families wrecked,' she remarked, and it was another glimpse into Rowland that surprised Jack. So there was some empathy lurking within. She was growing on him.

'That we know of,' he qualified. 'And then if we extrapolate, there could be women from Ireland and I'd need to liaise with An Garda Síochána—'

'You say that rather well,' she quipped. 'Most of us say Irish Police.'

He smiled, liking her even more. 'Then there's Wales, Scotland . . . Europe, even.'

He watched the Chief Superintendent drain her coffee to the last bitter sip and then sigh. 'Jack, I'll be straight. A full-blown joint operation with Australia would take some setting up.'

He couldn't help how his shoulders slumped, especially as he'd begun to feel that she might say yes. He began to stand and the familiar pain at the site of the stabbing knifed through his side at the movement.

'Stay seated, Jack.' It was spoken softly but it was a command nonetheless. 'I haven't finished.'

He sat, inhaling lightly and slowly through his nose so his frustration wasn't obvious. 'I worked a case a couple of years back connected with illegal immigrants—'

She held his gaze. 'I've read it.' Her tone was sympathetic. 'Your point?'

'I didn't think I'd run across a more insidious situation but if what I believe is happening here is true, then this is just as bad. The only one winning is the person with the bank account into which all the money flows.'

Rowland did a slow blink. 'Well, I imagine the couples who achieve pregnancy feel like winners and the method becomes irrelevant.' She looked self-conscious and he didn't hold her gaze, wondering if she'd had first-hand experience with infertility.

'No doubt,' Jack said, looking defeated.

'It's not my intention to take a facile view of this. There's scope for a more informal collaboration between our two countries. The Australians would have to be fully briefed so we can make a formal request for you to "help with enquiries" but I think they'd be very open to us working together, given the breadth of this potential black market you might have unearthed. I can start open liaison with the Australian Federal Police via Australia House.'

'I'd be seconded?'

'Let's just say we get you formally acknowledged so the Australians know what you're up to. Perhaps you'd be more agile if you were investigating without the harness of an op and its regulations?'

His eyes widened. 'You want me undercover?' he asked, surprised.

'No, not at all. I gather you have a sister in Australia. Why not go visit . . . part of your recuperation, shall we say? A holiday in the sun and, while you're at it, a visit to South Australia. What you do on your *holiday*,' she said, a slight rise in her intonation on the final word, 'is your business. But you are going to touch base with colleagues while you're there, aren't you? I'm sure you'll be welcomed into the bosom of the South Australian team that deals with organised crime.'

Jack's smile broke gradually but still he waited.

She shook her head slightly, a little dismissively. 'Of course, the Met will cover your "holiday" expenses. This would be part of our gratitude to you for your sterling work on the Colin Jarvis case last year, and reparation for the serious injury you endured in the line of duty.' It was her turn to smile – small and brief. 'Book your flights and off you go to warmer climes, Jack. And if you can track down that bank account owner, I promise you I'll get you the full support from both sides of the world. But trust me when I say that I believe you can work more expediently without others holding the reins. Trust your instincts and go hunt.'

'Right. Blimey. Thank you.'

She shrugged again. 'If we can, let's aim to avenge those deaths by nailing the perpetrator, but tread lightly, Jack. You're on someone else's turf – I'm sure I don't need to remind you of that.'

He nodded. 'I understand. Will I get any co-operation?'

'I gather you've already got some sort of carte blanche entry via Martin Sharpe's colleague based in Sydney, am I right?'

'Yes – that was to do a work sabbatical, I gather.'

'Well, I would let him know what you're up to. Tap into his network. Go and meet with some of the senior personnel in Major Crime as a courtesy. You never know who you might run into.'

'And if I get nowhere?'

She gave a look of surprise that had a cavalier quality to it. 'Nothing ventured, nothing gained,' she quoted. 'I'll cover your expenses – keep them modest – for two weeks. And I want you to report to me regularly. I must be informed; it's important that I don't look like I let my officers go rogue. I'll protect you as best I can but do not overstep the boundaries . . . If you do find proof of what we seek, then you step back and let me handle it from there. No threats, no arrests, nothing . . . You do not have anyone's sanction to behave in any formal way. Do we understand one another?'

'We do.'

'Then happy hunting, Jack. Let Jan know your travel details and I'll look forward to hearing from you.'

'Thank you, ma'am.'

She nodded. 'Martin mentioned you're a bit of a rebel. Please don't test my patience – or his faith in you that I'm relying on.' She paused to give him a tolerant half smile. 'Travel safe.'

8

ADELAIDE

Greg had been back to Europe twice since his request to Nikki and he kept following up about the upgrade. The first time, back from Belgrade, she'd fobbed him off, saying she'd mentioned it to Mr Gucci and heard nothing. The second time, when he'd returned from Vilnius with ten additional straws of eggs, his largest black-market transport so far, he'd hardened his enquiry.

'Look, Greg, don't badger me,' Nikki had snapped. 'I've done what I can. I'm not going to say anything else.'

'Then connect me to him, and I'll say it all myself.'

'No!'

'Why not?' he bleated. 'Ten extra straws . . . that's at least sixty, maybe eighty eggs, Nikki, and what are they worth? Thousands of dollars a pop. And that's just the latest run. Think of all the runs I've done.'

'Think of all the money you've earned.'

'I earn it as a genuine courier.'

'And then some! It's the black-market ones that really pay.'

'Oh, come on, Nikki. Please, tell me who he is and let me talk to him.'

That had been two nights ago. Their conversation had ended in a huffy farewell, with Nikki barely managing to find more than a silent, slightly hostile wave. They'd never exactly been friends – it wasn't as though he saw her socially, much as he'd like to, but even so, it felt like a barrier had gone up between them since then. A few months ago it might have niggled unhappily at him but after the most recent trip, which had seen long queues and delays, the knowledge that everyone in business class was being whisked off to overnight hotels or pampering in a lounge with showers and quiet areas was a tipping point.

A five-hour layover had become nine due to technical problems with the craft; another one had to be brought in from who knew where – who even cared. He'd boarded the plane with the taste of soured coffee in his throat and a furry tongue that disgusted him. And he'd still had to face a fourteen-hour flight, not in the A380, to Adelaide.

Even now, the memory of the trip ripened in his mind like an old banana, growing blacker over days. He wanted a better deal, simple as that. It was surely worth too much for them to compromise their underground operation over a better class of travel for their busiest, most reliable courier. He had never let them down; he'd never said no to a job that others might have avoided and he was now carrying more clandestine material than ever, for no additional money and no decent perks in the comfort department – but all the risk.

It had to change.

My case is strong, he thought, reversing like a boss into a tiny car space and barely breaking a sweat. He just wanted an opportunity to argue his case with the right guy.

Greg hadn't slept well and had decided he should wear himself out with a hike from Waterfall Gully to Mount Lofty Summit in order to have a good sleep tonight. It wasn't as busy as he'd dreaded and it lifted his mood slightly; he told himself it boded well and perhaps he'd be hearing from Mr Gucci any minute.

'Lucky us – not too crammed,' another walker said, emerging from the shadows of the morning twilight. The stranger was older than Greg but he looked strong, with well-shaped muscles on a lean body, precisely how Greg wished he might appear to others. The walker winked at his own quip before pulling off a windcheater to display biceps and pecs defined beneath his clingy Nike shirt, which sat over floaty shorts that reached the middle of his long bronzed thighs. He could be a trainer to the stars, Greg thought. Mr Fabulous, needing to look perfect in case the paparazzi were hiding in the scrub.

'Yeah,' Greg said, trying not to glance at the man with too much envy as he locked his car and moved to a small wall to do some warm-up exercises.

'See you at the top, mate,' Mr Fabulous said, grinning from a face that Greg was sure could attract any woman he chose. He loped off like a wild animal at ease in its surrounds.

'Bastard,' Greg muttered but stuck to his routine; if he didn't, he knew he'd suffer calf cramps and shin splints. Mr Fabulous looked as though his muscular calves wouldn't dare experience the sort of debilitating cramp that Greg's did. A bad one last year had caused his right leg to bruise from the force of the spasm, leaving him all but trembling from its power and fearful of a repercussion for days. He scowled. And there was yet another reason to travel in business class, he grumbled to himself as he stretched his right leg carefully.

Another guy had arrived now and was taking his time stretching. He too looked strong. Well, long-distance runners were traditionally weedy-looking, Greg comforted himself, together with the thought that one day soon he would pull the trigger and enter the London Marathon. If London was successful, he'd do the New York Marathon too. The final part of his daydream was to do a hike in Nepal and he knew from reading about it online that you needed to do some serious training to achieve a successful experience over there. But these regular jogs from Waterfall Gully to Mount Lofty and back were excellent conditioning – all part of his five-year plan.

He looked back at the newcomer and was impressed that he was taking so much time with his stretches. 'A man after my own heart,' he murmured under his breath. The guy looked European – Spanish maybe – and a bit too muscled for long-range running, but Greg imagined the Spaniard would overtake him quickly. It didn't matter; running was about personal bests. What other people achieved was irrelevant. Greg had already schooled himself to believe that he was not a racer but an achiever, and what mattered were his own times, his own successes.

It was April, one of the two best months in South Australia. The main heat of summer had finally passed and the mornings were cool – chilly even – but the autumn days were blessed by mild, heart-warming sunshine from a dome of cloudless blue. As the month drew on, the lifegiving rains would come and the days would slip into cold nights. Despite the nip in the air and the temptation to wear a layer or two against it, experience had taught him to tough it out for the first few minutes because all too fast he'd be fully warm and wishing he didn't have the burden of clothing tied around his waist. With a slight shiver, he set off in a T-shirt emblazoned with the original *Star Wars* cast – an old favourite from his school days and still going strong, if a little threadbare. He bent to swoosh tight the Quicklaces on his trail shoes, liking the zipping sound they made because they were still relatively new, then righted the very small and light backpack that carried his phone, water, bandaids and some lollies for a bit of sugar.

Greg hit his comfy pace before he'd even covered half a kilometre. He liked to jog for as long as he could – even if it did probably equate to a striding walk by the time the incline had raised the stakes and his breathing. But it was a near eight-kilometre trail there and back, so he needed to get some aerobic work in before he was helplessly slowed by the hillside.

The trail was a class four, considered 'hard' by whomever classed these things. That was reassuring because he'd never failed to complete it and always returned with a regular pulse and not 'fit to die', as some people claimed. Mind you, there were a lot of boomers on the track who could cark it with their dicky hearts and plethora of pills keeping their arthritis and high blood pressure at bay. Some people used it to train for an upcoming trip; the current favourite seemed to be the French Way, one of the Camino de Santiago routes. He'd like to do it too. As he got into his rhythm he began to plan maybe taking some annual leave while on one of his forthcoming work trips and spending a couple of weeks doing the walk. It sounded feasible.

He passed two women and gathered they were discussing weight loss by doing this trail at least once a week. *Not if you stuff your faces at the top though*, he thought, knowing it was uncharitable but not really caring. There was a café at both the summit and the bottom of the trail, always crowded, but he'd not visited either of them.

He sometimes saw members of the Adelaide Crows footy team changing up their training to jog up the hill. They'd never quite reclaimed their glory of those back-to-back premierships in the 1990s; he remembered the boisterous Grand Final parties and joining in with his parents, family and friends, screaming at the television. Even so, he couldn't deny he remained a fan and still got a ping of excitement if he saw the familiar colours whizzing past him. Not today though.

Greg now jogged around a couple who had paused at the boardwalk that formed the Waterfall Gully lookout. Their backpacks looked so heavy he pitied them. *How much do you need other than a bottle of water? It's only two hours to the top at a steady pace, not even fast.* At his clip, he'd be back at his car within three hours, and maybe he could knock some minutes off if he jogged a bit faster. He intensified his stride and thought he caught sight of the celebrity trainer guy's black outfit, recalling that he had run off with only a bum bag around his waist, probably carrying just his phone. Hard-arse!

Greg snatched a glance over his shoulder. No sign of the Spaniard. Maybe he would beat him to the top. He cleared his mind and ran as hard as he could, knowing he would slow within a minute or so. Someone had once told him that going full out, even for a count to twenty, and doing that several times, could rapidly improve fitness.

But the all-out thing didn't work for him – not uphill, anyway. It made him feel nauseated. Time to find the groove and a steady rhythm to the summit. He hit play on his iPod Nano, found his happy pace again, which he knew was around eight kilometres per hour on an ascent, and dug in. He clicked through his playlist until he heard a powerful loop of strings signal the start of his current favourite song by Coldplay and tempered his pace to match its rhythm. He sang softly alongside lead singer Chris Martin, and then left it to Martin in case people heard him singing out of tune. He'd treated himself to the new tech – the third gen of the iPod – while waiting in Dubai for a dewar flask to be returned to his hotel. He'd never thought about where the dewar was taken or returned from; it was not his role to query such things. But now, for the first time, he wondered where in the glittering, sci-fi-looking city the precious cargo, which he had dutifully carried out of Vilnius, was tampered with. There would have to be a laboratory attached to a clinic somewhere that could retrieve eggs.

He blinked, finding it hard to imagine that Arabic women were selling their eggs. That seemed unlikely in such a wealthy country, so that would leave the foreigners. Most of the Europeans in Dubai were living high-end lifestyles, employed by big companies with plenty of fringe benefits. So that would leave the people working in Dubai who originated from all over Asia, many of them in situations of hard labour as construction workers or cleaners, housekeepers and babysitters. Maybe it was women from that group, never paid enough, perhaps having to send money home to their families. That made sense. But how did the operation ensure the physical characteristics of the eggs being sold? He'd never seen any special labelling on the straws that set the black-market material aside from the legitimate.

Greg frowned as he jogged, no longer concentrating on the terrain other than an absent awareness of crags and boulders, or the slippery parts of the narrowing pathway. Suddenly his mind was intent on his illegal activities. He'd never questioned the logistics of it all. He liked the money and for the last couple of years had been happy with just that. But suddenly, in his restless mood, keen to improve his working conditions, earn more and get closer to the chain of command, he was bewildered. It just didn't make sense that the material was sourced in the United Arab Emirates. On some vague level he accepted that a couple desperate for a child might not be so choosy, but he presumed they'd like their potential child to resemble them in a general way so as not to draw attention or questions.

On the rim of his mind he was conscious that there were no other walkers around him; he'd left everyone behind, and going by the catchy song he was up to in his playlist – 'Low' by

Flo Rida — he'd lost around half an hour in his own mind. He didn't remember overtaking many people but clearly he had, and he was past halfway. His time would be great today.

His pace had naturally adjusted to match Flo Rida's rhythm and he lost himself again in the beat, returning to his musings. So if the material was not sourced in the Gulf, why was it being added to his dewar in Dubai and where did it originate?

Greg was aware of reaching the very steep bit, the section where, if someone was on the brink of giving up, they would, but experience had taught him to just push through and not think too hard. Just run. Wait, was there another courier doing the same delivery run? The thought hit him so hard he stopped moving momentarily. How cunning! It made sense though. Run two couriers, one bringing legitimate material, the other bringing illegal material. If they were put on separate flights, never meeting, no traceable links between them, no one would be any the wiser. Someone at Dubai would collect the legitimate dewar and add the contents from the illegal dewar — and off goes the courier to Australia while the other returns to their base . . . Maybe Europe or Britain, or even America or Canada. Brilliant! Perhaps that was how they kept the material moving safely, seamlessly, and their workers in the dark about each other.

Three other songs had now passed, he realised, since the rapper had sung about getting low. He felt a slap on his back that was more like a shove.

'Hi, mate!'

Startled, Greg jumped, pulling at his right earphone to dislodge it. 'What the . . .?'

'You're a bit slow,' Mr Fabulous said, looking as fresh as he'd looked in the car park.

Greg frowned. 'Then why wait for me?' he asked, hoping it sounded as sarcastic as it did in his mind.

The man slapped him on the back again, harder this time.

'Stop, will you?' Greg growled, annoyed at having his run interrupted and his time compromised. 'I don't even know you.'

'Aw, don't be like that,' his companion said. 'I saw you in the car park, remember?'

Greg pressed a button on the side of his Garmin Forerunner 50 that he'd bought duty-free and paused the timing. 'So what?' Greg said, his annoyance intensifying. He thought he heard footsteps behind him but Mr Fabulous clicked his fingers in front of Greg's face to annoy him beyond all get out. 'What the f—?'

'Listen, can I see your car keys, mate?'

Greg's forehead couldn't have creased more deeply in confusion if he'd tried. 'What?'

'Your car keys.'

'Why?' He glanced behind and saw the Spaniard arriving. He looked fractionally puffed but not struggling. 'Listen,' he said to the newcomer. 'This guy's acting weird. Maybe we need to call someone.'

Fingers were snapped at his face again. 'I'm perfectly lucid, loser,' Mr Fabulous said to Greg before looking towards the Spaniard. 'We need his keys. I'll leave that to you.'

Greg felt trills of alarm now, like dozens of snakes suddenly let loose in his body, prompting gooseflesh and rising of the hairs on his arms. He swung around to confront the Spaniard. 'Are you together?' he asked, knowing how stupid that sounded given that Mr Fabulous had addressed the Spaniard.

The newcomer simply strode up to Greg and ripped the small shoulder pack off him. Good thing he'd fed his earphones through his shirt or they might have been broken. He yelled, 'Hey!' It sounded angry but it had no effect on either man.

'I have a message for you,' Mr Fabulous said, refocusing Greg's attention.

'A message?' Greg felt like a parrot, but the guy was seriously annoying. 'From who?'

The man smiled, revealing a perfect row of impossibly white teeth, and Greg could only hate him more for it but somehow hated him still more when the man put a finger to his lips and made a shushing sound. 'From someone you're *dying* to meet.'

Greg looked around wildly. There was only the Spaniard, still rifling through his pack. The sky had only recently lightened sufficiently to call itself morning and a glance at the summit told him there was no one else at the top. He licked his lips and realised how dry his throat had become.

'Nervous, Greg?'

'Yeah, you are making me nervous. I don't know you but you seem to know me.'

'We know all about you. You've been wanting to make contact.'

Greg at last made the connection. 'You're from Mr Gucci?' His voice sounded high, a bit too excited.

Mr Fabulous laughed. 'Hear that, Ric? Is that the name you use? Hilarious. Yes, from Mr Gucci.'

Greg swallowed, thrilled. At last. But why were they approaching him here? Perhaps they were simply taking precautions, making sure no one saw them together. Seemed a bit rough but he would forgive them. He watched Mr Fabulous unzip his bum bag. 'What's the message?'

'We'll just get your keys first. Ric? You got them?'

The man shook his head.

Greg obliged. 'Er, they're not in there.'

'Ah, you could have said so. You want to be with the higher ups, don't you?'

'Yes,' Greg snapped, unzipping the back pocket of his shorts to lift out the keys. 'I don't understand why my k—'

Mr Fabulous snatched them and threw them to Ric, who caught them deftly. 'Apartment keys on here?'

'Yes, why? Give me my stuff back.'

Ric zipped up the pack and threw it back to Greg.

'What about my keys?'

It was Mr Fabulous who sighed, then said, 'You don't need them.'

Greg presumed the man meant he didn't need them for now, but he didn't understand what the plan was. 'Where am I meeting him?' Through the one earphone still in his ear, he heard a song coming to an end. Soon he'd hear the moans of Leona Lewis and her song of heartbreak.

He was ignored. Instead, Mr Fabulous looked over at Ric, who had jogged away and was checking the path. 'Are we good?'

'So where am I meeting him?' Greg repeated, intensifying his demand. What was going on?

'At the bottom,' Ric said, popping up right at Greg's side, making him feel extremely uncomfortable.

Ric nudged him and for a heartbeat Greg regretted that his run had been interrupted, especially as he had been on track to make a good time, but he moved nonetheless, keen to have this meeting. He moved instinctively in the direction he was being urged, even though he didn't like that he was now walking closer to the edge.

He paused suddenly and frowned. 'You said there was a message?'

'It's this,' Mr Fabulous replied, pointing.

Greg turned automatically to follow the direction of the man's finger, a wave of vertigo taking over as he looked deep into the gully. But a second later as he regained his bearings, he realised Ric had seized both his arms, pinning them behind him viciously; he was sure he felt something give.

Pain powered in. Was that him shrieking? Before he could work it out, a new sensation took over – this time a cool damp against his mouth and nose. He wanted to touch his face but he couldn't move from Ric's grasp. It couldn't be sweat. It felt like a wad of something pressed to his face but something wasn't right . . . He gasped with shock, pain, confusion, experiencing more vertigo now, which turned into sustained dizziness and a narrowing of his sight. He could taste something salty and metallic.

Suddenly his arms were released and the wad pulled away and he could now taste an odd sweetness, something chemical and gassy that he recalled from a childhood trip to the dentist. Greg tried to turn but cutting through the blur was the realisation that he was being held at an angle over the abyss and only by the strap of his pack. It wouldn't hold.

Greg glanced back into the gully. 'Wait!' he thought he said.

'You should have stayed satisfied,' Mr Fabulous said. He stepped back and Greg had the presence of mind to realise it was the Spaniard – Ric – who held his life by that fragile strap.

'Bye, loser,' Mr Fabulous said.

And then Ric let go.

Greg's arms cartwheeled as he felt himself floating. He was over the ridge, angling down the gully, the rocky crevasse waiting to welcome him with an unforgiving landing that would crush and smash his weedy frame in every imaginable spot. Just before he hit he could swear he heard Leona Lewis begin singing her song about bleeding, which seemed altogether appropriate as the first of the granite outcrops rushed to meet him.

9

Jack had spent a couple of days acclimatising to the new time zone. He'd never visited South Australia before so he was intrigued to find himself in a place that couldn't be more different to the high-energy, sparkly harbour city of Sydney that he was familiar with. Adelaide felt more like Melbourne, he thought. Actually, he decided, it felt like a country cousin to the Victorian capital, which sprawled like any big city to its unique beat. While Melbourne prided itself on sport and cultural pursuits, Adelaide, he gathered, had experienced some sort of culinary revolution since the 1970s and once boasted of being a foodie capital – some even claiming it was the nation's leader in culinary expertise. Back in the eighties and nineties, he was told by locals with long enough memories, it had been crowded with superb restaurants – Mezes, Nediz-Tu, Mistress Augustine's, just to name a few – and so much innovation in food that the bigger cities looked on with longing.

And for every rise there is a fall, he had thought, walking around the city, wondering where all these famed places of gastronomy had fled. That said, Jack was happy with Adelaide's café scene, a very good number two to Melbourne's incredible coffee culture. He was seated now in Rundle Street East, which felt like a happening place, with plenty of shops and eateries and a steady stream of pedestrians walking towards the main shopping mall. He had not enjoyed the mall much, wondering why cities all seemed to end up with a soulless parade of shopping centres with no natural light and all boasting the same shops, undistinguishable from anywhere else. He was in the midst of this observation with a fellow single espresso drinker on the neighbouring table. They'd both put down their newspapers to be polite.

'I far prefer this,' Jack continued, waving a hand. 'There's something reassuring about roadside shops and cafés, don't you think?'

'You're preaching to the choir, mate. I hate that bloody mall. By tomorrow afternoon it will be filled with a crowd of school-kids, acting loutish, not buying anything, just hanging around with each other. I don't blame them – we all know what it's like to be young and needing somewhere to go with friends. But there's so many of them, plus it's fast becoming a haven for drug pushers. And then at night it becomes a ghost town, a place for skateboarders to have some fun.'

'It's happening all over England too. I think malls are ghastly places,' Jack remarked. 'But this is great,' he said, finishing his first coffee of the day.

The man shook his head. 'It was even better a decade ago.'

Jack wondered if he was going to hear again the list of fine eating establishments now closed but the fellow simply drooped into his short black, momentarily lost in memory, no doubt.

Jack took his chance. 'Are drugs a big problem in this state?'

'Yeah,' the man said, as though it was a stupid question. 'Our innocence is long gone. What's that stuff they inhale from glass things? Ice, is it?'

'Crystal methamphetamine,' Jack said, wishing immediately he hadn't sounded so certain or so knowledgeable.

'You know about it, do you?'

Jack nodded. 'A little. I'm a teacher,' he lied. 'It's in schools all over England. And it can be snorted or swallowed, smoked or injected.'

'This bloody generation is going to drug itself to death.'

Jack turned his palms face up. 'We've got to be more optimistic than that.'

'Why? I lost my son to drugs.'

'Oh, I'm very sorry. I didn't mean to sound glib.' Jack looked mortified.

'I've made my peace with it, mate. We did everything . . . everything. It wasn't enough. I know there wasn't more that we could personally do – I think he needed to be sectioned or something, but his mother was determined she could win through by keeping him at home. Of course she's broken. But it's so quickly addictive, you know. He went from a straight-A student to a school dropout by Year 12, a liar, thief and ultimately someone who overdosed and choked on his own vomit. He was a private school student – they're not immune – but it's even worse in the poorer demographic areas.'

'Are the drugs being brought in?' Jack asked, deliberately trying to shift the conversation away from grief, but unable to prevent the detective in him from kicking in.

The man drained his espresso and shook his head. 'Probably the bikies who move it around. I really don't know. From what the police told us, there are clandestine labs all over the suburbs. I gather you don't need much tech to make it – it's easily homemade in a bedroom.' He sounded disgusted.

Jack nodded. 'It's true, sadly, but in this region the bulk is probably coming from China and South-East Asia.'

'Like everything else,' the man grumbled.

'I'm really very sorry about your son. I hear Australia's border security is getting more cunning,' Jack said.

The man shrugged as he stood. 'They'll just find new ways in. Look at South Australia's massive coastline. They can come in via our harbours . . . Even somewhere innocent like the Yorke Peninsula – Wallaroo, for instance – would be just so easy. That's what I hear on the grapevine. There are no real eyes on it.'

Jack had no idea what or where that was, but he returned the man's knowing nod.

'Anyway, didn't mean to get you down, mate. Enjoy your holiday. You should get over to Kangaroo Island or head north to the Yorke Peninsula I just mentioned. It might be perfect for smuggling, but it's also very good for some top fishing.'

'I will. Thanks.'

As the man departed, Jack caught the eye of a wandering waitress.

'Piccolo again?'

He smiled, impressed she'd remembered, although the small glass was likely the giveaway. 'Er, let's make it a macchiato, please.'

'No worries,' she said, clearing away his saucer, teaspoon and glass. She left no bill and he noticed most patrons simply walked up to the café's open window to pay before leaving. It was an honour system for anyone seated. He liked that people were trusted. Jack leaned back, allowing himself to relax fully into the lazy enjoyment of being a foreigner, sitting beneath an umbrella on a strange street, not feeling cold and knowing a good cuppa was on its way.

London and its recent sorrows felt a long way away, although it still stung to recall the conversation with Chief Rowland. She'd riled him, but she was right. Beginning romantic relationships with three women all connected to cases hadn't been deliberate but it didn't change the facts. He needed to be like Kate – find a teacher or hairdresser to date, someone with far more distance from his line of work. Go home to what Kate described – a warm house, a meal, glass of wine being poured, and someone else's day that had nothing to do with death or crime. He sighed. That did sound good.

Later in the day, he strolled the River Torrens, deciding that the excellent belt of parkland was delicious, especially here, where a fine zoo luxuriated. He had already visited the Adelaide Botanic Gardens and been delighted by its lushness and the autumn colours. He'd watched the busy activity of the gardeners preparing the beds for spring, and had enjoyed strolling the pathways around the huge old fig trees. And like London, Adelaide families seemed to make good use of the parks. With so much space and so fewer bodies, it trumped the crush of the London parks for him. He had spent one afternoon reading beneath an old Moreton Bay fig and only seen a handful of people wending their way around the paths.

Finally it was time to make his way to a pub called the Wakefield Hotel. It sat on a wide boulevard of the same name that cut through the city centre from east to west, beginning at East Terrace in the posh end of town, Jack presumed, going by the beautiful bluestone homes. It ran into Victoria Square, the most central and grandest of the five public squares the city boasted. If he was honest, Victoria Square looked a bit sorry for itself, almost an inconvenience for the traffic that had to cross or circle its circumference to get to the western edge where the Adelaide City Markets resided.

He strolled unhurriedly until he found the corner entrance. The pub smelled like every other pub – of yesterday's beer drinkers. The floorboards were long in need of a resurface; they were trashed. The walls were painted in an unremarkable cream paint that led his eye to tattered furniture and burgundy bar stools, where perched the backsides of patrons who looked to be predominantly blue collar, going by the row of dirty denim and grubby, mustard-coloured, steel-capped boots. A few men were taking turns at a pool table by the large windows, groaning when they missed or laughing in unison at a good pot. The horrible blooping of poker machines floated in from a room nearby and the distant smell of smoked cigarettes spoke of the ban that Australia had bravely introduced.

This pub, or hotel as these establishments were called down under, was the local watering spot for city detectives and he saw one face he recognised now: Ron Mason. The man raised a hand in welcome as he put a schooner of beer back on the bar.

'Here he is,' he said, grinning broadly and walking towards Jack with a hand extended. 'You found us all right?'

'Easily,' Jack said, returning the smile. 'Hello, Ron.'

'Welcome again to Adelaide,' Ron said, 'mind-blowing place that it is.'

Jack chuckled. 'Actually I like it.'

'Good. You can tell us why,' Ron said, slapping Jack's arm. 'We're all ears. Actually, I jest. None of us would live anywhere else if you asked us. We like its slower pace. Good place to raise our families.' He grabbed his beer and led Jack deeper into the pub, gesturing for him to take a seat at a table. 'What are you having?'

'Er, what's the local beer?'

'Coopers. This is a pale ale,' Ron said, pointing to his glass.

'I'll have that,' Jack said.

'Schooner?'

'Thanks.' He nodded, glad to know what one was.

'Coming up. In the meantime,' Ron said, gesturing to the table, 'meet Len Coles and Johnno Barnes. We all work together. Guys, this is Jack Hawksworth. He's over from Scotland Yard.'

Jack had asked him not to use his title; he wanted to keep any conversation as casual as possible.

They shook hands while Ron fetched Jack his beer.

'An exchange?' Len asked, sitting back in his chair opposite Jack.

Jack shook his head. 'Nothing official . . . Not yet, anyway.'

The men gave knowing nods. 'What are you after?'

He gave them a generalised version of what he knew. Ron returned, sat next to him and joined in the explanation; no detail, just that he had a potentially far-reaching syndicate in his sights. 'Bill Davies in Sydney asked us to help if we can. I picked Jack up from the airport to find out how we can assist without actually assisting – if you get my drift?'

Another couple of knowing nods. Jack sipped his ale and gave a sigh of appreciation. 'Ah, that hits the spot,' he said. 'Thanks.'

'Hungry, mate? We were just going to order some counter meals. They're not Michelin-starred, I'll warn you now,' Ron said.

Jack laughed. 'I'm up for it,' he replied, using another expression he'd learned from his sister. They pondered greasy menus for a moment, though Jack presumed these men knew the menu by heart anyway. 'How's the whiting?'

'Passable only at a pinch. I reckon it's crumbed and frozen at some factory somewhere,' Johnno cautioned him. 'You're better off with their toasted wraps. All fresh ingredients. Save your whiting for a proper fish restaurant and really enjoy it.'

'Okay then.' Jack grinned. 'I'll have a chicken and tomato wrap.'

They ordered four of them, all slightly varied.

'What are you all working on?' Jack asked to ease the wheels of the conversation into motion.

'Heard about the murdered woman in the septic pit?'

Jack nodded.

'I'm working closely with Mount Gambier Police on that case,' Len said, also keeping it general, Jack noted.

Ron sighed. 'I'm part of the team working on The Family . . . You heard of them?'

Jack sipped his ale. It was cold, bubbly and delicious. 'I have. Grisly business.'

'We seem to be getting a name for our state as the one where all the weird crimes happen.'

The three detectives chuckled but with no mirth.

Jack put his glass down on the cardboard coaster promoting a different brand of beer. 'I read in the paper this morning about the guy at the bottom of the gully. Suicide?'

'It looked that way originally,' Johnno said, taking a large swallow of his beer. 'But an old-school mortician, out of retirement and hosting some training at the funeral home the guy was released to, felt something was on the nose.'

'On the nose?' Jack repeated.

'Yeah,' Johnno grinned. 'You know, smelled dodgy . . . suspicious.'

Jack wanted to laugh; he made a mental note to remember that marvellous phrase.

'Anyway, he queried it with the local boys at Burnside, who consulted Adelaide CIB. No one's convinced it isn't suicide but there's just enough doubt that they've made it a tier two, which means Major Crimes is now involved. Only in a supervisory manner at this stage. The body's been transferred via the coroner's office to state pathology, so hopefully that will reveal more. My brother-in-law is the supervisor on the case, which is how I know all this,' Johnno said. He shook his head. 'Seems the guy had a good job, solid parents, good life. No history of depression, no recent relationship breakdowns . . . no current girlfriend or boyfriend that his close contacts knew about. Didn't take drugs. Bit of a fitness addict – did the Mount Lofty summit whenever he was home.'

'Home from where?' Len asked.

'Oh, I don't really know the details. Matt said he's one of those international couriers.'

Len frowned. 'Transporting what?'

'Human material or something.'

'Kidneys and things?' Ron wondered.

Johnno shrugged. 'I suppose. What else do you manually transport across borders other than organs?'

They all shrugged, except Jack, who frowned. 'Blood, skin, eyes, perhaps . . .' He blew out his cheeks. 'Even reproductive material. Who did he work for?'

'Search me, mate,' Johnno said, as the wraps arrived. 'Ah, great. Thanks, love.'

The waitress smiled. 'Someone having mayo in theirs?'

'Guilty,' Len admitted, raising a palm.

'And another with cheese?'

'Mine, thanks,' Johnno said.

'So this must be yours, Ron,' she said, placing one serve before him, 'because I know you don't like salad, which means, handsome newcomer, this is surely yours, then?'

'Ooh, you've been noticed, Jack. If Rena likes you, you're set in this pub.'

'Thank you, Rena.' Jack gave her a smile.

'You're welcome, my darling. I'm not used to tall, dark and handsome strangers in our pub. It's usually blokes like this lot.'

They obviously knew her well because Jack's companions didn't look offended in the slightest and laughed with genuine amusement.

'You should have seen Len in his day, Rena,' Ron said. 'Full head of shocking blond hair. Now look at the bald bugger.'

'Oi, oi, speak for yourself. At least I can do up my belt, old timer.' Len grinned. 'Mmm, lovely. Thanks, Rena,' he said after taking his first bite.

She winked at Jack and left.

He watched his trio of companions tuck in and followed suit, waiting for the moment to jump back in to their conversation. 'Johnno, do you reckon you could find out the name of the company that this guy who fell off the cliff worked for?'

'I'm sure I can. Not sure how it lines up with what you're hunting, though.'

'Neither am I, but if he is confirmed as a courier of human material, then that does potentially tie in with what I'm researching. I might take a walk to this summit.'

'It's no walk, mate,' Len said with a smirk. 'It's a hike.'

'Here,' Johnno said, wiping his mouth with a paper serviette. He took another from the holder in the middle of the table, pulled a pen from his jacket pocket and began scribbling. 'That's my brother-in-law, Matt. Tell him I sent you.'

'Thanks. It may lead nowhere,' Jack admitted.

Ron swallowed. 'Maybe. But there're certainly cleaner, surer ways to commit suicide than jumping off a mountainside.'

10

'Who are you?' Nikki frowned, speaking into the intercom.

'I'm the courier.'

'From where?'

'GDG.' He said no more. Obviously he didn't feel he had to, especially as she was expecting a delivery from Global Dangerous Goods.

'Where's Greg?'

'Who's Greg?'

'The other courier.'

'Listen. I've flown from Europe with barely any sleep. I'm wrecked. Can I just make my delivery or shall I ring and say the lab won't let me in?'

Nikki used the lift to meet him at the doors and usher him through. 'Sorry, can't be too careful.'

'That's okay. Sorry to be grumpy. It was a hellish journey.'

'Are you new?'

'Nah. Just a different route for me.'

'Since a week ago?'

'Yeah. I don't mind. It pays more than the Europe to UAE route.'

She led him up to the lab. 'How many straws?'

He checked his paperwork. 'Er, looks like twenty-five.'

'That's what we're expecting at MultiplyMed,' she said, knowing she sounded dim for stating the obvious.

He shrugged. 'Good. Our paperwork tallies.'

'No . . . er, extras?'

'What?' He looked perplexed.

She had to manage this quickly. 'No extra stuff? They've some-times surprised me by adding in some semen we weren't warned about, and once some embryos,' she lied.

'No.' He sounded dumbfounded. 'Not as far as I know. When I signed, I checked everything was on here.' He read it aloud again, annoying her. 'Twenty-five straws, with six eggs in each.' He looked up. 'That's it.'

'And this dewar hasn't been out of your sight?'

'Why the inquisition? You know how this works.' At Nikki's intense stare, he sighed, suddenly too tired to bother. 'No! Not for a moment.'

'During transit?'

The man's expression changed. 'Suddenly the lab technician is the dewar police,' he sneered. 'I said no. I sat it out in the Dubai terminal with this backpack between my legs. And before you ask, no, I didn't sleep. Who would tamper with this shit, anyway?'

'Okay.' She forced a smile. 'Just being diligent. And just for the record, I'm an embryologist, not a lab technician . . . a few more qualifications.'

'Putting the new guy through his paces, eh?'

'That's it,' she said, hiding her bafflement. She'd need to check in with Mr Gucci. Something had gone tits up.

And where was Greg?

★

Greg was lying on a stainless-steel tray in a fridge at the back of a building in Divett Place.

It was brutalist, Jack had decided minutes earlier, staring at its bulky geometric form unashamedly promoting all the concrete used to achieve its ugly height of seven levels. It dwarfed what he considered to be elegant and highly desirable bluestone buildings either side of it.

This stubby tower was the home of the state's forensic science centre and headquarters to the coroner's pathology unit. Jack was standing in an anteroom facing a single high desk running the length of a long-shuttered window. The room itself was sparsely furnished, save stools, a microphone on a stand, and some tech equipment in the corner. His contact, Matt, a senior detective, touched the microphone and grinned.

'I always want to ask for a cleaner in aisle three on this thing,' he said.

Jack gave the chuckle that was required as he watched Matt reach forward to open the narrow venetian blinds, revealing the viewing room to the pathology theatre where people looked busy at their tasks, prepping for the day.

Jack leaned over to Matt and murmured, 'Listen, I didn't get the chance over introductions to say thanks for this.'

'No prob,' Matt replied. 'Dr Moore is one of the good ones. She won't care who you are or why you're here so long as you don't waste her time. Oh, and she doesn't appreciate us eating or kidding around back here. We'll get a firm look of disapproval if we do.'

Jack shook his head. 'You can rely on me.'

A mortuary assistant was working quietly in the background, checking off equipment, it looked like, and another was standing closer to them, rubbing the details of a previous pathology exam from the whiteboard.

Matt nudged Jack. 'There are smaller rooms like this one and then the other one, over there'—he pointed—'is bigger and can see into the main theatre where they can perform three autopsies at once, if they need to. I prefer this space; means we can get closer to the pathologist and the body.' He gave Jack a sidelong glance. 'You won't throw up your breakfast, will you?'

'I'll be fine.' Jack grinned, remembering the story he'd told his class. He'd done so many of these now he'd lost count.

'I don't know how they do it in England but the pathologists here record everything on that board. And it stays on there for twenty-four hours.'

Jack nodded. 'So that when they write the report, if they can't remember something or their notes are illegible, they can come back to the original details recorded at the time. Yes, we have an identical system.'

The corpse was wheeled in on a gurney, his body enclosed in a bright tropical-blue plastic bag.

Dr Moore arrived, moments later, wearing scrubs of navy.

Jack noticed the cyan floor and decided there was a distinctive theme going on in the Adelaide Forensic Studies Centre. He decided not to mention it.

The pathologist's white gumboots squeaked on the lino as she pulled on electric-blue gloves. Her hair was tied up in a hood and her mask was on but sitting beneath her chin. She was a study in the fifth colour of the spectrum, Jack thought, as she looked up towards the detectives with a bright smile that warmed the otherwise clinical surrounds.

'Matt. How are you?'

'Great, thanks, Dr Moore. Er, I have a colleague over from England. This is Detective Superintendent Jack Hawksworth from Scotland Yard. He's on holiday as it happens, so this isn't a formal visit, but I invited him. I hope you don't mind?'

'Not at all. The more the merrier. Hello, welcome to South Australia, DSU Hawksworth.'

'Jack's fine. Thank you for this.'

She smiled and it reached intelligent eyes the colour of dark steel. 'Want to get closer?'

Jack hesitated, keen to make sure no one was pulling his leg. Australians liked a joke, especially in macabre situations, he'd discovered. Their gallows humour was reliably top-notch. He looked at Matt, who gestured for him to go ahead with no guile. 'Love to.'

'Come on, then,' Dr Moore encouraged him. 'I know your companion would rather stay behind the glass, right, Matt?'

The Adelaide detective nodded back at her.

'Scrub up, Jack. I'll wait.'

It didn't take him long. Jack knew the routine and within a few minutes he was ready in navy scrubs and squeaky rubber boots. He inhaled through his mask, tasting the familiar sterile air of the mortuary. The smell of bleach was strong, but rode above a nastier one: it was the smell of decomposition and not one Jack had ever been able to fully wrap his mind around to describe. When asked once by his sister he'd said, 'Imagine the orchestra is playing and there's a consistently off note being sounded.' At her laugh, he'd shrugged. 'To try to pinpoint it is tricky. I could trot out the usual descriptions – you know, stale boiled cabbage, the hum of chicken gone off or sulphurous eggs, but nothing quite touches it. Your senses just know it's wrong and it can override everything else.'

That off note surrounded him now, climbing through his mask, reminding him that death and its secrets lived here. It joined the hard sounds around him, metal mainly, and the creaky wheel of the gurney being moved and his spongey boots on the lino surface. The gurney was being plugged into the sink so bodily fluids could be drained effectively.

'Ready?' Dr Moore began, looking to her assistant, a bearded man who had sidled up beside them. Jack watched him nod. 'Let's meet Mr Greg Payne. Tell me more, Matt.'

From behind the glass, Matt read from the file. 'Mr Payne is thirty-three. He travels frequently for his work as a medical courier and he is single, lives alone at Dulwich, no previous convictions or issues with the law. He has two parents alive and an older sister, and the local police have noted that interviews with family and neighbours suggest nothing was out of the ordinary in Mr Payne's life. Should I go on?'

'No, that's enough. Thanks, Matt.'

As Dr Moore pulled back the covering, Jack saw a man's body that was slim, face hideously pale with slitted eyes that were still slightly open to reveal no distinctive colour. Like all in death, they were a murky and light greenish grey.

'If you stay there, you can remove your mask. You only need to wear it if you get as close as we do,' Dr Moore said to Jack before continuing. 'I like to think all of us who perform a pathology report are truth seekers,' she murmured and Jack presumed this chat was for his benefit, because one glance told him Matt was already reading the newspaper.

'I like that,' Jack remarked.

Dr Moore was carefully inspecting the feet. The vague smell of rot intensified as he lowered his mask; no amount of antiseptic could wash away the traces of the conveyor belt of cadavers that must have passed through this mortuary.

Moore was scrutinising the corpse's toes. 'I attended a PM at Guy's in London that was being performed by Dr Richard Shepherd. Heard of him?' She glanced Jack's way.

'Er, yes, I have. I've met him.'

'Is that right?' She sounded impressed and swung around to look at him. 'And?'

'I found him brilliant, empathetic. Very helpful in the case I was working on.'

'How did you come to meet?'

'It was back in the nineties when I was a detective sergeant. Still a bit green, but it was an important case and I was exposed to plenty of solid investigative work. He was part of that process. I see you subscribe to his method.'

It was a risk to say this to the pathologist, who was probably of a similar age to Shepherd.

'Oh yes, what's that?'

'To not begin with the obvious,' Jack replied and his gaze travelled with the doctor's to the head, where they both knew a shocking wound existed.

'Well, Jack, you're quite right. And I'm not ashamed to sound like a fan – he was indeed the pathologist who convinced me to carry out my post-mortems in the manner you're witnessing. I stay well away from any major wounds to begin with.'

Behind the glass, Matt shrugged, clearly baffled, and hit the microphone button. 'But why, Dr Moore? It's so clear that blow likely killed him.'

'It's correct to use the word "likely",' the doctor said. 'But it's a presumption. My role is to give you facts about this body. I'm trying to get to the truth of what actually killed him and while that head wound *may* be the reason, it may only be part of it, or it might be incidental. The truth of death could well be something hidden, like a brain aneurysm that happened to choose that moment to rupture. Then it'd be the weakened artery finally giving up and major bleeding that killed him, while the other wounds were inflicted by the fall.'

'Ah,' the detective said. 'Got it.'

Moore continued. 'It's about not leaping to what seems straightforward, taking time to explore and be sure there are no signs of anything else that might have caused this man's death. Of course,' the doctor added, moving up the body to inspect the calves, 'he could have been pushed, he could have fallen, he could have had an internal episode or he simply could have jumped. I'm going to do my best to rule out natural causes or foul play, but I may not be able to give you anything unequivocal. This isn't going to be fast – we may need to do toxicology tests, et cetera. You might like to come back, or we can call when there's something to tell you?'

Jack nodded. He wouldn't like people staring over his shoulder as he worked either but then again, a forensic pathologist would likely be used to it. Matt's phone sounded distantly through the glass and he excused himself by holding up a finger, stepping away to avoid distracting the pathologist, who had now reached the arms.

'What do you think so far?' Jack asked.

'So far a healthy male in his thirties,' she replied, checking over each of Greg's elbows. 'No needle marks, no old bruising, but plenty of contusions consistent with his fall. He's not overweight and while I doubt he pulled weights, I suspect this gentleman exercised regularly and ate less takeaway than he did nourishing meals cooked from scratch. Very good muscle tone.' She'd reached Greg's hands. 'I'm going to check for fibres, skin, anything else under these nails.'

Jack fell quiet. Matt returned, wearing an expression Jack couldn't immediately read. It was halfway to being smug, as though he was suppressing a secret. He beckoned eagerly to Jack.

The pathologist sighed. 'What's up, Matt? I can see you gesturing.'

Matt hit the microphone button. 'Sorry, doc. I've got some news for my colleague.'

She cut Jack a grin. 'I'm going to be a while. I would say you'll miss the exciting bit,' she said, reaching for a scalpel, 'but it sounds like there's exciting news waiting for you – even though you're not here in any formal capacity.' Their gazes met and she gave him a knowing look; she clearly understood he was here chasing down clues but couldn't have an official acknowledgement. 'Go ahead. I'll call Matt if we find anything interesting.'

'None of the injuries say much?' Jack asked.

'Too many TV shows suggest a pathologist can tell that a blow like that one on the head was inflicted by an assailant and not achieved from falling down a steep, rocky gully. Blunt force trauma is blunt force trauma, and I doubt very much that I'll be able to tell you whether it was done with a cricket bat or from the fall. There's nothing particularly inconsistent with how the police have described this death. All these injuries'—she gestured up and down Greg's body—'speak of toppling down that gully and bouncing off rock. When we open up this gentleman I might learn more, plus bloods might give us clues as to whether there's been any foul play, but not necessarily. Short of a boot's impression between his shoulders, I can't tell you if he jumped or was pushed, but I will search and I will have some answers for you.'

Jack nodded. 'And do you think you'll be asking for a toxicology report?'

'Tox takes weeks unless I specifically request it be fast-tracked.'

Jack again lifted his gaze to meet the doctor's over their masks.

She rolled her eyes. 'You're persuasive, Jack, even when you're not saying anything.'

He gave a smile. 'Hugely appreciated. Thanks again for letting me watch. Sorry to desert you.'

'I'm not offended. Sounds like duty calls even though you're not on duty.' She laughed, as though amused by the absurdity of their pretence. 'Nice to meet you.'

Matt ushered Jack from the cool of the mortuary into the long corridor with the geometric pattern on its grey floor that led them back to security. They signed themselves out and stepped into midday sunshine and the now-familiar territory of Wakefield Street. Jack reached for his sunglasses to shield himself from the sharp glare of another bright, mild day. He couldn't remember the last time in England he'd needed sunnies, as the Aussies called them. Probably the last time he went sailing a year or more ago and he'd lost that pair – brand new – that weekend.

He was following Matt, unsure of where they were headed but his colleague jangled his keys.

'Come on, let's go somewhere quiet, out of the city,' Matt said. He nodded towards the small sedan they'd arrived in. 'Hop in.'

Jack obeyed, imagining they were about to go on a one-hour drive to find countryside; that's how long it would take from his base in London to negotiate traffic and leave parking problems and crowds behind. Instead, the drive took under ten minutes from putting on his seat belt to climbing back out in front of a lone café in a leafy street, which sat high, overlooking a neighbourhood park with tall trees. They were somewhere in the suburbs but Jack had no idea where. They had parked directly outside the café. He shook his head, impressed.

'You'll love this guy's coffee. I'm happy to drive out of the city for it,' Matt said, making it sound like a trek. 'I come here regularly on the weekend with my cycling club.'

His slim build and shorter-than-average hairstyle made perfect sense now.

'Oh, you're one of those,' Jack quipped with a look of feigned distaste, before grinning.

'I know, I know. Everyone hates us until the Tour de France is on or the Tour Down Under. Then we're in vogue for a few minutes.'

'Let me get these. How do you take it?'

'Flat white, mate, thanks. Oh, and don't try and make conversation. The guy's a champion barista, won some global competition. But he's a sulky bastard.'

Jack smiled at the casual way Aussies threw around insults in jest, even affectionately. He also liked the name of the coffee that Aussies or Kiwis had coined – they fought between themselves over who was responsible – which the rest of the world's espresso drinking crowd had frowned over for a while. *Flat white.* He frequently patronised a tiny café in London's Soho that went by the same name, set up by an Aussie.

Jack walked inside to a small counter where a single guy was manning a machine. Jack was wondering what news Matt wanted to tell him; he'd remain patient. One other person, who looked like a uni student, cleared tables and stacked a dishwasher. It was a hole-in-the-wall operation and far too nice a day to cram into the small, slightly gloomy and limited seating space inside.

'Two flat whites, please.'

'Coming up. That's four fifty, thanks.' Jack handed over a five-dollar note and gestured for the change to go into the tips jar.

'Thanks, mate, we'll bring them out.'

Jack returned to join Matt outside, where they sat against the café wall on two small chairs with an equally petite table between them. 'All those houses circling the park are living the dream,' Jack said, pointing to the wide expanse of grass they faced, where people were exercising their dogs and a small gang of women were doing fitness training with an instructor.

'Yeah, Burnside is a lovely suburb. Actually . . .' Matt paused his speech to raise a finger. 'If I wanted to be precise, we're in Stonyfell within the Burnside Council. Base of the foothills – everything is up from here. My bike club rides up Greenhill Road, just over there, and it takes us all the way up into the Adelaide Hills.'

'I could live here,' Jack remarked as their coffees were delivered. 'Thanks.' He nodded to the young student.

Matt rubbed together his thumb and two fingers, the universal sign for money, and Jack nodded.

He believed it would cost a king's ransom to live out here. But he couldn't make small talk any longer. 'So what did you want to tell me?'

'The idea of our boy taking his own life just got murkier. The local police found his car last night. It took a while to establish which was his because his parents insisted that their son usually rode his bike up to Waterfall Gully because it's hard to get a park up there, even before dawn when he always went. So they weren't looking for a car at first, especially as there were no keys on his body or in his small backpack.'

'Was the car locked? No keys inside?'

Matt nodded. 'That's the mystery.'

'They could have fallen out of his pocket,' Jack mused.

'Or he could have deliberately tossed them in a sort of up-yours to life if he did suicide. Someone could have picked them up and hasn't yet got to a police station to hand them in.' Matt gave a gesture with his hands that said it could be one of many reasons, then stirred and sipped his coffee, sighing with pleasure.

'Or they were taken,' Jack finished for them. They both frowned at this notion. Jack reached for his small flat white and was delighted by its taste. Why couldn't they do this all over England? Maybe he should open a coffee shop.

Matt shrugged. 'Exactly. And that idea may have some weight, given a neighbour said she saw Greg going into his unit at around nine-thirty that morning.'

'Is she sure it was him?'

'No, that's the thing. She became more doubtful when one of our lads questioned her and now only thinks it *might* have been Greg. Her words: "Well, it was a man and he was in those sporty sort of clothes that Greg wears when he goes running." So I'll keep an eye on it. Keep you informed. I should have the name of the company he worked for soon, too.'

Jack held up the cup in a small 'cheers'. 'Thanks for all of this. I have no idea if this will lead anywhere for me but I'm like that old mortician . . . I've just got a hunch that it's worth following.' He shifted topic, or so it would have sounded to Matt. 'If you needed to transfer goods into the state but weren't going to use the airports, how would you do it?'

Matt didn't flinch, obviously used to his colleagues throwing around what-ifs. 'I'm guessing it doesn't need a truck?'

Jack gave a rueful smile. 'It's a small package, about this big.' He lifted his hands, approximating the size of the dewar flask he'd been shown at a clinic in London.

'And you need to transfer these goods without the watchful eyes of the boys and gals in blue?'

Jack nodded, then waited while Matt considered.

He shrugged. 'Truck could work.'

Jack gave a shrug of acknowledgement. 'What if you wanted to minimise the number of people involved . . . avoid a driver or courier, for instance?'

'Then it has to be by boat. We have a huge coastline. Where is it coming from?'

'I can't be sure.'

'Perishable?'

'To a point. Probably a shelf life of up to a few days for peak but maybe up to a fortnight.'

'Asia then.'

'Possibly.'

Matt swallowed the rest of his coffee and Jack followed suit.

'Doesn't need a big harbour obviously, although you have a better chance of hiding something illegal on a bigger ship.'

'I doubt the criminals I'm after are even hiding it,' Jack said with another shrug. 'You can walk off any boat, any plane, any truck with it hidden in a backpack.'

'What the hell is this stuff?'

'Human reproductive material,' Jack admitted.

Matt blinked. 'What?'

'Eggs harvested from women mostly, but it could be embryos, and certainly semen.'

'Get out of here,' the detective replied, looking back at him in disbelief.

'Got family, Matt?' He was hard to age because he looked youthful from a distance. It was only up close that Jack could see a silvering of the hair around his ears. So they were probably around the same age, staring down forty.

Matt nodded. 'An eight-year-old and a five-year-old, about to start school. Would you believe my wife wants another? Don't ask me how we'll cope, but Maggie's a brilliant mum.'

Jack smiled. 'So I'm guessing you didn't run into the situation of needing help with fertility, but there are thousands of couples who do. Human reproductive material criss-crosses the world daily.'

Matt shook his head, clearly shocked. 'And that's what you're chasing?'

Jack gave a potted version of what had triggered his investigation. 'Caught the scent of someone in Australia but, as I've explained, I'm not here formally. I'm here to discover if we can set up a joint op.'

'But since 9/11, border security is super finicky. Surely they'd pick up this flask thing immediately. There would be questions.'

'Yes. I have to think that through.'

'Well, I'll help anywhere I can. We all will.'

'Thanks. I've got to be careful though – I can't be seen to be asking for any formal assistance, not yet. It all must be off the books.'

Matt nodded. 'Yeah, happens all the time, mate. No worries. I'll see what else I can find out about Greg Payne. Come on, I'll drop you back.' His phone rang again as they were both getting back into the car. He mouthed 'Moore' to Jack, who nodded and stayed quiet, listening to the one-sided conversation. When Matt paused, Jack could just make out a tinny voice on the other end. 'Right . . . right. Ah, okay. Interesting. When can we have that? Yeah, thank you. Appreciate it. Thanks again. Bye.' Matt looked at Jack with raised eyebrows. 'Seems our retired mortician was on the money.'

'What have they found?'

'The pathologist is yet to complete her report and all her findings – the internals, you know.' Jack did. 'But she's discovered that both shoulders have a partial dislocation. Muscles are torn too symmetrically in her opinion to be achieved by random injuries from a fall. So she's referred it for an urgent tox report.'

Jack mimicked his arms being pulled backwards. 'Someone restraining him from behind?'

'Sounds like it. But we have to wait for toxicology and all the other jazz.'

Jack nodded. 'My hunch has got a fresh tingle.'

Matt grinned. 'Careful, we'll start calling you Nostradamus.'

'I think you mean Quasimodo, don't you?'

The error made them both laugh but it didn't stop The Tingler, as Jack liked to think of it, which was the name he gave the feeling he had when all of his animal instincts went onto high alert. The strange, creeping sensation of alarm tended to travel up his spine and reminded him of the terrible 1950s B-grade horror movie of the same name. It usually didn't end well.

11

Jem brought her new shimmering glass platter, which she'd splashed out for at the JamFactory, to the table outside for lunch. It was a design by the hottest new talent in local glassblowing and she'd been dying for an occasion to use it. It was perfect for her Moroccan couscous. She'd eaten the dish in Marrakech and had been sorely disappointed by how bland it had been, with thick carrot halves lining the mound of plain cooked grain . . . but little other colour or flavour.

Couscous was such a good carrier, and hers was full of garlic, shallots and chopped green and red chilies. She'd added pine nuts and perhaps gone a bit berserk by throwing in some dried cranberries, but she loved the hit of tangy sweetness they brought. Peas and freshly steamed sweetcorn added extra colour, while chopped mint and parsley added the final flourish and flavour. It looked fabulous turned out as a large and colourful dome onto the new platter, and it occurred to her as she set it down that next time she might even drizzle some thick pomegranate syrup over it.

'Beautiful,' Alannah Petras cooed in her slightly accented voice that Jem wished she could emulate. 'Ooh, I'm going to steal that glass platter. Where did you find that?'

'It's a Llewelyn Ash,' she said, as though it should register immediately with her wealthy guest. She was surprised when Alannah's eyes widened.

'Ah, I have one of his Lucky Drops,' she said, 'but this is magnificent.'

'It's called The Wave.'

'And it looks just like the perfect surfing wave,' Alannah replied before lifting her voice. 'Come on, you men. Jem's cooked a feast for us.'

Alannah's husband, Alex, was standing next to Mark, watching him brush down the barbecue.

'Leave that, Mark,' Jem called, now arriving with the last of the side dishes. 'I hate lamb going cold.'

The men took their seats beneath the pergola, whose roof was open today because the sun was mild and there was no wind.

'Quiet without the kids around,' Alex noted. Jem had organised sandwiches and finger food for the youngsters, including Alex's child from his first marriage; they were in the family den with a pile of DVDs. 'But you have a beautiful trio,' he said, smiling directly at her. He lowered his voice and leaned right in towards Jem. 'I mean that. Marguerite enjoys their company and I wish we had a brood.' Now he slid a glance at his wife, who was busy serving Mark some couscous and laughing over something with him. 'But sadly, we're unable.'

'Oh, I'm sorry,' Jem said.

Alex put a finger to his lips as though he'd just revealed a secret. 'Here, Maddox,' Alex said louder now, reaching for the wine in the nearby bucket. 'Try this sauvignon blanc we brought. It'll blow your mind.'

'Marlborough?'

'Where else? This is Clos Henri.' Before offering the bottle to Mark, Alex looked at Jem with a query and she nodded, only now realising how attractive he was. Certainly not traditionally handsome, as Mark might be described, and which was why so many women managed to find various ways to tell her how lucky she was. No, what was it? His slight European accent was quite sexy, she thought, but it wasn't that . . . It was his eyes. They had an ability to penetrate, to blank the noise and surrounds, like a camera lens focusing purely on the subject and blurring out the background. When he offered her his wine, it felt as though no one else mattered in that heartbeat.

'Yes, please!' she said, handing him her tall wineglass. When he handed it back, his fingers touched hers in a fleeting manner. He didn't seem to register it, but she did, still trying to work out what the specific attraction was that he possessed. Apart from that gaze of his, his skin was pale, his features unremarkable within the squarish face. His hair was blond, kept trim and traditional, parted on the side. He was clean-shaven and, although it was the weekend, there was no ghosting of yesterday's growth like she could see on Mark, who tended to be lazy on a day off. And who could blame him – he worked so hard, always on call, it seemed, for other women.

She glanced at her husband; no one could deny this was a traditionally attractive man in every respect, from his enviable muscular shoulders and slim hips, which he earned at the gym, to his effortlessly handsome features. His strong jaw and wide, white smile looked hand-picked for maximum impact, and his eyes sparkled like the summer waters off Wallaroo where she'd spent her childhood summers.

'This all looks amazing, Jem,' Alex said, as though he'd been aware of her scrutiny. 'Thank you again for having us round.'

Jem flicked her gaze back to see him pouring out the other three glasses as Mark was busy carving the lamb. 'An overkill of garlic,' she said with a grin, glad her tone sounded easy and casual.

'An overkill of treats,' Alannah remarked, adding, 'Phew, we'll need to hit Mount Lofty to lose the kilos I'm going to gain today.'

That reminded Jem. 'Did you hear about that fellow who fell off the cliff?' she asked the group.

'I suppose it was a pretty spectacular way to end it,' Mark quipped, pausing his carving to flap his elbows. Alannah cackled a laugh that sounded cruel to Jem.

Jem frowned, pleased to note that Alex had not cracked so much as a smirk. 'Come on, Mark, that's not cool,' she admonished him, but tried to keep it light. 'If it was suicide, imagine how deep into his depression this guy had to be.'

Mark looked a little annoyed but didn't respond.

'You're right,' Alannah agreed, glancing with amusement at Mark while taking a delicate serving of couscous. Her diamond rings and bracelet glinted fiercely in the sunlight. Jem figured their guest was wearing fifty thousand dollars' worth of jewellery just on her hands. She looked at her own hands, which were naked save for her wedding band; her solitaire engagement ring was on the shelf above the sink where she'd put it after taking it off to wash the lettuce for today's salad. She had plenty of jewellery and Mark had mercifully stopped buying her more.

'I need two sets of hands and several necks to wear it all,' she'd tried to jest. 'Mark, I love my solitaire and I love my bracelet, and I will never want to wear anything around my neck other than this diamond-studded heart. It makes me anxious to have options and I feel like a spoiled brat if I don't wear it all. Truly, darling, I'm really happy with what I wear.' He'd just presented her with some gobsmacking pearl teardrop earrings. 'I will wear these because they are astonishingly beautiful and when we go out I do like a drop earring, but no more, Mark. Really.'

He'd shaken his head in soft disbelief. 'Trust me to pick a wife who doesn't lust for jewellery.'

It had felt like an accusation, another wedge in their marriage forcing them apart. She looked over at her handsome husband, playing the fine host, and wondered if he was seeking affection elsewhere. Was divorce in their future?

Alannah was still pondering the trail jumper aloud. '. . . and trekking up there, he'd have had so much time to talk himself out of it.'

'Or plenty of time to talk himself into doing it,' Mark rebutted.

'The thing is, I've heard it may not have been suicide,' Jem said, refocusing on the conversation. She contemplated her plate of food, proud of its colour and variety, and cut into the meat. 'Oh, Mark, perfectly cooked.'

She looked up to find him staring at her. There was something odd in his expression but it was fleeting; he quickly re-arranged his features to his easy, charming grin, the one that had won her from the moment it had first landed on her. 'Oh? Where did you hear that?'

'Hmm?' She chewed. 'Oh, the dead man. Well'—she waved a hand in front of her mouth to show she needed to finish chewing and swallowing—'you know the Kemps at school?' She was aware of the others tuning in too now that everyone was eating.

He shrugged impatiently. 'Probably by sight.'

'Oh, I do,' Alannah said. 'The father's in car yards, right?'

Jem nodded. 'The wife is Sal and her brother's wife . . .' She pulled a face of puzzlement as she mentally checked the familial links.

'Her sister-in-law?' Alex helped out.

She laughed, raising her glass to him. 'Yes, indeed. Thank you, Alex,' she said, aware without looking at him that her husband was becoming irritated. 'So Sal's sister-in-law works in the Attorney General's department. And she mentioned to me yesterday at pick-up that Major Crimes might be getting involved.' She took another neat mouthful and when she looked up, her husband was still staring at her, his food untouched. 'What?' she asked him as she remembered her grandmother's words: *Never say what, say pardon.*

'What did she say?' her husband queried far too intently, she thought.

She shrugged, looking at the others, who were chewing happily but watching them. 'Nothing more. There's obviously something fishy enough about the case that they're not going to formally sign it off as suicide, or whatever it is they do.'

Mark shook his head. 'But Burnside Police signed the body over to the funeral home. That means the police had signed off,' he persisted.

Jem shook her head, slightly baffled. 'Mmm, then you know more than me.' Why was he acting so strangely about this? She hoped he wasn't getting into one of his moods, not in front of their friends – or people she wanted to become friends with, anyway. 'Look, I've probably got it wrong or maybe Sal's misunderstood. All I know is apparently there are questions, and it's being referred.' She took a breath as though that should be the end of it. 'Her words, not mine,' she added, hoping she wasn't showing the embarrassment she felt.

'Anyway, cheers,' Alex said, raising his glass. His arms were long, like his body. He was noticeably taller than Mark, but wasn't as muscular. 'To good health, good companions, good food, good times.'

'Cheers,' they said in unison, but Jem noted that her husband was the only one not smiling.

★

Much later, after their guests had left, she felt Mark arrive next to her as she stacked the dishwasher.

'I suppose I should say well done, Jem. Everything was delicious.'

'Except your mood, perhaps,' she said, annoyed that she couldn't let it go.

Too late. He leaned away, frowning. 'What do you mean?'

Why couldn't she hold her tongue? Jem could barely look at him, disgusted with herself for picking an argument when all she had to do was take his compliment and maybe try to turn the rest of the evening around.

She shrugged. 'Nothing, really. I just don't know why you made the temperature drop and let it stay that way.'

'I don't know what you're talking about.'

'No,' she said in a flat tone, trying to rein it in, but the sigh that followed was a giveaway. 'It's just . . .'

'Just what?'

'It's hard work, Mark.'

'Then get the cleaner to do more hours.'

She gave him a glare. He wasn't getting it. 'That's not what I mean. I'm always happy to have people over and I like all the preparation. But what I don't need is you getting into a bad mood and then leaving me to do all the heavy lifting for an entire after-noon, entertaining the guests that you wanted to have over.'

'Oh, *I* wanted them?'

'It was your idea. Listen,' she said, trying to smooth things over, 'I think they're great and I am very pleased you invited them, but while you know him quite well, I don't know either of them beyond them being parents at school. You tuned out and I was left to babble.'

'I don't recall tuning out, as you put it.'

'Mark, you completely disappeared mentally and then physically left me to it.'

'I had to make a phone call.'

'Why? We were in the middle of lunch. What was so urgent?' It wasn't like her to be so demanding and she half wondered herself what was happening. 'I understand you getting calls, Mark. We've always lived our lives around someone else's emergency, and I never complain, but I do object to you leaving our guests in order to make a phone call.'

'I was checking up on something.'

'Who did you call?'

'Really, Jem, you need to take a lie down or go out for one of your long walks and get rid of this shit on your liver, or is it *that* time?'

'Don't do that!'

His eyes narrowed. Ah, yes, there it was. The Mark who emerged frequently these days, no longer smooth but hard and jagged. If you set aside the handsome face, the larger than life personality, the quick-witted tongue, the money, the status, the power . . . That's what it was, the attraction to Alex Petras. He was powerful too, but he kept it within, didn't show it off. That was the quality that had evaded her all evening. She liked it in him, but it made Mark ugly. Mr Hyde, she thought. And it was her fault.

'Don't do what?'

She returned to Mark's scowling. 'Don't belittle me. Don't turn your poor behaviour on me and, especially, don't deflect my question. I asked you something. After nearly eighteen years of marriage, you can do me the courtesy of a direct answer.'

'You want to know who I called?'

'I do.'

'It was the midwife at Calvary, if you insist, who is looking after one of my mothers. Mrs Campion was in labour; presumably still is, given they are yet to call me in. She's struggling to dilate, if you must know the gory details. I plan to go in shortly.

And as you seem so incredibly interested, during that phone call I instructed them to administer thirty mils of oxytocin over the hour.' He glanced at his watch. 'That was nearly three hours ago. I came in here to say goodbye, that's all.'

Jem sighed audibly. 'I'm sorry.' She didn't mean it but it was the only way to end this before it turned a lot uglier.

'You should be. All I do is provide for you and the kids. Why am I being made to feel like a villain?'

She needed to stay firm, even if she was allowing him to believe her apology. 'We've had a lifetime of you racing out on functions or not being present. The children are growing up with a father they cannot count on to be where he says he will be . . .' Before he could interrupt she softened her expression. 'And we know why. We have all learned how to live with your work, Mark. And let's face it, we all enjoy the lifestyle it affords us. I am not ungrateful.'

'You sound it, Jem.'

Oh, he always played such a cunning victim to make her feel bad. She reminded herself of how chilly he'd become at lunch. 'I want you to at least make us as important as your patients. I know we must step aside when one is in labour and needs your presence, but honestly, Mark, what you did today was unforgivable.'

He waved away her complaint; he'd lost any patience he'd had for the conversation. 'I don't even know what you're talking about. I rang the hospital to ask—'

'I know, I heard it the first time. What I don't know is why you brought the mood down so hard. It was after I mentioned the guy falling off the top of Mount Lofty. You made a poor joke and I'm surely allowed to have an opinion on that? I didn't embarrass you, I didn't say much more than "Oh, come on, that's not cool".'

He looked lost. 'I've already forgotten it.'

'No, don't lie. I've lived with you for too long. You haven't forgotten it. It's still burning in there.' She prodded his chest lightly and he batted her hand away.

The roughness of his gesture made her freeze. That was a first. Mark was never physical with her unless amorous and *that* was a distant memory now.

She knew she was glaring at him open-mouthed. 'What's going on with you, Mark? I'll be honest, you've been unreachable in recent times but these last few days have been unbearable.'

He reached for his keys on the counter. 'I'm going to the hospital. You can clear the rest on your own. Get your kids to help you or leave it for the cleaner, I don't care.' He strode away.

'Hey!'

He turned.

'Maybe don't bother coming home.' She regretted that show of temper instantly.

'Careful what you wish for, Jem.' And he left.

12

In another, more ostentatious home, Alex and Alannah Petras were sharing a nightcap. After checking Marguerite was sound asleep, Alex had switched on the fire and large, pale pebbles now looked like they were aflame. It didn't throw out much heat without the fan boosted up but sitting beside it tricked him into feeling warmer and he was grateful they'd had it installed.

'Warming you up?' Alannah remarked, holding up her brandy balloon.

'I can count on a lovely Remy Martin to warm my insides.' Alex swirled his cognac around. 'Or maybe I should let you warm me all over?' He raised an eyebrow in question.

'Ooh, not tonight, darling, please,' she begged. 'I'm cold too and don't even feel like changing, let alone getting naked.'

'I was hoping for one of those skimpy silk things you tease me with.'

She laughed, moving from the plush sofa to snuggle up next to him, kicking off her shoes and folding her long legs up like an insect. 'I'll put you on a promise.'

He put his arm around her and stroked her face with his free hand. 'You said that last time . . . and the time before that. My darling, we seem to be—'

'Al . . .'

'Okay, okay. Can't a man fancy his wife?'

'Yes, please, but we don't always have to act on it, do we?'

'We used to,' he replied, unable to hide the disappointment in his tone. Her coquettish voice wasn't working on him.

'We were trying for children then.'

He cut her a look. 'Tell me it wasn't only about children.'

She shrugged. 'At the time I must admit that's all it was about. Nothing to do with you, Alex. It was just having to get the timing right and always feeling so tense. The worst part was, neither of us ever felt sexy, right?'

She was right, and he shook his head.

'So it became a chore. I hated it.'

'Not now though?' he asked.

'No, not now. But if we're talking about *right* now, my belly is still swollen with food and I'm happy just here with you.' She nestled in deeper. 'We girls like the cuddles more.'

He broached the topic that had been weighing on him. 'I know you wish you had a child to love.'

Alannah paused and he didn't fill the silence. She finally sighed. 'I think I'd be so different if we had a child of our own. I love Marguerite but it isn't enough. It just isn't.' There was only sadness in her expression.

He nodded. 'I don't expect it to be, though you're very good with her. I wish with all my heart you had your own baby.'

'Or two, or three,' she replied, sounding sadder still. 'I always wanted a big family around the dinner table.'

'You say you'd be different, but different in what way?'

'Oh, I don't know. I think I'm angry, Alex . . . actually, I'm not sure angry touches how I feel. I've got all the money in the world, my father could hire ten men to kill for me if I asked and yet no money or muscle can provide what I most want. I've been cheated out of something that everyone else takes for granted. Why me? Why do I have to miss out?'

'You have so much to be grateful for, though. And I don't mean money, darling. Look at you. Women would kill to look like you. I think every man envies me.'

She shook her head. 'I'd trade it.'

'You would?'

'I adored my grandmother, Alex. I worshipped my mother. They were both strong women who stood up to their men and made great partners. I wanted to continue that. I'd like a daughter to look up to me, someone I can teach to know she doesn't need a man to reach her potential. Don't get me wrong – I love men. I love you, I adored my father, as you know, and I was as close as a sister could be to my brother, but that matri-archal line was important to me. Those women were the ones who gave me my confidence, taught me how to stand tall, be strong, believe in my own power . . . not Dad. Dad just indulged me, adored me.'

'It was more than that. I've met your father. You impressed him more than your brother.'

She nodded. 'That's true. Lukas was softer than me. He didn't suit Dad's tough image, but I did.' She laughed. 'He used to say I should take over the business.'

'But you chose me instead.'

'I did. And listen, it's my body that won't obey – don't ever think I blame you.'

'I don't ever think that. I know we've tried everything. No stone unturned, as they say. You know I would have adop—'

'No!' she all but snapped. 'My baby has to be mine. Grown in my womb, birthed by me. I want what others seem to have so easily. It's my right.'

'Well, we nearly had it,' he tried but it was the wrong memory to trigger.

'Losing her changed me, Alex. I hide it but I've become angry. And even knowing that doesn't help me to stop feeling that way. I want to punish someone.'

'I know, darling, but we can't get her back,' he said gently. 'You must find contentment in other parts of your life. Your design business and this new idea to import furniture from Europe is surely satisfying?' He held up a hand. 'I'm not saying it's a replacement – it can't be. But it can make you feel happier, surely?'

'I don't know any more, Alex. I'm probably too twisted, failing her by not hanging onto her.'

'The clinical team told you she wasn't viable.'

'Just listen to that word – *viable*. It's hideous. She was our *child*. She was meant to become my new world. Just a few months more and I'd have had her in my arms.'

'But she may not have survived, and somehow I think that's worse, Alannah.' He turned to stroke her face. 'Do you want to try again, darling?'

She shook her head and he saw both sadness and no little rage. 'No.' She sounded emphatic. 'I'm done with it. Mark said my body's hostile and that's that. Apart from the humiliation of failing again and again, I can't cope with the mental anguish of getting my hopes up, or the potential to lose another at the last gasp.'

'That was two years ago.'

'I can still touch it though. There was so much pain and I feel it every day, Alex. I wake up and the hollow feeling arrives. Jem Maddox has pumped out three children, perhaps without believing there's anything so special about it. Everyone does it, right? That's one of the clever tricks to being a woman. Except I can't.

I can't do the one thing that my superb body was designed to do. I want revenge but there's no one to take it out on.' She gave a mirthless laugh. 'But I'll find a way to fill the void.'

'Well, that first shipment was a terrific success, right?' he said, obviously trying to change the subject.

She nodded. 'Not a piece left. Sydney and Melbourne took it all.'

'So double your consignment from France.'

'Maybe.' She shrugged. 'Hey, Al, why don't we take the cruiser out before it really gets too cold?'

He frowned. That was a shift he wasn't expecting. 'Isn't it already?'

'A last hurrah. Nowhere far – perhaps we can hug the coast. I love being out there with you. And just us, no Mags . . . no offence. How about somewhere like Wallaroo? You've always said you'd like to do some fishing around there. We can look up the Maddoxes at their beach house and hope they've sorted out their differences, but essentially just us and the sea.'

'Sounds romantic.'

'I promise to bring skimpy stuff despite the cold.'

He chuckled into his brandy. 'Done.'

13

Jack had rented a studio called Athelney Cottage on the rim of the city's green belt, in a leafy and salubrious suburb that was best known for the rather grand, 160-year-old St Peter's private boys' college that sprawled in the neighbourhood's heart. The main house to which the cottage was attached looked out into historical gardens where the youngest of the junior primary students safely played.

'Probably to burn off all that effervescing energy,' Rosie, his landlady, had said when she handed him the key with a soft smile. 'Technically, the main house is in St Peters, I gather, but the cottage is apparently noted as Hackney.' She gave a shrug to say it didn't matter much.

They had stood in the courtyard, which, despite her gentle protestations to the contrary, possessed a Mediterranean flavour, with concrete tiles that evoked pavestones and overhanging foliage that Jack could almost believe were vines. Stone plant pots were haphazardly placed, giving a carefree atmosphere to the outdoor setting, complete with table and chairs. He imagined he'd want to eat outside for every meal, though his landlady had laughed when he'd voiced this thought.

'Brr, bit cold for that in the evenings,' she said. 'But look, Mr Hawksworth, you please yourself. However, Percy will insist on sharing that time rather noisily.'

They glanced at the parrot. His appearance defied a bland title of green, which was the dominant colour; against iridescent hues that included traffic light red, the green was turned up to an unreal level, like an artist taking liberties for impact. And yet there Percy stood, outrageously bright, watching them, listening to them, head cocked.

'Hello, Rosie,' he said on cue, making Jack laugh.

'He's an eclectus parrot, from the far north,' Rosie explained. 'He'll chat constantly, I must warn you, and he's a marvellous mimic, so no burping unless you want me to know about it.'

Jack grinned. 'His plumage is incredible.'

'It is. You should see the girls. Scarlet, blue, violet and those marvellous coral beaks.'

'He's priceless. I'll enjoy him.'

'We'll see, Mr Hawksworth. He's very nosy, and once he starts impersonating the squeal of the garage door closing, you might change your opinion.'

They chuckled together. 'Call me Jack,' he suggested.

'Then you must call me Rosie. I've laid out some cool drinks at the house. Would you care for some?'

He couldn't refuse the elegant woman in her senior years. Her hair, like fragile wire of aluminium, was loosely pulled back behind her head, where owl-like sunglasses were perched. A vivid splash of cerise lipstick cut through her otherwise muted palette, and she wore a dramatic, artistically wrought necklace of silver suspending a large oblong of what could be quartz or potentially opal. He didn't know either stone well enough to guess.

'That would be lovely,' he replied. Rosie escorted him back to the house and into the front courtyard – the owner's private space – with comfy chairs beneath a lush natural canopy. 'It must be so cool under this shade during summer.'

'I do live out here during the hot months,' Rosie admitted, pouring lemon squash into a pale blue glass and nudging it towards him.

He smiled inwardly. It made him think of the lemon barley water of schooldays after tennis or hockey matches; he hadn't tasted it since.

'I love this garden,' Rosie said, gesturing to the quirky space behind where they sat. 'I had hoped to make it meadow-like, but'—she laughed with a shrug—'that didn't work so I'm letting it develop as it chooses.'

'It's a creative space,' Jack remarked.

'Thank you. As an artist that's reassuring. I call it my opinion garden because everyone who visits has something to say about it, given freely without solicitation, but I note your English reserve.'

'I think it's rather wonderful,' he said, 'especially the perfectly sculpted tin chickens. They're so real.'

'We call them chooks in Australia, Jack.' She smiled. 'So tell me about yourself.'

He gave her the fashioned lie, not enjoying being untruthful with his delightful host. After fifteen minutes he took his leave and returned to his new private space, grinning at Percy, who gave him a rousing welcome back. The studio was surprisingly large, with a separate fully fitted kitchen and bathroom. French doors, painted blue with shutters of a rich buttery cream, completed the look and created the keen impression that he could be somewhere in Provence. He wished he could live here, under happier circumstances, and take full advantage of its superb location.

It was a pleasure to stroll through the botanic gardens again. He had just finished a phone call with his sister in Sydney, leaning back on the park bench to tip his chin towards the morning sun, when his mobile rang again. 'Hawksworth.'

'Morning, mate. It's Matt.'

'What news?'

'Well, you're not going to believe this . . . or maybe you will.'

Jack leaned forward to pat the head of a friendly dog who had run up to him. 'Go on.'

'Sorry,' the dog's owner mouthed to him, whistling at her pet, and he smiled but remained intently focused on Matt.

'Firstly, we do have fingerprints in Greg Payne's unit that don't match his or his family. It's not conclusive, of course, because it could be any friend or visitor. However, the prints are focused around his computer, desk, drawers, et cetera.'

'Did you find out which company he worked for?'

'Ah, well, you'll like this. Greg was a full-time medical courier for a company called Global Dangerous Goods, which has clients all over Australia, including many that are fertility clinics.'

Jack mentally punched the air. 'What else can you tell me?'

'He was either paid very well or he had some sort of extra income. A look around his place shows he didn't skimp on anything. New-looking laptop, high-quality desktop, the kind of TV that I dream about . . . We found a receipt for a new iPod and his computer history shows he was planning to invest in a new hi-tech watch and a new phone. He wears quality clothes. His running gear is all branded – no Kmart here.'

Jack didn't know what that was but understood what Matt was intimating. He waited.

'He was never late with rent and his parents tell us he was about to buy a small house up around Burnside where we had coffee. That doesn't come cheap. They said he was going to buy it alone, so he's obviously good at saving, but when we look at what he spends . . .'

'Not adding up?'

'You could say that.'

Jack blinked. His interest was more than piqued. 'So, are any of those clinics in Adelaide?'

'Down here GDG has contracts with two of the major reproductive medicine units.'

'Good work, Matt.'

'Gets better. This guy was attached to only one of them, an outfit called MultiplyMed. Totally above board as far as I can tell – it's been around for nearly forty years.'

'Well, it's a starting point and I'm very grateful.'

'Remember, you haven't heard any of that from me.'

'Tread lightly?'

'Please,' Matt said.

'Like a butterfly on hot sand, I promise.'

'Okay, keep me in your loop.'

'Will do. Thanks again.'

Buoyant at what felt like a little breakthrough, and becoming aware of the sun's bite, Jack moved to another bench that was conveniently placed beneath a big old Moreton Bay fig tree. He'd learned from the Gardens' information boards that these giants – the Australian banyan – hailed from eastern Australia and were planted nearly a century and a half ago. The fig's roots, called buttresses, he'd discovered, twisted out like ancient tentacles searching for food and to a width that almost seemed to echo its height. It was cool and dark beneath its leathery leaves, and Jack felt like he was in a secret world here. He was far from the world he knew with its familiar places and faces, so a sense of perspective came easier. The death of Anne McEvoy, for instance. He'd not allowed himself to dwell on it, though he'd spoken about it a little in the mandatory psychology sessions organised by the Met, and it sat in his mind like a glowering presence that probably needed to be confronted. But not yet. If things had been different, they might be married right now, perhaps even with little Hawksworths charging around. In truth, he'd never stopped loving her, and all the women since had been a temporary substitute – Jack could see that now. Each was a brilliant woman, but none of them could make a claim on him, either because they were committed to someone else, lived in a different country, or, as with Lauren, they'd agreed their relationship was friendship, offering solace and companionship at a time when they both needed it. Perhaps Lauren was the one who got away? But it was too late now.

And then there was Kate. Jack loved DCI Kate Carter, but not in the way she craved. He had often wondered just how destructive their friendship was on her psyche. Had it been cruel, for instance, to invite her back for the last op? Perhaps, but there were few other detectives he trusted as much as her and none who would have his back as single-mindedly as she did when they were on a case together. It was frightening to contemplate that he had been aware, in that split second of danger, that Kate was prepared to risk her life for his.

Jack shook his head and absently rubbed his scar, a touchstone for reliving the sensation of the blade slicing into his skin, miraculously missing organs but creating damage nonetheless. He had never regretted that he'd taken the wound, because it had saved his friend's life. He checked his watch and calculated the time, then pulled out his phone and made a call to London.

'It's me,' he said, when it was answered.

'Jack! Long life to you. I have just poured myself a nasty late-night coffee and could hear you tut-tutting on my shoulder.'

'Still at work?' he asked. 'I thought you'd be home and tucked up with . . . er . . . ?'

'Dan.' She laughed and it was a reassuring sound. 'Yes, I was asking myself just that: why am I still here in this grim office when I could be eating spag bog near the fire, watching *Dancing on Ice*?'

He grinned, knowing full well that Kate would rather cut off a limb than watch one of those competitions. 'Good to hear a voice from home, Kate.'

'Homesick?'

'Not really. Just, oh, I don't know, having more time to think.'

He heard her chuckle, knew she'd be chuffed he called. 'Actually, I rang to ask if I might chew something over with you.'

'And there I was flattering myself you were missing me.'

He didn't bite. 'What are you working on?'

'Two stabbings after a football match.'

He'd read about that and wondered who was on it. 'I'm sure you'll catch your guy.'

'I live in hope,' she replied flippantly, but he was ever careful with Kate's remarks that might have a double meaning and this was certainly one of those. 'Anyway, chew away, while I sip my awful coffee.'

He told her what he'd discovered.

'Mmm, right. Well, you've caught the trail, perhaps.'

'Maybe. But why kill a lowly foot soldier, assuming my gut is right that this wasn't a suicide? Why draw the attention to the operation?'

He imagined Kate's agile mind racing around the possibilities and waited. 'Well,' she began and he heard the softly distant squeal of a desk chair protest as she sat. 'Setting aside all the other noise, I suspect we can presume that this foot soldier had become troublesome somehow.'

Jack nodded, having reached the same conclusion. 'How, in your opinion?'

'Well, I've had some experiences with couriers through my airport days. They're not exactly big wigs, but they are privy to the illegal workings of whatever the operation is – drugs, weapons, you name it. The men and women who are the mules, if you will, are taking all the risk in the world for relatively little. They are paid a fee and their expenses are covered for accommodation, transfers, meals and all that, but it's a pretty lowly task when you shake it out. There's no glamour and barely any thanks, given they're facing an intensive correction order as a minimum if caught. Even fully legit couriers will tell you that while the job *appears* glitzy with all the travel and hotels, there's a lot of hanging around getting bored. They generally stay in relatively low-priced accommodation, they eat in small-time restaurants and they fly economy.'

'Moving with the herd?'

'Exactly. And all of them are worn down through time-zone changes and having to queue for everything, getting to airports so much earlier these days for security, waiting for endless hours roaming terminals like lost souls when disruptions occur and on it goes. They tend to come to the realisation that they are simply a bum on a seat with a piece of luggage or package that a company is waiting on at the other end. That person, who has a name, a heart, feelings, a life, starts to feel inconsequential, irrelevant, and that's particularly so for illegal activities. They don't really matter to their employer, could be anyone.'

'So maybe this fellow, Greg, got bored?'

'Ground down, perhaps, by his job. Changing time zones constantly would mess with your mood, I'm sure. And it's a pretty thankless task even when it's legit.'

'You think?'

'Jack, when did you last personally thank the bloke on the motorbike delivering a parcel to you at work? You just accept, sign and want the guy gone, especially these days when we're all anxious about security. A medical courier would be just as anonymous and, if he's moving illegal gear, that anonymity is what he's counting on.

She was right. 'I hear you. So, do you think perhaps he was pushing for some recognition and they didn't like it?'

'Well, if it's true, for them to go to the trouble of murdering him, then I think it would be more than recognition. To get that sort of reaction, he must have threatened to expose them, whether it was deliberate or inadvertent.'

'Blackmail?'

'It wouldn't have to be that blatant. Grumbling about conditions or lack of thanks in a small, tight-knit operation that depends on everyone just doing their job and never questioning anything . . . That might be enough to make the person in charge nervous, and question this guy's loyalty.'

'Why not give him a warning?'

'I've worked in organised crime, Jack, and I'm telling you there is a rule book. It's not written down, but everyone in an organisation, right down to the lowliest courier, understands that a loose mouth earns the most serious of consequences. Warnings can work but once you're on that road of complaint or rocking the boat, you're in the sights of the powerful guys at the top. Easier to get rid of you than warn you.'

Her words were chilling. 'Right.'

'One more thing I'll mention.' She didn't wait for him to respond. 'It will boil down to money. Ninety-nine times out of a hundred, when I've attended a crime scene with a body within an organised crime situation, it will be about money. Not being paid enough for the risk, not being paid enough for the eventual haul, the split isn't fair, blah blah. They know enough, they've done it long enough, they want to get closer to the big table. They become a liability without realising it. If this guy was murdered, it was almost certainly over money.'

'Follow the money,' they said together and shared a laugh.

'Good,' he said. 'Then I need to find some of his legit colleagues, see if they noted him feeling unhappy about his work. I do frown though, at the idea of an organisation killing their golden goose.'

'What do you mean?'

'Well, they could have just paid the guy more if that's what would shut him up. Why kill someone who's prepared to take all the risk to transport your illegal goods? I mean, you'd have to re-invest trust in someone new. Break them in. Show them the ropes. Frighten them sufficiently into understanding that this job is not the kind of job you walk away from. There's absolutely no way that this guy, if he was a courier for an illegal side business, didn't know what he was doing, right?'

'No way. He would deliver the legitimate consignment and then do a second delivery, I presume. So if they're prepared to kill this guy, it means they have others to fill his shoes. That sounds easy enough but, as you say, there's a lot involved in letting too many people into the circle of trust. Or . . .'

'Or what?'

'Erm, or,' she began again, sounding thoughtful, 'they've got a new route, or a new way in and they don't need him or others like him.'

It triggered a fresh path in his mind but Kate continued.

'Follow the money, but also the trail back to whoever's taking the delivery. And Jack?'

'Yes?'

'Be careful, eh? These guys don't muck around, as you can gather.'

'Thanks, Kate. I wish you were here working it with me.'

She gave a small sad laugh. 'Come home safe. Lunch is on me.'

'All right, bye for now.' He made a kissing sound, knowing it was risky but he hated to be anything but authentic with her;

if she had been standing in front of him, he'd be hugging her or pecking her cheek goodbye. 'Toss out that ghastly muck that you're sipping and go get yourself a good espresso.'

'Have you tasted these new freeze-dried granules called Arabica Royale?' She laughed when she heard him give a sound of horror across oceans. 'Lots of love, Jack.'

Ending the call with a smile, he decided he might as well do a second London call now. And although fully expecting to leave a message with her assistant, he was put through to Chief Superintendent Rowland immediately.

'Jack. Enjoying the sun?'

'Actually I am, ma'am,' he replied. 'I'm sitting in the Adelaide Botanic Gardens and contemplating life.'

It was reassuring to hear her chuckle. 'I presume you didn't ring to share just that, though?'

'No.' He gave her a succinct brief of his discoveries and summed up his thoughts following his chat with Kate. 'Of course, none of this puts me closer to the source but it does make me believe that we might be onto something.'

'I agree. You've got another what . . . nine days?'

'That's right. I'm thinking of heading north to the regional ports. It's a busy shipping coastline of South Australia. I'd like to explore the potential for bringing in illegal goods by ship.'

'I thought you said this material was coming in via air?'

'It was. It is. But there are other ways in, and maybe this guy's death signals something. I'm covering all bases.'

'Australia has one of the tightest border securities in the world,' she reasoned.

'It does but, ma'am, we're talking about something that could come in on a pleasure craft and walk ashore inside the backpack of a perfectly normal-looking daytripper.'

'Mmm, okay. So what are you asking me?'

'If I'm going to keep up the pretence of being a tourist, I'll need to rent somewhere close to or at the beach. I'll have to do my sleuthing in the most indirect way I can.'

'And am I still paying for the place you're renting in Adelaide?'

'I'm afraid so, ma'am.'

He heard her give a sigh from within the crushing overload of teak veneer in her office.

'Is it raining there, ma'am?'

'It's not just raining, it's miserable, and you're doing little to improve my mood, Jack.' She sighed again. 'Right, do what you must. Thanks for checking in – I'll wait to hear from you the same time next week unless something breaks.'

'Thank you.'

'And Jack, if you are onto something, it's important that this is handed over to the Australians. We can't wait too long to formally brief them.'

'I know, ma'am, but I have skin in the game. I want to find the person whose actions led to the death of my student.'

'I understand. But Jack, you risk what has been your Achilles heel through several ops. Don't let this get personal.'

'No, I shan't,' he said, carefully ignoring the fact that it was already too late; Amelia's death had become personal long before his chief had heard about the case.

14

The Maddoxes sat in a taut silence that was punctuated only by polite responses to each other as they navigated breakfast and getting ready for the day. Jem didn't think the children were picking up on the chill in the kitchen; she tried to convince herself that the civility would fool their youngsters that all was normal enough.

It wasn't.

Mark was still holding yesterday's grudge, and Jem was feeling uncharacteristically sour that he'd managed to pull on the martyr's robe. Even so, she knew all too well that it needed to be her who puffed on the peace pipe first. Mark didn't know how to say sorry. In the past he'd seemed to think sex solved all issues, and she blamed herself for surrendering to physical attention rather than showing him that the issue was not over between them just because they'd had sex, and that when he rolled over and slept, the problem – whatever it was – was still oozing acid into her thoughts.

Was feeling privately miserable about her marriage now the default? It seemed so. Was it time to be brave, call it quits? How would the children cope?

She wanted to make a stand – wanted to make it today, and still her good sense told her to stay in neutral until she had a plan. Time would explain what his strange behaviour had been about. But she needed to apologise to their guests; they had surely sensed the awkwardness.

And so they continued through the hurdle of breakfast without upsetting the children.

'Do you want some toast?' Jem asked Mark.

'No, just a tea.' He looked away immediately. 'Listen, Hugh, we need to leave in five, okay?'

'That's early,' she remarked as her son sighed and left the breakfast table with his cereal not quite finished. 'Let him eat.'

'No time. I've got an early one.'

'I can't even brew you a pot in that time,' she said. They had a thing about pots of tea – no dunking of teabags in mugs for the Maddoxes.

'Then don't worry,' he said, and she watched him conjure up a smile for the girls' sake. 'I'll grab a takeaway on the way in.'

Jem watched him bend to the golden head of each of his daughters and kiss them. 'Be brilliant today, Izzy. Remember what I said about the introduction to your English essay.'

'Yes, Dad,' she said, pushing him affectionately as he gave her ponytail a soft yank.

He kissed her twin sister. 'Good luck with the flute test, Hols.'

'It's an exam, Dad. Grade three.'

He mimicked playing a penny whistle and grinned. 'You'll ace it, and there'll be a reward if you do.' Mark glanced at Jem. 'See you later.'

She nodded. No kiss. No smile.

Not from either of them.

★

A couple of hours of brooding later, Jem sat in a reception area she'd never been in, waiting to catch Mark. It was a risk, but Jem was determined to deal with the stand-off head on and quickly. This needed to be put behind them. But he had to explain what she'd done wrong and own yesterday's awkwardness.

Both of them stewing was unwise. She'd comforted many a friend who, when prodded, couldn't remember exactly what had set off a situation that had escalated until it called a long-term relationship into question, causing hurt and damaging words that couldn't be taken back easily. She'd always believed they were better than that. But she wasn't sure they were that good together any more. She'd sat on the edge of the bed after Mark had left that morning and asked herself whether, if there was a way out, she would take it. When she'd forced herself to confront the dilemma, a small voice had said, yes, she would, because she was so intolerably unhappy and sick of putting on this facade to others that they were the perfect family.

The children would understand. No, that was a lie for her own benefit. They wouldn't, because they adored their father. But they would learn to live with the separation of their parents, as so many others at school had done.

You must keep working at marriage, her mother's voice had sounded in her mind. *At least give it another try.*

Jem had stood with purpose and let out a breath. 'All right,' she said into the silent house, and won a response from their little dog, who came scampering into the bedroom to see if this meant a walk. 'One more try, Mark. I'll make the effort.'

She'd rung his rooms and found out that he was working that morning at MultiplyMed on Greenhill Road. After a short jog with the dog, she'd showered, washed her hair, blow-dried it and found her favourite jeans of the moment, no longer those low-waisted horrors that gave even the trimmest of women a muffin top. These were mid-rise, in a comfortably distressed pale denim, straight legged but not too clingy. She teamed them with a plain baby-doll blouse in white that showed off her angular shoulders and, not wishing to overdo the skin on show, she grabbed a cropped tan leather jacket. A pair of tan slip-ons and a handbag in pewter Mark had bought in London at LK Bennett completed her look, along with a sheer foundation, a dusting of powder and a tiny smudge of stick rouge. Black-brown mascara, no eye liner or colour, with just a sweep of near-nude lip balm from her favourite Kiko store in Paris.

The waiting room was busy.

She flicked absently through today's newspaper and the story of the dead man at the bottom of the gully was still taking up plenty of space. She read now that his name was Greg Payne, age thirty-three, and he had lived at Dulwich. A photo showed his parents standing forlornly at the edge of the gully, his father's arm around the slumped shoulders of his mother.

Again she felt the glumness circle her, because either way, jumped or pushed, it was a terrible way for anyone's life to end. Jem took a deep breath and turned the page, looking for something shallow and upbeat while she waited for her husband to finish his present appointment.

'He's doing a transfer,' the receptionist had told her when she'd arrived without warning. 'He shouldn't be long.'

Jem only vaguely knew what a transfer was. She had always thought her husband cared for pregnant women and then delivered their babies. 'Golden Hands', the midwives called him apparently, because he was skilled and gentle, especially with the anxious new mums. But no, he had more ambition and had branched out into reproductive medicine, helping childless couples start their families. Now he spent a morning and afternoon most weeks working with MultiplyMed.

Considering the ease with which she'd fallen pregnant with their three children, and taking a measure of the invisible but palpable anxiety of the women waiting in the reception area, who all wanted what she had, she allowed herself to like Mark a fraction more in this moment despite her vexation at his recent behaviour. He was doing something important. Something that brought joy and happiness.

It made her wonder why Alannah and Alex Petras hadn't started a family together. He'd been married briefly before, and there was Marguerite whom Alannah was clearly involved with; she picked her up from school a few times each week, which was how Jem had come to know her, discovering when she'd mentioned her to Mark that he played golf regularly with Alex. She didn't make it her business to know Mark's every move but it did seem odd that he hadn't mentioned Alex, given their daughters were not just in the same year but the same class and house at school.

Her musings were interrupted by the arrival of a tall, good-looking man and she became even more diverted by him when she heard his English accent asking for her husband.

'Do you have an appointment?' the receptionist asked.

'I don't, Lisa,' he admitted, and Jem smiled inwardly, realising that he must have read her badge in a nanosecond. He was smooth.

The receptionist flashed a smile, gazed momentarily at the computer screen and shook her head. 'I'm really sorry, but Dr Maddox is booked out.'

'Popular guy,' the Englishman said with another smile.

'He is,' she replied, melting a little further, Jem noticed. *Blimey, who wouldn't*, she thought. *That kind of package doesn't walk through the doors often.*

'Are you . . . er, selling something?' Lisa asked.

The man laughed and it was a lovely sound in the otherwise

tense atmosphere of the fertility clinic reception; Jem guessed that was normal, people waiting in a state of anxious quiet. 'No, I'm a writer, actually. Perhaps I could make an appointment?'

Just then, Jem saw Mark push through a door to reception. He'd been told she was waiting and spotted her immediately. But as she smiled, the visitor swung around, obviously recognising him.

'Oh great. Dr Maddox?'

'Yes?' Mark frowned.

'I'm sorry, I don't mean to ambush you. I was just asking Lisa here if I might make an appointment?'

'For a sperm sample, or . . .?'

Jem watched the man's smile break wide, white, entirely amused. 'Er, no, nothing like that.'

Mark glanced her way and put a hand up. 'Look, could I just ask you to wait a moment?'

The visitor shrugged generously. 'Sure.'

'Thanks. Excuse me.' Mark took a couple of steps in Jem's direction as she stood to greet him warmly, but she was met by a wall of tension. His voice was tight. 'Jem, what are you doing here?' He sounded distracted, interrupted. 'I'm working.'

That much was obvious but she hated that she was having to explain herself in front of others. This had been a bad idea. *Try harder!* She risked kissing his cheek, which felt tense and unwelcoming. 'Well, I figured you might like to go for lunch . . . a quick sandwich, a chance to chat?' She shrugged, horrified by how small she suddenly felt in front of an intently listening Lisa.

Mark gave her a smile, clearly for the benefit of others. He couldn't touch the warmth that the English guy generated, even though she knew Mark was more than capable of that sort of charm. He was obviously still stewing.

'I can't.' He shook his head emphatically.

'Okay,' she said, lifting a shoulder in a soft shrug and deciding to cut her losses quickly. 'Just an idea. I thought it would be nice for us to—'

'Absolutely not,' he cut in. 'We're flat out.'

'Yes, I really should make an appointment.' She looked at the man still patiently waiting. He must have heard her comment and twitched the barest of smiles. 'Sorry to interrupt. I'll see you at home.'

'I'll be late.'

The cold emanating from Mark shocked her as effectively as being dunked into a pit of ice, and she simply nodded.

'Of course you will. Bye, then.'

Everyone had heard, including the receptionist and the patients waiting in their chairs to be called in. And the Englishman, at whom she cut a look as she moved towards the door. He held something in his expression that spoke of empathy. Before she stepped through the huge sliding doors that squealed a little as they opened, she heard Mark say to the cold-caller, 'Now, Mr . . .?'

'Hawksworth. Jack Hawksworth.'

The doors squealed closed behind her and she skipped down the steps, wanting to be gone. She was horrified to discover that her eyes were stinging with tears. No one must see. Glad to turn into the soft breeze, Jem made for the side street where she had parked. She couldn't keep up this pretence. Maybe it *was* time to tell Mark she didn't want this life any more. It was a failure. Such a shame. They'd had everything going for them.

Finally at the car, she snatched away the tears with a quick flick of her fingers and began to dig into her bag for the keys. Why did they always disappear like this?

'Mrs Maddox?'

She turned and was surprised to see the Englishman striding easily in her direction. He appeared taller now that he stood before her and even more darkly attractive square on. His chinos hung off narrow hips to encase long, lean legs and his amused gaze landed on her from eyes that were unfairly blue, outlined by killer dark lashes to boot. She couldn't look away from his kind expression.

'Yes,' she said and instantly dropped the keys, cursing.

'Here, let me,' he said, bending easily. 'Why are car keys always so heavy?' he remarked as he handed them to her, and that cultured yet not pompous accent did funny things to her.

She wasn't dim. Knew she was vulnerable to a kind word, a handsome smile. But she couldn't have asked for a better combination than what this fellow was offering.

'You were in to see my husband,' she said, flicking away the last tear. The remark was obvious and she wanted to bite her tongue. 'Did he give you the short shrift too?' She might as well not pretend.

'I'm afraid so.'

Glad that the tears had dissipated, she tried for the levity she could usually rely upon. 'Did I really just say short shrift? I don't even know where the saying comes from. I think my granny used to use it.'

He grinned. 'I can probably tell you where it comes from.'

'You're fibbing.'

'I'll bet you a cup of coffee I can.'

She paused, watching him. She was sensing no guile in his open face.

'You look like you could use one,' he said, but somehow it didn't sound judgemental.

'All right,' she agreed, mildly surprising herself. A coffee sounded good, as did some fresh and fun conversation with this handsome stranger. 'But we'll pay for ourselves. There's a café behind us in Dulwich, if you don't mind walking.'

'Not at all.' He gestured for her to lead.

Jem paused, caution kicking in. 'Listen, you're not hitting on me, are you?'

'Definitely not,' he said, raising his hands in a gesture of apology. 'And hardly so close to your husband's office. I need coffee and . . . I suspect so do you.'

'I feel awkward that you heard that.'

He shrugged. 'I wasn't following you. I parked my rental here too.' He pointed to a small hatchback just two cars away from her own and pressed the switch of his keys. The car, true enough, squeaked its answer and its tail lights winked.

'Instead you're feeling sorry for me? Maybe that's worse,' she replied, trying to sound light-hearted but not quite making it.

'It's not charity,' he assured her and she noted he evaded the question. 'I don't know anyone in Adelaide and so it will be pleasant to order some coffee, perhaps a bite to eat and not sit alone for once.'

She liked the honesty. 'Come on, then. It's not too far. I'm Jem, by the way. Short for Jemima.'

'Jack,' he replied. It suited him.

They were soon seated. On the way he'd answered all her questions and she learned he was visiting his sister in Sydney but had wanted to explore a different part of Australia for a week or so.

After ordering she asked more questions, enjoying watching his mannerisms as he spoke. He had an economy of words but his hands – well cared for – matched his eyes for expressiveness. His voice was even, with a pleasant grittiness; he would sound soothing over the phone, she decided, feeling like one of her daughters with a crush. She hoped she wasn't blushing.

'But why Adelaide, for heaven's sake?'

He shook his head with wonder. 'You know, I think you should work for the tourism office in this state. You're truly nailing it.'

She laughed and it felt like a lovely glow, warming her up after feeling frozen out by her husband for the last twenty-four hours . . . no, the last couple of years. 'Most of the English tourists head for Queensland, don't they?' she asked, pouring half a sugar stick into her coffee and twisting the top to close off the other half, which she lay on her saucer.

'Do they? I wouldn't know. And why not Adelaide, I say? Last visit I did some touring out of Melbourne, so that box is ticked for now. I'm not a fan of humidity so I'll leave Queensland until I can visit in wintertime. I didn't have long enough to do Tasmania, which by all accounts is incredibly beautiful, so I'll probably organise a hike next visit when I can take my time, rent a car.'

'It's every bit as lovely as people tell you, although it can look a bit like England at times – or Scotland, maybe. Perhaps you see enough of that?'

He nodded. 'Yes, so here I am. The dry state.'

'We like to think of ourselves as the festival state or, better still, the winery state,' she corrected him as the coffee and panini they'd ordered arrived. The sandwich had been cut in half, as requested, so they could share it. 'So, why on earth did you need to see my husband?'

She watched his lips pucker to blow gently on the coffee before he sipped and sighed his pleasure.

'I'm writing a series of articles about life in a modern marriage.'

'Really?' She glanced at his left hand.

'No, I'm not married,' he said, ahead of her question. 'But I have loads of single women friends—'

'I'll bet you do, Jack,' she said with a playful smirk.

He smiled back. 'I was going to say, who are building careers and holding off on settling down. And when they do, fertility is one of the problems they often run into.'

'Ah, okay. Why here though? Surely the same problems exist in England?'

'They do, of course. But I'm on holiday and my mind is floating free. And my sister is pushing me to write the piece. Ideas roar when you're away from home. I only came up with this idea last week and my editor has given me the go-ahead. I saw your husband mentioned in a magazine, and he looks like the poster boy for fertility.' He shrugged.

Jem laughed; it was true but she decided to turn it back on the boyishly handsome writer. Why did men at this age look so good in pale blue shirts and simple chinos? His tie was now loosened, and she was looking at a neat V of smooth skin below his Adam's apple, which pulsed with his heartbeat. Was she staring? She cleared her throat. 'That's rich coming from you.'

He looked back at her, puzzled.

'Oh, come on. Tell me no woman has remarked on your looks before. The receptionist back at the office . . .'

'Who tried to give me the short shrift, you mean?'

She laughed. 'I'm going to hold you to that explanation but yes, her and'—although she didn't turn, she nodded in the waitress's direction—'even she is staring. She would have undressed if you'd asked her.'

Jack looked genuinely pained and she wished she hadn't teased him. The problem was her. She was compensating for Mark's lack of interest in her by behaving like a lioness on heat. *Stop*, she told herself.

Jack was talking. '. . . can't help the genes and how they arranged themselves,' he reasoned, sounding affable. 'I don't trade on it.'

And Jem believed him, especially as she'd managed to make him look about as discomfited as anyone ever had in her company.

'I'm sorry. I think I'm in a bad mood.'

'I would be too. He could have let you down a little more gallantly.'

She nodded. 'I'm also sorry you and everyone else had to witness that.'

'Nothing for you to feel sorry for. We don't have to talk about it.'

Jem sighed, suddenly wanting to talk about it, tired of bottling it up and faking her life. Why couldn't she be honest with herself? 'We've fallen out, but I don't really know why,' she blurted. 'Today, I thought I'd surprise him, try and mend it somehow. But that all went horribly wrong.' How had they arrived here already? She was opening up her heart and her dirty laundry basket to a perfect stranger. But maybe that was good – what did it matter what she told him? She already felt lighter.

'To be fair, he did look busy,' her companion said.

She nodded. 'And I did ambush him. It was already tense in there without me adding to it.'

'I'm sure he's already regretting it,' he assured her.

Together they bit into their panini halves as though orchestrated, their gazes meeting, and Jem knew he was just trying to make her feel better. She didn't believe Mark was regretful. He probably hadn't considered her feelings at all; he was careless with her these days. What mattered to Mark was Mark's feelings alone, or perhaps the children's; there didn't seem to be room for her. How had it come to this?

'Tell me about him.'

She frowned. 'Why?'

'Looks like you need to talk and I'm a good listener,' Jack said. 'Besides, this is a good sandwich,' he jested.

It couldn't hurt. And the truth was, she wanted to talk. If she'd had a close girlfriend, that's exactly what she'd be doing right now, picking over the last two years and what had triggered this slide. It would help organise her thoughts. She gave him a potted version of their life while he chewed.

'So life's good, otherwise?'

'Well, yes. We don't seem to have the financial strain that others have to juggle, though don't ask me how he does it.'

'What do you mean?'

Jem shook her head. 'Mark lives extravagantly, I've always thought. You know, three children at top schools, the cars, the clothes, the holidays and general lifestyle . . . It all screams to others what you're worth, or want them to think you're worth.'

'And you don't like that?'

'Mark's always had a healthy ego. He likes praise − he thrives on it − and yes, he's always wanted people to notice his achievements. I'm different, but also I'm not the breadwinner. I'd be happy in a little cottage, making my own curtains.'

'You would? Curtains?' He raised an eyebrow.

'Well, maybe not the curtains, but I mean it. Past a certain point, I think money corrodes. It's great when it flows enough to make you feel secure. But how much does one need for that security? Mark needs a lot more than I do. I'd take a love-filled marriage and having to scrimp a little over what I went through back there. It's belittling. I think the money and him providing the lifestyle seems to give him that right. It also makes him more tense, more unreasonable. It's a mistake to believe that money always brings a more relaxed approach to life.'

Jack met her gaze. 'You have the power to make changes,' he offered.

'So says the unmarried guy with no children,' she said in dry accusation.

'Actually I have several,' he said, and then laughed at her look of dismay. 'Sorry, I thought I should lighten the mood. I don't have children of my own, just a niece and nephew, and no broken marriages.'

'Plenty of broken hearts, though?'

He shrugged, didn't respond.

'Anyway, I didn't mean to unload all that. I think I owe you an apology.'

'Not at all. Maybe unburdening it will help you confront it.'

She gave a small shrug. 'I don't know if I want to.'

He nodded. 'He must earn very well to provide as he does.'

'I suppose so. He seems to be doing much better than his peers on that front.'

'How do you mean?'

He really knew how to keep her talking. 'Oh, just that in the last couple of years we seem to be pulling ahead. You know how people talk. I'm not that interested in it all, but he seems to be doing something right, if I look at what he spends in any given month. He never skimps on anything for the family.'

Jack was a good listener and she was saying far too much. Time to wrap this up. She watched her companion dab his lips with the serviette and wondered whether he'd be a good kisser.

She suspected he would be.

15

Jack pressed a serviette to his lips, buying time and covering any flash of interest that might reflect in his eyes. That little nugget from Jem Maddox about her husband earning more than seemed normal would now sit in his craw, he was sure. He wouldn't be able to leave it alone, but experience had taught him to let it sit and bloom in his mind for a while. But he wanted to find out more. He needed to keep her engaged, yet not sound too intrigued by her husband.

'Really? Do you feel the other wives' jealousy at how much he spoils you?'

She laughed but he saw little mirth in it. 'I don't really know them, if I'm truthful. Mark keeps me separate from his workplace. You know, I didn't even know he spends two half days a week there in reproductive medicine until recently.'

'Truly?'

'I think it's wonderful. I'd like to learn more about it – it must be so satisfying to help all those couples. I can imagine he finds that powerful, and I'm surprised he's not mentioned it.'

Tuck that away too, Jack decided. 'Too modest,' he remarked.

'Mark, modest? All these clinicians have big egos, as you'll discover if you interview a few. I don't criticise them for it, but when you live alongside it, it can be . . .'

He waited with a question in his expression.

'Well, wearing,' she said, grinning self-consciously. 'They call him "Golden Hands" in the maternity wings of the hospitals he works at. And'—she shook her head—'his mother used to refer to him as Golden Boy.'

'Only child?'

'Only son. Treasured.'

Jack nodded. 'And you? Does he treasure you? I know you said things have been a little rough lately . . .'

'I think we're drifting apart,' she said sadly.

'Maybe more achievement simply brings more stress. That can affect people in so many ways.'

'You're right, of course. But in a few years we'll have older teens in the house doing their own thing, planning to move out even or move state. That leaves just us and I'd hate to think we have nothing gluing us together other than absent children and a dog. We used to be great as a couple. But now we barely reach for each other. And the last two days . . .' She looked down at her plate and fiddled with her sandwich.

'What triggered the cold shoulder?' he asked gently, probing but not expecting much. He was surprised when she didn't deflect his question.

'We had some friends – more acquaintances, I suppose – over for lunch. We were discussing that guy who fell off the top of Mount Lofty.' She lifted her gaze to him from the nibbled panini she'd lost interest in. 'Have you read about that?'

'Of course. It's been in the news plenty.'

'Right, well, it's one of Adelaide's typically bizarre deaths – we're sort of known for them, unfortunately. In a week when there's not much news around, they get a lot of airplay. Naturally, it came up.'

'And?'

'The conversation around it was short, but Mark turned instantly cold from thereon. There was no reason for his sudden change in mood, as far as I could tell.'

Jack couldn't help pushing it a bit further. 'What was said as your husband became upset?'

'I wouldn't even say he was upset.' She shrugged. 'Oh, it was the usual stuff . . . why choose that way to suicide, that sort of thing. He made an off-colour joke about it and I gave him the look, you know – the sort of wifely look that says that wasn't necessary.'

He nodded. 'But he didn't like that? I mean, it is a topic on most people's lips in this city,' Jack said, wanting to prolong the conversation but not have her notice that he was fishing.

'Well, yes, it is. But I don't think it's something to joke about. I do remember saying I'd heard that it wasn't confirmed as suicide and might be considered suspicious.'

'Oh really? Where did you hear that?'

Jack listened intently as she told him about her connection to the Attorney General's department.

'And I'm sure it was about then that the temperature dropped to zero and never recovered.' She dropped her shoulders, deflated. 'I mean, Alex Petras is Mark's friend and I hardly know Alannah.'

He nodded and she suddenly sat up straighter.

'Oh, look, Jack, I'm sorry. You have been extremely polite and charming.' She glanced at her watch. 'Why are you listening to my problems? I'll make tracks. I've got some errands to run before school pick-up.'

'I told you, I'm a good listener. But before you go, I need to make good on my promise. Short shrift comes from the verb to shrive, connected with penance and usually just before death –

you know, someone on their deathbed seeking absolution. Shrove
Tuesday, for example, which most of us prefer to think of as
pancake day, was a day to be shriven,' he said. 'Too boring?'

She laughed. 'Not at all! I think it's fascinating.'

'Anyway, centuries ago, when prisoners were hanged in England
for crimes we'd consider borderline trivial today, they were sent to
the scaffold immediately upon sentencing, so there was no time
to seek the long form of absolution. Instead, they were given what
was termed the short shrift by the priest. And so it's come down the
ages to have the meaning of cursory consideration.'

She gave a small clap, making him smile. 'Brilliant! You must
find chatting up women effortless.'

It was his turn to gust a laugh. 'No, actually, they've been known
to yawn in my face,' he said, thinking of his favourite colleague.

Jem gave a soft smile. 'So what's next for you, Jack, on this
working holiday?'

'Some facts to check for this article and then I'd like to go to
the beach for a few days,' he said with a casual tone, reaching into
his back pocket for his credit card.

'Oh, lovely. Whereabouts? Kangaroo Island, I'm assuming?'

'Why's that?'

'Because it's incredible, especially for an overseas visitor. You
can experience the bush, see the wildlife, enjoy the wilderness at
its best.'

'Do ships call in there?'

She laughed. 'The ferry does.' It sounded like she said 'fairy'.

'Er, no, no ferry for me.' He grinned, rubbing his belly to
signify the lie that he suffered seasickness. 'Any other suggestions?'

Her eyes widened and sparkled. 'Well, yes. We have a beach
house at a place called Wallaroo.' Jack realised this was the same
stretch of beach being mentioned again. 'And it's not at all crowded
this time of year. Sandy beach . . . gorgeous water. It belonged to

my family and now it's mine, at the southern end of North Beach.'
She blinked. 'I was thinking of going up there for a couple of days
myself.' He sensed the lie as she grinned softly in thought. 'I have a
friend who rents her house out — it's called Horizon. Do you want
me to call her and see if it's available?'

'Wallaroo?' he queried, to see what she could tell him.

'The Yorke Peninsula,' she qualified. 'Beautiful coast. Used to
just be quiet fishing in my grandad's time. But it's got a busy grain
port.'

There was that coast mentioned again. It could not be coincidence, he decided. Definitely worth a look. He watched her give
a casual shrug.

'You'll love it. I'd be glad to show you around if our paths cross.'

Jack sensed coercion. But it suited his situation so well that he
couldn't turn her down. 'Er, well, if it's no problem?'

'It's not. Give me a number where I can reach you,' she said.
'I'll text the details. When do you want to go?'

She was pushing. He wrote the local number he was using on a
serviette. 'Tomorrow, probably. I'll stay around to the weekend.'

'Well, I hope you enjoy it. It's a special place, known for being
where the outback meets the sea.'

'That sounds romantic.' He didn't mean to catch her gaze but
did, and it felt like an accidental trip.

Both he and Jem Maddox looked away quickly and she
immediately began fiddling in her bag, pulling out keys and
checking her phone.

She cleared her throat. 'Well, I never fail to feel rejuvenated
after even a weekend there. I'll send details.'

'Thanks for sharing a coffee and a bite.'

'Let me pay for—'

Jack put his hand up in a warding gesture. 'Let me. It was my
idea, and my pleasure.'

'But we agreed.'

'Okay, then we can have another coffee in the distant future when I'm next in Australia,' he said. 'It's fourteen dollars, Jem. It won't break the bank.'

'I owe you seven dollars,' she said, with a smile that allowed him to go ahead and swipe his card.

'And I promise not to let you forget it,' he warned, grinning back.

'Maybe I can buy you coffee in Wallaroo if our paths do cross.'

'Sure,' he said, deliberately not loading his voice with promise. This was for her protection as much as his.

'Anyway,' she continued; he hoped he had avoided giving offence. 'Thank you for getting me over the grumps. I'll put in a good word for you with my husband, and maybe you can still get that interview.'

He shrugged, though inwardly he was cheering; he couldn't have planned it better. 'That would be great, if Dr Maddox doesn't feel cornered.'

She shook her head. 'Cornered? No. I told you. Big ego.' As they made their way back onto the street, Jem Maddox cast him another soft smile that told him in another life, on another day, they could be lovers. 'See you, Jack.'

Jem picked up the girls first, hoping her cheeks were not reflecting the burn of guilt she was feeling as she waited at the gates. What was wrong with her? She had all but thrown herself at Jack. *Why didn't you just lift up your top and ask if he liked what he saw?* What an idiot! And yet . . . there was something about him that had got beneath her guard.

Easy to talk to. Funny. Mild. He didn't overstep. Either he was a Lothario or he was just incredibly adroit at talking to women and making them feel at ease. She preferred to think it was the latter, and that she had controlled the conversation and where it had ended. He certainly hadn't encouraged her flirtation, she was relieved to recall. If anything, he had been careful in how he spoke to her. What was all that silly accusation about the women he connected with? Gosh! Either she'd lost her touch or she was desperate.

Yep, desperate was likely how she'd come across. He'd witnessed her embarrassment and had rather chivalrously tried to ease her pain, and what did she do? All but invite him to bed. Well, not quite. She was overreacting. This whole day was a bad one and she needed to put it behind her.

She'd promised to contact Maria about the beach house, though. Wouldn't hurt. While she waited for the girls, she tapped out a message on her phone. Jem anticipated not hearing until tomorrow but as the girls emerged, she heard a ping and a glance at the screen told her Maria's house was available, and the details for booking.

It was time to step back and take a breath. *Don't do it.*

She did it.

Jem forwarded the message to Jack's phone number and felt sick. She blinked, frustrated with herself, and yet she was strangely excited. Was this her seeking a pathway away from Mark? Was she practising no longer being with him, allowing herself to be intrigued by another man? She couldn't answer herself – dared not.

She watched her daughters' golden heads tipped towards each other as they walked side by side, waving goodbye and now and then hugging friends farewell. She'd never done that. Young girls were so emotionally demonstrative these days. Someone said something and both Holly and Isabelle shrieked with laughter. They looked so like their father it hurt. They adored him . . . Would they forgive her if she left him? Would they want her?

Isabelle spotted her first and waved, grabbing Holly, urging her to speed up. Jem smiled. It was a good sign.

'Mum, you're not going to believe it!' Isabelle blurted.

Jem laughed, smoothing Holly's ponytail. 'What won't I believe?'

'Maddy Evans is having a hot air balloon party for her birthday.'

What's in her mother's head? Jem thought. 'Where?'

'The Barossa Valley,' the girls chorused.

'You don't expect me to sign off on you two going up in hot air balloons with a dozen screaming girls, do you?'

'Yes!' Isabelle shouted. 'We can't be left out. Maddy's parties are the best.'

'They're show-offy and you know it.'

Both girls began to whine at once.

'Look, I'll call Pat Evans and find out. Until then, stay calm. I'm not saying no, I'm just saying I want to find out about safety.'

'Dad would say yes in a heartbeat,' Izzy challenged her.

'I know, but Dad doesn't adore you as much as I do,' she joked, knowing it wasn't true. 'And how would either of us live without you if something should happen?'

'Nothing's going to happen, Mum,' Holly said.

From his car Jack rang MultiplyMed and asked to speak to Dr Maddox.

'I'm sorry, sir. Dr Maddox has left for the day but you can probably leave a message at his rooms. I would be happy to give you the—'

'Er, no, that's fine. I am interviewing him,' he lied. 'There were just some queries for the article I meant to get sorted out, but I think it's probably more suitable for a lab technician.' He knew that wasn't a question and she was waiting. 'Would it be possible to speak to one of your embryologists?'

'No, sir, that would likely require permissions. Could I put you through to Lorna Davis? She's our communications manager.'

Before he could answer he was transferred and could hear an extension ringing.

'Lorna Davis.' The tone was singsong. Would he get what he needed?

'Oh, hello,' he began and explained all over again, this time refining his pitch to leave no doubt in the mind of Ms Davis that Dr Maddox would want him to have this information.

'That's fine. I can probably help if it's not too technical.' She had a smiley sort of voice that he tended to expect from anyone involved in public relations.

'It really isn't . . . let's try and see how we go. Can I run through it with you now?'

'I have . . . um, ten minutes before a meeting. Would that be enough?'

'I can sort it in half that time.'

She laughed. 'Excellent, then shoot.'

'Great. So, with the reproductive material that is brought into this country, I'm right in saying it can be coming from anywhere in the world?'

'Yes. We receive material from the US, Europe and Asia regularly, but other places too . . . just less frequently.'

'Good, that's a tick!' he said, keeping it light. 'Let's take material coming from Europe,' he said, pretending it was just the first example that leapt to mind. 'May I check how it is carried and what is its longevity? You can keep this very general, Lorna. It's just so readers feel they have a handle on how everything is transported.'

'Oh, okay,' she said, seemingly unfazed, and gave him a succinct overview of the dewars and how the contents could be carried easily over thousands of miles in liquid nitrogen.

'And the material isn't at risk of being compromised?'

'Not at all. I gather that, if push came to shove, the material would be fine even up to three weeks, but we'd never require that time – not even half that. From the moment it is signed off in the dewar, it will be where it needs to be – hand delivered – within forty-eight hours.'

'Wow, that's impressive door to door,' he said, stroking her feathers. 'And so the journey is never interrupted?'

'The journey might be, but the seal is never broken.'

'Right, and how do you ensure that protection?' She explained about seals and plastic ties, barcodes and so on. He made all the right noises of interest, even though he knew it from his own research in London.

He gave a light laugh. 'Forgive me for asking, but couldn't someone cut the plastic ties and re-attach them?'

There was a tight silence before she answered. 'But why would someone do that?'

'To tamper with the contents.'

'I ask again, why would they, though?'

'Just a hypothetical query, Ms Davis – pure interest. My parents always said I was too curious.' He laughed again.

'Well, hypothetically then, yes, I suppose. But you'd need identical ties, you'd need identical contents with all matching names and code numbers . . . and I still can't imagine why anyone would bother to tamper with this material. If someone wanted to destroy it for malicious reasons, it would be inconvenient, but we could have fresh material delivered within the next two days.'

He could almost see her shrugging in his mind's eye, and was surprised when she continued.

'And theft wouldn't work, because we'd notice immediately that the straws containing the material were missing. Besides, you'd need a very well-equipped lab to take care of the fragile material, and that would be hideously expensive.'

'An excellent and comprehensive answer,' he said, trying to keep things light. 'Thank you for indulging me.'

Jack continued with a few more inane questions, but the one answer he needed he'd now received.

It was possible to tamper.

Not only possible, but entirely plausible . . . One could set up a laboratory somewhere along the traditional route of the dewars, intercept the package, clip the ties, and insert the cuckoo's straws, as he now considered them, containing rogue material. It didn't sound too tricky to top up the liquid nitrogen, seal the dewar and re-attach identical plastic strips, and then the dewar would continue on its merry journey as though it hadn't been touched.

'One last question, Lorna, please?'

'Sure.'

'The couriers are always the same and always use the same route?'

He heard her hesitate, presumably because of Greg Payne's death. 'Not always the same, but from the same global company – it specialises in the transport of this material. The route is the same though, as the best connections are from the UK or Europe to Dubai, which is such a busy hub, and then same day through to various airports in Australia.'

'Yes, that's the way I came too,' he said. 'Just a few hours in the UAE. I suppose they could kill the time with good shopping.'

She laughed. 'I doubt it. They're not allowed to let that dewar out of their sight . . . and I can assure you they don't. As you say, it's only a matter of hours – I think they depart Europe around midnight or so, and the layover is at most ten, maybe twelve hours. You'll have to check that. Anyway, they're used to it. It's part of the job.'

And there it was. Dubai. That was the clue he needed. The layover gave more than sufficient time for the dewar to be collected and material to be added. So long as the courier was in on the scam and well paid for their co-operation and silence, then MultiplyMed and its courier company would never be any the wiser.

Of course, the embryologist in Adelaide would have to be in the know too. They would see the extra straws, would know something was wrong, which meant the embryologist was also in on the black-market activity – and no doubt being paid handsomely to look the other way.

16

Nikki Lawson checked her reflection in the mirror and admired the new streak of red she'd had the hairdresser put through her hair. She'd been going to Style du Jour, on Walkerville Terrace, not too far from where she lived in Evandale, for years.

'Now, you're sure?' Kyla had asked her in the salon while snapping on black gloves to mix up the colour.

'It's your suggestion!' Nikki had laughed with feigned exasperation.

'Yes, but it's your head!' Kyla gave a loud laugh in return, tossing back the mane of thick blonde hair that spoke of the proud German ancestry she'd shared with Nikki over the years. 'You're the one who will be walking around with it. You could put it beneath, for instance,' she offered, lifting the top layer of Nikki's curling hair. 'And then it would show as you walked or moved your head, without being too obvious. But bright red is certainly bold.' The hairdresser's white smile widened as she nudged her robed client. 'But you're hardly shy, Nikki. I've never seen you without your trademark red lippy. If anyone can pull it off you can. It's edgy.'

'Let's do it. But underneath as you suggest, so at work it looks relatively normal.'

Kyla laughed again. It was such a loud and infectious sound to match her sunny personality. 'If you can call bleached blonde normal.'

'You know what I mean,' Nikki said, joining in the amusement.

So now she was off for a night out. Her destination was a club that wasn't exactly invitation-only but not many people knew about it, tucked away in an old cellar in Thebarton. She needed to lose herself after the news of Greg's death, and dancing for hours, accompanied by something she might swallow to force her spirits up, was the best way she knew how.

But first she was meeting Mr Gucci. The appointment was unplanned – she'd received an invitation out of the blue and, while surprising, it was exciting nonetheless. She'd phoned during a quiet moment earlier in the day. She'd been meaning to ever since reading about Greg in the newspaper and got the answering service as anticipated. Nothing out of the ordinary there, except this time she left a coded message. What did surprise her was a return phone call within half an hour.

'Nikki?'

She'd frowned, not recognising the number or the voice. 'Yes?' She looked around to see how many people were in the lab: two others. Personal phone calls were discouraged in the work area but sometimes they were necessary and no one took offence.

'You phoned.'

There was a pause and Nikki didn't fill it, her mind scrambling.

'About our special arrangement,' the caller prompted.

'Oh!' She didn't expect *that* voice on *this* topic. Usually some minion returned her call. 'Uh, yes. I was wondering if I could talk to someone about what happened?'

'Sure. You can talk to me. I'm the boss. I don't like phones, though. How about we meet? Let me buy you a drink somewhere nice.'

Another surprise. She felt her chest tighten with anticipation. 'That would be great, actually. Who would I be meeting?'

'Exactly the person you want to speak with. I believe you call me Mr Gucci?'

She gave a nervous laugh. 'I'm sorry, I had no idea that—'

'Please. I find it amusing.'

Nikki let out a low breath. 'Um, great. When?'

'How about this evening? Are you working late?'

She shook her head instinctively, knowing the red beneath would be showing as she did so, even though the caller couldn't see her. She cupped a hand around the microphone, glancing over her shoulder as one of the lab technicians fiddled with a computer nearby. 'No, I've got an early mark. Not much happens on Friday afternoon around here, and there are no deliveries today.'

'Good. How about the Hyatt? Do you know it? North Terrace, near to the station and casino.'

'Oh yes, I know the hotel.' She felt way out of her depth. Why was she acting so dumb, instead of like the smart person they thought they were working with? 'That's fine. Sorry, I'm a bit distracted.'

'No problem. You're at work, I understand. Shall we say nine? You can bill the taxi to me.'

'Oh no, that's all right,' Nikki blustered. 'I'm going out tonight in the city so I can carry on from there.'

'See you in the Atrium Lounge.'

'How I will know you?' she asked, too hurriedly.

'I'll know you,' Mr Gucci said before the line went dead.

That had been mid-morning. Since then, all her usual defences had crumbled. She knew people thought she was prickly but she'd been raised to be private, not overly demonstrative. None of that reservation had helped her today. She'd been feeling uncharacteristically nervous ever since.

Battle dress helped, she told herself; getting frocked up could create a different persona, achieve some distance from the quieter soul she usually enjoyed being. So now that she had her make-up on and her new red streak looking impudent when it revealed itself, she was feeling bolder. She'd deliberately tempered her clothes for Mr Gucci, choosing not to wear her favourite shoulder-less, mini fru-fru dress that showed off her tattoos, and her Doc Marten boots, which allowed her to slide between edgy and feminine. Instead, she wore a simple black lurex dress with sleeves – and no flesh on show – with a shiny black belt so wide it was like wearing weightlifter's protective gear. But it highlighted her tiny figure and, with her new hair, no one would miss her. She slipped on a cutaway black leather jacket and wore heeled shoes, yearning for her boots. At least they weren't skyscrapers, because she'd definitely slip.

The concierge pulled back the doors to the five-star hotel with a smile that felt authentic as it landed on her.

'The Atrium Lounge?' she queried.

'Right over there, madam,' he said, pointing. 'Enjoy your evening.'

She walked carefully across the shiny tiles, aware of the thin row of diamantes sparkling around the neckline of her dress; when she hit the dancefloor later, they would flash and dazzle. For now, she hoped they lent an elegance to her look.

Nikki was welcomed into the lounge by a woman behind a small counter and was shown to a table and pair of club chairs by a window that looked towards the Adelaide Oval. She was reaching for a menu, for something to do, when a voice said, 'Nikki?'

She was startled but didn't show it, smiling instead and nodding. 'Yes, I'm Nikki.' Finally, Mr Gucci. How extraordinary.

'May I?'

'Of course.' She watched, intrigued, as her host eased into the seat opposite.

'I don't come into the city very much. Do you?'

'Not during the week. But it's Friday night and once a month I go clubbing.' She figured it was a time to be open.

'Where?'

'Thebby . . . er, Thebarton. There's a little-known club called Axis.'

Secretly, she wanted Gucci to like her, but she was a little scared – intimidated – by the tall, immaculate person before her, as relaxed in these surrounds as Nikki was not.

'You go alone?'

'I do.'

'Impressive. No man?'

'Who needs a man to have fun?'

Her companion laughed. 'Whatever floats your boat.'

'Anyway, there's always people I know around.'

'Why alone?'

'Not everyone likes to dance as much as I do. It's like a workout, but it also helps me to get rid of the month's build-up.'

'Work stress, do you mean, or personal anxiety?'

Be honest. 'Right now, a bit of both, but mostly the latter. I don't want to share it or be watched. I know how to alleviate stress, and it's on the dancefloor.'

Her companion nodded knowingly. 'Let's order,' Gucci said, glancing at a waiter who had sidled up. He was handsome, with dark hair and a tan, and Nikki caught the flash of a diamond stud earring under the hotel lights. 'My guest is having . . .?'

'Erm . . .' She glanced at the list of beverages.

'How about a champagne cocktail, Nikki?' Her host's eyes sparkled back at her with encouragement.

She dared not look at the cost but her treacherous gaze told her anyway that a flute of something effervescent and alcoholic was going to beggar her before the night got started.

'On me. Would you like me to choose?'

'Oh, thank you. Yes, please do.'

'Two Air Mails, Ricardo.'

Nikki watched the waiter retreat to fetch their drinks. Their name meant nothing to her. 'It's lovely here. I feel a little conspicuous though.'

'Nonsense. The night is young. The party-goers haven't yet arrived and you're dressed for clubbing. You look dazzling.'

She laughed. 'Sparkly dresses are fun beneath the club's lighting.'

Mr Gucci shrugged. 'You say once a month?'

'Sometimes I leave it longer, maybe two months.'

'Well, that hardly makes you a party animal. So why not dazzle when you have the chance? And where exactly is Axis?'

Nikki explained not only the address of the venue but how to find the entrance, which was concealed. 'Very few people know about it. I can hardly remember how I came to find out about it, to be honest.'

'Drugs?'

'Always in the clubs.' She shrugged as if it was an obvious answer.

'And do you partake, Nikki?'

She sensed this was a test. *Continue to be candid*, she told herself. This was someone who paid her handsomely to fib a bit. It didn't take much from her, if she was honest, and it was allowing her to consider buying her own apartment soon. Maybe tonight was about paying her more, now that Greg was gone and she'd have to start working with someone new. She was here for assurance, though. She needed to know she was protected.

'Now and then, depending on my mood,' she replied, keeping her tone light. 'I don't need it like some do, but when the mood is right, it can be wonderful, I'll be honest. Frankly, it's cheaper to swallow a tab than booze the night away, and you don't feel like shit all weekend. I can't afford to still be under the weather on a Monday, like some can at work. I hold down a responsible role and I need to be professional. Anyway, I only use good stuff that's clean, out of my system quickly.'

'Heroin?'

'Hell, no!' she snapped. 'Sorry.'

Her host shrugged that no offence was taken.

The cocktails arrived, fizzing and joyful. They were golden in colour, and Nikki was surprised by the two blocks of ice luxuriating in the champagne. She wondered if it was a French wine. A beautiful bright green twist of lime peel was impaled on a metal stirrer in each glass.

'Ever tasted an Air Mail?'

Nikki shook her head.

'It's rum, lime juice, honey and . . . what have I forgotten, Ricardo?'

'Er, the French champagne perhaps,' the waiter offered with amusement.

They all laughed. 'Indeed. A nice brut gives all that sweet and sour its beautiful dry finish. Enjoy, Nikki. Cheers.'

They clinked glasses as Ricardo withdrew once more and they sipped in unison.

'Scrumptious,' Nikki admitted, trying not to smack her lips. She could get used to these cocktails – and this lifestyle. And it occurred to her only now that perhaps Mr Gucci was going to offer her a new role, perhaps elevate her standing within their operation. How could she make sure she impressed?

'Glad you approve. So, if not heroin, then I'm guessing methamphetamine?' Mr Gucci said, returning to their previous conversation.

'Ecstasy, yes.'

'Do you carry your own? Forgive all the questions – you can tell from my age this is not my scene, but as a parent I should educate myself.'

'Oh? How many children do you have?'

'Just one. I want her to grow up safe, informed, confident . . . make it past twenty-one. That begins with her parents being fully informed about what's out there, what you young things get up to.'

Nikki obliged with a small chuckle, grateful to be considered a 'young thing', and relieved to know her host was married with children and likely not hitting on her with the talk of how good she looked tonight. Again, she was honest. 'I imagine she'll probably try some drugs – her friends will put pressure on her, even if she's not immediately inclined. But ecstasy, used properly, will just enhance her evenings.'

'You seem convinced.'

She shrugged. 'I don't really know how it's different to swallowing this . . .' She raised her cocktail. 'Grog is still a drug. But it's very expensive and I find that to get the same effect as one pill, I pay a much higher physical price the next day. If you can make sure you're not judgemental, your daughter will probably tell you a lot more.'

Mr Gucci nodded. 'Have you got the ecstasy on you now?'

Nikki tapped her small handbag. 'Yes. As I say, I'm careful. I always bring my own, and I insist on knowing where they've come from. Then I feel safe. I use a very reliable dealer and I stay in control.'

'Good. I'm glad to hear how careful you are.'

She needed the small talk over. 'Do you mind if we talk about Greg?'

'No, of course. A very sad business. Were you friends?'

'We were friendly,' she qualified. 'As people who see each other during work hours regularly are. But I didn't see Greg socially.'

A neat eyebrow raised itself. 'I'm surprised at your concern then.'

Nikki frowned. 'Er, well, it's awful to learn that someone I know has died, especially someone still so young. And under such tragic circumstances.'

'Well,' Mr Gucci began, 'we both know he was worried about earning more. You told me so.'

That took Nikki aback. Was this an accusation?

Mr Gucci was still talking. '. . . perhaps he was in debt, or maybe he didn't feel he was getting ahead with—'

Nikki interrupted. 'There's rumours he was killed.'

Mr Gucci gave a slow blink. 'Yes. I think the parents are pushing that message rather strongly because, quite understandably, they don't want to accept that their only son committed suicide. They don't want the stigma. Again, as a parent, I get it. I might do the same in their shoes.'

'So you're confident he jumped?'

'Who would kill him?'

Nikki shrugged, looking uncertain.

Her host caught on and laughed. 'Me?' More chuckles. 'Why?'

'Because I left the message that he was asking questions, asking for more. I warned him against it, but he insisted. I suppose I did wonder whether he'd become a liability . . . a sort of loose cannon.'

'Well, if you're thinking that, you know others would too.'

'I didn't think he'd let up until I could put my hand over my heart and say I'd passed it up the line.' Perhaps she was now revealing too much, but it was already too late for Greg and she needed to protect herself.

'You thought you were doing the right thing.'

'Yes. But now I'm worried the police are about to come sniffing around our laboratory to find out more about Greg. Should I be?'

'The police won't be coming, don't worry. It's all taken care of.'

'So you didn't have him . . .?' She couldn't say the words.

'You sound frightened, Nikki.'

She swallowed a large sip of her champagne cocktail, listening to the sound of the ice clinking against the glass. Her heart was pounding. 'Could you blame me?'

'We'll never know why Greg did what he did. We don't know what was going on in his personal life, or what stresses were on him.'

She nodded, taking another swig of her delicious drink as she let Mr Gucci's reassurance settle. 'I didn't know him that well, it's true.' Nikki frowned. 'Wait, you said I *thought* I was doing the right thing. Do you not believe I did the right thing in bringing Greg's complaints to your attention?'

Mr Gucci shrugged. Sipped. Watched Nikki intently. 'Perhaps your judgement was clouded by Greg's insistence. He didn't have your status or my ear. I think I would have preferred it if you'd nipped it in the bud yourself.'

Why did that sound threatening? Nikki wondered. The tone was amiable, the words neutral, the body language calm. And still she felt suddenly as though she was teetering on the edge of something dangerous.

A distant ringing began in her ears and, strangely, time seemed to be slowing, with far too long between Mr Gucci speaking and her response. She took another swallow of the champagne. It was probably time to leave, and things were getting weird. Greg, for whatever reason, had committed suicide. It was not her business. He was not her responsibility.

Nikki glanced at her watch. 'I'll be more cautious from now on, but you can rely on me.'

Mr Gucci smiled and nodded in a benign way.

'Well, thank you for the lovely drink and for making time for me,' she said. 'I appreciate our arrangement and I have no complaint.'

'That's good, Nikki. You've always been solid.' Mr Gucci sighed. 'Isn't it a bit early to go clubbing? I thought you young-sters only left the house when the rest of us were going to bed.'

Nikki smiled. 'It's almost ten. By the time I get down to Thebby, the music will be cranking up.'

Her host smiled. 'It was good to finally meet. You get going, I'll sort this out.' A finger was lifted to signal to Ricardo that the bill was required. 'Goodbye, Nikki.'

It was only now as she stood, feeling vaguely dizzy, that she realised she was none the wiser for their meet. She still didn't know what Mr Gucci's real name was. The nickname she'd attached wasn't appropriate any longer, but it was best not to linger; she still felt slightly unnerved by Gucci's rather overwhelm-ing and powerful presence. No, she needed to get away and think it through. There had been no offer of more money, no mention of being brought deeper into the syndicate. It would come later, perhaps. She had proven herself reliable and open with them. She would continue to behave that way and the rewards would arrive.

She gave a polite nod and turned, feeling another wave of dizzi-ness go through her. The alcohol had really gone to her head. She should go to the bathroom and wake up, splash some water on her face. She did so, holding a damp paper towel to her neck. Why was she feeling so foggy? It was time to rev up and dance.

She left the bathroom and stumbled out to the foyer, cursing her shoes and toying briefly with the idea of going home to change.

'Taxi, Miss?'

She nodded. 'Thanks.'

'Going to?'

She urged herself to utter 'Evandale' and go home, but 'Thebarton' was what came out in her voice, which she was feeling somewhat disconnected from.

As the doorman whistled to the taxi driver, Nikki was aware of Ricardo from the bar arriving to whisper to the doorman. She flopped into the taxi as it pulled up, rubbing at the side of her forehead while the doorman spoke to the driver. They eased around the drive and entered North Terrace. It occurred to her they were going in the wrong direction but the taxi driver spoke over her thoughts.

'Sorry, what?' she asked.

'I said where to in Evandale.'

'Thebarton,' she corrected him.

'No, I was told Evandale.'

She was so confused suddenly. That's where she'd wanted to go but she was sure she hadn't said that out loud.

'You okay, love? Not going to be sick in my cab, are you?'

'No,' she said with disdain. 'Slight headache, that's all.'

'What address, kiddo? Looks to me like you've had a drink tonight, eh?' He chuckled.

'Yeah, I have,' she answered and looked out through the window as the cab surged forward at the King William Street intersection. The lights of the Adelaide Festival Theatre were all aglow. There was a big musical event on but she couldn't bring it to mind right now. She felt so dull.

'I wanted to go dancing,' she said. Nikki knew she sounded like a resentful child. Who had told him Evandale? Had she said it?

He laughed at her. 'I think it's best I get you back to your home, love. Safer, eh? Your mother would thank me.'

'My mother doesn't care about me.'

'Don't say that,' he said. 'I'm a Greek boy and we love our mothers.'

'Do I look Greek?' she slurred.

'Not with that hair,' he quipped, eyeing her in the rear-vision mirror. 'What've you been drinking, anyway?'

'Cocktails. Actually I only had one.'

'Then you shouldn't drink, my girl.'

'I was looking forward to dancing,' she said, falling over in the seat.

He said no more or if he did, she didn't hear any words. Her last vision was of the Botanic Gardens' main gate on North Terrace sliding by.

When she stirred, the driver was hauling her out of the cab. 'You're here, love,' he said, trying to lean her against the car.

She could barely stand but she tried to focus. Evandale. So much for her big night. She began pawing at her bag, still slung around her body. 'Pay you . . .' she began.

'No, no, all done,' he said.

'What?' She frowned through the haziness.

'They paid at the hotel.'

'Why?'

He shrugged. 'I dunno, love. Look, I have to get on. It's going to be a long night, but hopefully not for you. Go to bed. Sleep it off. Ah, here we go.' He looked towards the door of her tiny house.

Nikki squinted into the darkness to see a man emerging from her home. Her home. That wasn't right.

'Nikki!' he said, sounding relieved. 'There you are.'

'You'll take her?' the cabbie said.

'Yes, sorry. She wasn't sick, was she?'

'No. She just needs to sleep it off.'

'Who are you?' Nikki said. It took a lot to string those three words together and her mouth felt thick and dry.

The stranger laughed. 'I'm her husband,' he said to the cabbie. 'She's really losing it! Thanks, mate.'

'But you're Ricardo,' she struggled to say, somehow making the connection. 'How did you . . .?' She didn't finish, because she was being manhandled towards her cottage door, which stood open, the hall light on. 'Stop it!' she tried, squirming.

'Bye,' Ricardo said over his shoulder and she was aware of him lifting a hand and the sound of the taxi departing. 'Get in there, Nikki,' he said and all but flung her across the stoop.

Someone had put music on. It was a synthesised dance track, tuneless in its pounding, endless beat, not loud enough to annoy the neighbours but, Nikki noted, loud enough to cover the sound of their voices. There was no song as such – just a rhythm to pick up on and move to.

'Here she is,' said a new voice and Nikki followed its direction to see her hotel host again. Mr Gucci.

'How did you get here?' she thought she said.

'Ricardo's fast,' came the reply.

'Why is the waiter here?'

There was laughter, cruel and blunt. 'Nikki, why don't you take one of your pills?'

'Why?'

'You look tense.'

Ricardo was fussing in her bag. 'Where are they?' he growled but then he found the zipper and pulled out a tiny square of fabric. 'This?' He shook it for his boss to see.

'That looks about right.'

Ricardo reached down to her coffee table where a bottle of water waited at the ready. 'Take it,' he said.

Why not? she thought. *Might as well be high when Mr Gucci tells me why everyone is in my house.*

She swallowed the soft grey tablet stamped with what looked to be a flying insect; she'd never been sure what the image was, but it reassured her that it was one she trusted. She'd seen them in all manner of colours with stamps ranging from birds to question marks. They were very pretty, some of them, designed to appeal to young women in particular, she was sure. But her supplier only had these: plain, grey – pretty boring if she was honest – but expensive, attesting to the quality. What she did know was that despite its dull colour, it gave her exactly what she needed to escape.

'Good, now we can all relax. In fact, you look nearly asleep. Seems that cocktail worked better than we could have hoped.'

The cocktail? Nikki shook her head. *Of course, they'd drugged her.* 'Why are you here?' she ground out.

'You're a loose thread, Nikki. I'm very sorry. Both you and Greg. He's dead. And now it's your turn. The combination of drugs in your system will look like an accidental overdose.'

Nikki's vision began to swim as the alcohol combined with the depressing sensation of the sedative. She felt like she was floating but also like she was underwater, unable to surface. She didn't feel frightened; in fact, she felt curiously safe despite the familiar sweats beginning. And while nothing was making sense, she understood those last words loud and clear.

They're not here to talk to me, they're here to kill me. Just for a moment she wanted to laugh. *I'm going to die with a red streak in my hair and really infuriate my mother. Good.*

'Okay, Nikki.'

The voice she now despised was coming from a long way away now. The beat of the music seemed to match the new pounding of her heart. It was racing, or that's how it felt. Maybe she'd cheat them and die of a heart attack. Nikki felt a cool hand stroke her face and then hold her chin, almost tenderly.

'A real pity,' she heard. 'You're a smart operator.'

She didn't have time to think about it. The response was animalistic. Primitive. Fight or flee? Even in her current state, she knew it was too late to flee.

So, fight!

Nikki grabbed the hand that was touching her face and operating from pure instinct, closed her jaws over it. She bit with more power than she'd ever bitten down on anything, knowing it was the only weapon she had. Her jaw ground down hard and her teeth, hurt though they did, cut through skin.

She tasted metal, as though she had a mouthful of nails, and she tried to bite still harder. Distantly she heard screaming. She could feel strong hands trying to pull her away but now she began to grind her teeth. Her jaw ached, her head still throbbing, her heart still pounding. But this was survival and her instincts refused to let her capitulate.

Now they were hitting her. She bent over to shield herself from their blows and as she toppled forward, she took the hand and the monster who owned it with her to the rug in her sweet cottage, her jaw still locked.

Finally the hand was wrenched from her mouth, a single finger the last to leave her grip and she felt a string of flesh come away to the sound of a fresh shriek. Good. *Hope you die of sepsis, you psycho.*

A human bite is a dangerous thing, she heard her old uni lecturer say and then she was falling.

17

Mark took a deep breath and made the call. 'Hey, it's me.'

'Hello, Mark.'

Be direct, he encouraged himself. 'Listen, Al, things are unravelling between me and Jem.'

'And?' There was a small, embarrassed chuckle on the other end. 'I don't mean to be heartless, but your marriage is your business. It's not part of ours.'

'It is, though. She's getting suspicious.'

'Of what?'

'Of me! What else? She turned up at the clinic the other day. Look, if she's suspicious it could be dangerous.'

'It's always been dangerous. Your job is to manage the danger at your end as I manage it at mine. Sort your wife out.'

'I think we should cool it.'

'Cool it?' The tone was scathing.

'Just for a while.'

'No, Mark. We can't just *cool it* when we have a list of eager, desperate couples – who've paid in advance – and embryos awaiting collection, some already en route, as you well know.'

He sighed audibly. *Say it. There'll never be a better time,* the small voice in his mind urged. 'Al, I think I want out. I didn't sign up for this.'

'For this?'

'Divorce for starters . . . but I mean the deaths. It was meant to be a side earner, but it's become something else that laughs at the oath I took, the ethics of my work, and my conscience. I want no further part in it.'

'No.' Now the voice was calm. 'You turned your back on ethics the moment you realised how much money could be made from this little "side earner", as you describe it. You don't just walk away because it gets a little tough. You're out when I say so.'

Mark frowned. 'Tough? This is murder. And don't threaten me. This whole venture revolves around my participation.'

'There are other fertility experts. You're not unique.'

'Perhaps my ability to keep my mouth shut and kill for you is unique though. I won't do that again. Threaten me or mine once more, Al, and I won't just walk, I'll do far worse.'

Al's tone changed again. Conciliatory now, ignoring the threats. 'Do you want me to speak with her?'

He hesitated. 'Jem? How might that help?'

'Well, you want her off your back in terms of snooping around your business affairs, right?'

'Right.'

'I'll think of something. Where is she now?'

'Threatening to go to the beach. I got the impression she's leaving tomorrow, although she didn't come right out and say that.'

Al let out a low chuckle. 'Okay, I'll try to catch her at school. And the beach could play in our favour.'

'What do you mean?'

'Invite us over for another barbecue.'

'Why?'

'Are you forgetting what's happening this week?'

Mark frowned. 'No, but why would you involve our other halves?'

'Because it looks innocent and it gives me a reason to be in Wallaroo where I need to be. Just trust me. Ring your wife and tell her that you're coming up to the beach to sort things out and you've also invited us for a meal to make up for last time.'

'But why would I invite others when I'm trying to repair our marriage? She really got stuck in to me about disappearing at lunch last time you were over.'

'Tell her you're embarrassed about the other night and you want to make amends. We won't stay. We'll bring the cruiser; we've been talking about getting away for a couple of nights on it before winter sets in. This is perfect. Now, ring me back and leave a message to that effect on my voicemail. In the meantime, I'll have a chat to Jem.'

'Okay, but Al, she's not stupid. Don't assume that she's dim, just because she wears active gear and no longer works.'

Mark heard a soft laugh before the line went dead.

Jack was on his way to his beachside abode that sat between two gulfs – Spencer and St Vincent – on the Yorke Peninsula. Jem had come through with the booking; Jack had received instructions via text and the house known as Horizon was his for the next few days. It was on North Beach, where Jem's house also was.

It had occurred to him that Jem might have a vested interest in him staying at Wallaroo. Even though she was married, she was clearly vulnerable, and he hoped he hadn't triggered something in her by being sympathetic to her situation. However, one too many people had mentioned this part of South Australia's coast for him to ignore its potential in the case, and she'd all but delivered the opportunity to visit to him on a platter. If he could gather some solid evidence of activity within South Australia, he could get the dual op underway.

Wondering how the town of Wallaroo had earned its curious name, he had looked into it the night before while waiting for his meal to warm in the oven. In this regard, Australia could be wildly different to England. Driving into rural areas of his home country, he'd find wonderfully quaint names like Barton in the Beans, Nether Wallop, Mudford Sock and other intriguing titles that leaned hard on charm and amusement. But in Australia, the non-colonial names tended to be Aboriginal – like Woolloomooloo. He thought it was brilliant, but he'd needed an Aussie to kindly explain how to say it with speed and ease. In Sydney, you'd show yourself as a foreigner immediately if you said 'Coogee Beach' exactly how it looked. And then there was Nuriootpa in the Barossa Valley . . . another classic waiting to trap the unaware. Wallaroo, he discovered, came from the phrase 'wadlu waru', from the original inhabitants, the Narungga people. Translated, it apparently meant wallaby urine. He was sure his niece and nephew would find this entertaining. Early settlers had tried to pronounce it properly but their best effort was 'walla waroo' and they finally landed on Wallaroo.

His research had also revealed a gloriously Mediterranean-style climate and a laid-back lifestyle. He wouldn't tell his superior, but he was very much looking forward to a few days at the beach. He wasn't sure what he was looking for but if something was there to find, he would do so.

Driving along long, quiet country roads, enjoying the autumn air flowing through his open window, he had the opportunity to turn over in his mind everything that he knew; it wasn't much by an operation's standard but he felt there were some crumbs to follow. He was convinced the courier's death was not self-inflicted, and his gut told him that Mark Maddox was somehow involved. If this was the case, then snooping around one of his haunts was important.

When his mobile rang, he was more than an hour into his journey. 'Hawksworth,' he said, confident there were no police hiding in bushes out here to catch him on the phone.

'Hello, mate, it's Matt. Listen, toxicology is back on Greg Payne and I thought you should know that his blood shows traces of chloroform.'

'Ah!' Jack said. 'Not a suicide, then.'

'Exactly,' Matt said. 'It's been referred to Major Crimes.'

'Okay, good.'

'There's more.'

'Hang on,' Jack said, checking his mirror before slowing down and pulling over. 'Go ahead.'

'There's been another death.'

Jack sat up straighter in the car seat, as a family of magpies began to chat merrily to one another, the leader poised on the fence post nearby.

'At first it seemed unrelated,' Matt said. 'It's a woman, Nikki Lawson, age thirty. She was found at home on Sunday morning by a neighbour.'

'Okay . . .' Jack let Matt take his time.

'The neighbour was out walking her dog late Saturday night when she saw a taxi drop off this woman outside her house, a cottage in a suburb not far from the city. The curiosity is that a bloke stepped out from her home and this neighbour thought she heard him say he was the husband to the taxi driver.'

'And?'

'Nikki is gay and has no husband – she often looks after the dog for them. But the neighbour let it go. Sunday morning, though, out with the dog again and yes, being nosey, she decides to take some cupcakes over because Nikki hasn't answered her phone. Looking through the window she sees a pot plant on the floor, its planter broken. Music's playing. She goes around the back, where the back door isn't locked and she lets herself in to find Nikki dead in the bath. As far as the evidence went, it looked like a woman who'd sadly drowned after a drug overdose, and the local police gave her over to the coroner's care. She's now at the Forensic Centre in the city.'

'I'm intrigued as to how this relates to our case, Matt.'

Jack heard Matt's familiar chuckle. 'Stroke of luck, really. The way it works in South Australia is that the unit sends over one of its pathologists every day for a meeting with the coroner. They go through the previous day's deaths reported from all over the state one at a time and decide whether it warrants a post-mortem. Most don't, of course. They're signed off by doctors due to clear and existing previous conditions, old age, grave illness, et cetera. Anyway, yesterday it was Dr Moore who attended the meeting. Even though this woman's death was seemingly unsuspicious, they decided to be cautious; Dr Moore suggested that a post-mortem should be performed as a matter of course and a courtesy to the woman's family, and the coroner agreed. It was only when Dr Moore received the full details that she discovered Nikki Lawson worked for MultiplyMed.'

'Bloody hell!' Now Jack was focused.

The magpies seemed to pick up the excited mood in Jack's car and sang louder.

'I thought that would catch your attention,' Matt said. 'She was one of the senior embryologists.'

Jack frowned. 'So Dr Moore recognised the name from her examination on Greg Payne? What a tidy mind she has – and our luck she was on.'

'Right? Anyway, I've spoken to Dr Moore and she'll do the post-mortem.'

'Okay, thanks, Matt. So potentially now two murders, and connected through MultiplyMed.' Jack's mind was racing.

'I'll have more for you tomorrow. Where are you?'

'Er, I'm nearing somewhere called Kulpara. Not too far away now.'

'Well, safe driving. Have you packed your budgie smugglers?'

Jack knew the saying and grinned. 'Talk tomorrow.'

He farewelled the singing magpies and pulled out to continue his journey. He was tempted to pull into the next town but Kadina, where he planned to get some groceries, was barely twenty minutes away, according to the sat-nav. Besides, he needed to think this through and didn't want to interrupt his train of thought.

So, two potential minions dead.

A courier and the person in the laboratory. Why?

Did they know too much? What had triggered their murders?

Who else was in the chain?

What had broken?

Signposts for Kadina popped up into his line of sight and he allowed himself to start focusing on what he needed to buy. *Let it percolate*, he thought. Things were apparently going wrong for the black marketeers and if they kept killing their own, then whoever was in charge was going to trip up.

And Jack would be waiting.

Jem had moved through her day, to all intents engaged in all her maternal duties, even producing a macaroni and beef dish that each child pronounced delicious. Her cheesy bechamel always sucked them in. Mark had not returned until very late, slipping into bed beside her where she pretended to sleep, even feigning a slight groan. Except the eyes he couldn't see were wide open and alert.

He didn't kiss her shoulder as he might have done a couple of years ago and she sensed him turning his back on her. This was really bad. She helplessly inhaled silently, trying to catch the smell of perfume coming off him. Had he been with someone else?

Mark had never been a womaniser, but also she'd always been enough. He'd always promised her he'd never wander, joking that the price was always too much to pay. Too stressful, too expensive to keep various women content, too exhausting to keep secrets and everyone apart, and too potentially damaging to the relationships that mattered – her and the children. He was not going to split in half everything he'd worked so hard to build . . . or so he'd said.

'And I promise you, I would divorce you if I found out,' Jem had told him when they'd discussed infidelity. The subject had been raised because a couple they were friendly with had broken up over an affair, fracturing the family irrevocably. It was so sad to witness. But Jem's promise had been spoken with smiles and teasing kisses because she had been feeling so in love and secure at the time.

Now she felt adrift. She cleared her throat. 'Mark?'

'Yes,' he said tiredly. 'I thought you were asleep.'

'I was,' she lied.

'Go back to sleep.'

Jem rubbed her eyes. 'Where have you been?'

'Working. Where else?' he said, impatient.

'Who delivered?'

'She's still in labour. I'll go back in a few hours.'

'Which hospital?'

He sighed. 'Ashford. Why?'

'Who is it?'

'Angela Frame. What does it matter?'

'It matters.'

'Again . . . why?'

'Are you having an affair?' There, the doubt was out. And she was glad, no matter what that question was going to cost.

She felt him turn towards her and she mirrored his action.

He was frowning. 'What the hell?'

'Are you?'

'Don't be stupid, Jem.'

'I wish you'd stop accusing me of being stupid because I'm a long way from that. But you're certainly being stupid if you think what's happening to us feels normal or right in any way.'

'Because I couldn't have lunch yesterday?'

'No, because you're behaving so horribly. While it feels as though it began on Sunday with our guests, I still have little idea why. I think we've been coming to this for months and months.'

'So we're back to that.'

'Look, Mark, I don't want to fight.'

'Then let me sleep. I'm exhausted. And I've got to be up in a couple of hours to deliver a child. Just let me be, Jem.'

She gave a snort of frustration, and then without thinking further got up, pulled on the large, soft bathrobe she'd given him for his last birthday and stomped out of the room, not trying to be quiet. He made no attempt to stop her, which annoyed her more than it hurt. She opened the door and stepped outside into the chill of the early morning. An owl gave an eerie screech in the distance and a lone car drove down their street but then all was silent. She wished she smoked. In movies, the main character would be taking a long, thoughtful drag on a cigarette right about now.

The stranger called Jack Hawksworth arrived in her thoughts. He'd been a real charmer and, in a different life, she'd be in his arms right now. *What a loose and irresponsible thought*, she admonished herself, but she couldn't help it. The chemistry she'd felt over that coffee . . . She was sure he had too, though they'd both sensibly ignored it. It had felt the same with Mark all those years ago, and she wondered again what had happened to tip their otherwise solid relationship into feeling so unstable lately.

She was probably overreacting. But then traditionally, as a couple, they both knew they could count on Jem to take a pragmatic view of every hurdle; she was the one who found solutions, and she was the one who always made the first move towards making up. She had no answer this time though, because she didn't know what the problem was, other than feeling a strong sense of betrayal.

Be sensible, she told herself. This tension had begun only a few days ago. What were a few days in a lifetime? You didn't throw away eighteen years over a squabble. But she didn't know who it was sleeping in their bed upstairs. It was like being with a different man; so cold, so blunt, so emphatic, so uncaring.

And suddenly there was Jack Hawksworth. If she'd been told even a week ago that she could contemplate an affair, she'd have found it laughable. But now it wasn't amusing. Now it was unnerving to acknowledge that in this mood she would topple into Jack's arms in a blink.

She hated that just the right sort of man had breezed into her life just when the wrong sort of situation had presented itself. And she was in a strange mood. Reckless. If Mark could, she could. She needed to be touched. She needed some affection. She wanted to feel loved, to not be just the person who kept the house going and the children happy. Mark had to understand that she had needs too.

Jem shook her head; these were tricky waters to navigate. As it was, she knew she'd already begun a dangerous game, pushing some of the pieces around the chessboard just in case. Coercing Jack to go to Wallaroo meant she wasn't just titillating herself with the idea of an affair. This wasn't a silly schoolgirlish daydream. He would be there tomorrow . . . and so she could be there too, if she decided that's what she wanted.

She shivered, pulling Mark's robe tighter around herself, hugging her elbows. The scent of Dior's exquisite Fahrenheit wafted up and reminded her of the many hours of affection she'd spent wrapped in his arms. She owed him a chance to repair what was broken between them, but that didn't mean she shouldn't have an opportunity to taste the forbidden fruit too.

Jem sighed into the darkness. Perhaps she should ask one of Mark's colleagues about work — maybe something was going wrong at the clinic. Or perhaps Alex Petras might be a source of information. He wasn't a colleague, but a friend, and Mark might have confided in him.

A decision was made in the darkness; if she saw Alex at drop-off tomorrow, she would try to catch a moment with him. And after that, she'd think about Jack Hawksworth and whether or not she'd act on the chess piece she'd moved into place.

18

It was the early hours and sleep eluded Jack.

He sat now on the deck of the shack at North Beach, with only a tiny battery lamp on, preferring to let the inkiness of night close around him. He was rugged up in trackpants and a hoodie, plus a blanket, sipping on a Milo that he hoped would encourage sleep. For now he allowed himself to be soothed by the constant motion and restless sound of the water.

Here the sea surged and retreated with a rhythm that worked with his warm drink to settle him. He liked it better than the English Ovaltine or Horlicks, though he'd heated it too much so he blew on it as he looked up, enjoying the theatre of the night sky. The clear, vast sky explained the cold air, but the stars! Good grief, it was worth it. The people who lived out this way were blessed, having that as their ceiling every night. Was this one of the best places on the planet to stargaze? It had to be. The Milky Way was so clear in southern skies, he couldn't tear his attention from it.

Jem Maddox landed in his mind in this moment of awe, and

it was so unexpected, he forgot to wait and sipped, burning his tongue on the Milo.

'Bugger!' The expletive sounded wholly appropriate, sitting on an Australian beach. Now that would be several days of singed tastebuds. Damn Jem Maddox! Why was she in his head suddenly?

Because she's connected, that's why. His internal detective's voice was always happy to chat.

That's not a given, he answered. She was likely an innocent caught up in whatever her husband was.

This was how it usually worked for him and he knew to let the conversations in his mind play out. Connections came and he tested them before firm links could be made – or not. His mentor and former chief had counselled him from his first days as a detective constable: 'You've got an organised mind, Jack, a good policeman's nous, and your instincts are sharp. Trust them. Let them lead you but don't jump too fast. Keep testing.'

The back of his brain was shuffling cards, laying one out in front of him for his consideration: Jem.

All right, let's do it, he thought with a sigh, staring at a scraggy patch of grass on the sandy beach, illuminated by the tiny lamp on the deck. The light was attracting every insect for miles, he was sure. He stood to turn it off and now Nature took over, showing off; the glittering mantle above, the restless sea moving towards him and then backing off, the slim slice of light curving around the right edge of the moon, highlighting its surface even to the naked eye. He searched out Australia's famous Southern Cross. Someone – he couldn't remember who – had told him April was the best month to start stargazing.

Ah, it had been one of the police guys at the pub. 'Start looking from about eight and turn south east . . . Look for the two stars that point the way. You can't miss it,' Len had said with a wink.

Jack scanned the skies and to his delight found the two bright 'pointers', and he followed them upwards to pick out the five stars, one dimmer and smaller than the others, that featured on the Australian flag. He smiled. They did form the shape of a diamond lying on its side, high in the sky now, reminding him of the late hour.

He dipped his gaze back to the slow-heaving body of water in the distance. Everything around him at this level had been flung into grades of darkness, everything murky.

'So, what do we know?' he said aloud, but to the inner conversationalists. He smiled, allowing them free rein as he let his mind wander back to where it had been prodding: Jem Maddox.

Them being in the same place at the same time was hardly coincidental; Jem had forced his albeit willing hand. What she may not have known though was that their introduction was not coincidental either. Jack had deliberately made that happen to learn more about her husband without having to talk to him. He'd reasoned on his way to the clinic that if MultiplyMed *was* involved in something shady, then it was likely happening at the laboratory level. Some wily technicians, perhaps, who'd worked out how to override the system. But that had begun to make less sense to him. If someone like his student, Amelia, had lost her life due to careless procedures or over-zealous stimulation of her body's natural cycle, then that had to be happening at clinician level. Mark Maddox – and people like him – had the knowledge of reproductive medicine, the ability to order human material . . . and the power to coerce others – or perhaps charm them. No lab technician that he'd become aware of in his interviews back home had anything to do with the couples seeking fertility treatment, other than a cursory introduction – and only if the client was conscious. They simply prepared the material and handed it through to the operating theatre. Once the hatch was closed, the responsibility was all in the hands of the qualified gynaecologist.

So, people at a much higher level had to be masterminding this, Jack decided. People like Mark Maddox, with status and wealth. He had a public profile as one of the most eminent obstetricians and gynaecologists in South Australia, perhaps even the country. Someone as well-known and respected as him would attract patients. And he had that extra ingredient that was hard to quantify but very easy to see, the sort of presence that drew attention and people to him.

Difficulty in getting pregnant meant clinics like MultiplyMed were enjoying a stampede of clients, and they rarely visited just once. Even Jack knew from his investigation that couples struggling to conceive were like jackpot winners if they received happy news within a couple of cycles. In other words, it was rare. Some were on a treadmill of cycles, always hoping, always disappointed. It was heartbreaking stuff. And this illegal syndicate was feeding into that heartbreak. No doubt they would argue that they were simply filling a void in an unsympathetic system that was both expensive and limiting. The black-market eggs and embryos were presumably limitless, and a desperate couple might pay whatever was asked to have multiple attempts at pregnancy whenever they wanted, not just as and when a clinician advised.

So how might Maddox or someone like him fit in?

Jack prodded at this and decided it was probably wise for someone to set up a clinic that fronted as a legitimate one, but performed egg, sperm and embryo transfer as a black-market operation. Couples would presumably claim success naturally, to ensure they weren't incriminated in anything illegal. Even as he reached this conclusion, Jack realised that their discretion would make them a helpless part of the ring of silence surrounding the operation. Perhaps the syndicate found a way to threaten couples who might speak to anyone about having been 'helped'.

Jack frowned. Payments would have to be made in cash, so there was no paper trail. The money could be hidden and then laundered – perhaps through property, houses, jewellery or legitimate businesses.

But how did it work? The material was coming from Eastern Europe, the originating donors as far away as Scotland, and the ultimate recipients were, at least in this part of the operation, women from Australia.

Jack blinked into the dark. Yes, a hopeful mother could arrive at the South Australian clinic from anywhere in the country – or the world – feigning a holiday or seeing family and friends. A transfer wouldn't take long. He'd been surprised to learn that the transfer of an embryo took only moments. If it was a simple transfer, it was a fifteen-minute procedure and essentially painless, though he could imagine it being a little uncomfortable. It was no more invasive than a woman having her normal pap smear.

He sipped his Milo, now cool enough to enjoy, and continued pondering. He'd read the staggering statistics for Britain alone. One in seven couples experienced issues with infertility, which added up to approximately three and a half million anxious, sometimes desperate, people. Six out of ten treatment cycles were IVF, and eight out of ten donor insemination cycles were privately funded. These procedures were performed at roughly sixty registered clinics.

But how many on top of that number were happening unregistered? It was a frightening thought, where the old adage of supply always coming on the heels of demand applied. Cunning opportunists always saw the gap and filled it. Jack couldn't recall the exact figure but in the previous year, well above fifty thousand women had had one of these fertility treatments in the UK.

The percentage of the population undergoing the same treatment in Australia would likely be similar. Even if only one third of that number of women were seeking help, with multiple cycles per year, he could imagine how lively the black-market operation would be. Maybe three thousand eggs?

He let out a breath of frustration. Even if he halved his estimations, it meant fifteen hundred eggs needed to be collected from donors and transferred swiftly across oceans and into the wombs of eager women each year.

Fifteen hundred eggs, at maybe four or five thousand dollars a pop for a simple transfer, was nudging three quarters of a million dollars annually for this operation.

'And I'm being conservative with the figures,' he murmured, standing and tossing the dregs of his Milo into the sand. 'What if they charge double or even more?' This Australian syndicate could charge what they wanted, assuming people were willing to pay it, and if it was happening down under, it was certainly happening elsewhere.

So why were the very people who made the operation work being killed all of a sudden?

It had to be fear of being outed. That, or perhaps a more efficient way had been discovered to bring the material in, perhaps in greater volume, or a less risky manner, and the loose ends had been tied off.

Those loose ends were the courier, Greg Payne, and presumably the embryologist, Nikki Lawson, who'd just turned up dead. Were their deaths considered collateral damage, like all the women donating their eggs who had been left to die painful deaths when something had gone wrong? The procedures for the paying women seemed to be performed by legitimate, trained medical staff, but the same couldn't necessarily be said for the extraction of the material in the first place. Desperate women seeking a way to make ends meet, but finding only pain. Like Amelia.

Jack shook his head sadly; he vowed he would be responsible for finding the person or persons behind this syndicate and avenging the life of his student. All that ambition and potential snuffed out. All her family had now was memory and grief. He gave a sound of disgust as he forced his mind back to the method of transport.

So what had changed lately? Air might be the fastest way in, but if it was no longer the safest, then it had to be via sea.

Well, he'd begin at Wallaroo. It was a sleepy spot, but had a proper port, busy enough for leisure craft to come and go without drawing attention. If he were going to smuggle in a small package, this felt like an ideal spot.

19

Jem's mind was scattered. She'd rung off from the Ashford maternity ward, having spun a convincing tale of wanting to congratulate Mark's patient, whom she knew by chance. The nurse with whom she'd spoken was familiar with Jem and had passed on many a message to a busy Mark in days gone by, which was handy.

'Angela Frame hasn't gone into labour yet, Mrs Maddox. We haven't seen her. Er, let me check to be sure.'

Jem had waited, a snake of worry uncoiling, sliding up towards her throat.

'No, Dr Maddox hasn't been in these last few days but we do know she's having twins. I'm presuming they'll be delivered here, but it could be that another hospital has been chosen.' There was a smile in her tone.

'Oh gosh,' Jem said, feigning embarrassment. 'My mistake. I just presumed it was Angela. It must be another of his clients.'

'Maybe Mrs Frame was taken to Calvary?' the nurse asked. 'Do you want me to check? One of the midwives works there a couple of days a week.'

'Well, all right, it it's no trouble. I don't know who it might be though.' She hated being so conniving.

'That's okay. She'll know Mark's . . . er, Doc Maddox's list.'

Jem waited again, not daring to breathe; hardly daring to believe she was really doing this, poking around like a jealous wife. *I'm not jealous*, she told herself. *I'm concerned.*

The midwife was back. 'Are you there?'

'Yes.'

'Well, no, Angela's not at Calvary either. They haven't seen Doc Maddox there in the last few days.'

'Oh, look, don't worry any more, Sal. It's really not important,' she lied. 'Thank you, though. I'll ask Mark when I see him tonight.'

Now here she sat, in her car after drop-off, feeling hollow and blindsided by her husband. He'd lied. There was no other way to view it. The story about Angela Frame and Ashford he'd concocted was so plausible, why wouldn't she accept it? But she'd checked. Mark was covering his tracks for something she was not allowed to be privy to . . . either an affair, even though he'd denied that in such an offended tone, or something else he didn't want her to know about.

If the other mothers had sensed she was distracted she didn't care. Alannah Petras had approached, floating up on those long, lean legs of hers. 'We enjoyed lunch, Jem. Our turn next time.'

'You're so welcome.' Jem tried to stop the words but she couldn't help herself. 'I'm sorry Mark was so tense.'

Alannah nodded. 'I did notice. I'm sorry too. I hope every-thing's okay?'

Jem shrugged. 'Mark's in his busy times,' she said. *Now that was a throwaway*, she thought. Such a bland excuse. It didn't make sense either; babies didn't really have seasons.

'Yes, of course. His work must be so demanding. I imagine that's hard for you. I mean, him being distracted or having to dash off.'

'So long as it's not into another woman's arms and only to deliver her baby.' Jem had intended that to come out as droll to set her companion at ease, but unfortunately, her delivery wasn't quite there; she heard the false note but wasn't sure Alannah Petras had. Perhaps it didn't really matter. They were hardly friends. She couldn't be bothered to make any more small talk.

Luckily Alannah looked to be in a hurry too, heading into the school. 'Don't think on it again. We had a great time and I need that couscous recipe. Gotta run, girl.' She blew Jem a kiss and picked up her pace towards the main entrance.

Nope, she didn't care. That confirmed it. Jem turned, lifting a hand to someone else calling a hello, smiling absently. She made her way back to the car and got inside, and now here she was, still sitting there, unable to move on from that morning's discovery. Anyone glancing over might imagine she was looking at her phone or making a hurried list of today's tasks. A horn blew, and she looked up to see a familiar face grinning and waving. Another mother on her way, just what she needed.

Jem was feeling angry about being lied to so blatantly by her husband, angry enough that she just wanted to hit back somehow. The pain felt insurmountable, realising that the person she trusted most in the world, the person who knew all her secrets, who had shared every high, every low of the past eighteen years, was now lying to her face. Every sensible part of her was advising not to blow this up in her mind, and yet she was doing just that. She felt reckless. How could she deal with this?

She spotted Alex Petras walking back to his car and frowned. Why were both he and Alannah at school? They shared the drop-offs, and this was his day normally. She watched him get in and remembered the decision she'd reached last night. Was she bold enough? Yes, she would ask. Jem opened the car door, waving to him, and his face lit with a smile of recognition.

'Jem!'

'Hey, Alex,' she called, controlling her expression, making sure it seemed bright and delighted as she strolled across the street to speak to him through the car window. He didn't seem in a particular hurry. 'I just saw Alannah.' She pointed.

'Yes, I did my normal drop-off but she's got an appointment with the teacher about our daughter's maths. I hate those meetings, hate being told my child isn't measuring up. I'm a terrible chauvinist. I feel it undermines me.' He chuckled. 'Alannah's so good with confrontation of any kind. She's like a chameleon – she can be anything she needs to be.'

'Well, aren't you men lucky. Mark likes to leave that sort of awkward meeting to me as well.'

They shared a comfortable smile of agreement.

'Anyway, I'm glad you caught me,' he said, full of warmth. 'Look, thanks again for Sunday. It was great.'

'Oh, I don't know. I think we need a re-run, after Mark's turn of mood.' She gave a self-conscious chuckle.

'Don't worry about that,' he said and she noted he didn't deny it. 'Great food, delicious wine, good company – it's rarely perfect, but it was such a pleasure for us to all finally get together properly.'

'I do worry though. It was rude of Mark and I want to apologise if you and Alannah felt in any way awkward.'

'We're grown-ups, Jem. Grown-ups have spats.' He gave her a sympathetic shrug. He hadn't reached for the button that started the car yet.

'Except we hadn't had one,' she pressed. She needed him to open up. 'There were no bad words. Everything was fine and upbeat and then it wasn't . . . and I don't know why.' She didn't mean to start crying but the tears arrived to shock her too. 'Oh, look at me. Gosh! Sorry.' Was she acting? She didn't believe she was.

'Are you all right?'

She swallowed. Gave a shrug, not ready to answer.

His expression softened. 'Hop in.'

'Pardon?' she said, a nervous grin creasing her face and disappearing as fast as it had arrived.

'Let's go for a coffee.'

She waited a beat and then realised that this was exactly what she needed to happen in order to draw from Alex whatever he knew about Mark and the secret life she dreaded he was suddenly living. She got in and they set off, but it wasn't uncomfortable, strangely enough, despite barely knowing each other. Jem let Alex talk. He had a nice voice, the slight European accent she'd noticed at lunch pushing through as he chatted away, mostly about the school and certain teachers, clearly hoping to prevent any awkwardness.

'How about here?' he offered, gesturing to a coffee shop in Melbourne Street, north of the city. There was an easy park almost directly outside. 'It's not superb coffee but it's quiet and anonymous.'

'It's fine,' she said with a smile. 'Listen,' she began, carefully framing what she was about to say.

He waved a hand. 'Don't start. Friends do this, okay? We're out in the open and no tongues need wag. Two parents having a coffee and, besides, I don't like seeing any woman upset.'

She nodded, allowing herself to be guided towards the entrance. 'Thanks, Alex.'

'Find a seat. I'll get these. Latte?'

'Perfect,' she said and looked around for a quiet table near the wall.

Alex was soon sitting opposite, a plain espresso in a tiny cup before him. It nodded to his European upbringing. 'How's Mark anyway?'

'He's incredibly moody. Hostile in fact. I'm not used to it. We've been married forever and this is a new Mark.' She paused, using a teaspoon to play with the foam in her cup. 'Sorry to unload. How long have you known him?'

'A couple of years.'

'How's the trucking business? That is what you do, isn't it?'

'Mostly, yes.' He tipped half a tube of sugar into his coffee before stirring slowly. 'All transport. More recently we're getting into shipping.'

'Shipping always sounds enormous . . . global, full of billionaires.'

He grinned, sipping his coffee. 'Yes, by its very nature it usually is. But for the most part it's A to B, right? A ship leaves Europe and sails, destination Australia. Not so glamorous. And it's not just the big guys. Did you know that Alannah's using consignments as a means to bring in what she calls her "shabby shit"?'

Jem grinned at the play on words. 'She did say something at lunch about importing furniture – have I got that right?'

He nodded. 'She supplies various stores around the country with furniture that's either restored or ready for restoration.'

'She mentioned she brings in gear from France and places like Spain and Portugal. I hadn't thought of it as coming in a shipping container though. That's huge.'

Alex gave a shrug. 'It's a hobby. Keeps her interested and busy. But to tell the truth, I really don't need her worrying about income. I know that sounds a bit . . . tacky, but the fact is, I earn more than enough.'

She smiled. 'I noted her exquisite jewellery.'

Another shrug. 'She buys most of that for herself.'

Jem wanted to ask more but felt it would sound too curious so she nodded and took a sip of her coffee. 'Lucky that you know about shipping, then.'

'Been in transport all my life. But bringing in consignments is not really my thing; I help Alannah when she needs a hand with some of the transport queries but, personally, that's no challenge. I'm actually getting more interested in aquaculture.'

'Oh, wow. Tell me more about that.'

'It's a growing area. What used to be generalised as fishing, I suppose, now has a hi-tech term, and in fact it's a varied, high-income business. Lots of pitfalls for the unwary, though.' He smiled. 'But I'm not unwary and I like to be adventurous in business.'

She gave him the chuckle she imagined he might be waiting for. 'So it's fish farming, is that right?' Jem asked, wanting to show that she had more going on in her mind than shabby chic and jewels.

'Exactly. But not necessarily fish. To be honest,' he said, 'I'm not interested in the tuna, kingfish, et cetera, that are prized and farmed very well now by certain groups and corporations. I've decided to be bold and go down the exotic path.'

'Abalone?' She'd heard a little about that.

He shook his head. 'Again, that's very much advanced and already set up. No, I'm actually part of a syndicate.'

'A syndicate! Sounds a bit exciting and dangerous.'

Alex laughed but answered seriously. 'I think you're referring to a crime ring. This is more like a wine syndicate,' he said carefully, and she wondered if she'd overstepped with the humour. 'Oysters are popular, obviously, but also more risky and exotic things like spiny lobsters, seahorses—'

'Seahorses!' Her mouth opened with surprise. 'Really?'

He grinned. 'Yes. They're very much in demand for Chinese traditional medicine. But there's a black market for it, and sadly a lot of seahorses end up dead and wasted.'

'A black market. Are you part of that?' she teased.

He smiled awkwardly. 'No,' he said, not very convincingly. 'I operate above the law. We farm seahorses for export, and the rewards are good if we can get it right. Besides, I like being on the cutting edge in business . . . seeking new boundaries. Anyway,' he said, putting his cup down and seemingly bringing that part of their conversation to an abrupt close. 'We're here to make you feel brighter.'

'You have. Thank you for getting me out of my glum mood. You've known Mark a while. Have you noticed anything going on with him, or would that be compromising your friendship to speak about him?'

'Not at all. He has become more tense just recently on the golf course. His swing is normally effortless and he always beats me, but in the last couple of rounds, he's been a bit tight and I've come very close to toppling him.'

'Which would have made him mad,' Jem grinned. 'Mark loves to win at everything.'

'He's like Alannah. And I'm embarrassed to say we let them win most of the time, don't we?' He gave a shrug, meeting her eye.

She nodded. 'Makes for a happy life all round. So you agree he has been acting slightly out of character.'

He looked like he might want to temper that, but as he opened his mouth to object, she continued.

'What I mean is, it helps to know it's not just me he's been a bit off with – I haven't done something to make him feel tense. He's clearly out of sorts and it's probably something to do with work.' The lie about Angela Frame was still burning in her mind though, desperate to escape. She bit back the question and instead brightened her expression to cover her hesitation. 'Thanks for reassuring me, Alex.'

'You're welcome. I think every relationship has its dominant character, the one who, more often than not, sucks energy from the other.' He frowned. 'I've put that badly . . . I mean one tends to rely a lot on the other to do the heavy lifting.'

'I know what you mean. In our case, I'm the one who gives. Mark provides. They sound similar, but they're not quite the same thing.' She smiled.

He nodded. 'I am both in our marriage. I provide and I give. I've discovered over the years that Alannah takes.' He gave a little laugh; it sounded slightly self-conscious but he shrugged. 'I ensure she has all that she wants. I like to see her happy, but increasingly it's not enough . . . not for both of us.'

She wasn't sure where this was going. 'Happy wife, happy life,' she quipped, suddenly not convinced that all was well with Alex's marriage. It sounded like something was off balance at home. 'I've held you up long enough. You've been generous, thank you.'

'Don't mention it.'

Jem had bent to collect her handbag, signalling that she was preparing to move, and he caught her wrist, taking her by surprise.

'As we're being honest, I have to admit that I too have been wondering whether Alannah is straying.'

Jem swallowed. 'I . . . I didn't say anything about Mark straying.'

'But this is what your concern is about, aren't I right?' He gave her a sympathetic look. 'You're wondering if his strange mood and behaviour may be connected with him having an affair.'

'Yes,' she murmured, trapped in his intent gaze, unable to deny it.

He continued with his candour. 'I have no proof, only my feelings to guide me, my sense of the person I knew and the person I'm with right now.' He swept invisible crumbs from the table, looking down. 'It sounds like Mark's behaviour is more obvious. Alannah hides it better, but something subtle has changed.'

It was the way he lifted his gaze to meet hers . . . Jem felt some-thing split, like a balloon being punctured, spilling its air.

'You think they're together?' she whispered.

He gave a long, high shrug that spoke volumes.

'How? I mean—'

'No idea. Did you know it was Alannah who introduced me to Mark?'

Jem's mouth opened in surprise and she had to swallow because it felt so dry. 'No.'

'They knew each other initially as patient and doctor.'

'What?' He couldn't have shocked her more in that instant.

'Oh, yes,' he continued. 'He was treating Alannah for infertility. She has a very serious case of endometriosis, making it difficult to conceive. And despite all best efforts, she's had only failure in this regard.'

'He treated her,' Jem repeated, screwing the napkin she'd reached for into her fist. She let it go and it slowly unfurled, as though in agony, showing a pattern of fresh creases. 'Why wouldn't he have mentioned that?'

'I imagine he was being respectful of the doctor–patient relationship.'

He sounded far too reasonable and resigned. 'Except they're together, Alex! This is what you're saying.'

'Shh,' he cautioned her, looking around. 'I don't know that for sure. I have no proof.' He waited a beat. 'I do have magnificent rage though,' he said, his words defying how calm he sounded. 'I am not one to be cheated on and simply accept it.'

'Alannah was certainly easy in her manner around Mark,' Jem said, ignoring what sounded like a threat, because she was already thinking back to the luncheon. 'She was the one who laughed at his jokes, even the one about the suicide.'

'Yes, that was in poor taste, I'm sorry. I mentioned it later to my wife.' He grimaced. 'She said she was simply being polite. The truth is, Alannah lacks grace at times. I used to admire it as chutzpah, but now I see it for the arrogance it so often is.' He sighed. 'I worship my wife, but I see her faults all too clearly.'

'So I was the only person around that table who was an outsider. All of you knew each other.'

'Yes, and I'm sorry about that too. I would have said something, but Mark began acting oddly before our lunch had begun and I thought it better to get through the afternoon without any more awkwardness. I too was surprised by his behaviour.'

'But Alannah didn't act strangely, did she?'

'Not that I noticed, but then I was looking for different signs than you, Jem. I saw that you were baffled by your husband's reaction to the conversation about the Mount Lofty suicide, but I was watching your husband and my wife reacting to each other.'

He'd had an agenda while sitting at her table. 'Oh, Alex. This is intolerable.'

He nodded. 'I know. Last week I knew you only as someone I wave to across a hockey pitch. I didn't know how to suggest that our partners might be having an affair. But now you know my suspicions, perhaps we can work together?'

'What do you mean?'

'Well, we can both be on the lookout for signs. Compare notes, if that doesn't sound too awkward. There's only so much I'll tolerate before . . .'

'Before what?'

He sighed. 'I have no desire to stay in an unfaithful relationship, Jem. If what I suspect is true, and despite how much I love her, then I shall deal with Alannah in an instant. Lithuanian men do not take kindly to being cuckolded. And if she continues to flaunt her adultery, then I shall take the only kind of action her kind understands.'

'Her kind?'

Alex shrugged. 'I won't go into it. Alannah's background is rather . . .' he hesitated, searching for the right word, 'shaded.'

But Jem was past caring about Alannah and any repercussions coming her way. For her this was about Mark. 'Treacherous bastard. I don't care much for adultery either, Alex. Yes, I'll compare notes. Now, can you run me back to my car? I feel sick.'

20

Jack sipped his latte and tried not to grimace. It was too hot, which meant the ground coffee had been singed. It was also too milky but, he reminded himself in this sulky moment, he was not here for the coffee and the café owners were apparently new. He looked out over the Spencer Gulf and inhaled. The burnt flavour of the coffee lingered but Jack had to privately admit he was enjoying the salty taste off the sea breeze, which crusted with invisible stealth around his lips.

'Do you want to order anything more?' the café waitress asked hopefully.

He didn't but he did want to remain seated. 'Er, yes. Can you do toast with Marmite?' It seemed the easiest option.

'Marmite?'

He laughed. 'I meant Vegemite.' His error was deliberate; he wanted word to get around that an English tourist was staying locally. Just a lily-white traveller, searching for sun and relaxation. He'd drop a few calculated crumbs wherever he could about the pretend novel he was writing for an English publisher.

'Sure. We have sourdough, is that okay?'

'Great,' he answered with forced cheer. 'Do you mind toasting it well, and can I get the butter and Vegemite on the side?'

'I'll ask,' the waitress replied, clearly unsure.

'Sorry to be so specific,' Jack said, beaming her one of his 'brilliants', as DCI Kate Carter liked to refer to them. 'Oh, and perhaps I'll have another one of these, but just three-quarters full, please.' Jack touched the glass to show where the milk might fill to.

'Ah . . . yes, okay,' the girl said, returning his smile. She noticed the coffee glass was still full and made a face. 'It's just we've got a new trainee barista on. Sorry if that one wasn't up to the mark. I'll take it off your bill.'

Now Jack felt guilty and embarrassed. He protested, but the youngster wouldn't hear of it.

'The normal barista is just back on. Can I put your name on the order, please?'

'Sure. It's Jack.'

The waitress smiled again. 'I'm Charlotte, but everyone calls me Charlie. I'll get your order in.'

As Charlie departed, Jack looked out across to where he knew a sandy beach was hosting a calm sea this morning. He took out a notebook and flicked back through a couple of pages as though looking over research for his piece. Small towns like this had eyes everywhere; people were observant and noticed every anomaly, and he was one. A stranger.

Writers tended to attract interest and if he could cunningly prod the locals, citing research for the article – today's lie nothing to do with reproductive medicine – he might just find out some interesting background.

Background. That was the word his boss had used in a recent email. *Paint us a picture, Jack. We want the background before we bring all the pieces into the foreground and start playing with them.*

Jack had understood its message: he was not to charge into the viper's nest if it existed. He had no jurisdiction.

I'm referring to you as being undercover, Jack, simply because you're masquerading as a writer. But this is not a sanctioned operation. You're off the books, and don't forget that. Just find out if this syndicate exists.

'It exists,' Jack murmured to his notes, where he'd scribbled some details about the region. He had established that Port Lincoln on the opposing Eyre Peninsula was a huge, deep harbour, known for its excellent fishing and its famous son, weightlifter Dean 'Dinko' Lukin, gold medallist at the 1984 Los Angeles Olympics in the super heavyweight category. He'd become an overnight sensation that the whole country had embraced and, as a tuna fisherman from this region, it had drawn attention to the town. No one in this state cared that he'd been born in Sydney – as far as they were concerned, he was a South Australian hero.

He was also a celebrated millionaire, Jack had discovered. A haze of drugs had followed Lukin and his brother around, and Dean had been arrested for possession of cannabis. Although he'd been slapped with a minor fine on a lesser charge of hindering arrest, his brother had been convicted, sentenced and jailed for six months for cultivating hundreds of hemp plants. So the whiff of marijuana hung around the Lukins and attached itself to Port Lincoln as a result. None of that interested Jack in terms of his current case, but it did give a certain background to the busy harbour. Surely these southern seas offered an easy way into Australia and, more importantly, directly into the state where he was sure the mastermind of this syndicate resided.

Needing to blend in explained Jack's slightly ungroomed appearance. He'd donned shorts with a linen shirt and sneakers, deliberately not shaved for a couple of days and not bothered trying to tame his thick hair and present the crisp look he was known for. Right now he wanted those observant locals to see only another lazy tourist.

The house on the beach was perfect, its back doors opening directly onto the sand. It was private and quiet but gave him a good view of the port and the channel that would bring ships into and out of it.

'Here's your toast with butter and Veg on the side,' Charlie said, arriving back. 'And the three-quarter full coffee.'

'Looks good,' he lied. It looked more like four-fifths full but Jack knew this time he was the problem, not the barista. The discovery of high-end coffee in Melbourne had turned him into the worst sort of snob.

'Gosh, it's lovely out here, isn't it?' Charlie said, sighing. She didn't seem to be in a rush to hurry back to the counter.

Jack decided he might as well probe. 'Have you always lived here?'

'Yes. Can't wait to get away, actually, and see more of the world.'

'Really? I think it's idyllic.'

'Aw, I s'pose. But not when it's all you've known. Dad says I'll be back in a hurry once I see the real world.'

Jack chuckled. 'I think your dad's right, but you need to find that out for yourself.'

She nodded. 'That's what I told him.'

'So, what will you do?' he asked, beginning to butter the toast.

'I'm going to uni in Melbourne.'

'Wow. Big change.'

'Yep,' she said, looking excited. 'I could have chosen Adelaide but it would be so easy for Mum and Dad to reach me and fuss. So I'm deliberately making it harder.'

'Won't do you any harm, and means you can't run home when the going gets tough . . . and it will. Melbourne's a big city.'

'With good coffee,' Charlie said, glancing at the still untouched coffee near his plate. 'Are you on holiday?'

Jack explained about the novel he was researching, making it up as he went along, but sticking mostly to the same story he'd given others, like Jem's friend whom he'd rented the beach house from, and the lovely woman from whom he'd rented the car.

'Oh, I would have thought you'd want somewhere a bit more exciting than here.'

'Not at all – I want somewhere evocative and with heart. But I appreciate your interest.' He grinned, biting into the well-toasted sourdough. 'Oh, delicious, thank you,' he said, not having to lie. It was crunchy and just what he felt like.

'That's because I'm going to do film and TV studies.' She shrugged. 'Anyway, I'm really pleased you've chosen little Wallaroo. Port Lincoln would have been more obvious, I suppose, because the harbour is huge. Dad says Matthew Flinders came in during the early 1800s and named it after his hometown of Lincoln in England. I think even the French whaling fleets were snooping around this region, plus seal hunters of course. The only reason it didn't become the main harbour for South Australia back in the day.'

'Wow, Charlie, you're a surprise.'

She laughed. 'Why, because I'm a waitress?' She grinned. 'I love history and would probably study that if I wasn't so interested in making films.'

'Tell me more,' he said, crunching further into the toast. 'Only if I'm not holding you up?'

'You're not. It's very quiet today. Um, let me see if I can remember what I've learned . . . Er, the first governor of this state instructed Colonel Light – you know the guy who planned out Adelaide?'

Jack didn't but he nodded all the same. He applauded the fellow for making the city a grid, very easy to navigate.

'Well, he was told to find a capital for this new region. They'd all been looking for the right place with a harbour, somewhere for a settlement with so many immigrants clambering onto ships, and I gather there were lots of settlers already camping around Kangaroo Island, among other places.'

'Lots of pressure then,' Jack said; he could tell where this was going.

'It was considered seriously, because it had plenty going for it – a beautiful harbour and fertile lands surrounding it, but Light wasn't convinced there was sufficient fresh water, and the rocky reefs would make it difficult for the merchant ships to navigate. Plus we get howling gales around here.'

'So Adelaide was chosen,' Jack said, moving things along.

Charlie grinned. 'Exactly. They call this area Little Cornwall.'

'I can understand why.'

'You know Cornwall?'

'I do.' He grinned, sipping the coffee to please her.

'You'll see that Wallaroo has a lot of pleasure craft in the marina, if you haven't already.'

Jack waited, which encouraged her to talk on. She sounded proud of her hometown.

'But there's also plenty of tugs and prawn trawlers. It's busy enough, but not like Port Lincoln that takes huge ships.'

'So only smaller vessels coming and going.'

'Yep, lots of them, all the time. Lots of tourists, hobby fishing, and then the commercial boats for seafood and the large grain ships. I know I sound like I'm desperate to escape it, but Wallaroo's a really nice place. A good setting for a story – especially if it's a mystery.'

She was probing. That was good.

'It might be.' He grinned, putting his index finger to his lips. 'Do you think the town suits a mystery?'

'Well, if I was writing a screenplay, let's say, I'd choose here, because you can arrive and leave relatively anonymously via the harbour. We're so used to holidaymakers that if you posed like one and acted like one, no one would think further on it.'

'I'll keep that in mind,' Jack replied with another smile, while buttering his second piece of now-cold toast. Luck was running; she was answering his questions without knowing it.

'Glad to help. Well, I better get back to it, I suppose. Good luck with the book.'

'You too for uni. Do I pay inside?'

Charlie nodded. 'Yep, whenever,' she said, waving a hand. 'Take your time. No one's queuing for the table.'

Anonymity. Busy little harbour. The perfect place to set up a sly operation to get a single canister regularly into Adelaide, Jack thought. And if this was a global racket, then Wallaroo really was an ideal, nothing-happens-here sort of place to hide the activity.

Did he have it right? The crims had decided that the old method using corruptible couriers and embryologists working for legitimate operations was too risky? So they'd worked out a new smuggling route via tiny Wallaroo or similar? It seemed extraordinary, but there really was no limit to the creative minds of people who were playing in the underworld.

So if Wallaroo was the point of mainland contact, what was the route and how was it being managed? Jack scribbled another note in his book and sat back, deep in thought.

Jem was too angry, too bitter and too excited in all the wrong ways to just go home and wait for Mark.

She had called her parents to help with the children. She couldn't give a toss how Mark might react to his in-laws settling in at his home, without any warning, but they were all used to each other. Her father in particular was close to Mark, and they had enjoyed many an early evening in Jem and Mark's garden, sipping wine, solving the world's problems, while Jem and her mother got on with the food or caring for the kids. Besides, her parents preferred to stay slightly removed in the small guest house to one side of the garden. They would emerge in the morning with enough time to organise the children's breakfasts, make sure they had all their needs and to get them off to school. Frankly, Mark was lucky.

Now she scribbled him a note. *Gone to the beach, but then you knew I probably would. Need to think. So do you. I've left a note for the kids and M&D will take care of everything. See you sometime soon. Jx*

She thought about whether or not to end on a kiss or leave it conspicuously absent but as much as she wanted to make a pointed statement – especially with the bitter mood that had her in its grip – she decided not to be deliberately hostile. Ultimately, she decided, she wanted to save her marriage, if there was something to save, and he would notice that tiny 'x' not being there.

She did not want to be here when her parents arrived; it would only mean more questions. As it was, the conversation had been sufficiently strained.

'Isn't this all rather sudden, darling?' her mother had remarked after agreeing to step in.

'I think I just need a break, Mum,' Jem had tried.

It was never that easy though with her mother. 'From what? Motherhood, marriage, life?'

'All of it,' she said, hearing how blasé it sounded.

'Jem, you can't just run away when—'

'Why not, Mum? You and Dad love being with the children, I know you do. And they're not babies. They don't require the hard work they used to. It's more a taxi service right now, if I'm honest.'

'It's not that, Jemima. Not at all. We'll always help. But I'm worried about you. What's going on? Is it Mark? Has something happened?'

'No, look, you're getting this wrong. I've been feeling a little under the weather,' she lied, 'and a few days at the beach, some fresh air, some quiet time, will sort me. I promise. Please, Mum, don't worry. I'm not sick. I'm not giving up on anything. I just need this break.'

'Okay, okay. We'll take care of things here. So, you drive safely and we'll see you in a few days.'

'Thanks, Mum. I've left the usual list. The freezer is full and there's plenty of food in the fridge. All of them will cheer if you take them for a quick bite somewhere tonight instead of cooking. We never go out on a school night, so you can get away with it and break the rules.' Before her mother could say anything more, she followed up. 'Now, hug Dad for me and I'll call you when I get to the beach so you know I'm there.'

'All right. Bye, darling.'

Jem had left the house within moments of the call and fortunately didn't have to think about packing because she kept beachy clothes in their holiday home, and she knew its kitchen was well stocked with all the non-perishables. She'd just have to pick up milk, bread, that sort of thing. Now that she was in motion, she couldn't wait. The beach, the space . . . It was exactly what she needed right now.

And there was something else. Something that she refused to confront, or even acknowledge, skittering around the edge of her mind.

It was Jack Hawksworth's bright smile. If he'd followed through on his plans, then he was already at North Beach. And soon she would be too. Whatever was going to happen between them, she would leave to the universe.

★

Mark called home and heard his children's laughter on the voice-mail recording. Then he called his wife's mobile and listened impatiently through her sunny voicemail when she didn't pick up that call, either.

'I wish you'd answer when you see it's me,' he said, unable to hide his exasperation. 'Give me a call.'

He saw another patient, which took nearly forty minutes, and tried once more to reach his wife, only to receive the same upbeat voicemail. It felt like a sneer rather than the direct, uncomplicated message it was. He threw the phone down on his desk. When the phone rang a few moments later he snatched it up without looking at who was calling. 'About bloody time!'

'Mark, it's Al Petras.'

'Er, sorry, I thought it was—'

'Clearly. Jem, I'm guessing? What's wrong?'

He just sighed.

'She's upset. And let's not do the dance, Mark. She's specifically upset over your behaviour on Sunday and who knows what since. For someone not wishing to draw attention, I think you did a spectacular job of just the opposite.'

'Listen, she has no idea about—'

'You know it doesn't help our arrangement to have a wife who is so suspicious.'

Mark frowned. 'Of an affair I'm apparently having,' he quali-fied, sounding disgusted. 'I told you—'

'The last thing we want is your wife nosing around in our affairs. I agree with your original notion that it has serious potential ramifica-tions. I'm extremely careful, you know that, and I like to be entirely in control. But Jem is out of my control and if she's digging around, on the hunt for information, turning up where she's not wanted that could lead her into taking action that I wouldn't appreciate.'

'Action? What do you mean?'

'She could be reading your text messages, checking your computer, email, browsing history; she'll talk to colleagues, probably start talking to more of your friends and acquaintances. In fact, she's already begun, hasn't she?'

Mark, catching on, trilled with shock. 'She asked you about me? What did you say to her?' He tried to sound calm, even though the blood was rushing in his ears.

'I played along. What else could I do? I want her to see me at the very least as a friend. If she keeps talking to me, then at least I'll know exactly what she's up to, what she's thinking. But you need to sort this out.'

'I don't especially want you to know what my wife is up to, Al. It's actually none of your—'

'But that's just it, Mark. It has suddenly become my business. It's actually my very business you're now threatening – and my identity. Everything we set up has been secret, and that secrecy must be maintained at all costs or we're at risk. Your behaviour has brought unwanted attention.'

'From my wife? She's not going to . . .' Mark took a breath. 'This is escalating unnecessarily. I've spent my entire existence promoting life, bringing it into the world safely. And now you've turned me into a murderer.'

'Well, it's all very well to take a righteous attitude, Mark, but I know you've been enjoying the new wealth with your family. Holiday house at the beach, an apartment in Paris being negotiated, I gather. Your new car, the winery you've bought into. Three children at the top schools, top orthodontic care, music lessons, tennis lessons, designer labels for your clothes, overseas trips, a box at the footy . . . do I need to go on? We both know what's been adding the real lustre to your lifestyle. So don't be a pussy. You were the only person we could both trust to rid us of that courier.'

'I'm sure your guy, Ricardo, could have done it on his own.'

'No, I couldn't risk it. I take precautions – two against one was better. I needed both of you there.'

Mark ran a hand through his thick hair in a nervous gesture while Al continued.

'I thought it would be enough. But clearly, I've misjudged.'

'What are you talking about?'

'This will probably be in the news later today, certainly by tomorrow, so better you know now. With luck, it will be accepted as a tragic drug overdose.'

'What is this, Al? What do I need to know?'

'The embryologist.'

The silence was as sharp as the breath Mark inhaled with fresh shock. Nikki. He had liked her enormously, trusted her – it was why he'd recommended her in the first place.

Al had started talking again. '. . . I won't risk anyone going wobbly. That includes you drawing attention to something that should have remained a pure conversation piece. You did not play it cool at lunch, Mark.'

'So you'd kill me? Because I got a bit worked up?'

The laugh that brought did not sound at all amused and it didn't reassure him. He quickly moved on.

'Why did you have to kill Nikki?'

'She was a liability.' This was said matter-of-factly, with no ounce of sympathy or shame. 'I met with her and decided she was a risk to the whole operation. Don't worry. It was made to look like pure accident.'

'Just like Greg, apparently. So why is his death suddenly being looked at by the Major Crimes squad? That wasn't supposed to happen.'

'I can't speak to that. It's probably just a rumour. They can't prove it wasn't suicide. A pathologist would only see the wounds Greg would have received falling down that rocky hillside. I don't understand why it's even being looked at.' There was a pause. 'You did just push him, didn't you, Mark?'

'Yes.' He heard the shake in his voice.

So did Al. 'Mark, I need transparency now, or I can't protect us. What are you hiding?'

'Nothing. But I had to use some chloroform to make him compliant.'

He anticipated a swift, brutal response. Instead, the voice was unnaturally patient. That was worse. 'Well there's the answer. The pathologist has discovered an anomaly in toxicology. People don't often accidentally slip down big hills after inhaling chloroform.' Even the sarcasm was tempered.

'You weren't there. I couldn't risk being seen.'

'Fair enough. I could say the same. You weren't there when I met Nikki. She struck me as far too intelligent and humane to leave Greg's death alone.'

'So you decided her life was forfeit?'

'I decided my life was more valuable than hers.'

Mark couldn't believe what he was hearing. 'I could turn this on you, Al. All you've done is draw more attention to MultiplyMed. One death is a tragedy, but two is a little harder to explain.'

'She was asking questions about the courier. Much like Jem, she was suspicious. I had to deal with it.'

'Don't bring Jem into this,' Mark warned, feeling a tentacle of fear crawling up his body. 'I'm going to have to distance myself for a while. I won't be continuing with our agreement.'

Now the laugh was amused. 'No, Mark, I've told you – you don't make decisions.'

'I do when my family's being brought under the microscope.'

'We all want to protect our partners, our families, but they benefit from all that we achieve through this syndicate. Jem . . . she's complicit. If she doesn't stop this—'

'Complicit!' Mark's voice had risen. 'Al, are you threatening her?'

He heard soothing sounds, a tongue clicking. 'No, not at all. I'm simply trying to make you understand how important it is to take control of your wife.'

'What exactly do you want me to do?'

'Reassure her. Do what men do to make women happy. Pay her more attention, take her out for dinner, talk about getting away together, make love to her, Mark. Obviously that's lacking if she feels you have a mistress.'

Mistress! He could laugh at the quaint expression from the Lithuanian . . . if only it was funny. He sighed audibly. 'I'll do everything I can.'

'Good. We want all suspicion dissipating, especially as we're trying the new route this week. Now get yourself away to the beach soon, and don't forget we've been invited to join you the day after tomorrow. We're all friends. Happy. Nothing to see here.'

'And what about the two people dead?'

'Ignore them. They can't be traced to either of us. Show some spine now, Mark. No more wobbling.'

A dark chuckle reached him before the line went dead.

21

Andy Redford, ship's agent, was standing at the Wallaroo Dock, looking at the horizon where the grain ship would emerge tomorrow to sail down the channel. He'd witnessed it many times, but this one would have a different flavour to its arrival. The foreign vessels were dark, massive hulks, navigating their way between the twinkling red and green markers like slow-moving prehistoric sea creatures. He'd grown up here looking out at those illuminations; red for starboard, green for port and now he smiled in memory of his childhood notion of fairy lights over the sea.

The ship he would greet tomorrow was on a short trip – a positioning voyage – into South Australia to pick up a full load of grain. He'd put his hand up to meet it, since it was arriving the day after the long weekend, privately happy that no one else would want to handle it when they'd rather be taking an extra day of holiday with family or friends. As he'd anticipated, everyone had sighed with relief that he didn't seem to mind being around over the weekend in case anything needed doing before the ship's arrival.

Looking back down the wide and sweeping curve of white sandy beach that was Wallaroo's prime attraction, it felt like the whole of Adelaide had come here for the long weekend. He considered himself lucky to have got here early, because the café he'd just left, takeaway coffee in hand, was now full, with a queue snaking back. He decided to wander back down the jetty that he remembered leaping off as a youngster. The jetty was also crowded, with people setting up small chairs and eskies, gearing up for a day of fishing.

'What's biting?' Andy paused to ask one couple who looked comfortable, sipping tea poured from a flask. Being local, he knew the range, but he was always interested in what people might be catching.

'Ah, there's no wind today,' the bloke said, pointing to a rope near his wife. 'Not a single crab yet.'

'Still early.' Andy grinned. 'I'll buy some flathead off you if you catch some,' he half-jested.

'I'm expensive, lad,' the guy said with a wink. 'See how we go. There's a slack tide coming.'

Andy wandered on, sipping his flat white, recalling his own unsuccessful attempts at fishing off this very jetty. There was plenty to catch, but he'd never had the patience. Even so, those were such great days, he recalled, when the summers felt endless, school felt far away and he and his mates were starting to take a healthy interest in girls. But there had only ever been one for him: Keely Barker. He'd met her at kindy in the sandpit, when someone threw a bucket at her and Andy had taken offence. He was no fighter but he remembered giving Kevin Oatley a piece of his mind. And since that moment, when Keely had lisped a thank you, he'd been smitten until the day she agreed to marry him. And he still was very much in love with his wife, though he worried constantly that she could have done better.

Andy had read somewhere – probably an old *Reader's Digest* in the local GP's clinic – that it was the risk takers in life who got ahead. So here he was, taking a big risk, but he was beginning to wonder if he'd made a wise move.

'Make good decisions in your life, Andy,' his father had said on that final day of his life. The cancer had taken him swiftly but they'd had a wonderful final week together when he'd sat with his dad and reminisced. And his father, sensing the end was close, had become philosophical. 'The best decision you ever made was marrying Keely.'

Andy had nodded. No doubt about it.

'But now you've got real responsibility with Chloe, and every decision you make can affect her life. So make good ones.'

'Like what?' Andy had asked. 'My job?'

'No, you've got a good job, a steady one. But keep saving. Buy Keely a house – I could never do that for your mum. I blame myself for your problem. It was my downfall too. Give up the gee-gees, can you promise me that?'

'Oh, Dad, don't—'

His ailing father, visibly slipping away, had shaken his head. 'You've got to promise me. I didn't have the will to – I was weak – but learn from my mistake. I let your mother down, I let you boys down. Don't let your family down, Andy. Gambling is an abyss. It never stops. You'll talk up the wins, and never mention the losses that will cripple you. Promise me!' His father had all but growled the final two words, finding the strength to grip Andy's hand to convey how serious his advice was.

Andy had promised. His father had died. And Andy had not broken his vow, but the debt was already scary enough. Even the small inheritance he'd received after his father's passing couldn't touch it. Now he had a new baby on the way and it all felt unmanageable. Frightening, if he was honest, but he'd told Keely about his promise and she'd looked proud at his admission.

'I'll support you, Andy. We'll do this together, all right? Bit by bit we'll pay off what you owe, and we can start again from there.'

He didn't deserve her. But he was going to make it up to her.

I've never done anything unlawful in my life, he thought as the tingles of fear began to claw at him now that his task was imminent. *I don't even cheat at cards. Now this!*

Ever since he'd been approached he'd become edgy and it showed. He'd jumped at the opportunity to make some extra money – and untraceable cash to boot. But his focus had slipped at work with the fresh anxiety of what he was planning.

'Hey, Red? You haven't signed off here,' someone said last week, tapping a clipboard. 'Did you run the checks?'

'Yeah, I did. Sorry.'

Another had asked about something that should be in the file but wasn't.

'Isn't Pete in charge of that?' he wondered aloud, feeling dumb for asking and wishing he hadn't.

'Pete's on leave. You losing your marbles, mate?'

'Nah, I'm just . . .'

'Just what?'

'Oh, I dunno. Probably tired.'

The man had poked his shoulder. It wasn't hostile but it was a reprimand, and rightly so. 'Listen, you've had your head up your arse for a couple of weeks. Get yourself sorted, mate. Is there something I'm missing? Is it the baby? You can tell me; it's my job to make sure my team is feeling fine.' He tapped his temple. 'Up here too.'

'I'm fine, really. Just a bit tired. Chloe's not sleeping well,' he said, embellishing the lie.

'Okay, I remember those days too.'

'Sorry, chief.'

'Go grab a coffee and clear your head.'

But it was nothing to do with being fatigued, or even foggy. He was nervous. That was the truth of it – even he could hear the slight tremor in his voice these days. He was sure his hands might tremble too if he was asked to show them.

Keely didn't mean to, but the pressure was there. How were they going to afford another child when they could barely afford all that Chloe needed? Thank goodness she was out of nappies, which seemed to cost a small fortune, but now it was shoes and clothes she was growing out of fast. Day care was out of the question; Keely would have to work just to pay for it and then he'd cop flak from her mother, who'd look at him in that judge-mental way she had that told him he had never been the best choice and Keely really should have married Johnno Landy, the farmer who had shown immense interest in her. Landy was doing very nicely, thank you, as his family were generational farmers of the region. But he had inherited his business and property. Andy had nothing to rely on except honest work.

But, fortunately for him, there'd never been anyone else for Keely either, though he wasn't entirely sure why. Frankly, she was a dream girl for him. When he showed her photo around on occasion, other blokes would wolf-whistle or give appreciative noises of disbelief that this was his wife.

'What, you won her with your looks?' they'd say – or words to that effect.

He wasn't good-looking, not like Keely. He'd always thought her gorgeous with those eyes, almost too large for the rest of her features, and that almost alarming colour that was pale enough to win a double-take from most. Her hair shone dark, which only made her eyes seem more startling, and the dimple when she smiled was the final sequin in a round, sparkly face.

All he had going for him was his height – that's all he had over Johnno – but the rest of him was a bit gangly and, given they lived so close to the beach, his pale, freckled skin had always won laughs, even from his mates. His slightly reddish blond hair meant he burned rather than tanned and so he was always the one in a long-sleeved T-shirt when all the other kids were running wild and bare-chested.

But he had a talent. It was his poetry that had won her heart; she told him it made her feel romantic and special when she received his missives, which he'd leave in her family's mailbox several times a week. It was like old-fashioned wooing, his granny had claimed, making him smile. His clever words, and the fact that he was so good with Keely's baby brother, had made him a contender for her heart. She said she'd always known he would make a good father because of how he was with little Danny. He didn't get boozed each weekend like the other blokes either – Keely appreciated that, and she could tell the difference between blokes who fancied her and one who worshipped her.

He'd reminded himself many times that an ordinary-looking guy who loved a girl and only wanted to make her happy was surely worth a football field of good-lookers who'd sleep with her and then leave her for the next prospect. That's how he reassured himself, and he did so again now because he was feeling so uncertain about what he was about to do.

But how else could he provide? He'd tried to win extra money last month, and instead had lost his bet and a sizeable chunk of wages. So he'd agreed to the stranger's offer. He could see why they'd picked him; they must have studied his habits as well as noticing that he was one of the few Australians who boarded the ships arriving into dock.

The ships were all internationally based and used foreign crews, usually via cheap labour from Asia. There were no Aussies aboard until they docked, and then the ship's agent would run through the checks and administrative tasks needed to clear the ship.

'What do you actually do, Andy?' Keely had asked. 'I know your title and that you work the ships when they come in, but what's your job?'

It struck him that her mother was probably behind that question; Keely had never been that interested in his work before. 'Well,' he'd begun, 'it's a lot of different tasks. We have to make sure there's a berth at the port, and you know the tug that sits out off the jetty?' At her nod he'd continued. 'I make sure that's ready to help the ship move off. I arrange the pilot – he's the guy in Port Lincoln, who comes down and boards the ship to guide it in.'

She'd frowned. 'Can't the captain just follow the lights?'

That made him laugh. 'Yes, that would make sense, but the pilot knows the local waters and where all the problems might be, and he's responsible for the safe transit into and out of the harbour.' He grinned. 'And then there's a load of other stuff to bore you, from arranging any necessary repairs, to organising safe unloading or loading of cargo, to calling in cleaners if we need them, helping with provisioning the ship from local suppliers, and piles and piles of paperwork, sweetheart. Everything has to be authorised, cross-referenced, signed off as being in order . . . plus I may feel that the ship's hull needs cleaning to take the new load of grain, and that's about forty-four thousand dollars a day just for the cleaning vessel . . . So, it's many different tasks.'

'Makes you sound important.' She'd grinned, giving him that flirty look she had. 'I quite like sleeping with someone important.'

He'd beaten his chest to make her laugh out loud but it was pure bravado – he hadn't been feeling important or successful recently. He was failing her at every turn. Since Keely had stopped working to raise their family, it had landed entirely on him.

When Petras had approached him, he'd been vulnerable, desperate to pay off his debt. The money offered made his jaw drop, and he knew he would have to bring Keely into the conversation or she'd start asking uncomfortable questions about the cash – or worse, maybe her mother would get involved and that was just darkness waiting to swallow him. So he told her about the deal as they sat together on the couch one evening.

'What are you getting into?' Keely asked, worried, Chloe whinge-ing against her mother's bulging belly with yet another ear infection. 'I'll just get her some Panadol. Andy, it sounds illegal. Is it?'

He shrugged. 'Is it illegal to carry a flask?'

She slow-blinked. 'You know what I mean.'

'Look, I haven't asked too many questions. But I know it's not drugs.'

'How can you be sure?'

'The container I have to carry off is this size,' he said, holding his hands approximately twenty centimetres apart vertically. 'They wouldn't be arsed doing it for that little cocaine or ice, or whatever. They like to bring in bigger loads.'

'Well, whatever's in there, they're prepared to pay you thou-sands of dollars – it's got to be worth plenty to them.'

'I don't care what it is,' he assured her. 'I just want the money. It's simple. I pick it up when I board at Wallaroo and I carry it off and give it to someone before I even leave the esplanade.'

'What if it's a bomb?'

He laughed. 'Don't be an idiot, Keels. People build bombs, they don't carry the bastard around with them all that way.'

'It could be radioactive, or something that helps to build bombs.'

'This is South Australia! It's not anything like that.'

She nodded thoughtfully. 'You're right.' Then her face lit up. 'What if it's diamonds?'

'Well, then, it will rattle. I mean it, I don't care, Keels. We need this or we're going under. That money could cover our immediate bills and then there's another payment the following month. I could get us out of debt real fast. You wouldn't have to live in this place. You can have your own house, set up a nursery, Chloe can have her own room painted just how she wants, and a backyard to play in.'

She smiled and he watched her lips tremble. 'You know that's all I've ever wanted, Andy. I don't need to be rich – I just want our own place, a garden, a car that doesn't conk out every week . . . and us, happy.'

He shook his head, frustrated by his inability to provide for his family. 'And that's what we're going to have. You must trust me. It's easy, it's got no risk, and we can stop when we want.'

'Are you sure?' she said, rocking her body to try to get Chloe's droopy eyes to give up the fight and close into sleep.

He moved to sit next to her and stroked the wispy golden hair of his feverish daughter. 'I promise. And it's cash. If we're careful and don't splash it about, no one will be any the wiser, hon. You tell absolutely no one – not even your mum. So long as only the two of us know, then how can we get into bother? We just quietly go about paying our debts in regular chunks so they barely notice. And you go about your life as normal. I keep doing my job, but I'll accept a few of these side jobs and we'll save as much as we can. We're going to look up in a year and our lives will feel different, I swear it. And then I'll stop.'

She leaned in and kissed him gently. 'I trust you, Andy.'

Her words rang now in his mind as he contemplated what he'd be doing tomorrow. It was simple, the stranger had said, sounding so confident. Andy had insisted on sharing names or he wouldn't do it.

'Petras. Al to my friends. Are we friends, Andy?'

And that's when he knew they wanted him above anyone else. There's no way a name would have been given if he wasn't their first – and perhaps only – choice. It was why, in a curious rush of newfound courage, he'd pushed his luck in his new mindset of risk-taking.

Petras offered five thousand, but Andy shook his head. 'Double it.' He tried not to sound as though he was holding his breath.

'I can give you regular work for as long as you want it,' Petras said.

'Ten is my price.'

'Let's call it seven and a half. See how you go on the first run.' A smile. 'Deal?'

It was far more than he'd expected to be offered, and Andy had nodded over lunch in the busy travel stop of Port Wakefield on Highway One, where everyone's business wasn't everyone else's. They'd shared a drink and a simple meal of fish and chips at The Rising Sun, a local pub. It was small talk until their meals arrived, but within fifteen minutes the deal had been struck and his companion was making ready to depart.

'How will it work?' Andy had asked quietly, not that anyone was listening.

'You do what you do. All your normal routines, except you'll board with this backpack.' Petras had pointed to the bag leaning against the table leg. 'And you will swap it with an identical one that carries your money. I will send an SMS to a burner phone in this bag, telling you where it is. Ditch the phone when the job is done. You'll always be given a new one.'

Andy put down his cutlery, wanting to ask questions, but Petras held up a knife, just briefly, stopping Andy from saying more.

'The goods will be left for you in a simple spot, somewhere that is perfectly reasonable for a ship's agent to be moving around. I promise you this.'

'And if it's not there or I don't like where it's being left?'

'You will not object to where it's left, I give you my word. It will be there.'

'But what if it's not?'

'Then we've failed you and you'll get the money anyway.'

'All of it? No matter what, on the Tuesday after Anzac holiday weekend?'

'Yes, all of it.'

'How?'

'How what, Andy?'

'How will I get my money?'

'A man will wave to you on the jetty.' An image was shown to him. 'That's him. Can you memorise his face?'

Andy nodded.

'Good. So he'll wave to you and you'll act like you've met before. Make up a story if you're asked. You met him roadside and helped him to change a tyre.'

'Where did this occur?'

'Maybe just outside Kadina . . . Let's say over the Christmas hols when he visited last.'

'Okay.'

'Walk back together to the car park near the fish and chip kiosk. He'll be carrying a similar backpack. Put the backpack down near your feet as you talk. He'll do the same. When the moment is right, you each pick up the other's backpack and part company. He'll have the goods, and inside your new backpack will be the cash and a new phone.'

Andy nodded. 'Sounds clean.'

'It is. Very clean and simple. Don't look around, don't act suspicious – just be yourself. Get in your car and drive away. No looking back.'

'What am I bringing off the ship?'

'Do you really want to know?'

He hesitated. 'Is it dangerous?'

'Not in the slightest.'

'Can it be used to hurt anyone or anything?' he pressed.

'The opposite, in fact. I promise you, it is nothing that brings pain or injury. I'm in business, not terror. And it's not drugs.'

'Okay, I don't want to know any more. I just want my money.'

'Yes, I realise that. Keely's nearly ready to pop, and your expenses are going to skyrocket. I'm going now, Andy, but I'm leaving an envelope behind, and in it is a little taster of what you can look forward to. Go and buy Keely something lovely, and maybe a new toy for Chloe.'

Al Petras departed, stopping only at the bar to pay the bill while Andy stared at the envelope. It looked like a birthday card. So these people had been watching him, following his life. He watched the SUV leave the car park before he opened the envelope – which did have a card inside. It was a pretty picture of some country scene and when he opened it, Al had written, *Your lucky day, Andy. Keep the luck going.* And sitting within the card were ten crisp, green one-hundred-dollar notes.

They knew his weak spot.

22

It was the Anzac Day holiday, a Monday, and a last gasp for the fine days of autumn as it was surprisingly warm. Jack guessed South Australians everywhere were swarming to the beaches; Wallaroo was no exception. Too many cars to count lined the long, wide expanse of sandy beach whose curve was accentuated by a row of small beach shacks. The one he was staying in had been modernised, but some looked as though they hadn't been updated since the 1950s when they were likely first erected as fishing shacks. He'd since learned that farmers – or cockies, as they were referred to – owned most of them and would come in numbers after the January wheat harvest to relax with family.

Those who didn't have access to a shack had brought their cars and set up home for the day on the sand, it seemed. Jack found himself walking around large family groups with four or five cars and a dozen or more kids building castles or yelling back to their parents from the shallows. He couldn't imagine how they were allowed to drive cars onto the beach but apparently it was normal, because dozens of families had set up tents for shade and were using their cars as everything from changing rooms to kitchens. Boots were flung open and stuff was spilling out of the eskies that he'd admired since he first clapped eyes on one in Sydney. They were brilliant for keeping the beers cold, he thought, watching more than one father sip from a bottle or tinny and promise their wife and anxious children that they would go in for a final dip – in a minute.

Jack smiled to himself. It was the tetchy end of the day for families and especially mums, now hot, impatient, already imagining everything that needed to be done to get everyone readied for school tomorrow and off to bed. Could he ever live that life? He often believed he wanted it. The idea of holding an infant above the sea's foam, hearing them squeal with pleasure to feel its kiss while safe in their dad's arms, glancing back to where his wife might be smiling at them. A nice vignette in his mind, he thought, but then he caught sight of a mother, who probably didn't mean to be scowling. He watched her family, dog and all, making one last dash towards the water's edge, kicking sand back over the clothes she'd just neatly folded. He watched her pull her hair back with exasperation, the debris of their day's play seemingly her responsibility, and he wondered through how much of a rose-coloured lens he was daydreaming about parenthood.

He began to move on, but not before she made eye contact with him. 'Can I help you lift that?' he offered as she struggled to pick up an enormous esky.

She looked shocked and gave a laugh. 'I should have asked my husband before I sent him off for one final swim with the gang.'

'Here, let me.' He heaved it up and followed to where she gratefully pointed into the back of a station wagon.

'Thanks so much. Once that's in everything should fit, *Tetris*-like, around it,' she said, smiling and pulling back her hair again. 'Hope you win the lottery for that lovely gesture.'

He laughed. 'Drive safely,' he said, and left her behind, walking once again along the shoreline.

Apart from the absent pleasure of stepping on warm sand – he had removed his sneakers – his thoughts were as loose as the barely buttoned linen shirt that billowed in the soft breeze like a cloud. He was letting his mind wander again across all that he knew. London was waiting for an update and the South Australian major crimes team were now involved in the deaths of Greg Payne and Nicola Lawson, potentially drawing some connections, which meant any other clues he could feed them might just tip the scales for the joint op he was aiming for.

But he had to point a finger more confidently at a syndicate. If Major Crimes was involved, it meant the right people were now smelling something off, but all they had was the two deaths that felt suspicious simply because they were linked through their employer. If not for the sharp mind of the pathologist at the Forensic Science Centre, the link may not have been made, and that slightly off smell to the deaths might not have been sensed, let alone acted on.

Of course, no one knew yet, he presumed, whether the pair even knew each other. A courier and an embryologist?

'Unlikely,' he murmured into the breeze. 'But not impossible.'

Could he find that link? That would be sufficient to excite the South Australians into putting MultiplyMed under the micro-scope. He made a mental note to find out the procedure at the Adelaide clinic for delivery of material from overseas – its exact pathway from the courier touching down in Australia to the storage tanks in the clinic on Greenhill Road.

Right now he could brief London on his hunch about Mark Maddox, but at present that felt dangerously loose, and his gut feeling really was not enough. Jack sighed. It was too easy to dislike him for how he'd treated his wife in front of others, but he could have been having a bad day. Jack only knew Jem's side of the situation. He paused to shade his eyes and stare out to sea. It was curious though . . . downright intriguing, that she claimed Mark's behaviour was triggered by a discussion of the courier's death, particularly that it was being investigated, rather than treated as suicide.

But if Jack was wrong, then that family would be put under the microscope – with all the unwanted attention from police and media that came with it – without cause. Jack knew all too well the pressure that could put on a person, infecting their social life, work or school and so on. He sighed. He needed to get to Maddox to strengthen his case. He also needed to establish, beyond his existing suspicions, how the material was being smuggled into South Australia. His most recent email to the chief had asked her to use all the influence she had to establish whether there were any question marks over MultiplyMed's importation of human material. He trusted her to see that this information was vital and, as urgently as she awaited his news of real evidence, he awaited her call. He checked his watch again as he angled back, away from the shoreline towards the beach house.

As he arrived at the small sand dunes in front of his place, he was surprised to see Jem Maddox perched on his verandah. He hadn't notice her until this moment, blended as she was, small and still, into the neutral paint colour and backdrop of the house.

'Hello. You're here!' he said, wishing it were otherwise. Jem was a complication he didn't need. He could imagine Kate whispering to her, 'Watch out, you're his type.' He had no idea what his type was, though. The authentic romances in his life had been with wildly different women, although all of them had been particularly strong emotionally. Jem was beautiful, and he could imagine how striking she had been as a much younger woman. He couldn't imagine any man taking his gaze off her if she walked into a room. Despite having three children, she cut a neat, trim figure with slim legs that looked great in the carefree jeans and sneakers she wore beneath a loose-cut T-shirt that couldn't hide the swell of her breasts. Her skin was not freckled or wrinkled from childhood summers at the beach, like many others he'd seen, and her gaze, sliding quickly towards him, was as alluring as it appeared guilty. *Oh dear, here's trouble.*

'Hi.' She lifted herself off the porch and he watched her nervously push back strands of hair that had come free from a loose knot held with a clawed clip.

He knew he wasn't imagining her discomfort when she couldn't hold his gaze, looking away. Yes, she too was contemplating forbidden territory. Jack felt her painful indecision.

She shifted awkwardly in the sand. 'You must be wondering what I'm doing here.'

Her hesitancy at what he presumed was an attempt at seduction only made her more attractive. He needed to make this easier for her by giving her a way out. 'You have a house on this stretch, you said. Presumably you're having a break?'

She cut him a brief grin. 'Sort of.'

Jack could almost hear her scrambled mind telling her to run for it. He clung to the hope that if she was here, maybe her husband was too. He needed to create a distraction. 'Er, Jem, it's busy and warm out here. Would you care to come in?' he said brightly. 'I can do you a decent Italian coffee with my very reliable caffettiera,' he offered, knowing how comical that sounded. It was deliberately done and he hoped it would ease the conversation and, at the same time, her discomfort. Jack gestured screwing a lid on something and it won the smile he was after.

'Please don't tell me you carry one around. I can't see this beach shack providing one.'

'It doesn't,' he assured her. 'French press is the best it offers so, yes, I do carry a small caffettiera around with me when I'm travelling.' He slid back the big glass door. 'Have I told you that I'm a vigorous coffee snob?'

'Aren't we all just a bit pretentious about our coffee these days? Thank you. I could use one.' She looked self-conscious but followed him in out of the warmth. 'Storm's coming,' she said.

'How can you tell?' *Just keep the conversation light, Jack.*

Jem shrugged. 'I've been coming here since I was little.' She pointed up the beach, away from the port. 'My grandparents had a shack that my parents modernised and now I – well, we – own it. We've fully renovated, mainly because Mark insisted, and now it's far more glam than in previous generations.'

'I imagine your grandparents thought your parents were over-doing it,' Jack said.

'No, I think they liked what my parents did – just simple mod cons – but now . . . they'd see it as unnecessary embellishment to what was always a simple fishing shack. It's where Grandad would come to spend his day on the water, and us kids would play in the sand under Grandma's watchful eye.' She shrugged. 'It's not as though Mark particularly enjoys it here. He prefers an over-water bungalow in Bora Bora, to tell the truth. And I preferred how it was during my childhood. Mark makes us clean off the sand outside – it's such a drag. As kids we used to come hurtling in, pausing only briefly to dust off whatever we could, but Mum never made a fuss. She'd just sweep up each evening. The furni-ture was old and kicked around, we had no TV, just a radio and, well, we had the best times. Now the kids won't come unless they have their PlayStations or Xboxes and all that stuff. It sort of loses the point of being here. I want them to run wild like I did. And Mark's as needy as they are.'

Jack nodded, smiling at her memory but hoping to move her away from the subject of her husband. 'Were you waiting for me long?'

'No, not at all,' she replied quickly. 'I was just passing by,' she began and he sensed her fabricating a plausible story. 'I didn't know if you'd booked. I'm sure Maria is extremely happy the house is going to be occupied in the days after a long weekend.'

'It's terrific. Thanks for suggesting it.'

'It looked deserted and I wasn't going to wait at all, but then I saw you strolling back down the beach lost in your thoughts, your shirt undone and flapping around you.'

He let it slide that she had clearly waited for him and that she had probably come to Wallaroo looking for him . . . and especially that she was on the verge of something they should not pursue. It would do neither of them any good to press that button. He moved to the sink and began to run the water into his little coffee boiler. 'These cars are a shock,' he said, nodding towards the vehicles on the beach.

'Oh, it won't be long now.' Jem chuckled. 'As the sun starts to go down, they'll vanish. *Pfft!*' she said. 'Just like that and the whole beach will be yours.'

'Promise?'

'Well, yours and mine anyway,' she said, again not meeting his gaze.

He let that opening pass too. 'You were right about how lovely it is here. You're fortunate to be able to come here whenever you wish.'

She nodded but didn't reply as Jack got busy spooning in coffee, screwing the contraption together and reaching for milk from the fridge to heat.

Jack tried again. 'Did you bring the whole family?'

'Er, no. School tomorrow.' She shrugged. 'My parents offered to look after them.'

He smiled. 'Great. Just the two of you then.' He turned away to prepare the coffee, anticipating with dread that she'd come alone.

'Actually, just me this time.'

'Oh, right,' he said, not turning back. 'He'll join you, no doubt,' he said with hope.

'Yes, perhaps . . . depends.' She didn't say why and he didn't ask.

Jack put the coffee pot on the stove and saucepan of milk alongside, turning with a flourish. 'Biscuit?'

'No, thanks.'

'Well, maybe we will have these on the verandah. I'll be out shortly.' That wasn't subtle, but he needed to think.

She dutifully turned and did as he suggested.

Jack, Jack, Jack! He heard Kate's voice first, sounding disappointed, then his chief's with an I-told-you-so tone, and finally his own, full of regret. *Be careful*, the trio warned. He shook his head. Jem turning up could be helpful, especially if her husband followed . . . but dangerous all the same.

The milk began to tremble on the stove and he switched it off; the coffee pot began to bubble and sputter soon after. He took out two rather chunky mugs from the cupboard and was pleased sugar sticks were provided. He poured coffee into each, followed by hot milk. Jack carried out the steaming mugs and sugar on a small tray he'd discovered tucked away with chopping boards.

'Wow, Jack, how domestic you are.'

He could hear Jem had found her composure over the last minute or so. 'Living alone, I need to be. I'm sorry about the workman-style mugs. Half a stick of sugar – I remembered.'

She smiled and he deliberately didn't hold her gaze long, pretending to sigh instead and look towards the sea. He sipped his coffee as he heard her stirring hers.

'Mmm, lovely. Thank you,' she said. 'Just what I needed.'

'You're welcome,' he replied.

'Jack?' Her tone forced him to turn to her. He could see in her apologetic expression that she was feeling the pull too. 'I think I'm making you feel awkward?'

'Why do you say that?'

'Because we're both struggling to look at each other and I guess I could call myself perceptive.'

'You should have become a psychologist,' he quipped.

'You're avoiding my question.'

No point in pretending. 'I'm being cautious, Jem. You're not concerned about people seeing you here?'

'What, these people?' she asked, sweeping an arm out and shaking her head. 'No one's local here. These are daytrippers, if I can call them that – just here for the break. The locals might come down a bit later.' Jem sipped her coffee. 'Besides, I'm not doing anything wrong, am I?' She looked at him as though needing assurance.

'No, but these situations are always open to being interpreted the wrong way.'

'Meaning?'

There was a slight plea she couldn't hide in her tone, and he could tell that she needed him to say it, to help her walk away from what she knew she should never have walked towards. 'Jem,' he began in a patient tone.

She put her coffee mug back on the tray. 'I'm sorry, I shouldn't have come.' She stood, made to leave and he resisted catching her arm, instead stepping onto the sand slightly in her way.

'Come inside a moment,' he said softly.

'Why?'

'Because if anyone's watching, it looks more natural than us beginning any sort of difficult conversation in the open.' He shrugged, forcing a smile. 'People can read body language, so smile back at me and pick up your mug and let's just go back inside a moment.'

She didn't argue. Back in the kitchen area, he leaned against the back counter, well out of sight, which encouraged her to step away from the doors and any penetrating gazes. 'What's happened?' he asked.

It came out in a rush and he didn't interrupt, just let it rage, listening to all that had gone wrong for Jem since he'd last shared a coffee with her.

'An affair. Okay. And do you trust this Alex guy?'

'I have no reason not to.' She shrugged. 'Plus, he's as much a victim as I am in this situation.'

'You have no proof, right?'

Jem shook her head. 'But what Alex was saying made so much sense. I just wanted to escape. I had to get away from Mark. This is not something I would ever be prepared to forgive.'

'If it's true,' Jack qualified. 'Petras . . . Where does that name originate from?'

'Oh, I don't know,' she said, giving a soft groan of helplessness. 'Eastern Europe somewhere. One of those countries that if you asked me to pinpoint on a world map I couldn't,' she said, smiling sadly. 'I think he said Lithuania.'

Now she had his attention. 'And is this Alex Petras involved in reproductive medicine as well?'

Jem shook her head, frowning at him. 'No. Far from it. He's in transport.'

'What sort of transport?' Jack tried to keep his voice calm but all of his senses were on high alert.

'Trucking,' she said. 'Actually, he told me that more recently he's been getting involved in aquaculture.' She gave a mirthless laugh. 'Seahorses are in high demand, apparently.'

Jack blinked. 'Where?'

'Where what?'

'Where does he farm seahorses?'

'Here somewhere. In this region – Eyre Peninsula, Yorke Peninsula, I'm not certain. I really wasn't that interested. I was too busy worrying about his two-faced, bitch wife banging my husband—'

Jack interrupted her. 'You know this?'

She eyed him, puzzled. 'I don't have proof of his infidelity but—'

'I mean, do you have proof that Petras has shipping interests in this region?'

Jem frowned. 'No, he's cultivating some exotic sea creatures, so it's probably more like nurseries, I would think. Why on earth are you so interested in Alex?'

'I'm just trying to get the measure of the man,' Jack said quickly, but it sat halfway between convincing and lame. He wasn't sure which way Jem might lean but she was mercifully distracted by what he said next. 'After all, what he's suggesting might implode your relationship.'

Jem pushed away from the wall where she'd been standing and paced, angrily. 'Not might, *will* implode it if it's true. Infidelity is one crack I won't mend. These last two years have been so strange. Mark has been increasingly distant and I've been pretending, convincing myself that it's just a phase, that he's busy, that the children are demanding more and more time. But that's head-in-the-sand stuff. I must face it. I told you I didn't even know he worked at that place where you and I met – that's telling, right?' She didn't wait for his reply. 'There's other stuff too,' she said, tapping a nail against her mug and then putting the mug down in a show of frustration. 'He's become secretive. He's never been like that. So now I can't help but believe he's lying to me.'

'Why do you think that?' Jack hoped she wouldn't simply claim a wife's intuition; that wouldn't help him.

She described Mark's lie about the delivery of the baby that never happened. 'And before you ask, no, Mark doesn't make mistakes. His mind is like a vault. He deliberately lied. He confidently gave me the name of the mother and the hospital; it was so convincing.' She sighed, shook her head as if embarrassed. 'He presumed it wouldn't cross my mind to check.'

'So you think he was with—'

'That bitch, yes!' At his blink, she gave a bitter laugh. 'Sorry, but that's how I feel. She sat at my table only a week ago, smiling, schmoozing with me in that European accent of hers, and all the while she was probably planning when next to sleep with my husband. She came up and air-kissed me at school drop-off yesterday. Whore!'

Jack wasn't going to engage. 'You have no proof,' he repeated. 'Give him some quarter. Don't destroy your trust and marriage over someone else's suspicion.'

'No, Jack. It's too late. There are other things. The other day a friend said she saw Mark having coffee with a woman. When I called him he claimed he was at his clinic, but I could hear traffic, voices. He was quick to make me feel awkward about asking, saying he was seeing a patient to her car. I didn't believe him then, but I had no reason to mistrust him so I let it go. He was probably with Alannah the Lithuanian slut.'

Jack was sipping his cooling coffee in that second and he spluttered. She really was helplessly amusing in her anger.

'This isn't funny, Jack.'

He coughed, putting his coffee down. 'It's not, I agree.' His shirt was now stained with the explosive mouthful of coffee he hadn't managed to keep contained and he looked at the mess with regret.

She saw his glance. 'I'd get that into some cold water if I were you. In fact, the best thing for coffee is this,' she said, moving towards the sink and reaching for the dishwashing liquid. 'And some white vinegar, if we can find it. I've got some up at the house if you don't have it here.'

'I think I spotted some old apple cider vinegar,' Jack replied, beginning to rummage through a cupboard. 'Someone probably left it for the next guest.'

'That'll do. Here, get your shirt off first, and then look for it. The sooner we get this into water, the better.' As he hesitated, she looked back at him with exasperation. 'Hurry up.'

He tried not to appear overly self-conscious as he undid the two buttons that held his shirt on and slipped it off, immediately looking away and busying himself finding the vinegar. He handed the bottle to Jem, who had already plunged his shirt into the now slightly soapy cold water. 'That should do it,' she said, tipping two scant lids of vinegar into the water. The pungent smell of the fermented apples filled their immediate space and it was an excuse for him to step back.

'Now we wait,' she said and turned back to him.

Jack pointed his thumb over his shoulder in the direction of the bathroom. 'I'll just go and—'

'No, don't,' Jem said, placing a hand on his chest. Her fingers were still damp, cold against his warm skin.

Jack covered her hand with his. 'Jem,' he began in a cautionary tone. 'You'll re—'

'I won't. You don't know how angry I am, Jack. If you're in the mood, then I want this, to remind myself that I'm in charge of my life.'

23

Jack released Jem's hand to smooth a wayward strand of her honey-coloured hair as they stood in the kitchen. He nodded. 'I'm not going to be your revenge, or the source of despair later.' As she began to protest, he continued. 'No, listen to me. You have children, you have a family life you love, and you've got a husband – you don't know if he is having an affair, you simply suspect it on the word of another. And you can't necessarily trust that other person's opinion. Surely you'd rather trust Mark?'

Jem stared at him, uncomprehending for a moment. 'I hate you for making me feel responsible.'

He shrugged. 'You'll love me down the track for being your conscience.'

'And there was I thinking every man's a bastard, or a liar. But you're different.' She hugged him and it felt friendly rather than erotic. Jem turned her cheek against the expanse of his chest.

He was still yet to hug her back, feeling unsure about what he could do with his arms that would signal empathy but not encouragement.

'Mmm, not only are you not a liar but you smell damn good, Jack Hawksworth,' she murmured.

It was too much. Jack's healthy libido began to answer Jem's need as she pressed closer against his bare skin; now his body was calling on that desire to be answered. Adding to his discomfort was his knowledge that he was lying to her face, even though she suddenly trusted him more than the next closest man in her life.

'Jem, come and sit down.'

'You're not going to lecture me, are you? It's bad enough that you're behaving holier than thou. Here's a woman offering herself to you and you're saying let's talk. It's not doing my self-esteem any good at all.' Now her voice cracked.

He guided her to the worn leather sofa. It wasn't very comfy but he'd long ago accepted that holiday home owners tended to put in cheap furniture or that which had seen better days in their families. 'Just give me a sec,' he said. He raced into the bedroom and grabbed a thin blue windcheater, pulling it over his head as he returned.

'Spoilsport,' she groaned, her tone dark.

'You'll be calling me something else in a minute.'

She frowned. 'What do you mean?'

'I haven't been truthful with you and I think I should be.'

Her frown deepened. 'You're married,' she said, sounding careless. 'So what? So am I.'

'No, I'm single. I've never been married,' he asserted, adding, 'Nor am I involved with anyone at present.'

Her gaze narrowed, and she looked pained. 'Gay?'

He shook his head.

She shrugged. 'Then I don't get it.'

'I'm with the police.'

Jem Maddox blinked slowly, processing what she'd just heard. 'Police?' she repeated.

'A detective,' he said, unable to hide how bad he felt. He had no intention of letting Jem know just how senior he was.

'What?' She shook her head, confounded. 'Why? I mean, what's that got to do with me?'

'Absolutely nothing. If you hadn't come to visit, you'd be none the wiser and I wouldn't feel obliged to explain myself.'

He watched her breathe out, impressed by her composure. She'd felt comfortable enough to bare her soul to him, offer her body too, only to discover the man she trusted had been lying since she met him. He'd be fuming in her position.

'Why are you telling me this?'

'Because it's not in my DNA to comfortably lie, and it's not permitted in my job either. Can I add that I don't enjoy having to use guile with anyone, especially someone I like?'

'So why the secrecy? The pretence at being a journalist?'

Here it comes, Jack thought. 'I'm working on a case that began in London but has led me here.'

Her wrath was surely just a heartbeat or two away now. Jem's face contorted into puzzlement. 'So you're what, working under-cover? Is that the right term?'

'Not exactly. I'm from the Metropolitan Police Force in England, yes. I'm taking a holiday to see my sister in Sydney but I'm also following some leads from London that have brought me down under.' He tried to make it sound simple.

Nothing simple about it at all, Jack, he could hear Kate say. Suddenly she'd become his inner voice. *And by the way, she's not going to let you stay vague for much longer. When they sense a man being evasive, women need to know even more badly. So be direct.*

His conscience prodded, he came clean. 'I'm with Scotland Yard.'

'You're joking.' Jem's expression changed to wonder. 'So what is a Scotland Yard detective doing in my life?'

And there it is, Jack, Kate spoke again in his mind. *No more wriggle room, just some squirming away from yet another heart you've captured, even without trying.*

There was no easy way to say this and if he was going to be honest, as he wanted to be, then he might as well be blunt. 'I'm here following information that points to MultiplyMed. It's how I came to be at that clinic.'

Jem's expression compressed in concern as she tried to take in what he'd said. 'Following information that points to Mark, do you mean?' Her voice was small, her tone stretched.

'No,' Jack answered truthfully, but qualified his doubt. 'Not necessarily your husband. He was a starting point for me because he's so well known in fertility in this state, *and* he works at MultiplyMed.'

He watched Jem sigh in controlled shock. 'What's this all about?'

'I'm afraid I'm not at liberty to—'

'Don't you dare,' she warned him.

Jack lifted a shoulder in a regretful gesture. 'Jem, I'm not being deliberately obtuse. I'm not permitted to discuss a case.'

'No? You lied to my face over coffee the other day, coming over all chivalrous and . . .' She struggled to find the right words. 'Frankly, fabulous. You made me feel better about Mark, about myself and now—'

'Wait, Jem. Take a breath. You sent me here. And then you came to Wallaroo of your own volition, with your own agenda. I haven't contacted you since you sent me the information for the booking. Look, I'm not trying to humiliate you, but you came to this beach house to find me. I did not wish to involve you, or deliberately encourage you.'

Her lips thinned, a sure sign of suppressed rage. 'Look me in the eye and tell me you didn't strike up a conversation with me outside his clinic specifically to get to my husband.'

'I took an opportunity, yes. That doesn't mean I was insincere in what I said to you, and it also doesn't mean I believe your husband is a criminal.'

'Well, what the hell does it mean?'

He hushed her gently. 'It means I want to rule him out.'

'And me?'

He knew what she meant by that question and it wasn't whether he thought she was involved. Jack shook his head. 'I wish I could know you better, but that's not wise. I could easily have taken advantage of your vulnerability – if I was the bastard you now think I am, I would have pressed my advantage a few minutes ago. You're incredibly attractive, but I'm not a predator, Jem, or a home wrecker. I'm here purely in my capacity as a policeman.'

She let out a breath, looking down. 'All right. I can respect that. But what exactly is the crime you're looking into? It's not fair to keep me in the dark . . . and maybe I can help, point you in the right direction.'

'It's connected with the illegal trafficking of human reproductive material. That's all I can say, and that's already too much.' He didn't think he could make her much angrier, so why not press his point. 'You said Mark became upset and distant at the mention of the MultiplyMed courier's death.'

Jem crossed her arms. 'I did. But he could simply be upset that someone he knew committed suicide.'

She was defending him. Jack nodded. 'Yes, that's possible. Or, perhaps he was upset that someone he knew died as a result of crime.'

She didn't respond to that but her jaw was working hard, grinding with what he took to be a mix of anger and fear. The second death would be reported soon in the media, so he took a chance. 'The thing is, Jem, someone else from MultiplyMed has turned up dead.'

'What?' Her voice now had a squeak.

He nodded unhappily. 'Another tragic accident, apparently.'

'What do you mean, *apparently*?'

'It's all a bit too convenient to trust. There are suspicious circumstances, according to the coroner's findings. I can't say any more because, to be honest, I don't know much more.'

'Who was it this time?'

'Someone who works in the lab,' he said, keeping it vague.

She looked understandably distraught. 'And you're thinking,' she said, making a big leap that impressed him, 'that Mark's strange behaviour might be connected to all this bad stuff happening at one of the clinics he works at.'

'Is that a question?'

'It is.'

'Then yes. I do have to think like that.'

'And all this cover story, you writing a book, was simply to get to Mark?'

'To find the truth. Mark was never my goal – I'm not out to get him. He is simply one of the people I want to find out more from.'

'That's semantics, Jack. You've got Mark in your sights, haven't you?'

He shook his head, feeling relieved that he could be honest. 'I hoped he'd be a source of information, that's all.'

'Why not just question him formally?'

'I'm here by the grace of the Australian Federal Police. The South Australian police are being very helpful but I have no authority here; I am just collecting information and that's the truth. More importantly, Jem, if you're feeling unnerved right now, can you imagine what it would do to your family and your relationship if your husband was marched off to have a formal chat with police? How do you reckon you'd go with all the nosy school parents, your neighbours, the media, his colleagues? It's the last thing I or any other detective would want to do to someone. I thought if I could chat to him informally, I could learn more about MultiplyMed. That's all I was aiming for.'

It sounded convincing and Jack didn't allow himself to test how strictly true his words were. In his heart he felt that someone of Maddox's calibre – and probably Maddox himself – was involved. It was just as likely to be him as any of the other senior clinicians, but Jack kept his counsel.

Jem's expression fell from angry to despondent. She sighed. 'I'm sorry. This is a shock.'

'I completely understand, but I could use your help to—'

Jem's complexion blanched and she froze. 'Shit!'

Jack turned to see what she was reacting to. Mark was walking across the sand in front of the house, framed by the sliding doors.

'Good. He's here and no doubt looking for you to repair things,' Jack said. 'Be calm.'

'Calm? I was just about to climb into bed with you!'

'I see no evidence of that. You were out walking and saw me dozing on the deck. I invited you for coffee. That's all you've done, Jem. Now step out and greet your husband – use all that surprise. It's authentic.'

'But, Jack—'

'There's nothing to feel worried about,' he assured her, ushering her towards the door. 'Call him.' He stood up and reached for his mug that fortunately still had some dregs in it.

Jem ducked out onto the verandah. 'Mark!'

Her husband turned, surprised, then lifted a hand in acknowledgement.

She looked back at Jack but he was not watching her. Instead, he smiled at Maddox in a neighbourly way and lifted his hand too, emerging onto the deck right behind Jem.

'Jack,' she murmured, just for his hearing. She sounded fretful. 'What about—?'

'Hi there,' Jack said over the top of her doubt, preventing her from asking anything more. 'This one caught me dozing on the deck.' He grinned, knowing the doctor had recognised him instantly; not even a nanosecond of trouble recalling or placing him. Jem was right. Her husband had a sharp mind.

Mark strolled up, his expression at ease, left hand casually in his pocket, although his right hand, clenched into a half fist, said otherwise. Jack knew he'd have to tread with great care now. Whatever tension there was between these two, he didn't wish to get trapped in it, but he had to use the situation to his advantage.

'Do you two know each other?' Mark asked, a smile of query stretching across his mouth.

'We do now,' Jem said and Jack felt relief zip through him like a drug. Her tone was pitch perfect; effortless and comfortable. He wondered how difficult it was to maintain her facade. 'I thought I recognised this guy,' she said, flicking a glance Jack's way. 'But it took a while to work out that we'd seen each other in your clinic's waiting room.'

Jack stepped off the deck to shake Maddox's hand, deliberately tipping the remains of the coffee from his mug into the sand. He hoped it would signal the innocence of Jem's presence. 'Before you imagine this journo is stalking you, I have to admit that this is one hell of a coincidence.'

Mark gave an obliging gust of amused disbelief.

'He was reading on the deck when I walked by,' Jem added.

Mark looked nonplussed. 'So, are you staying long at Wallaroo?'

'Just a few days,' Jack replied companionably. 'My sister organised the rental of this place as a surprise,' he lied. 'She knew I needed some quiet time.' He hoped that Jem would quickly contact her friend Maria and stop any leakage of the truth.

'And I barge in, saying, "Hey, aren't you that guy chasing my husband?"' Jem shrugged. 'Anyway, sorry again for the interruption and thanks for the coffee,' she said, nodding at Jack's empty mug, now casually dangling in his hand.

'You're most welcome.'

'Should I feel obliged to do that interview now?' Maddox asked in a droll voice.

Jack grinned. 'I mean, if you can. Half an hour tops.'

'Who do you work for again?'

'Well, I work for myself,' Jack said, returning to the original lie. 'But the feature is to be syndicated through a variety of publications. Essentially it's a weekend magazine feature across England.' None of that really made sense and he could imagine an English journo snorting with laughter at how ridiculous he was, but it sounded credible in the moment. 'It will do your profile no harm at all, especially with that huge international fertility conference coming up next year.' He was glad he'd done his homework. 'The one in Switzerland.'

'Yes, I was toying with attending that. Take Jem, even, turn it into a European adventure.'

Jack nodded enthusiastically. 'Great idea. But after this feature, they'll be hunting you for a keynote or similar.' He hoped that would fire up the ego that Jem had mentioned.

'You should come up to the house,' she suggested, obviously deciding to help. 'Share a barbecue with us before you go.'

Jack looked at Mark, his expression open. This was actually going better than he could have hoped.

Maddox sighed. 'No, sorry. I'm only here for the afternoon. However, Jem, because I couldn't reach you, I wanted to let you know that I did intend to join you – I'll come back tomorrow – but I've also invited Alex and Alannah.'

Jem looked surprised. 'Really? Why?'

'Well, you told me our recent get-together was a bit of a flop, so I thought we'd try again. Apparently they want to take the cruiser out before winter sets in, so I suggested a trip up here. They leapt at it – you don't mind, do you? Anyway, look, I'm sure Mr Hawksworth doesn't need to share our domestic chatter.' Mark looked at Jack. 'But you might as well come up to the house while we're here if it's not going to take long?'

It was dismissive, but Jack reacted with gratitude. 'Brilliant. Honestly, thirty minutes, no more.' He looked at Jem. 'And thank *you* for saying hello. It got me my interview.' He made sure his gaze slipped off Jem quickly and returned to Mark with a smile.

'That's all right – glad to help,' Jem said in a breezy tone. 'He's a busy man, my husband, and even I have to queue up sometimes.' It was meant to be lighthearted but Jack knew she was having to work hard to sound so civil. He hoped she could maintain it.

'Jem will organise it. I presume you have Mr Hawksworth's number?'

'No,' she said with smiling puzzlement. 'I didn't even know his surname until this second,' she lied. 'And my mobile is dead,' she said. Another lie. Jack had seen it happily light up earlier. 'So you two had better sort that out.'

'Do you mind giving me your mobile number, please, Dr Maddox?' Jack asked, sure he did mind. 'It makes it much faster. I can text you.'

Jack noted Maddox didn't look pleased as he reluctantly recited his mobile number and Jack entered it into his phone. *Got you,* he thought. 'Thanks,' he said, already turning back to the house as Jem waved and fell in next to her husband. As they began the walk back up the beach, Jack was grateful that Jem, no matter how tempted she might have felt, didn't look back. But he noticed the distance between her and her husband as they made their way towards their home, just broad enough that it would have been awkward to hold hands, and it spoke of the crack that was now likely widening between them.

24

Jem hadn't lied. Thunder had begun grumbling in the distance around four and by four-thirty, Jack could see pillars of rain on the horizon, in line with the vast grain silos at Wallaroo Harbour. They were stacked side by side in an imposing block, softened by the curve of their design to store the grain. Jack followed the conveyor belt, painted spearmint green for some reason, that reached from the silos across the jetty out to where the grain ships were berthed, waiting to be filled. From talking to locals, he understood that in the past few years, something like half a million tonnes of cargo were loaded annually.

'It's an endless stream of trucks during harvest,' one of the fishermen said. 'The cockies from all around the region send in their grain.'

Jack had pondered this. As small as Wallaroo was, it was a busy enough port, which meant lots of comings and goings when a ship was in. It surely presented an ideal cover for bringing in the human reproductive material. Regular, too. That's how any trafficking flourished, he'd learned through his work; it needed a secure route, but most importantly, it needed volume. And volume could only be achieved through regular arrivals.

It made sense. A small town, quiet and friendly but used to tourists and strangers. Sailors from foreign ports could clear swiftly and easily, leaving their ship and heading into the town in search of fresh food, money conversion, beer – anything but the heave and roll of the waves.

But who was the Australian connection and how was the cold chain that kept the material safe and at the right temperature preserved? A ship was due in tomorrow. Perhaps he could find out more.

The thought of Jem had interrupted his musings, and he felt relieved that her desire to seduce him had not been fulfilled. He'd promised his chief he would avoid all such 'complications'. He'd spent the rest of the afternoon after Jem's departure researching the cold chain he'd learned was required for transferring human reproductive material across the globe. He rang his sister.

'What's up?' she asked after they exchanged hellos.

'Do you know anyone in reproductive medicine?'

'No, Jack. How random is that question?'

'Well, you never kn—'

'Oh wait, I do know someone. Margie Boyd, the receptionist here where I work, was on an IVF program, I'm sure of it . . . Would the name of her clinic be any good to you?'

'Yes. Could you ask her?'

'Okay, hang on. It's the oddest question, though.'

'Does she know what I do?'

'She doesn't even know you exist, Jack.'

'Good. Well, if she asks, let her think I'm a journo doing a feature story about reproductive medicine and then play dumb. You'd be good at that, wouldn't you?'

She laughed with him. 'I'll get you for that. Hang on.'

He waited several minutes until she came back on the line. 'It's called North Shore Fertility, apparently.'

He scribbled it down. 'Thanks. I'll call back soon.'

'In a hurry as always?'

'I promise. Bye, Amy.'

'Lots of love, loser.'

Ending the call, he looked up the number of the clinic and dialled again.

'Good afternoon, North Shore Fertility.'

'Hello, my name is Jack Hawk, and I'm an English journalist with *The Weekend Feature* in London.' Again, he could hear a collective sighing in his mind at the name he'd invented.

'Oh, right. Um, it's a public holiday so there aren't many of us here. But how can I help, Mr Hawk?'

He chose to ignore that. 'It's a curious one. I'm writing a spread about fertility worldwide, and I wondered if I could speak with one of your laboratory team on a technical query about the transport of material.'

She gave a chuckle. 'Well, that isn't a question I get every day, Mr Hawk. Let me see what we can do, and if there's anyone around who might help.' He heard the muffle of her covering the mouthpiece and the distant sounds of a short exchange. She came back. 'I'm going to put you through to our admin manager, if that's all right? She's the most senior person in today.'

'That's fine,' he said, inwardly sighing.

'Thanks, Mr Hawk. I'm a lab assistant so forgive me if I cut you off – I just happened to pick up the phone. Please ring back if we lose you.'

He waited through the clicks and then heard a new voice. 'Mr Hawk? This is Patricia Adams. I'm the administration manager for the clinic. I had to call in today to pick up something so I don't have long. Can you tell me more about your article, please?'

'Yes, of course. Thank you for helping,' he said and rolled into a monstrous lie that now included innocent Margie Boyd. 'Margie mentioned that the clinic was exceptional in its services, and so I thought I should include some comments. This story will go national, and might even be picked up internationally,' he lied, feeling he really should blush at his audacity.

'I see. That's impressive.'

'Oh, well, what you clinics do is impressive, and the number of people on the program is staggering, I've discovered. That's a lot of emotional baggage to manage.'

'It certainly is,' she said, sounding more open. 'And you have a technical query, I gather?'

'Yes. A couple actually, but one in particular that is quite a simple one, I hope. I can run it by you but I think one of your embryologists would be best placed to answer it. The thing is, Patricia, I'd like to include your clinic in the acknowledgements.'

'I understand. Let me think. Er, our lab manager, Dan Cornwell, is on holiday just now, but . . . er, yes, maybe his deputy, Peta, is around.'

'Wonderful. If you're happy to put me through to Peter, that would be terrific, thank you.'

'All right, let me see.'

More clicks, a longer pause this time, and then a woman's voice came on the line. 'This is Peta, Mr Hawk.'

Oh, Peter was actually Peta. 'Oh, hello, Peta. Thanks for taking the time to speak with me. Did Ms Adams explain?'

'She did. Ask away, I'll see what I can do.'

Over the next few minutes he learned plenty, but especially that the containers – dewars – were never tampered with from point A to point B.

'We fill the dewar here at the clinic, which is point A,' Peta explained. 'If they're eggs, for example, the material is collected in our theatre and then transferred into tiny straws, put into cold storage in liquid nitrogen and then, if they're being shipped, put into dewars – also filled with liquid nitrogen, sealed, tagged, and off they go.'

'How long can the cold chain be maintained?' Jack asked.

'Ah, I see you know the lingo. Good. Well, the cold chain can't be interrupted, which is why those dewars are sealed and tagged. Untampered, they could probably, at a push, keep material at the right temperature for two weeks. Maybe even longer, not that we would want to push that far. We never risk compromising the material, so we wouldn't want to use the dewar as the main storage for much more than ten to twelve days.'

'And that's enough to get them where they need to go?'

'Oh, yes. These dewars are generally moved around the world by professional couriers within forty-eight hours on reliable flights, but there's room in there for all sorts of delays.'

'Never moved by ship?'

She gave a sneering gasp that he forgave her for; she couldn't possibly know what he was digging around in, and that meant his question did sound dumb. 'No. Absolutely not. Across the seas is far too long and complex.'

'But it *could* last a voyage?'

'Yes, if required, but it would never come to that. This material is hard won and precious. If we need to move it, we take the fastest, most reliable route, and we use the best and most profes-sional couriers to cross the globe. We have to.'

'Right, understood. And those dewars could be re-charged with liquid nitrogen if necessary?'

'Could be? Yes. They never would need to be though, and I would be horrified to discover any dewar I seal, tag and sign off for transport had been tampered with.'

'What if they *were* tampered with?'

'Pardon?'

Jack laughed. 'You know, Peta, every journalist I know is a frustrated novelist in the making. And I'm thinking this could make a really good crime novel.'

He was reassured by the smile in her voice when she replied. 'Ah, I see. Well, yes, of course it *could* be tampered with. Let's say the crims wanted to add a few extra straws—'

'Or take some out?'

'No, that wouldn't work, Jack, because everything's checked and cross-checked. Each straw is recorded with a unique number and we know exactly what's in each straw – right down to each egg, for example, and they're traceable back to a donor.'

'Wow,' he murmured, genuinely impressed. 'Okay, so no removal but you're saying more could be added?'

'Well, yes. You could add some, so long as you had someone at the other end who was willing to look away. They would see them immediately, know there were extra straws without the proper paperwork.'

'Got it,' Jack said, and it felt like clouds parting in his mind, allowing sunlight through. 'Peta, you've been fabulously helpful. I think I shall have to include you in the acknowledgements of my novel if I ever write it.'

'I hope you do. But in the meantime, good luck with the article. I'd rather not be quoted in the article on the illegal stuff, though.'

He chuckled. 'I promise. That was purely for my interest.'

Jack was reassured, as he put the mobile down and closed his laptop, that bringing the material in by ship from somewhere like Singapore was easy enough. And he was now convinced he knew how the syndicate was working, certainly in this part of the world.

It was time to share his hunch with London and get the SA police briefed. But before he called his boss, he made a final phone call, this time to Matt.

★

Mark had left almost as soon as he and Jem had got back to their house.

Jem sighed. 'You're not staying then?'

'No, I told you I had to get back.'

'I think if you want to save our marriage, you should consider your next step carefully.'

'Jem, how did it go from a simple spat yesterday to our marriage being in tatters today? It doesn't make sense, or am I just not being sensitive enough?' When he said the word 'sensitive', he made air quotes with his fingers to annoy her.

How dare he do that. She half-expected him to ask if she was having her period; then she really would lose it and toss him out. She took a low breath to force herself to calm down. 'You're probably going to tell me that Al and I are wrong?'

She watched his face blanch, all the colour emptying swiftly beneath the collar of his shirt. His Adam's apple bobbed as he swallowed. She felt a vague concern he may need to sit down.

'Mark?'

He seemed to shake off whatever had shocked him. Even so, he sounded nervous as he asked, 'What has Al got to do with this?'

She shook her head. She might as well be honest. 'Well, he's like me, suspicious of your behaviour. We've both noticed something's wrong.'

Mark blinked rapidly, looking as though he was trying to make sense of what she'd just said. 'You and Alex Petras have been talking about me?'

'Talking about you and his wife, yes!' Jem felt mild pain and looked down to see Mark's fingers gripping her slim arm.

'And what are you both concluding?'

Jem shook him off. 'Don't do that, Mark. Don't hurt me, and please don't act the victim in this. You're the one behaving oddly. You're the one having an affair.'

He stood back and straightened, raising his face to the ceiling and inhaling through his nose. His eyes were closed, as though asking the heavens for strength and patience. 'Jem, what will it take for me to convince you, prove to you, that I have never been unfaithful to you?'

She hadn't expected this. She'd anticipated another row, and then the admission and probably him leaving, slamming a door on her and their marriage. But not this. He sounded earnest, almost shocked that she was levelling the accusation. 'You're denying it?'

'Hotly. I'm not even going to bother telling you to prove it, because there's no proof to find.' His tone softened. 'Fuck! Jem! Why would I want anyone else than the mother of my children? We chose each other long ago. We made promises. We've come through the hard years and can enjoy life, and *now* you're wondering about my fidelity? You know I'm not going to share this with anyone but you.'

It was her turn to swallow. 'Why have you been behaving so oddly, then? You've been acting edgy for ages. I've been trying to work it out, figure out when things changed. And now I think about it, you haven't been the Mark I thought I was living with for more than a year. Something happened over Anzac weekend, do you recall? In Turkey, when we went to see the beach at Gallipoli where your grandfather died. I put your odd behaviour, which seemed to begin when we flew into Eastern Europe, down to you feeling melancholy. But you have been behaving weirdly since then.'

'Define weird, Jem,' he said, shaking his head.

'Distant. Snappy. Impatient. Talking in your dreams. Not sleeping well. Elusive. Secretive. Do you want me to go on?'

He looked down and sighed. 'No.'

'Mark, talk to me.'

'It's work,' he said, shutting her down. 'I have no other excuse, and no other secrets.' He made no eye contact as he said this, instead sweeping a hand through his hair. 'Anyway, look, I want you to know I'm not betraying you. All right? Everything I do is for us, our family. I'll come back tomorrow. And I do want to have that barbecue with Alex and Alannah. Is that a problem?' As she began to object, he continued. 'I think it's important. Let's lay that beast to rest. Let's all be friends. I have never slept with Alannah Petras – please believe me – and I have no intention of ever being with another woman but you.'

She felt trapped. There was a lie here, she knew it, but he was walking her around it. 'I don't want house guests,' she said neutrally.

'No, that's fine. I told you, they're bringing their cruiser. They can anchor out there and join us for a meal.'

'Mark, this feels so odd, hot on the heels of what's been going on.'

'It's not. It's better to confront it – be honest, repair any damage. Whatever Alex's worries are about his wife's fidelity, you don't have to consider me in that equation. I swear on our children's lives.'

Jem swallowed. Why couldn't she trust him? She shifted topics to buy some time to think. 'Look, I hope you don't mind me inviting the journalist to dinner so you can do your interview?'

Mark shrugged. 'I don't really care for a stranger stepping into our private domain, but the interview will only take half an hour and it'll get him off my back. Besides, it sounds like it can't hurt my international profile.'

No, and I trust him more than you right now, she felt like saying, remembering his lie about the mother in labour at Ashford Hospital. That point she'd keep up her sleeve for now. She shrugged. 'Look, you'll have other people around, so that puts pressure on him to keep it short and sweet. I just wish it wasn't her!'

'Jem,' Mark began again with exasperation.

She held up her palms in surrender. 'Okay, okay, but you need to show me it's true, Mark. I'm only suspicious because you've acted so oddly.' She rubbed her arm to make her point. 'Give me old Mark back, and I'll have nothing to complain about.'

He nodded. 'All right. I'm sorry for making you feel uncertain.'

'Sorry isn't enough. Actions speak louder, right?'

He gave her a look of reproach but he clearly still hadn't grasped how much he had hurt her. It was time for Mark to do some of the heavy lifting in their marriage. She was not ready to forgive and sweep it all away into some dark corner, could still feel his fingers squeezing her arm. What had that been about? He'd never touched her in any way other than in affection, but that grip had had something else driving it. Fear, perhaps? Jem wanted to trust him, but Jack and his interest in Mark was still at the back of her mind. Could her suspicions and his be linked? She needed to find out and feel one hundred percent sure about her husband's activities.

'Okay, I'm going now,' he said.

She shrugged. 'See you tomorrow.'

'So I'll confirm with them?'

'Whatever you want. I'll get some food in, but I'm not putting on a show, Mark. I did that for them last time and look what happened.'

'Snags on the barbecue is fine.'

'Good. All right. You'd better go, there's weather coming in.'

He hesitated as though he wanted to kiss her goodbye, but the cast of her face was probably not encouraging and he simply nodded and left. She watched him get into his car, reverse out into the narrow road and then he was gone.

Now she stood at the large picture windows that faced the deck over the beach, watching the storm she'd promised roar in. The few hardy beachcombers who hadn't yet left were soon scampering for their vehicles and the beach became the sole domain of the seagulls now hunkering down. The rain was determined in its trajectory to the land; driven and angry, it splattered in a heavy, addictive percussion that defied anyone to look away. While the rain drummed on her tin roof and the timber boards of her deck, Jem's thoughts wandered down the beach to where a man in a blue windcheater was probably mesmerised by the same scene. He had knowledge. He had suspicions. And she wanted to share both.

When the rain stopped she intended to act on her desire, and she hoped with all her heart that it was simply to find out what he knew.

25

After his phone call to Matt, Jack had sent off a quick email to brief Chief Superintendent Rowland, suggesting the notion of a formal joint op had firmed up. Matt was going to advise who they might bring in from the Organised Crime Division. Jack signed off with a note that he'd call her tomorrow.

He stared out across the bay. The tide had come right up and he only noticed it because it had been so far out this morning that people had been wading in the shallows about a kilometre from his door. Right now, the shoreline was barely fifty metres away. Disgruntled seagulls were shaking themselves off as the sunset turned the skyline into a fiery cauldron that he found hard to tear his gaze from. It changed by the moment. Clouds that had looked like grey battleships sailing on an upside-down sea turned purple as the fireball sun kissed the horizon and farewelled him with one final scorching ray of neon. He marvelled at the heavy and billowy shapes, like a Renaissance master at work using his paints to promote transcendence. Wallaroo Beach was surely the domain of the gods as sunset darkened the skies. And below, the now calm sea was striated with dark lines stretching across a blazing surface, reflecting all the colour above and shimmering as evening twilight shifted to dusk.

It came as no surprise to him to see a lone figure approaching. He'd hoped she wouldn't come, but somehow this felt inevitable.

'Hi, Jem,' he said, standing in the narrow opening he'd left at the sliding door.

'Jack.'

He pushed the door wider. 'Are you all right?'

She shrugged. 'I have questions.'

'Can I get you a drink? I have a pinot gris in the fridge.'

'Sure, thanks.' She smiled.

As he returned quickly with two glasses, she nodded towards the sunset. 'Did you enjoy the show?'

'I did, including the fireworks. The lightning strikes at the horizon were fabulous.' He paused. 'And how did you go?'

Jem shook her head. 'He wants to make amends.'

'Good.'

'But he's lying, Jack. I know he is. I no longer think it's about an affair, but he's not telling me the truth. There are so many ways to betray someone, aren't there?'

Jack nodded. 'When did you notice him changing?'

She told him about Gallipoli. 'You know, I only brought that into focus today,' she said with wonder, 'but I know now it was on that trip when the rot started.'

'Did you notice anything else at the time?'

She stuck out her bottom lip slightly in thought. 'I suppose that he was rather extravagant on that trip.'

'Meaning?'

'Mark is not one to deny us anything, but I felt he was being a bit flashy. I don't need a lot of stuff. I've got a good life and plenty in it, material and otherwise, but Mark was talking about investing in real estate on the Dalmatian Coast, maybe buying a cruiser. He even said we should invest in some diamonds, maybe go to Amsterdam or Antwerp and buy some stones. "So portable," he said. But that's not us . . . certainly not me. I can't deny we live in a big house in a fine street, and we have all the trappings of success. But I'm content – I don't need anything else. Mark wanted more, though. So much more. He was talking excitedly . . . big plans, you know?'

'You said you went on to Eastern Europe?'

Jem sipped. 'Mmm, yes, we did.'

'Where?'

'All sorts of places.' She must have noticed his slight frown, because she continued. 'Erm, we did quite a few cities, as I recall. Budapest, Vilnius, Prague, Krakow, even Buch—'

Jack jumped on that. 'Vilnius?'

She nodded. 'Nice hot chocolates there. Mark bought me some amber. I didn't particularly want or like it, but it's what it's famous for, apparently . . . Well, that and some rather nasty-looking Russian underground torture chambers.' She made a face.

'What did you do in Vilnius?'

'Why?'

Jack hesitated.

She met his gaze. 'I demand your honesty. I'm being open with you.'

'All right. There's solid evidence that Vilnius is one of the places where the rogue clinics are operating in Eastern Europe.'

Her gaze hooded. 'Tell me what that means.'

'That's one of the places where women are being encouraged to allow their eggs to be harvested.'

Jem shrugged. 'So? Each of us has more than enough for a couple of lifetimes.'

'Yes, so I gather.'

'And since when was it against the law to donate eggs or sperm or embryos? Is it illegal?' She looked genuinely interested.

'Not illegal to donate, no. However, paying a woman to harvest her eggs is illegal, and selling your eggs specifically for payment is illegal in this country and in England – and no doubt elsewhere.'

Jem nodded. 'Ahh, okay. That makes sense but I didn't put that together in my mind. Even so, Jack, there's so much heartache around pregnancy; you know, getting pregnant sounds easy, and our parents raise us to believe it can happen if you so much as kiss a boy, but I know from Mark's career that it is incredibly difficult for a huge chunk of the female population. And it brings incredible anguish and mental health problems.'

'I understand,' Jack said. 'Truly, I've encountered so many stories like that in my research, and it's why so many accredited fertility clinics have sprung up around the globe. Their technology is not only a blessing but essential for some couples. I have no issue with the science.'

She raised her brows in query. 'So why are you investigating?'

'What I do have an issue with is non-accredited clinics taking advantage of that vulnerability.'

'Aren't they simply filling a gap in the system? If people want to do it . . .'

'You could view it that way,' Jack said, 'but that suggests there's something philanthropic – you know, "cool" – about it, rather than it simply being cold, hard money that drives it. Very soon, I gather, a new global egg bank will come online, allowing clinics and, I imagine, individuals to pursue what they need in a regulated, authenticated way, with a paper trail, maybe barcodes, tracking and the like. But right now it's the wild, wild West with a lot of cowboys doing exactly what they please and making fast money at the expense of other people's misery.'

'Whose misery?' Jem asked.

'Well, the women who are desperate for the money. What I've learned is that they're prepared to risk a procedure at a dodgy clinic in order to sell their eggs. And then there are the women who need those eggs, who are prepared to pay large amounts of cash to buy them illegally. They are also going through proced- ures at unaccredited clinics.'

Jem's expression changed as she registered how serious this was. 'Right. That doesn't sound good. And so, meanwhile the brokers get rich, is that what you're saying?'

'Well, I don't know about rich, because I don't know what the going price for an egg on the black market is, but I suspect the middle man is taking a significant amount. If they have enough traffic, shall we say, then it's potentially a lucrative scam. Any underworld operation depends on volume. Couples who want children will presumably pay whatever is asked, given that the accredited clinics might only offer them a few cycles per year. All of this is privately funded too. It's not on the NHS yet, and I doubt it's funded by Australia's Medicare.'

She shook her head. 'I just don't see why you'd pursue this so hard. It's doing good.'

'Is it?' Jack queried over the top of his wineglass. 'We know of two deaths just in Adelaide, and I know of at least another half- dozen overseas – women who have undergone procedures that went wrong. Let me tell you about just one.' He told her about Amelia Peters. '. . . and that's where this all began.' He shrugged. 'She was just a child herself, first year uni, all excited to be living away from home and feeling grown-up. The world at her feet – bright, pretty, smart, intelligent and funny. Amelia was one of those kids I imagine most teachers would relish in their class. Now she leaves behind traumatised friends and a family in pieces.'

'I'm sorry,' Jem admitted. 'I can see in your eyes how it hurts.'

'It does. But Amelia's just one of many across the UK alone who are dying for the not exactly exorbitant money they're being paid for taking the risk. I'm sure there are dozens of women who pass through these illegal clinics with no lasting side effects, but for every few dozen, some are probably going to have lasting complications – they might be risking their own fertility – or worse. All that for the kind of money that might just cover yours and Mark's restaurant budget for a couple of months.'

She cut him such a look that if it were attached to a blade he'd be haemorrhaging. 'Oh, go fu—'

'I'm sorry, that wasn't fair.' He put down his glass.

But she'd already hurled her glass of wine towards the sand. It missed, bouncing off the deck and handily breaking in two rather than shattering. By the time he looked back, she'd stomped off the deck and was striding down the beach. It didn't take much to draw level with her on his long lope and he caught her arm.

'Jem . . .'

'Ouch,' she bleated and stopped; Jack pulled his hand back as though burned.

'Sorry, I wouldn't dream of hurting—'

'No, it's okay,' she said, sounding reluctant. 'It's already bruised. That wasn't you.'

'I'm really very sorry for what I just said. You don't deserve any blame, and I have no right to make you feel guilty for any of this.'

'And still I do,' she snapped, sighing out her frustration. 'I don't know who to trust. Which of you is telling me the truth? I feel like I'm surrounded by people with their own agenda, each feeding me the version they want me to believe.'

He nodded. She deserved more clarity. 'Well, I'm a senior detective at Scotland Yard and in the course of my official duty, it's my job to uphold the truth. I will not lie to you, Jem.'

'Senior detective now?' She hadn't missed the clarification.

'Detective Superintendent,' he added, feeling like he'd been hauled up in front of a scowling headmistress.

'Wow. Jack. Really? Doesn't that make you more of a pen pusher?'

'No, I wouldn't describe it that way.'

'How would you describe it, then?'

'I lead major investigations, supervising all aspects of the operation – everything from setting strategic tasks to deploying team members.' He'd simplified it, but it was the essence of his job.

'And yet here you are, renting a beach house in Wallaroo, far from home, all alone with no back-up, just to spy on a single guy who may or may not be involved in some international scam.'

'You'd make a very good Chief Inspector,' he tried to jest, but the cast of her mouth told him she was not amused.

'I suppose you explaining your seniority is to assure me that you alone are telling the truth. Is that it?'

'I'm telling you everything I'm permitted to by law. There are aspects I'm prevented from sharing with anyone, including other police, but especially the public, because it might compromise witnesses or pervert the facts in some way.' He looked away, feeling awkward for saying what came next: 'And it may threaten my life if I say too much.'

Jem blinked. She looked chastened. 'Well, I'm going to ask you again. Is my husband a suspect?'

Jack took a chance, judging that his life potentially being at risk had only just sunk in for Jem. 'Tell me what happened in Vilnius.'

She did.

'So you were left to your own devices in that city. Is that a fair way of putting it?'

She sniffed. 'Yes. Mark said he had work to do at a local clinic – he was offering some special training in Vilnius and in Budapest he did the same.' She shook her head. 'I didn't mind.

They were cities I'd never seen and I enjoyed myself exploring, shopping, sipping drinks in cobbled lanes. Why would I be suspicious of the hardworking husband I trusted? Your turn, Jack.'

He nodded, and she allowed him to turn and lead her back to the house as they walked.

'Do you think Mark's involved?' Jem pressed before he could begin.

'I do now, yes.'

She gave a groan of despair.

'There are too many factors coming together for it to be coincidence any longer. Add it all up yourself, Jem.'

As they arrived back he bent to pick up the broken glass.

Jem looked at his hands. 'I'm sorry about that. I'm not usually that dramatic.'

Jack stepped back up onto the deck and leaned against the post. 'I'm guessing you've always wanted to slap a man's face, like in those old movies from the forties and fifties?'

She gave a sad chuckle. 'I have, actually.'

'Go on, then. Slap me,' he said, sticking out his jaw and screwing his face up. He closed his eyes, tempting her to deliver her blow. 'I deserve it.'

There was a pause, but he kept his eyes tightly closed, knowing he looked comical. He hoped it was having the right effect of lightening the heavy mood. After a moment he felt her lips brush his lightly, and his eyes snapped open to meet her gaze. She looked back at him in question.

'My turn to apologise,' she said. 'I hope that was the ideal way to say I'm sorry.'

He stared at her and now there really was no resistance left. To turn her down again would insult a lovely woman far more than she deserved. And still he tried to caution her. 'Jem . . .'

'I'm a big girl, Jack. I make my own decisions. And I want this. I've wanted it since you picked up my car keys and began your seduction. Uh-uh,' she cautioned him, holding up a finger. 'Don't deny it. It doesn't matter that you didn't plan to make love to me, Jack. You still set out to seduce me in some fashion. I'm showing you that there are consequences when you set something in motion. Now, kiss me and show me how truly sorry you are for being so beastly earlier.'

He took her hand. 'Just so we understand each other, this is a kiss of apology.'

She gave a small laugh. 'Okay. That'll do.'

'No, I mean it. I don't want to hurt you.'

'You'll hurt me more by rejecting me. Now, shut up and kiss me, Jack, unless you're worried about those two seagulls out there watching us and reporting back?'

He relented, flinging the glass halves backwards onto the sand and pulling her to him, trying not to think of his boss in London and those pursed lips while he pressed his gently against Jem's. It began tentatively, Jack pausing just long enough to give her a chance to change her mind, but when he felt her slim arms loop around the back of his neck, he knew they were toast. Their kiss deepened and lengthened, while the wind of the storm dissipated entirely. When Jack gently broke the long kiss and tasted salt on his now softened, swollen lips, the sky had turned from dusk to night.

She gave him a long look that suggested she didn't entirely trust him, despite all of his admissions tonight. 'Tell me something, Jack. Are you really unattached? I've had enough of lying men in my life. Don't join the list.'

He looked back at her with gentle offence in his expression. But she wasn't letting him off the hook.

'You're an ace kisser.'

Jack began to shrug but she continued.

'You must get a lot of practice. Us long-term couples get less and less, and I miss kisses that last for minutes . . . hours! I want that back; just for a moment. In fact, I want your mouth all over me.'

He gave a shocked laugh. 'Shameful wench!' he declared.

It made her toss back her ponytail and laugh, exposing her neck, which he smothered with small, light kisses, working down from just below her ear, mumbling, 'I love the sharp dip of your suprasternal notch.'

He knew it would make her guffaw and it did.

'Is that you talking dirty?'

'What do you mean?' he asked, pausing his kisses with feigned puzzlement. 'The suprasternal notch,' he said, pointing, 'between your clavicles.' He drew a finger along it lightly and felt her tremble beneath his touch. 'Yours is very deep, like a hammock. I'd like to curl up in there and rest.'

Still amused, she cupped either side of his face. 'You make me feel good, Jack. You make me feel reckless and desirable again.'

He returned to her neck. 'You are desirable, or did you think I'd picked up some driftwood and stuck it in my pocket?' he murmured from her jaw now, as he pulled away the scrunchie that held her hair up.

She giggled again. Her amusement was intoxicating for him. 'How do you expect me to focus when you are joking around.'

Jack stopped and looked injured, pointing south. 'My lad is no joke.'

'Lad?' She convulsed with laughter. 'Well, you and the lad need to take me to bed this moment. I adore you.' She put one hand over her heart.

He felt his laughing expression falter. Did she think this was something it wasn't?

'Oops, no, don't hear me wrong.' She looked back over her shoulder. 'You saw those grumbly clouds earlier, all that purple above us?'

He nodded.

'That was me, and my life at the moment. Dark, expectant, suspicious, unsettled. But that fiery sun on the horizon . . . that's you. Bright, full of warmth, and sort of dazzling. I know, like that sun, you are going to leave me. I know it, so don't fret. I'll stay here in the southern hemisphere while you slip over the horizon and head north.'

He looked back at her with soft thanks and nodded, glad that she understood.

'I haven't been kissed like that in so long. I know it's transient. I know this feeling will leave me soon but for now it's electrifying. Can we just enjoy it a little while longer?'

None of the charming symbolism was lost on him. 'You want day and night to cling to their embrace a little longer?'

She grinned. 'Absolutely. I do. And let's not forget the lad. We don't want dusk falling too soon,' she added, with a look of wickedness.

Jack took her hand and led her back into the house.

Their lovemaking was unhurried. As much as their ardour was demanding urgent satisfaction, Jack deliberately took it slowly. He wanted Jem to have this memory, something that carried resonance for her, as he suspected she had never been unfaithful to her husband. He didn't celebrate that he was the reason for it; if anything, he was daunted, but he justified breaking faith with Rowland by assuring himself that to not give in to Jem's needs was to hurt an already hurting woman more.

And that contravened his personal code.

So he let go of the cerebral and handed himself over to something primeval. Given their heightened desire in the moment, it took some management on his part, which he attributed in no small way to the looming vision of his tutting boss in London, to hold back when he most wanted to let go. He imagined Rowland shaking her head with disappointment over him allowing another case to bleed into his love life, letting her stay in his thoughts long enough to prolong Jem's and his enjoyment of each other until he sensed Jem wanted him to allow her to ascend that invisible mountain in the mind, until they both trembled and groaned out their pleasure at tumbling back down from the summit.

Later, tangled in the sheets and each other, they began to talk again about the situation with Mark.

'I don't want him associated with something he's not part of simply because I've cast guilt on him. And I don't want him hurt.'

Jack's hand was entwined in Jem's tousled hair, and he allowed the silky strands to wrap and unwrap around his fingers as he let his thoughts move. 'I understand,' he said, carefully.

'How do I help him?'

'Just be yourself. I'll come over for the barbecue as planned and find out what I can. That's my role. I'm not here to arrest anyone, Jem. My single goal is to establish that there is a crime being committed.' He chose not to tell her that he believed the mastermind of the operation might be South Australian . . . and could quite likely be Mark Maddox, given his behaviour.

'I asked you before if my husband is a suspect and you didn't answer me. I'm asking you again.'

So she wasn't going to let him off the hook. Jack sighed. 'There are no suspects. There's not even a case yet. I'm trying to build one. There are laws being broken, and deaths have occurred – deaths I find suspicious. But until I find a hard link in the chain of events, then no, Mark is not a suspect.'

Jack was able to hold her gaze but inwardly he cringed, unsure himself whether he was lying. Until he had more information, he was going with innocent until proven guilty.

'Thank you. Even though I think Mark's up to something, I can't imagine it's what you think. But I don't recognise him right now and this . . .' She waved a hand at the bed they were lying in. 'This is not something I'll ever refer to again, other than privately. I have, however, had a wonderful glimpse into a world I'd forgotten.'

He knew he didn't need to say anything in this moment, so he held his tongue.

She gave a smile as she continued. 'I know I cornered you – and I rather like your reluctance . . . it's sort of sexy. But I have no regrets and, curiously, I don't even feel guilty.'

He gave her a gentle kiss. 'I'm sorry your world is being shaken.'

She nodded. 'Time for me to get back to that unstable world.'

He sighed and disentangled his hands from her hair, which smelled of something spicy and exotic.

'You get out first,' she ordered. 'Women who've had children don't like handsome, single men watching their war-torn bods from bed . . . after the fact.'

He laughed, twisted out of bed and, not wanting to act suddenly modest, gave a stretch. He was aware that she was enjoying looking at him naked. She would never watch him again like this. He reached towards levity to help them move past the moment. 'Right, I'm showering. Be warned – I sing. Hope you like Perry Como.' At her look of horror, he shrugged. 'Blame my parents. We were fed a steady diet of easy listening.'

Jack switched the taps off several minutes later, hoping he'd annoyed her with his rendition of a famous song by the old crooner. As he stepped back into the bedroom, rubbing his thick hair vigorously with a towel, he sensed he was alone. His instinct was confirmed when he padded across the smooth timber floors to the kitchen where she'd left a note.

I couldn't take another chorus, but I enjoyed our magic moments. Decided not to prolong them. Back to the real world now, but I'll see you at the barbecue tomorrow. 6.30. Don't be late. Now please burn this note.

Jack smiled at the play on the title of the song he'd belted out happily in the shower and he was pleased that Jem didn't seem to be expecting anything from him that he was not in a position to give. He liked her all the more for her strong, independent manner. He wished her husband was not going to let her down, but every instinct that he'd honed over his years as a detective told him Mark Maddox was knee deep in this operation.

He went hunting for matches to burn the note, smiling once more at Jem's message.

26

The next morning, sipping a coffee on the deck, Jack watched an enormous cargo ship begin its docking procedure into the port of Wallaroo. Far out in the channel it had looked huge, but now, up close, its enormity gave it a sort of lumbering innocence, which only made his new theory seem more plausible. What better method to bring in illegal goods than a mundane cargo ship?

He threw the dregs of his coffee onto the sand, reminding himself to pick up the broken glass on his return, and went looking for his car keys. It was a pity he couldn't use the beach as a shortcut, but the council's decision to put in a new marina and open up a new slab of the beachside region to housing meant the beach was cut off by the ferry. It took passengers on a two-and-a-half-hour crossing to a place called Lucky Bay, which apparently cut hours of driving off the trip to Port Lincoln on the other side of Spencer Gulf. But as a result, he'd have to loop around and make his way past the terminal.

He drove past the ferry terminal before angling towards the main jetty, where he found parking nearby a café. That would do him. He ordered a takeaway coffee and waited, choosing his moment carefully after sussing out a couple who looked like locals. They were settling a small chihuahua, apparently called Pepper, beneath the table and between their legs.

He made eye contact and smiled. 'I have a chihuahua,' he lied. 'Mine's called Goliath, but we call him Golly for short.' He chuckled.

'Loyal but vicious,' the bloke said. 'It's Pam's dog,' he said, pointing at the woman.

'Oh, Don, don't fib. I see you playing with her all the time,' Pam said, smiling back at Jack. 'Don't listen to him. He's a big softie.'

'You live here?' Jack asked. 'I'm holidaying up the beach.'

They nodded. 'Are you on your own?' the wife asked, sounding surprised.

'Yes. I'm a writer,' he said, hoping that would explain everything.

'Ah,' they both said, as though it did in fact explain every other logical question that might follow.

'I see the big grain ship is in,' Jack remarked. It was an obvious statement but the sort of small talk that strangers might exchange.

Don nodded. 'Yes, mighty things, aren't they? He'll be loaded and gone by morning, although the slack tide forecast might keep him here another night. Expensive business to dock overnight. Tens of thousands of dollars per night, apparently.'

Jack nodded. None of this was useful. 'You seem to know a lot about the industry.'

'This used to be a town that sent copper ore to faraway places. We had plenty of west country miners in the early days. Well,' he paused, giving a shrug, 'they had all the knowhow, eh? Now it's all about the grain.'

Jack smiled and nodded, while Pam gestured to the waitress, catching her attention. She then returned her gaze to Jack.

'Have you read that we used to be known as part of the Copper Triangle? Little Cornwall, they called us.'

'Yes, I have,' he said, feeling sure he'd noted that somewhere in a brochure. Charlie, the young waitress, had referred to the name as well. 'And these grain ships come in regularly, I presume?'

'Oh, yes,' Don said, thanking the waitress as she arrived with their coffees.

Pam began tipping two packets of sugar into hers while Don continued chatting.

'Those silos are never empty,' he said, tilting his head back towards the tall sentries behind them.

'And I imagine the crews bring good trade to the town?' Jack asked.

'Aw, not really. I mean, they get off and all that, but usually the blokes just want to call home, do some shopping and stock up on the sort of rubbish their canteen probably doesn't provide. They keep to themselves. A few of them might try a pub but, you know . . .'

Jack waited.

The man gave a wry grin. 'They're foreigners, so they probably feel a bit awkward, I reckon.'

That surprised Jack. 'No Australians?'

Don laughed. 'No, mate. These are crews from Asia. They're sending money home, not drinking it.'

As Pam joined his laughter, Jack felt obliged to throw in a chuckle. 'I don't know why I felt it would be Australian sailors.'

'Not a one, not on these ships. Only Aussies you'll see on these big hulks would be the cleaning crew if they're ever sent on, but more likely one of the blokes from the ship's agents.'

'Ah, of course,' Jack said, feeling like his brain was lighting up with that tiny flash of information.

'Wait around long enough and you'll see them. He'll be lurking . . . Of course, you might be lurking all day, waiting for that ship to come in, but the hope of beating the slack tide will hurry things along.'

Jack nodded. 'Makes sense. Anyway, nice talking. I might walk down the jetty,' he said, keen now to detach himself from the chatty Don and Pam. 'Enjoy your coffees.'

They waved and he strode off as though he hadn't a care in the world, but as soon as he was out of earshot, he reached for his phone and dialled.

'Matt, it's me again. Sorry for filling your voicemail. Who is the ship's agent in these parts? I'll tell you more when I see you. Also,' he said, squinting as he searched for the giveaway equipment, 'are there cameras at these docks? If so, any chance we can view footage?'

The voicemail ran out and he had to dial in again, waiting for Matt's message to finish.

'Yeah, sorry, so, the cameras. There's a grain ship in. It would be easy to use it to bring the material in, but I need eyes on the comings and goings. Any chance?' It rang off again and he decided he wouldn't put in another call.

He walked down the jetty and deliberately began making idle conversation with the people fishing as he waited for Matt to call back. The locals there ranged from a ten-year-old to one eight times older, both men and women, some seated together, sharing stories and cups of something warming. Jack wished he could join them for the morning, but he was convinced now that Mark Maddox trying to repair his marriage, the visiting friends and the grain ship were no coincidence.

Ricardo's phone vibrated in his jacket pocket next to his heart. He knew who it was. His phone for everyone else was in his trouser pocket.

'Yes,' Ricardo said as he answered the call, and waited.

'Have you heard any more?' the familiar voice was terse, abrupt.

'The girl was green-lit for a post-mortem.' Ricardo kept his own words to a minimum, his tone blunt to match. He listened to several low muttered expletives and knew to not say anything at such a time. He was an obedient henchman, and had proved himself smart enough to anticipate the moves before they were commanded and to offer suggestions if he was asked for them. But until then, he kept his own counsel and remained silent.

'Who's doing it?' the voice asked.

'I gather it's that woman doctor who did the courier.'

'Any way to change that?'

'No. We have no infiltration at State Forensics. Certainly not at this short notice.'

'Right. Is there a way to contaminate or even get rid of the Lawson corpse?'

Ricardo shook his head. 'Nope. Too dangerous.'

'You realise having the same pathologist allows for continuity.'

'There's nothing to find.'

'There might be.'

Ricardo frowned, fiddling with his earring. He hadn't seen anything that needed any special clearing up at the scene, even though the girl had fought like a cat to her final breath. He went back over those moments in his mind, looking for a clue.

The embryologist had writhed for far longer than he'd anticipated and never gave up trying to scream, despite his boss's hand clamped firmly over her mouth. She'd bitten and scratched viciously, but they were both far too cunning to let her near their faces. And then, at last, the drug finally took full effect and she'd begun to lose what pitiful strength she possessed in her tiny frame.

'Drown her,' came the command and it was done. He had stripped her, filled the tub, added bubble bath he'd noted on the side and even lit a few candles to keep it all authentic. And then, watched by his boss, he had pressed Nikki Lawson beneath the frothy water and held her there until she'd kicked twice – some ancient survival neuron firing through the blunting drug, but it was ineffective. He held her under, smelling rose and jasmine from exploding bubbles, until he was sure she was dead.

They'd left everything else as they found it, even had a cover story with the neighbour, so what had he missed? It had felt seamless, save the knocked-over pot plant and the rumpled rug it sat on, which they'd left because it looked like she'd been dancing to the blaring music, rather than kicking furiously to stay alive.

Ricardo blinked as a recollection eased into his thoughts. He remembered now how his boss had plunged a hand into a pocket for the journey home and, even when dropped off, hadn't removed it.

Realising his boss was still waiting for him to speak, he finally asked, 'What do you mean?' even though he could guess the answer.

'That skinny little bitch bit me.'

Jack was leaning on the edge of the jetty, watching the grain ship, still lost in thoughts of how to trap Jem's husband into revealing more than he planned, when his phone trilled.

'Hawksworth.'

'Morning, Jack. It's Alison Moore, from Forensics in Adelaide.'

'Oh, hello.' He frowned, waiting.

'Look, sorry to ring out of the blue like this, but we've found something on that young woman who supposedly overdosed and drowned in her bath.'

'Okay, should you—'

'Matt left your number with me in case of a breakthrough moment like this. I've got the engaged tone twice now, so either he's on a big case with lots of calls, or he's having a lengthy discussion with his wife.'

Her remark made him smile. 'In that case, how can I help?'

'It's how I can help the police . . . and you in your informal capacity.'

Jack could almost see her drawing inverted commas in the air as she uttered 'informal'.

'I figured you'd want to know.' Her voice had a conspiratorial tone now; she seemed to be enjoying what she'd perceived as a cloak and dagger situation.

'I do,' he admitted.

'Then let me tell you what I've found. I've got some time, so I might rather enjoy explaining it all.'

Jack was in no rush either. 'Go ahead. All ears.'

'Okay, from behind the front teeth of the deceased, Nicola Lawson, I have extracted a narrow strip of skin that I'd describe as roughly rectangular and measuring fifteen by five millimetres.'

Jack frowned as he imagined that size in flesh. 'Behind her teeth?' he repeated, full of puzzlement. 'Oh, a bite?'

'Ghoulish but oh-so-fabulous. Discoveries like this so rarely come along. Most of the time it's all pretty straightforward, as you'd know, but just sometimes there's a surprise and it flings you into a different direction. Anyway, as soon as I saw it, I knew this was what we term a "significant finding". So I took stock and made a plan. I needed to know whether the skin was simply trapped behind the teeth, or whether it was caught *between* the teeth.'

'The latter suggesting a deliberate bite, I'm presuming? So this is no accidental overdose.'

'Precisely. So, after careful photography, a pair of sterile forceps told me that Nicola had well and truly meant to bite this hand, and no doubt her attacker pulled away, alarmed and hurt, making the injury worse.'

'How much worse? Are you able to tell?'

Moore paused and he imagined her frowning. 'A human bite can be dangerous because of the raft of infections it can lead to. And on the hands the infection can threaten joints, tendons, bones, which I'm very much hoping is what is going to happen.'

Jack grinned. He really liked this pathologist and wished he could transport her to London. 'Go on,' he encouraged.

'Not much more really. Without a tissue match I can't make any further conclusions, although it's always tempting. After extracting it, I put it on a sterile theatre drape for measurement and more photography, so we've got a pile of accurate evidence to rely on should we need it. It's a wonderful piece of DNA if we ever do catch up with the killer. Would you like me to describe it in technical terms?'

'Please,' he said. He had nothing to do this minute except remain watchful for the ship's agent. Being on a phone call made it look less like he was loitering.

'The skin was from the back of the hand – the dorsum – and I can confirm it's from a left index finger, from the area overlying the distal interphalangeal joint. Want that in layman's terms, Jack?'

'I do.'

'That's the joint closest to the fingernail.'

Jack looked at his left hand to see where the skin would have been torn. 'Got it.'

'Look, its superficial,' she qualified, 'but it would have hurt like hell, would have bled and would definitely be ripe for infection. Between us, I'm now convinced she *was* killed, by the way, which probably enhances your theory and perhaps points to the reason why you're so far away from home. And I know you can't talk about it, or whatever you're hunting, but good luck. I hope this helps.'

'It will, Dr Moore, I'm sure of it. I'm very grateful you break the rules.'

'Oh, gosh,' she said, dropping her professional voice. 'Where would history be if we all just followed the rules?'

'Still gathering nuts and berries, I think,' he said, laughing. 'Thank you for telling me.'

'I'd have thought you'd have a more dramatic response – even an expletive – for that incredible finding, Jack,' she said. 'It was tucked right behind her front teeth . . . quite the miracle that I discovered it.' She laughed.

'I didn't want to offend you,' he said, smiling into his mobile phone and wishing she could have seen the genuine surprise lighting his features.

'That's near impossible. I work and live with men, and they're not all as polite as you, Jack. Anyway, I'm rather chuffed with the discovery and secretly very proud of Nicola for her fight. She didn't give up her life easily. Now we have a lovely piece of DNA.'

'And we're looking for someone with a bandaged left-hand finger.'

She laughed again. 'Exactly. Don't ever say we pathologists don't make your job easy for you.'

'No, but really, it's another jigsaw piece . . . a fascinating and potentially damaging one.'

'My thoughts too. Whoever took her life, brave girl, will be hurting. Having measured the flap, I'm guessing he'll need a plastic surgeon, because stitches are not going to close that wound. Let's hope he's already feeling deeply unwell; he might even go to a hospital.'

'Brilliant, Dr Moore. Thank you.'

'My pleasure. Hope you catch the bastard, but you didn't hear me say that.'

'We haven't even spoken.'

She rang off with a soft chuckle.

★

Jack moved to another spot on the jetty that jutted out from the main section to form a right angle. Obviously this wasn't the best fishing spot, as most of the people with rods were working off the main walkway. His stance was casual and he was glad he was dressed unremarkably, although he hoped his sunglasses weren't too *Mad Men* in this part of town. It meant he could turn his head slightly, as though watching the sea and the people fishing, while actually keeping his gaze on land to see who was coming and going.

He sipped on the takeaway coffee that had long turned cold to add to the illusion of him being a holidaymaker with no urgency. But his mind was working overtime.

How would this go? If the syndicate had coerced a ship's agent, that meant one of the foreign crew members had been paid to bring the goods in. From where? Singapore or Malaysia, perhaps? Indonesia? The Philippines? It was easy enough to do, but it had to be somewhere with the infrastructure of a lab, and some sort of legit clinic in which it could disguise itself. Or was nothing legit under this new method?

He frowned, trying to put it together in his mind. So was the material originally from Asia? Unlikely. So if it was coming from, say, Eastern Europe, that meant the illegal set-up would now potentially piggy-back legitimate courier services into Asia. There, another compromised lab technician, somewhere like Singapore, would look the other way as the illegal material was removed and taken to a small lab to be topped up with liquid nitrogen in a new dewar. Then it would be returned to the new courier – a sailor now, Jack presumed – who continued on their merry way into South Australia to do what? Hide it somewhere to be picked up?

Jack sipped his cold coffee again. Its ugly taste nearly caused him to wince, but he used it to sharpen his thoughts.

A ship's agent could be handsomely bribed to board the ship and, in the course of his routine, acquire the material and walk it back off the ship to pass it forward. A long, illegal chain. It worked in his mind, but for the moment it was all hypothetical. He didn't know if the syndicate had changed their method of importing the black-market goods. He didn't even know for sure if there *was* a syndicate. But Greg Payne had died. Something had changed. And his gut was telling him he was right.

Jack saw a car swinging into the small car park. Soon a lanky guy unfolded himself; Jack noted his pale, freckled skin and hair the colour of cooked honey as the man slipped a cap with a prominent logo on his head.

'Is that you, Judas?' Jack murmured. The historical myth had bubbled up at the sight of the red hair: the Spaniards and Italians had always painted Judas Iscariot with red hair. 'Are you betraying your firm?' he whispered under his breath, amusing himself as he waited.

He watched the fellow lock the car, heft a small backpack over his shoulder, straighten his cap and emerge from the car park with his gaze firmly on the ship. His short-sleeved uniform had an official-looking government badge embroidered prominently over the breast, matching the logo on the cap. He was stopped by someone and they shared a brief word, a small laugh, and then Judas kept walking. He pulled his cap a little lower, adjusted the backpack.

You look nervous, Judas, Jack thought. He watched his prey until the pale man disappeared onto the ship. He couldn't wait here any longer without looking conspicuous, so he strolled back down the jetty to the coffee shop. He ordered a toasted sandwich, which he had no intention of eating, but it gave him credibility, a reason to be hanging around. He took a corner seat that faced away from the ship, into the car park, so he wouldn't miss Judas leaving.

Jack dialled Matt again and left an urgent voicemail, repeating what had come to light from pathology, and asking for an update on his own progress. 'Things are potentially turning hot,' he finished.

He found a discarded newspaper and pretended to read, all the while watching the car park. Soon a dark SUV arrived and pulled in. The windows were tinted, and Jack suspected the level of opaqueness was illegal.

'Got you!' he murmured into his newspaper and dipped his head lower, but the shades he still wore hid his gaze, which was firmly on the muscular-looking man who got out of the car. He wasn't tall but he looked strong, showing off delineated biceps beneath the sleeves of his white polo top. He looked Latino, and Jack noted the glint of a diamond stud in one ear. Jack watched him take out a phone and punch in a message to someone, then slip the phone back into his pocket. He looked like a patient cat waiting in the bushes for some poor creature to stroll by, though he surprised Jack by opening the car door, withdrawing a backpack and walking away from the car, out of the car park. That alarmed him, but he wasn't prepared to follow the guy and risk being clocked or losing sight of the red-headed agent, who he presumed would soon be returning with the goods.

His control was rewarded. The Latino guy, whom he mentally nicknamed Ricky Martin, returned with a small brown paper bag and something that looked too hot to eat, going by the way the fellow tentatively bit into it. It looked like a Cornish pasty or 'parstee', as it was pronounced in South Australia.

It took an hour of patient pretence: Jack reading the paper and nibbling on the toastie he didn't want, the beat of 'Livin' La Vida Loca' surging through his brain; Ricky Martin giving the impression that he was simply stopping somewhere convenient for a bite to eat. And then Jack caught the unmistakable flash of copper, like a newly minted penny of old, and then Judas was striding back down the jetty, headed for the car park. Again, he was stopped by someone he knew; they shook hands, exchanged pleasantries. Did he look nervous? Jack thought maybe the frequent adjustment of the hat and running his hand through his hair might be a sign of it, but then it was a floppy style. They parted and Judas made quick work of the distance to his car.

'Now, let's see,' Jack whispered. He raised his newspaper in case they glanced his way but stared over the top.

Ricky Martin stepped out from around the charcoal SUV and Judas halted as though stung. Now he looked just short of frightened. Ricky Martin suddenly smiled, though it looked forced.

Even from where Jack sat he heard the salutation.

'Hey is that *you*, Andy Redford?' Ricky Martin called loudly.

Judas, whom Jack now knew as Redford, nodded and said something, trying to smile but not doing a very good job. Jack couldn't hear him but at least now he had a name.

Ricky Martin strode over and hugged him. Jack blinked in surprise, while Redford looked terrified. Jack wished he could read lips because Ricky Martin was saying something now. Redford seemed to obey him. He slipped off the backpack and put it down.

They talked for no more than three minutes, Jack estimated, before Ricky Martin shook the agent's hand with a bright smile. Lots of nodding, a couple of shoulder slaps and the fellow was getting back into the driver's seat of the SUV. As he drove off, the passenger-side window slid down and Jack was surprised to see the brown bag from the pasty flung out.

Either Ricky Martin was a good shot over two seats, or someone else was in that car with him. He felt a thrill of excitement; maybe the passenger was the one he hunted. 'I'm coming for you,' he murmured.

He returned his attention to Andy Redford, who had now picked up his backpack and put it into the passenger seat of his car. Soon he too got into his car, reversed out and was gone.

Had an exchange been made? Jack hadn't witnessed it.

Redford had got on the ship with his pack, got off with it and got into the car. What had just happened?

Jack had to hope that Matt would reveal that CCTV was available and they could see the footage to figure out what had actually taken place.

Disappointed in himself, he checked his watch. He should go. There was enough time, though, to drive into Kadina and hunt down something to take to the barbecue. As young as he'd been when he lost his mother, he could remember her advice never to arrive as a guest empty-handed.

He never had.

On the way he rang a florist in Adelaide and asked the shop to send Dr Alison Moore a bouquet of flowers in the morning.

'I can organise that. We have three options,' the woman said, rattling them off, starting with the lower-priced options. '. . . or there's the seventy-five-dollar package, which includes David Austin roses, hydrangea and white tulips, and this bouquet is sent in a very lovely vase wrapped with cellophane, ribbon, a card and a smile.'

He grinned at the telephone. 'I'll go with the last one, thanks for your help. Let me give you my details and the address.'

Jack hoped there might be a florist in Kadina as well.

27

'These are for you,' he said to Jem when she stood to welcome him. He had walked along the beach until he reached their place, where Mark and Jem stood near a barbecue and an outdoor table setting made more elegant by thick candles enclosed in open bell jars. He had a keen sense of anticipation about the evening but told himself to remain calm. Find the information, brief London and let Matt know. That was his remit.

'You shouldn't have,' she said and then gave him an air kiss, presumably for Mark's benefit. 'I adore pale pink, thank you,' she said, taking the small bouquet of roses. 'And you,' she murmured quickly and only for his hearing.

Jack pretended he hadn't heard her final words. 'And Dr Maddox, for you . . . Thank you for having me at your home,' he said, handing over two bottles of wine.

Mark took the bottles with a genuine-seeming smile. 'Mmm, Barossa Valley. Shiraz, no less. My favourite.'

'Drinking very well according to the pimply teenager behind the counter in Kadina,' Jack replied modestly. He'd taken some

time choosing, and the teen was surprised that he'd bought such
an expensive red and then decided on a second bottle. His quip
made Maddox smile.

'Come on up,' Jem said as Jack hovered politely on the sand,
awaiting the signal to join them on the deck. 'Mark has invited
some guests – they're inside.'

'I'll still give you your interview, Hawksworth,' her husband
assured him. 'I need to get it over with, as I'm just too busy from
here on.'

'Make yourself comfy,' Jem suggested. 'The rest of us will be
out soon enough. Mark, you know I like those sausages well
cooked,' she warned with a knowing glance at her husband.
'I'll just check on Alannah,' she said, her gaze now turning and
lingering on Jack just a fraction too long, and he looked away,
smiling at Mark as if he hadn't noticed.

As Jem disappeared, Mark turned back to the barbecue and
another man emerged from the house. 'I think for the purposes
of this evening, Mr Hawksworth, we should call you by your first
name. Is that all right?'

'I'd prefer it, in fact.'

The new arrival came over to join them, resting a hand on Mark's
back and peering at the sausages. 'How are they coming along?'

'Jack, this is Alex Petras, a good friend,' Mark said. 'Alex, meet
Jack. He's an English journalist who I seem to have promised to
give a very brief interview to later.'

'Welcome,' Alex said, warmly extending a hand. 'An interview
on what?'

Jack shook the man's hand, noting his soft European accent. So
this was the Lithuanian guy who had been feeding Jem the doubt
about Mark and how he was potentially having an affair with his
wife. Petras was tall, with close-cropped blond hair and casual
clothing, but Jack wasn't fooled; the brands were expensive, going

by the small but conspicuous logos. He looked to be in good shape for his age, perhaps nearing fifty, and had an alert, pale gaze. His smile was warm but had a slightly strange cast due to a scar on one side. It looked as though it had been achieved by a blade, and he intended to find out what had caused the wound. Hopefully there would be an opportunity over what Mark was calling the 'snags', clearly an understatement. The sausages looked and smelled expensive, sizzling enticingly in a fug of garlic, onion and herbs, without bursting or bleeding oodles of fat.

Jack brought his attention back to the question. 'My piece is about infertility. It's a global issue. Women and indeed couples all over the world want the science to move at a hectic pace, so there's less trial and error, it's not so expensive, they have more options . . . they want more births, essentially,' he said. Alex was smiling; it touched his eyes, which Jack wasn't expecting and thus it felt genuine. Was he disappointed? He wanted to believe these two men might be the bad guys, and Alex Petras his prey.

'But here, in little Wallaroo, a journalist?'

'I'm a novelist in my dreams,' Jack assured him.

'Jack got the bum's rush from my clinic for turning up unannounced, so he cunningly stalked my wife instead. Isn't that right, Jack?'

'Pardon . . . What?' He swung around to see Mark watching him carefully. 'Bum's what?'

That made Alex laugh; Jack had deliberately defused what could have turned into an ugly exchange. His nephew had taught him what 'bum's rush' meant.

Mark continued conversationally. 'She mentioned you took her to coffee after seeing her in my clinic.'

Jack kept his features neutral, knowing he had to tread with care now that Jem had come clean about knowing him. 'I wouldn't colour it quite that way,' he said with a smile.

'Oh. How would you, er, *colour* it, then?' Mark asked, a vague sense of menace in his tone.

Jack refused to bite. 'We were parked all but next to each other and your wife dropped her keys. I was raised to be polite, so I picked them up, noticed she was upset and, after checking she was fine, I offered to buy her a cup of coffee.'

'Ah.' Mark sounded as though he'd trapped Jack.

It was Petras who came to Jack's defence. 'What's so wrong about that, Mark?'

'I was simply being chivalrous, Mr Maddox,' Jack appealed.

'I feel ambushed,' Mark remarked.

'And I suddenly don't feel welcome,' Jack countered.

'Only suddenly?'

'Look, I didn't like that yesterday your wife failed to mention us sharing a coffee. It was all very innocent but I played along.'

'Why? So odd to lie.'

Jack shook his head, feigning embarrassment. 'I am not privy to the dynamics of your marriage and neither do I wish to make it my business. I simply want the interview, but I figured she was embarrassed to say anything about talking to me after I visited MultiplyMed and it just didn't matter enough to me,' he lied.

'And so the booking here was a coincidence? You want me to believe that?'

'I told you, my sister booked it a while back. I had no idea your family have a beach place here. That's why your wife was so surprised to see me dozing on the deck.' Jack shrugged. 'We got chatting again, I made a coffee and then you arrived. I think your wife was just a little taken aback to see you on the beach.'

'And felt guilty, you mean?'

'Hey, hey, Mark,' Alex soothed his friend, frowning. 'Don't do this to a guest. You invited him. Have your interview. Let's not spoil the evening or upset the girls any more than they are already.'

'Sorry.' Mark surprised Jack with the apology. 'I'm a bit on edge.'

Jack waited.

'Work's been a bastard.'

'That must be stressful.' Jack turned to Alex. 'What's wrong with the women?'

'Oh, my wife's had a bit of a turn,' Alex explained, letting out a sigh. 'She'll be all right. Strong Lithuanian stock. She must be sick to be missing out on the socialising.' He gave his odd grin.

Jack was getting used to it but remained desperately curious about how it had become so crooked.

'You see that cruiser out there, Jack?' Mark said, turning to point with his barbecue tongs.

Jack politely followed his trajectory. 'I do.'

'That's Alex's boat. He likes to call it a boat in an attempt at modesty, but personally I think it's a crime to call it that.'

Jack heard Alex chuckle behind him.

'It's a beautiful ship,' the obstetrician continued. 'These two sail all around the country – the world, in fact. They drop anchor at any lovely bay they see, wherever they like. That's my idea of a perfect life.'

'And today it's Wallaroo,' Jack said, turning to watch Petras, who sighed.

'Our last trip out in South Australian waters before they become a little too rough for my liking.'

'Where might you go next?'

Mark answered. 'They're talking about Fiji, Tahiti, wherever the wind and longing takes the lucky sods.'

Alex gave a smirk.

'No children, I'm guessing?' Jack enquired, trying to sound innocent.

'No, sadly. Not of our own,' Alex replied. 'I have a daughter from my first marriage. I wish dearly I could have had children with Alannah. One is not enough, and the one I have is not hers, so it can make for tough times now and then.'

'You tried everything,' Mark assured him.

Jack observed the men carefully.

'We did, but that's cold comfort; she's all about family. Comes from a very powerfully bonded one back home.'

Mark was still staring at the boat. 'I know, but you have complete freedom. Financial independence. It's an achievement.'

'It can be yours soon enough, my friend,' Alex said, 'although you'll soon realise it isn't enough. Family, faith in your loved ones and trust is all that matters.'

Jack wondered if they were speaking in code, although Mark looked just as confused by Alex's suddenly philosophical mood and firm look. He moved the conversation on.

'And that belongs to your cruiser, I'm guessing?' Jack gestured towards a motorised dinghy that was the colour of a banana. It was sitting carelessly on the sand, quite a distance away for something that was clearly valuable. Jack already knew it belonged to Alex, having seen the cruiser arrive at the beginning of the day, and was just making polite conversation.

'Yes, only way to get to and from without getting wet,' Alex said with a grin.

Jack gave the obligatory smile in return and tried not to look delighted to see Jem stepping out from the house.

'Right, wine. This is from Jack.' She began pouring the bottle's near-purple contents into fresh glasses.

'How's my wife doing, Jem?' Alex asked.

'Well, as inappropriate as it is to say this right before dinner, she's just heaved and is feeling a tad brighter for it. She's not seasick, is she, Alex?'

'I doubt it,' he scoffed. 'Alannah has better sea legs than all of us put together. She's the ocean freak, not me.'

Jem shrugged. 'Are you sure you didn't eat something odd? I would ask her, but she's been feeling so off that I don't want to mention food just yet.'

'We ate on the boat,' Alex answered. 'It was all fresh. We ate the same thing too. And it wasn't seafood. She did go off mid-morning, though. She said she wanted to walk along the beach and the jetty. I don't know why she didn't ask to borrow your car – she hates to walk, prefers to work out with equipment for her exercise. Anyway, perhaps she ate something then.'

'You let her go alone?' Jem asked.

'Well, she wasn't sick then. She said she was meeting a friend or something. You know how Alannah is – always has her own agenda. She wasn't gone long.'

Jem looked nonplussed and Jack had to admire just how well she was handling having Alannah Petras in her house, given her earlier suspicions. And then it registered. One could not get to the jetty via the beach because of the marina – he'd found that out the hard way. Alannah could not have walked there.

'There's a café at the jetty,' he offered innocently. 'Perhaps she picked up something to eat or drink there?'

Alex shrugged. 'Possibly. She keeps so fit, I can't believe she's the one feeling so miserable.'

'Come on, let's eat,' Jem said. 'I'll just get the salads and bread. It's simple fare tonight, folks. Mark, can you grab the sausages?'

As they found their seats, Jack wondered about the dinghy. He pointed. 'You're not worried about it so close to the water?'

Alex laughed. 'I have to admit I wondered the same, but my wife – who hates to walk, as I said – explained something about a dodge tide. I don't know what that means, but she said not to trouble myself with moving the dinghy. The water's hardly moved all day.'

Jack frowned. 'Dodge?'

Mark turned and set down the pyramid of very good-looking sausages, scattered with nicely caramelised onions. In a different situation, Jack would have remarked on his culinary skills, but their mutual dislike for one another was obvious and he didn't see the point.

'How have you got through life living on that tiny island of yours? Dodge tide, often called a slack tide, is when the sea remains pretty still for several hours, and the tidal change'—Mark gave an up and down gesture with both hands to insult Jack further—'doesn't fluctuate terribly much. I've never sailed myself but I think I learned about this at school.' He shot Jack a disdainful look.

Jack gave a droll smile. He had sailed plenty since childhood and still enjoyed getting out on the water with friends whenever time permitted. 'Ah, I get it now. Mark, you probably don't realise that in the rest of the world we call this a dead tide. I know exactly what it means. Dodge is obviously specific to Australians, although slack tide is used more commonly. It's just another oddity I've noticed in this state.'

'Oh, yes? Like what?'

'Like . . .' Jack gave the impression he was innocently searching for a good example. 'Some people from Adelaide I've noticed say "show-wen" for "shown". They add an extra syllable on those tricky "wn" words.'

Before Mark could respond, Jack continued. 'And then there's that curiosity for any French word . . . reservoir, abattoir. Some South Australians I've met don't pronounce it the French way, instead choosing to say "reser-vor" or "abba-tor".' He put a finger in the air. 'That said, South Australians sound more English than the rest of Oz . . . to my ears anyway. "Cultivated" is probably a good way to describe it – perhaps because the region was populated with free settlers rather than ex-convicts, who might have come from the rougher end of town. Less Irish here, more Cornish and Scottish.'

He was deliberately showing Mark he knew a little of the local history and wouldn't be condescended to by an arrogant medico. He saw Mark take a breath and kept going so he couldn't jump in. 'You say "chance" the way I would, rather than the more American way that, say, my niece and nephew in New South Wales might.' He smiled, still keeping his tone neutral, so Mark could not be sure whether he was having a go, and continued.

'I like the way South Australians speak. I like the way *all* Australians speak. You can't miss them in a crowd, but they're not loud like Americans, simply distinctive. And that's good. You're a proud country and you have your own way of speaking English. Us lot,' he said, now in a more disdainful tone, 'our dialects change within fifty miles of each other. People from Manchester have an entirely different accent to people from Liverpool, and they're not even as far away as Adelaide is to here. Intriguing, isn't it?'

Again, he didn't allow Mark to answer. 'Anyway, I do know a little about sailing and for a wife who doesn't like walking,' he said, turning back to Alex, 'you might want to set off early.' He winked at Alex, for whom the joke clearly meant nothing, as he frowned, then smiled and passed it off politely.

'I don't know what you mean.'

'A dead tide lasts a few hours, but then you may find—'

Jem stepped back into their orbit, unwittingly cutting off any opportunity for further discussion. 'Here we are,' she said, placing two platters down. 'Let's eat before those snags get cold.'

The conversation turned to the best butcher in Adelaide for sausages, the deliciousness of Jack's wine, which no one around the table could dispute, and onwards to the exchange rate between Australia and the UK. Later, over a bottle of Pedro Ximenez sherry that Jem dug out of the drinks cupboard, much to Jack's approval, he and Mark remained on the deck while Alex helped Jem clear up inside.

The sun had set in another of this region's boastful, gloriously luminous ways and as the gulls fell silent, the sea's rhythm was calm and soothing. Evening twilight crept around them as the water shook off the slumber of the dead tide and began to turn.

28

'So, let's do this quickly,' Mark said, sounding bored.

The table had been cleared, and it was just the two of them seated with empty coffee cups and a refill of Pedro Ximenez.

'May I record you?' Jack asked. 'Easier than scribbling notes.'

'Sure, why not?' his host said with a careless shrug.

Jack posed some general questions, which Mark, to his credit, answered fully.

'Around the world, infertility treatment is a rapidly growing area of research and clinical practice. What is the average number of cycles a woman might go through?'

'To be honest, that is one of those "how long is a piece of string" questions. It depends on the woman's situation – her fallopian tubes might be blocked or damaged, she could have uterine fibroids or endometriosis, she could have an ovulation disorder, or have undergone sterilisation. Then, we look at the man. Does he have a problem with sperm production, or perhaps function impairment? And then a whole raft of other complications for either parent,' Mark said, as if the subject was far too big to tackle this evening.

'Such as?'

'Such as . . .' Mark blew out his cheeks. 'Well, if someone is having treatment for cancer, then they may want to preserve their opportunity for pregnancy by harvesting eggs and freezing them, or even fertilising them before freezing. Or, a woman who doesn't have a functioning uterus might have another woman carry her pregnancy on her behalf.'

Jack nodded. It certainly was a complex arena. 'So, the cycles – there must be a limit to how many you can do?'

'Some women are more aggressive in their determination, but in the main we urge women not to do more than three per year.'

'Why?'

'There's wear and tear on the body, plus we're forcing an otherwise natural system to behave unnaturally.'

'By forcing her ovaries to produce more eggs than is natural, you mean?'

'Correct.'

'And that's dangerous?'

'Of course.' Mark gave a look saying that should have been obvious.

'Any of the procedures fatal?' Jack thought of Amelia.

Mark made a scoffing sound. 'Not in my hands, no.' He continued, warming to his topic. 'Let's take an average heterosexual couple struggling to conceive. They've tried all the less invasive procedures over several years. Now she's thirty-four and her body clock feels like a time bomb inside. The maternal drive is so strong it starts to play with her mind. There's massive emotional stress and that doubles – triples, even – once they're on the program. They want magic on the first cycle. The lucky ones are pregnant within a year.'

'And the not-so-lucky?'

'Years of cycles and buckets of tears. A lot of misery, often leading to depression. Big strain on the relationship, potential

break-ups. Getting pregnant is harder than a lot of people think –
even when the couple have no problems.'

'And then there's the cost, of course.' Jack brought Maddox
around to where he needed him.

'Hellish on the household. The financial strain, on top of the
mental and emotional, is enormous for both of them.'

'And in your opinion, how widespread is the use of this
technology?'

'In the order of one in six heterosexual couples seek help for
conception.'

Jack nodded as though he'd heard that figure from others.
'Yes, it's about the same in the UK – France, Germany, too,' he
replied. He sat back. 'Is there an average number of cycles these
couples do?' he asked, raising his eyebrows, appearing innocent.

'It's logistics, Jack. The more cycles you do, the more the
chances increase. It's like any form of gambling. The wealthy,
the determined, the out-of-their-mind with stress will demand
more cycles to increase their chances. It's not healthy, but desperate aspiring mothers don't care much about their own mental,
emotional or physical health at this point.'

'Do you personally prevent them from taking an unreasonable
number of cycles?'

'At MultiplyMed, I do take a strong stance, yes. But I can't
speak for other clinics.'

Jack marvelled at his slipperiness. Mark spoke so confidently,
so professionally, but he was specific and cunning. Jack tried a
different way. 'So there must be unregistered clinics that offer
the same service when MultiplyMed, for instance, is not open to
doing more cycles, to keep pushing their bodies and their bank
accounts?'

'I have no information about that.'

'Off the record, Mark, does such a black market exist?'

He didn't miss a beat, reaching to turn off the recorder that lay on the table between them. 'Off the record, where there's a gap and a quid to be made in any market, someone will fill it.'

Jack didn't make too big a thing about the positive response, nodding to himself instead. Then he gave the impression that a new thought had struck him. 'What if a woman can't supply her own eggs for all those reasons you've mentioned?'

'That's all right. She can use a donor egg.'

'What if she doesn't have someone to donate one? Are they easy to come by on the black market?'

'Supply and demand, Jack – you said it.'

'And what sort of fee might she pay for that cycle with a "donated" egg?' Jack made it clear he was talking about the black-market ones.

Mark sighed, inhaling noisily. 'Is this what your article—'

'No, no, not at all,' Jack interrupted. 'You've piqued my interest, that's all.'

'Your article really shouldn't be about the industry – you can quote me on that. It reduces something emotional and socially important into something mercenary, certainly commercial. I'd put it another way,' Mark said. 'Quite simply, the people who formerly had to face life childless now have the ability to outwit Mother Nature's rather cruel efficiency.'

'So how much are we looking at for a donated egg?'

'It's never just one. And remember, these women who have the money for this sort of thing, who are going to risk illegal purchase of eggs and services . . . Well, they want to control who their donor is.'

'They can choose?'

'Like looking at a menu and ordering at a restaurant.' Maddox chuckled. 'I'll take the egg donor with dark hair and hazel eyes, thanks,' he said. 'If it's an embryo, they not only check the mother's details and history, but they can choose the sex of their baby, and they'd ask for a rundown on the father's appearance too. I wouldn't put it past some of the wealthier ones to want to know the IQ of the parents.' Now he laughed more fully. 'Poor sods.'

It was this final callous comment that convinced Jack that Mark really was involved. Was he the top dog? He couldn't be sure. Something instinctive told him Maddox was still aspiring. He remembered the remark by his friend, Petras, suggesting Mark was on his way but not there yet. Was Petras the man he hunted? The one who needed to pay for killing Amelia? The Lithuanian connection felt irresistible.

Maddox was still talking and Jack jerked out of his thoughts to pay attention. '. . . probably a thousand to fifteen hundred per egg, on top of the cycle costs.'

'Per *egg*?' Jack confirmed.

Jem's husband nodded. 'And we put in two, minimum.'

'So it's often more?'

Mark shrugged. 'Look, they're paying, right?'

'Right,' Jack said. He was pleased to realise Mark was forgetting himself, saying too much, feeling confident that the recorder wasn't on. He was experienced enough with interviews to know a journo had to respect the confidentiality of remarks made off the record. Jack switched on the recording device again. Nothing of what he was about to ask felt important. 'Just a couple more,' he said, frowning as if in deep thought. 'Now, I've been hearing about the World Egg Bank.'

'Yes,' Maddox began again breezily. 'What a clever conception . . . no pun intended.' And he laughed at his own joke.

Ten minutes later, Jem tapped on the glass doors in gentle interruption before poking her head around. 'Nearly done?'

Jack nodded. 'Done,' he said, looking at his watch. 'Seventeen minutes. Thanks, Mark. You've been insightful.'

He nodded, giving a grudging smile. 'Hope it all helps.'

'Oh, it does,' Jack said. 'I'll need to organise a headshot, or perhaps you have—'

'Yeah, plenty. Ring the clinic.' Jack was being dismissed.

Jem opened the door and behind her, Jack could see two people now.

'Don't be in a hurry to leave, Jack. Alannah's decided to surface,' she explained.

'I'll say hello,' he said, as if wanting to please, but signalling that he would be leaving soon.

He watched Alex Petras escort a willowy blonde onto the deck. She was taller than Jem, with a figure that spoke of never having had children. Even unwell, devoid of make-up, she was attractive, with naturally stunning features. He couldn't confirm the colour of her eyes in the low light, other than noting that they were pale and watchful, flicking to him once too often.

'Er, I'm Jack,' he said, as no one was doing any introductions.

'Oh, sorry,' Alex and Jem said together.

'And you must be Alannah,' Jack continued. 'I'm sorry you've been under the weather.'

'That's one way of putting it,' she murmured wryly, sighing. 'But I needed to get up. I think the fresh air will help.'

'Are you comfortable, darling?' Alex wondered. 'Can I get you—'

'Oh Alex, don't fuss,' Alannah said with aggression, waving a hand.

Something snagged in Jack's mind. It was vague, skimming at the edge, trying to win his focus, but the others talking all at once distracted him. Suddenly water was being poured, fresh coffee being offered and other topics were being talked about and he lost the thread that he had tried to keep a grip on a moment or so before.

'I hear you're a journalist,' Alannah directed at him.

Jack smiled. 'Features more than hard news.'

'Have you been spilling your secrets, Mark?' Alannah asked, looking over at him with a smile that struck Jack as almost sly, certainly one that only people well-acquainted with each other might share.

'None to spill, Al.'

Jack watched a glance bounce between Maddox and Mrs Petras. He couldn't read it properly; Mark seemed slightly defensive in that glance.

'And I hear you're something of an old salt,' Jack said to Alannah as everyone settled into seats.

'Old salt?' she queried.

He laughed kindly. 'A silly term for a good sailor where I come from.'

She beamed a smile back at him; she really was stunning and he had little doubt as to why Jem might feel threatened by the suggestion that her husband had fallen prey to Alannah Petras. Most men would likely enjoy her attention. Jack's well-honed senses, however, told him that her smile was cold, contrived to pay him the compliment of her attention, which she could choose to lavish – or not. 'I've always loved the sea. Do you know Lithuania?'

'I've never visited, but I know it's on the eastern shore of the Baltic Sea.'

'Then you know more than most Australians.'

'He's not Australian,' Jem said.

Jack watched Alannah give a blink as if she couldn't care less, like everyone here was simply for her benefit. In fact Jack believed that, apart from himself, they probably were. She might be unwell, but she commanded attention.

Jem was certainly doing a great job covering up how she felt about this woman. He needed to think, backtrack, find out what had caught his attention earlier. He also wanted to call his boss; he needed to excuse himself.

His phone conveniently pinged and he checked. It was a text from Matt. At last.

'Right, well, I'd better go. Thank you, everyone – a most enjoyable evening. Dr Maddox . . . Mark, you've been very generous with your time.' Jack offered a hand and Mark shook it. He then turned to Alex, who already had an outstretched hand that Jack shook too. 'Good to meet you, Alex.' He looked at his bored wife. 'Mrs Petras, I do hope you're feeling much better by morning.'

She gave a grimace. 'I want to get off this beach, to be honest, and get back on our cruiser, no offence intended, dear Jem.'

'None taken,' Jem said, cutting a look at Jack. 'Oh, listen, Jack. I think I might have left my cardigan at your house when Mark and I were there.'

'Oh, did you?' he said carefully, immediately presuming Jem needed him to say just that. 'Erm, how can I get it to you?'

'Mark, do you fancy fetching my cardi for me?'

'Not really, Jem. I'm tired. Can it wait?'

'I'll go,' Alex offered in his kind manner.

'No, no, please. Stay with Alannah.'

'I don't need babysitting by my husband,' she said.

'It's fine,' Jem assured them and looked to Jack. 'Do you mind if I walk back down the beach with you?' she asked. 'I do actually need it. It's the only one I brought.'

He was impressed by her calculated risk. She'd played it well, especially as either of the men could have been gallant enough to say they would go. 'I shall feel obliged to walk you back here.' He grinned.

'No way,' Jem said. 'I'll bring a torch and text Mark so he can look out for me.'

Mark nodded. 'Wave your torch about and I'll know it's you.'

'Right, I'll just get it,' she said, ducking back inside the house as Jack stepped down onto the sand with another round of polite farewells.

Jem was at his side with a small tote bag slung around her shoulder. They kept a marked gap between them, just in case anyone was watching them as they trudged off into the darkness. She dug into the bag for her torch and switched it on. 'We don't really need this, but it means Mark can watch us innocently walking back. Tide's going out.'

'So I note. What's up?'

'Apart from the fact that I hate them all right now and would rather be with you?'

'Jem . . .' Jack began.

'I know. It's all right, I don't mean to make you feel responsible. I'm just angry. And I need to say it aloud or I'll explode. Having that sour-faced bitch in my house with all her disdain is testing me.'

'You're doing amazingly well despite it. Do you still believe she's sleeping with your husband?'

Jem shook her head. 'No.'

That explained her tolerance. 'What about Alex? Does her husband trust her?'

'I can't tell. I don't know him well enough, but from the little contact I've had, I think he's a traditional sort of guy who won't want his manhood threatened. Either way, I do think Alannah has got some sort of hold over Mark.'

Jack had seen it too. 'She probably has over most men she meets.'

'You?'

He chuckled. 'In a different situation, perhaps, yes. She strikes me as being used to absorbing all the attention.'

'I think I despise her,' Jem said, making a face. 'She has a powerful magnetism for women as well. The mothers at school crowd around her like flies to roadkill; they like being her friend.'

'But not you?'

'I didn't really know her until very recently. So now I'm being polite and observing the manners my parents might expect of me on this occasion for Mark's sake. If I'm to save my family a lot of heartache, then I have to save my marriage and it starts here with horrible Alannah. Her only defence today is that she's clearly unwell. She was running a fever earlier.'

'Still is, I reckon,' Jack said. 'That's not food poisoning, that's an infection. Her eyes seem glassy.'

'She swears she and Alex ate identical food and, let's face it, it doesn't look like she eats anyway, the thin skank.'

Jack laughed aloud. 'Don't let her get under your skin, Jem. She may be attractive, but it's in a very cold way.'

'Well, I hope the fever intensifies and she has to go to the local hospital and share a ward with some drunks,' she jested.

'What's the infection from, I wonder?' he said as they strolled.

'I'm no nurse but probably whatever damaged her hand.'

Jack felt The Tingler creep up his back. It came without warning; gooseflesh accompanied by a momentary sense of an alarm ringing distantly. 'Wait! What?' But his mind was racing. That was it. The tiny bandage around a finger.

She'd kept it covered with the sleeves of her jumper pulled low, but he'd caught sight of it when she had waved her hand at everyone fussing. The image now came roaring back with the pathologist's warning that whoever had suffered the wound would likely be feeling unwell, with the potential for infection unless it was properly treated. And that injury would be as good as Nikki Lawson speaking from the dead, pointing her finger in accusation at her murderer. He needed to confirm this, but how?

'Jack?'

'Keep walking,' he said, pulling her arm gently before letting it go.

'What's going on?' Jem asked.

'Her hand is hurt, you say?'

'Yes. She hurt it on the boat, apparently.'

'How?'

He could feel her frowning in the darkness. 'She didn't say.'

'Did you see the wound?'

'Yes, briefly, when she cleaned it. Why?'

'Quickly, what did it look like?'

They arrived at his beach house and started walking up the sand towards the low dunes that backed onto the verandah.

She grinned. 'Don't be ghoulish.'

'Jem, please,' he urged.

'Er . . . okay.' Jem realised he was serious. 'It's here,' she said, pointing down the length of the index finger of her left hand from the fingernail. 'She's taken some skin off. Looks quite nasty.'

'Shit!' he murmured.

'Jack! What?' But he was already reaching for his phone.

29

'You need to go back,' Jack urged Jem. 'Did you really leave anything here?'

She shook her head. 'No, I just wanted to be with you a little longer.' She shrugged. 'I don't say that to be needy; I just wanted to get away until everyone's gone home or to bed and the trial of having to be around them in my bleak mood is nearly over.'

'Switch your torch on, send Mark the text and you'd better head off. Here, stuff this tea towel in your bag to pretend you picked something up.'

'It's okay, I brought one. I'll wear it back. He won't notice.' Jem shrugged again.

'Right, well—'

'Jack, I'm not leaving until you tell me what's going on.'

'This isn't—'

'Listen to me. I'm trying to save my family. When I thought Mark was seeing someone else, I needed to feel desired too . . . and perhaps it was some private revenge. I'll say again, though, I'm glad I followed my instincts with you, Jack. If Mark isn't being unfaithful, then I'm going to attempt to repair my marriage. To do that I have to be able to trust my husband from here on. I told you that I still sense lies somewhere, though, and you withholding information is not helping me to make that decision to give him a chance.'

Jack didn't for a moment think Jem's marriage would survive what he now believed Mark was deeply involved with. He couldn't tell her that. She'd need to reach her own decisions that were best for her and her children. 'I think you're right that Alannah's injury is making her so unwell.'

'And?'

'And I don't think she was injured by accident. If my hunch is right, she got it while involved in some clandestine activity.'

Jem began to speak but Jack continued. 'I can't say more. It would compromise everything I'm trying to do here and, more importantly, it may put you in some jeopardy. You not knowing any more will keep you safer. Now, I need you to go back to the house before anyone starts getting suspicious.'

'I want to know—'

'I know you do. But I can't tell you any more than I have. Go home, Jem. By tomorrow, I promise I'll be able to tell you plenty.'

That seemed to placate her; her features slackened and he could see the tension leave her body. 'So I will see you tomorrow?'

'I'll say goodbye for sure, and I'll have more to say.'

'All right. I'm counting on you keeping that promise, or I'll hate you from afar forever.'

He leaned in and kissed her cheek. 'We can't have that,' he said gently and, knowing what she needed, he allowed his mouth to stray to hers, kissing her tenderly. 'I want to say thank you, but I don't want you to take it the wrong way.'

She smiled, kissed him softly back, savouring the moment. 'I won't. I don't regret you for a second.'

'Good.' They shared one final affectionate peck and hug. 'Go wave your torch and, Jem, don't say anything about that wound on Alannah's hand. Will you promise me?'

She nodded. 'Is she dangerous?'

He hadn't expected her to make the connection. 'I'm not sure yet. But say nothing, just let Alex and Alannah leave as soon as you can organise it, if they haven't gone already.'

'Alex was in no hurry though. Anyway, all right, I'll keep all of this to myself. Bye, Jack.'

'Night, Jem.'

After she left, he stood in the dark of his house, listening to the sea drawing itself back as if inhaling before sighing out and allowing the foam of its edge to dribble back to shore. All he could do was wait now. He'd called Matt, told him everything. He stood there for hours as night drew into the early morning. Absently, Jack thought the inhalations of the ocean felt longer, stronger and louder than the former soft sighing, but he was fully preoccupied by the thoughts at the front of his mind, which were now all about Alannah Petras.

He rang Matt back.

He answered brusquely. 'Yep?'

'Where are you?'

'Sorry, did you get my text? I got delayed with another case. Another hour maybe.' Matt sounded tired.

Jack, on the other hand, was wide awake. 'What's the plan?'

'Eyes on, that's all. We've put them under surveillance. I've got our team applying for warrants to listen in to phones, and all that other stuff. Just be our eyes for now, Jack, and don't do anything heroic. I've organised to download that CCTV footage from the port, and—'

'His name is Redford,' Jack cut in.

'Who?'

'The ship's agent. Andy Redford.'

'We have to be sure first that—'

'I am sure. But if the material was brought off the ship, and I reckon it must have been, I can't tell you how it was handed over, because I didn't witness anything that resembled an exchange, just a meet.' He hated having to admit as much, but he continued. 'That's why we need that footage, now.'

'Right, well, it's on its way. Have to say I'm pretty impressed with Dr Moore's discovery.' Matt's voice sounded warmer now, more like his usual self.

'She's very chuffed and deservedly so,' Jack said. 'I know she probably pushed our barrow in the background to get that post-mortem, so I've sent her some flowers with our thanks.'

'Good on you, Jack.' He could almost hear the smile in Matt's voice. They rang off.

Hearing someone else's voice, knowing Matt was driving towards him, had brought fresh focus and it was time to get organised. It was with a sense of wonder that Jack began to slot the pieces into place. He knew they all needed to fit snugly or Carol Rowland would not acquiesce to bringing about the full-blown joint op.

He decided to record his thoughts so he could leave a file with the South Australian Major Crimes Unit and send a copy to Rowland. Saying it aloud also made it feel real to him. He moved through the dark house and turned on a single bedside lamp, which illuminated the room with low light but flung the outside into darkness. The picture windows became a mirror reflecting him as he found the small digital recording device. He meant to turn the light back off so he could look out past the moonlit beach to the inky depths of the far distance, where, on this dead tide night, the cruiser belonging to Alex and Alannah Petras had been anchored. But he forgot and instead stared unseeing at his own reflection.

Without moving from his seat on the bed, he began to organise his thoughts. This was important. If he got this right, the dual op would happen – he had no doubt about it – and he could leave Australia knowing he'd delivered a withering blow to the insidious and shadowy enterprise that had led to the death of bright, ambitious Amelia Peters. He'd never thought of himself as an avenger, but this knowledge he'd built that would tear down the architecture of the black-market operation felt powerful.

When Jem had arrived back at the house, a fresh storm had brewed. The conversation started out innocently enough, but quickly turned dark.

'I thought you were leaving,' she said to their guests, who were sitting around the deck.

'Suddenly Alannah's in no hurry.' Alex sighed.

'You and your English guest look close,' Alannah said. Alex gave her a look.

Jem knew the woman was stirring trouble and didn't respond.

'Don't start, Alannah,' Alex said.

'And don't you tell me what I can or can't say, Alex. You're not my keeper.'

Jem saw that land. She felt sorry for him. She wished they could all go to bed, but Alannah seemed to have found a second wind, having taken enough painkillers to satisfy an elephant.

Alannah shrugged. 'It all seemed cosy, that's all I'm saying.'

'Cosy?' Jem repeated, glad the darkness would hide her blushing.

'He's handsome.'

'Is he?'

The laugh that came in response was edged with ice. 'I found him very handsome and interesting. I'd sleep with him.'

'Alannah!' Her husband looked genuinely furious. 'Don't speak like this.'

'Oh, darling, you're not jealous, surely? I'm allowed to find other men sexy, aren't I?'

Jem was horrified. Surely Alex Petras wasn't going to let that go? She jumped in, not wanting a scene between the couple. 'How would you know he was interesting? You were vomiting in the bedroom for most of our evening.'

'Jem, cool it,' Mark murmured. 'Don't get involved.'

Alex looked as though he'd smelled something awful. 'You know, Alannah, I love you, but be careful not to poke the bear.'

'What does that mean, darling? Should I feel threatened?'

'I'm a man. No man likes to be disrespected.'

'I told you years ago, you should never trust a beautiful woman, Alex darling. They're always going to be desired by others.'

'I won't be mocked, Alannah.'

'Or what?' Alannah said, in a horribly saccharine tone, stroking his ear.

He pushed her hand away. 'You'll see.'

'Oh, how curious. Shall I phone my father and say I'm feeling frightened?'

'Do what you like. I'm tired of it.'

'Don't you dismiss me like that, as though I don't matter,' Alannah said. She looked crazed suddenly. 'My father could have you killed in a heartbeat for that alone.'

'Your father's an old man now. And he can't reach me out here. Be careful. Don't threaten me. The snake will turn.'

'Snake? I thought you were a bear.' She laughed and looked to Mark, perhaps hoping to drag him into the fray to laugh alongside her. He didn't. No one was laughing.

'Okay, I'm finding this turn of conversation very uncomfortable,' Jem said. 'I think we should call it a night.'

Alannah turned her gaze on Jem. 'Why invite us if you don't want us here?'

Jem's patience had deserted her. 'I didn't,' she said, feeling uncharacteristically mean. 'Mark insisted.'

Alannah smirked. 'Actually, I was only being polite because dear Alex wanted the four of us to be friends. To be candid, I don't need new friends. But a word of advice, Jem, honey. Look out or lose him to someone just like me.'

'Goodnight, everyone,' Alex said, looking angry now. 'Thank you, Jem, but I won't be staying.'

Jem wanted to say she hadn't offered for them to do so; perhaps Mark had suggested it. It annoyed her to think he might have, but Alannah jumped in before anything further was said.

'Good. I don't want you near me, Alex,' she said with terrible disdain.

No, she couldn't tolerate this a moment longer. 'Actually, Alex, I think you should take your wife with you,' Jem said. 'And when you emerge from your fever, Alannah, I hope you'll remember how horrible your behaviour has been. I doubt you're well enough to get to the cruiser, so I suggest a motel in town.' She absently heard Alex excuse himself and move indoors, hopefully to gather up their things and make a quick departure to a nearby motel, as she rounded on her husband. 'This dinner was a mistake.'

'And you inviting the journo was a mistake too. We can call it quits.'

'Yes, let's talk about that, shall we?' Alannah drawled. 'An interview? At night, over a barbecue? How odd. Tell me about it,' she demanded.

Alex came back out. 'Alannah, are you coming with me?' he asked. 'Last chance.'

'No! And don't "last chance" me. You're nothing without me on your arm,' she said, her tone still oozing disdain. 'Let's face it, darling, I am good for your ego and public reputation. It would not be in your interest to snub me, my love.'

Alex shook his head. 'You presume too much. Your father's reputation doesn't stretch to here and I'm not quite as in awe as you imagine.'

Alannah just laughed. 'I don't believe that.'

Jem had to hand it to her. What wouldn't she give for just a smidge of that confidence, or was it simply arrogance?

Alex nodded at the Maddoxes. 'Right. Well, I'll find a room somewhere local. Good night.' Alex turned on his heel and departed.

Alannah didn't bat an eye. 'I want to know what you said to the journalist, Mark,' she pressed.

Jem couldn't help bristling at Alannah's demands of her husband. 'Why? What interest does reproductive medicine hold for you?'

'You don't know what interests me. You might be surprised.'

Jem rolled her eyes. She *was* surprised that her husband felt compelled to obey Alannah's demands.

'Nothing much to say,' Mark said, sounding annoyed. 'Just an interview about reproductive medicine and the demand for it.'

Alannah nodded. 'How does he know you?'

Mark explained briefly, his expression conveying that he didn't think it was important.

'How coincidental he found you, Mark. Did you check his credentials?' Alannah asked.

'What's it to you?' Jem whipped back. 'Mark can talk to whomever he wants.'

Alannah ignored her, eyes on Mark. 'I want to know. Did you check him out?' Jem noted the hard edge in their guest's voice as she continued her questions. 'Who does he work for?'

'I don't know,' her husband snapped, his arms wide in ignorance. 'He's a features editor for some magazines in England. Probably a stringer, I imagine. It was fine. It helps my international profile.'

Jem felt the urge to spill the beans and envisaged Jack threading a needle to stitch her lips together. She couldn't betray him.

'What's his interest in you, specifically?' Alannah asked.

'Mark is one of the foremost minds in reproductive medicine in this state, that's why,' Jem interjected, feeling it necessary to support her husband. 'Now, can I suggest you join your husband in the motel he's obviously left for? I think it's time for you to go.'

Alannah didn't even look at Jem before saying snidely, 'What did we agree about lying low?'

'It's nothing, Alannah,' Mark snapped.

'Lying low?' Jem asked, feeling like a caged parrot repeating what she heard, with no idea what was being discussed. 'Are you talking in code now?'

'Shhh,' Alannah hissed, her eyes glittering with fury. Jack was right; infection was definitely raging through her body. 'Just shut up, Jem.'

Jem's mouth opened in shock. 'You did not just say that to me. On my deck, of my house, after lying in my bed?'

'I could buy this house ten times over, you stupid creature.'

Mark drew in a breath. 'That's enough, Alannah! You need to drop this.'

Jem stood. 'Well, you two seem to know each other pretty well – this cosy chat is intriguing. You know Alex thinks you're sleeping together.'

Alannah laughed. 'My husband is a dolt . . . just like you, Jem.' She waved a disdainful hand. 'So naturally he'd think someone like me would be sleeping with someone like Mark.'

'Alannah, please. This is my life,' Mark bleated.

Jem frowned. What was she missing?

'Tell me what you told him,' Alannah demanded.

'Nothing! Everyday general stuff about infertility. It was a regular interview, nothing out of the ordinary.'

'I want to know if you checked him out before you said a word to him.'

'Look, he's a hack, looking for a story and a quick buck to pay for his holiday down under. He ambushed me at my clinic and I sent him packing.'

'So why was he eating sausages at your beach house then?'

Mark explained how Jack had run into Jem.

Alannah's laugh was unkind. 'You fool. You don't smell a rat in this?'

Jem was spent. 'The only smell around here is your hand, Alannah. I think you should go to the hospital and get the hell out of our lives. Go back to importing your shabby chic, or whatever it is you do.'

Alannah met her gaze. 'If you only knew.'

Jem blinked. *What did that mean?*

But Alannah hadn't finished. 'And I think you should go inside or shut your stupid mouth, because I'll close it for you if you don't.'

'And that's okay by you, is it, Mark? Her speaking to me like that?' Jem asked, thrilled to hear her voice dripping so much sarcasm. She was glad she hadn't lost her temper again.

'No, it's not okay. Alannah, did you get what you came to Wallaroo for?'

'Yes.'

'Then leave before this gets out of control. I think the tide is moving.'

It's already turned, Jem thought. What had Alannah come to Wallaroo to get? She wanted to leave too, but this was her house.

'Let me worry about tides. I know the sea. I'm not leaving until you tell me everything you told your handsome guest, because, Mark, he is not who he says he is. He's probably an undercover cop.'

Jem stepped back into the darkness, shocked. She slid out her phone.

Mark looked shocked too. 'What do you mean?'

'I told you who my father is, and who my grandfather was. They say I'm every inch in his mould.'

'Why are you telling me this?' Mark said, looking confused.

'Because I grew up at Arkan's knee, watching how he cunningly avoided the police.' Alannah glanced at Jem. 'He's a mob boss, if you didn't know.' She gave a little shrug before turning back to Mark. 'And if there's one trait I learned better than most from him, it was to be suspicious of everyone, even family, but especially newcomers who seem to come into your world innocently. This journalist is much cleverer than you think. I had a few minutes in his company and I can tell you, I could smell police all over him.'

'Rubbish!' Mark said. 'Jem will tell you—'

'What will Jem tell us, Mark? Look at her. It's probably him she's texting right now.'

Jack's phone pinged once in his pocket but he'd just started recording. He would check it shortly; it was likely Matt, giving him an update on his progress.

Jack began with the date and place to formalise his report. He paused; he thought he saw something out in the dark but it was hard to see past his own reflection and he didn't want to lose his train of thought right now. It was likely a lone seagull swooping low towards its nest in the dunes.

'This is Detective Superintendent Jack Hawksworth of Scotland Yard and I'm here under no official title, but receiving support from the South Australian metropolitan police as I build the background for a potential dual operation between the UK and Australia. The plan was for me to pose as a tourist to establish that there is an organised crime syndicate operating out of Adelaide. My hope was to pinpoint the leaders of this black-market operation, who are promoting the collection, storage, transport and use of human reproductive material across borders from the UK to Australia, involving clinics in Eastern Europe and the United Arab Emirates.'

He outlined the information he had about the women involved, then took a deep breath and continued. 'Alannah Petras, with the help of obstetrician and gynaecologist Dr Mark Maddox, have, I believe, set up an operation in South Australia that has quickly broadened its reach, like any successful enterprise that sees a gap in a market where demand is far greater than supply.

'I imagine it has widened into greater Australia and perhaps into New Zealand. While to the best of my knowledge it is servicing a domestic market, it has the ability to reach sinister and dangerous tentacles across the globe, all the way into Europe, further still to the UK in order to get original material from as far away as possible.'

What a cunning operation, he thought, then continued. 'The sly beauty of this syndicate is that it sources eggs from, let's say, Europe for use on the other side of the world. I think any police operation should be looking at whether that plan is also done in reverse and eggs are being sourced for use in the UK and Europe, perhaps even the US. It makes sense, as they have the infrastructure set up. This group have established laboratories in Eastern Europe – and we have a witness who will attest that Mark Maddox visited both Vilnius and Belgrade at the time the clinics were established.'

He nodded to himself. 'We must scrutinise Alannah Petras and her travel habits. I would not be surprised at all to discover labs in places like Singapore, Malaysia, Thailand, India and other Eastern European countries.

'The syndicate collects money from desperate, infertile women who are prepared to pay whatever is asked to have a shot at pregnancy. They exploit expertise from presumably undervalued laboratory clinicians and pay them to overlook the illegalities of the situation. And they have worked out how to hitch a ride with the legal courier transfers coming into Australia, although I am yet to establish how that's done.

'I have a suspicion that the two people behind this syndicate believe the slick transport they've had going for the last few years may come under scrutiny due to the deaths of two key people – a courier, Greg Payne, and a senior embryologist, Nicola Lawson, who knew each other and worked together via MultiplyMed, where Dr Maddox also works. These deaths suggest to me that something went wrong with the plan. I am hazarding that the courier and embryologist were asking questions or perhaps making threats to go public and have paid with their lives.'

The sound of clapping startled him and he turned. Standing at the door of his bedroom was a smirking Alannah Petras. Behind her, looking anxious, was Mark Maddox.

'Where's Jem?' was all Jack could think of to say.

30

Alex Petras had left the beach house angrier than he could remember feeling since he was a young, hot-tempered man in Vilnius. He'd known from his late teens that Alannah Rubis was trouble. Off limits. She was the daughter of a notorious gangster, but she was irresistible.

They'd met at a nightclub. She'd looked dazzling and he was the only young man who'd had the courage to walk over to the booth where she sat with her wealthy friends and ask her to dance.

'Do you know who I am?' she'd asked, blinking those cool seawater-coloured eyes lazily.

'I do.'

'And you're not scared?'

'Clearly not.' He'd smirked. 'Do you want to dance or not?'

'My father doesn't like his seventeen-year-old dancing with strangers.'

'Introduce us then . . . and we won't be strangers.'

She'd laughed. He liked that. And she'd danced with him.

They danced all night and then he took her to her home and didn't even try to kiss her goodnight.

This surprised her. 'Not trying to steal a kiss, Alex?'

He shook his head. 'I'm too smart.'

'How smart?'

'Smart enough that I'll be a very wealthy man by twenty-five. By thirty I'll be a millionaire. By forty, a multi-millionaire.'

She laughed again. 'How?'

'Watch me . . . or, better still, marry me.'

'We only met tonight!'

'I don't want anyone else.'

'Maybe I do.'

'I doubt it. No one will be smart enough for you. But I am. And I'm not scared of your father.' That last part was a lie. He was indeed scared of Galeti Rubis, who was known to be ruthless in his dealings.

She smiled that cool smile of hers. 'Come to dinner tomorrow night. Meet the family. Seven. Don't be late. My father likes to eat promptly at seven-thirty.'

And that had been the beginning of something he'd thought unbreakable. Not only had her terrifying father made him earn the right to be at his table, putting Alex through a forbidding and relentless conversation that could only be termed an interrogation, but he'd ended it with a threat over the honey cake, made by the cook to Alannah's mother's family recipe. Rubis had lifted a finger and the cook was called in to taste from a slice that Rubis had chosen. Alex learned later this was normal practice; the cook had to prove each day that none of the family's meals were poisoned by sampling them in front of Rubis.

Satisfied, Rubis had shovelled a large forkload of dessert into his mouth and then pointed the fork at Alex as he chewed. 'I can see you like my daughter.'

'I do.'

'She tells me you want to marry her.'

'I do, sir.'

'You're nineteen. You're nothing.'

'Maybe. But I will be.'

'Prove it. Take your time. Impress me and then we'll talk about my girl.' He put down his fork. 'And one more thing, Petras.'

'Yes, sir?'

'If you ever hurt her, I will flay you. Do you know what that means?'

Alex met his gaze. 'You'll strip the skin from my body.'

Rubis had smiled with a mouthful of honey cake behind his teeth. He finished chewing and swallowed. 'That's right. And then, not dead yet, I'll impale you on a stake in the forest and the wild animals can finish you off. Do you understand?'

Alex nodded. 'I will never hurt her. I adore her.'

He had indeed taken his time – seven years. In that time he'd slept with other women, got one pregnant, married her and then promptly divorced her as soon as Marguerite had been born. There was only one woman for him. When he presented himself back to Rubis, Alex's bank account was bulging from his wily transport business through Europe. In that time, Alannah had not married but she'd had a lot of fun, it seemed, and her parents now wanted her to settle down. They chose Alex for her. And he chose Australia to move her away from her father's influence and reach. But not without Rubis reiterating his threat.

'I haven't forgotten,' Alex assured him. 'But I'm opening up new routes,' he'd lied. Australia would be safe. South Australia in particular would be sleepy. They could have a family, raise their children and live a good life without the gangster tag.

It hadn't worked out how he'd planned but it had come close – he'd even shifted Marguerite and her mother out to Australia so he could look after them properly. Perhaps he should have thought it strange then that Alannah had not given a moment's care to the woman and child from his past being so close. He now realised this was because Alannah simply didn't care about anyone – or not since they'd failed to create their own family, anyway.

And now her adoration of him had disappeared. Alannah was affectionate when she felt like it, but often treated him so badly a physical pain could erupt. But he kept his promise to Rubis. He had never disrespected the powerful man's daughter; he had made more money than twenty men might in a lifetime, and he had lavished that money upon her for all her wants and desires. He sent her home two, sometimes three times a year to be with her family, and he had shown her only faithfulness and affection. Until it became clear they could have no children, their marriage had been solid and affectionate. But it had turned when she'd met Maddox, whom Alex had stupidly introduced her to in a last, desperate bid to fall pregnant.

Once he observed the familiarity between them, he had immediately assumed the worst, that she'd fallen for her doctor, but now he couldn't tell whether Alannah was sleeping with his friend, or whether she was using all of them. He'd always had blinkers where Alannah was concerned; he gave her so much rope to do as she pleased, so long as she never betrayed him. But now Alex was convinced he was being betrayed in more ways than one, and his old temper, which he'd kept in check for so many years, was back. It had begun easing out of its shell a year ago, maybe. He'd managed to calm it, but today it was out and raging, angrier than ever.

He knew she was lying about her hand. She said she'd torn it on a rusty nail and had given him some half-baked tale that he'd accepted but not trusted. Acceptance began to subside when she refused to go to hospital to have it treated – why wouldn't she want to have it looked at by a professional?

'You may need plastic surgery,' he'd tried. 'Your hands are beautiful. Why risk one being defaced by this injury?'

She'd ignored him. And that annoyed him more than anything. In the last few weeks Alannah had become dismissive of him, disrespectful, as though only her needs mattered. Sex had stopped. Her affection felt contrived. She was acting secretive, no longer consulting him about her business interests when she had always relied on his proven skills. He'd initially helped her with her shipping questions, and gladly, but then she'd become evasive, intolerant of him knowing much about her dealings. Now she was openly insulting him, making fun of him in public . . . in front of Mark Maddox. Showing off. Earlier, she'd left him to go and do something at the jetty. Something secretive. Was that where she'd met her lover? Maybe he'd organise to have her followed next time.

But tonight was the final straw. Her behaviour and her disdain were no longer things he could tolerate. His pride was no longer bruised but broken. She was treating him like a loser and he wouldn't stand for it. But why? Maybe she blamed him for her lack of children rather than the proven endometriosis. He knew her sadness over not being a mother was genuine, even if little else about her was.

Alannah was becoming worse as she aged, he'd noticed. More arrogant, over-confident, still believing her gangster background could frighten everyone in her path. She wanted everything her way. Oh, there were moments when he glimpsed her vulnerability, like the other day after the lunch with the Maddoxes, and yet why did he feel it was purely for his benefit? She didn't want him touching her, had knocked him back when he suggested they go to bed early and enjoy one another.

Yes, she was enjoying someone else touching her, he was sure.

And that just wouldn't do.

He stared at the new phone in his hand. If she didn't call him soon and find out where he was . . . and if she – heaven help her – decided to leave on the boat without him, that would be the decision made. He would deal with her in the only way Alannah's kind might understand.

Alex moved back into the dark alley between two unoccupied homes halfway up the beach, presumably holiday houses, now quiet, curtains drawn. He sat on one of the decks, not too far from the yellow dinghy, which gave him a panoramic view across the landscape, all the way to the sea and the small light left on in his beloved cruiser.

'Where's Jem?' Jack repeated.

'She's here,' Alannah said, and reached beyond the door to drag a gagged and bound Jem into view. 'I must say, Jack, I'm truly impressed with how well you've put that all together. Don't you agree, Mark?'

Mark said nothing. He looked as though he was trying to avoid the murderous stare coming from his wife, and Jack suspected a lot was running through Mark's mind: children, wife, family, their life before all this, but most especially that he had never intended his sideline business to become so dangerous and out of control.

Jack moved off the bed to face Alannah, deliberately not looking at Jem and her fear. 'So I gather you murdered Nicola Lawson, Alannah, but who murdered Greg Payne?'

'Nikki drowned and Greg committed suicide. I didn't know either of them and I am not aware of anything criminal.'

'The fact that you say "Nikki" and not "Nicola" incriminates you,' Jack replied.

Alannah gave him a sly smile, as though acknowledging he'd trapped her that time. 'Are you recording?'

'Not any more.' He tossed the device onto the bed.

'It was one each. I was involved in Nikki's death, and Mark pushed Greg off the cliff.'

Jem squeaked behind her muzzle, and Mark's expression turned from stormy to thunderous at Alannah's admission.

Jack shook his head. 'Fill in the blanks for me. Why did they need to die?'

Alannah sighed as though it was tedious to answer him but she didn't mind because she had no intention of allowing him to live. 'They were becoming liabilities. Your presumption was correct – they knew too much, were asking questions, were no longer necessary.'

'Am I right you've shifted to bringing in the material via grain ships?'

She smiled. 'You're really very smart, Jack. I knew it. See what you let in, Mark?' she said over her shoulder. 'It was such a clever idea too, but you've blown it now. I'll have to think of something else.'

Jem began to cry. Quiet tears.

'I intend that you'll never get the chance to reinvent yourself. Where's Alex? Is he part of this operation?'

'No. He's too straight. He's at some motel, none the wiser.' Alannah gave another smirk.

'So what now?' Jack asked.

A bottle of pills was tossed on the bed. 'Now you swallow those,' Alannah commanded.

'Why would I do that?'

'I want you, shall we say, compliant.'

'That many will kill me.'

'Good. One less nuisance,' she said with a shrug. 'We'll stage a suicide.'

Jack shook his head, tutting as if admonishing a child. 'Really, Alannah? No one would believe that, and you don't have time for it anyway. Think clearly now.'

'I am thinking clearly. According to you, I have two murders to my name—'

'Actually, quite a few more than that,' he corrected her. 'Although a good barrister would ensure that those I refer to were seen as only manslaughter. While your actions caused the deaths, you didn't deal the blows yourself.'

She frowned. 'What are you talking about?'

'At this stage? Eight women across the UK that I'm aware of, who have died as a result of botched harvesting of eggs.' He told her about Amelia.

Alannah couldn't hide her surprise fast enough, and Jack caught the look of betrayal that flashed in her pale eyes, again glittering with fury. 'Oh, Mark. You should have checked his credentials and then we'd not be in this situation. It seems we're part of an international sting.'

Jack ignored her. 'I was never going to let go until I got to the bottom of Amelia's death. And now all roads lead to you, Alannah . . . and you, Mark. Sorry, Jem. Your husband is every inch a criminal, like his Lithuanian sidekick here.' He knew the sidekick remark would infuriate her and he watched her face carefully.

She kept her expression even. 'Swallow your pills, Jack.' She pointed a long finger with a dark painted nail towards the bed.

'Or what?'

She pulled out a mean-looking switchblade and pressed the button that released its full nastiness.

'That doesn't scare me,' Jack lied, remembering all too vividly the feeling of another blade not so long ago.

'Yes, but it's not for you,' Alannah said, barely taking a breath before viciously stabbing Jem in the shoulder.

Jem shrieked in shocked surprise. Both men yelled in alarm.

Alannah was breathing hard, but Jack saw only pleasure in her expression. She was a predator torturing other animals simply for sport. 'And now she's in pain, Jack, because of you.'

'Alannah, what the f—' Mark began but his words died in his throat because she'd whipped around and threatened him with the blade too.

'Don't push me, Mark. You're the weak link, I'm afraid. Now, get your pathetic wife to stop her moaning and get her back on her feet. I have to go and, frankly, I've suffered more serious wounds than that as a child,' she sneered.

Jack swallowed his fear for Jem; he had to pretend he wasn't intimidated. He forced his voice into neutral. 'Why does the world owe you any favours? Why should it reward your suffering, whatever that's been? Do you believe you can somehow not be held accountable?'

'Take your pills,' she warned, 'or I'll hurt her again.'

He switched tack, buying time. *Come on, Matt!* 'Whatever pain relief you've taken will only work for a little while,' Jack said. 'The infection in that wound of yours is only going to get worse. I can smell you from over here and it's not pleasant.'

'How do you know about my wound?'

'Bites are the worst, aren't they?' He enjoyed seeing surprise flash in Alannah's cold eyes. 'Full of nasty germs, and because you didn't get it seen to at a hospital, the infection is about to have a party in your body, Alannah.' He kept his voice calm, almost like he was speaking to a child.

'I asked how you know.'

Jack tapped his nose. 'You're as smart as I am. I know you'll work it out next time you take a long look at that oozing, festering wound. It's lost about, um,'—he measured a couple of centimetres in the air between thumb and forefinger— 'about this much skin. Perhaps if you leave it long enough and luck's on our side, it might kill you and do the world a favour.'

Her lips flatlined at his remark. 'Take the pills!' she shouted, lurching towards Jem again.

'Okay, okay!' Jack put up his palms. 'Let her be.'

'See, Mark? There *is* something going on between your wife and the detective. He cares more about your wife than you do.' She sneered at Jem. 'You poor idiot.'

Jack cut a look Jem's way too. 'Hang in there.'

Jem shook her head, begging him with her eyes not to swallow the medication. But Jack reached for the bottle, snapped open the top and shook a couple of them out. Next to his bed was a half-drunk glass of water. He picked it up and put a pill in his mouth, letting it sit under his tongue, then swallowed a sip, tipping his head back as though allowing the drug to drop down his gullet. But he could feel it nestling against his frenum. How he could even remember that term at this moment baffled him, and he fought the urge to laugh.

'Now what?' he said, focusing on staying alive to joke later with Kate about the word.

'Keep going,' Alannah said, and he watched her wipe her forehead. Her face looked clammy. She was going downhill fast without realising how sick she was. Good. He needed to leverage that, keep her talking, keep her lingering here and hope she passed out. That was the best hope he had right now, but at worst, if she was weakened, he could at least try and get that knife. Thoughts whizzed by like fast-moving trains. If he managed to knock it out of her hand, then Mark might overwhelm him – he looked strong, if a little distracted. He was probably weighing up his part in all of this. If Jack wasn't mistaken, he could sense the bravado leaching from the doctor, quickly being replaced by fear and regret. Was that something else he could leverage? The problem was Jem and that bleeding. How could he get her out of the fray? She was Alannah's weapon and she knew it. All of his options screamed past in a couple of heartbeats.

Alannah nodded at the pills again, then at him.

He took another pill, again feigning swallowing it, but he knew this couldn't last. The tablets would begin melting in the warmth of his mouth – not fast, but they would have an effect and he couldn't hide many more under his tongue before it became obvious when he talked. 'What are these, anyway?'

'Tranquillisers. You can thank Dr Maddox for those. Frankly, I'd have preferred the chloroform, but Jem told us you're a martial arts expert and we'd never get close enough, although I'm not sure I believe it.'

Jack glanced at Jem again. He liked her pluck under the circumstances; she must have been terrified when the truth began to reveal itself, but she'd still found the courage to lie. Right now, though, her pallor was greyish and she seemed unresponsive, staring at the ground. Blood was dribbling slowly through her fingers. Alannah had chosen her spot well, painful but not life threatening. He tried to unsettle Mark instead.

'Maddox, check your wife. You let her bleed out, and I'll make sure it's on you.'

'She won't bleed out,' he said, his professional knowledge speaking, but Jack could hear the fear in his voice.

'Wow, your care factor is enormous,' Jack said with an eye roll. 'Alannah, even so, her wound needs—'

'Shut up. Don't be rattled by him, Mark. They train these arseholes in this sort of countermeasure.'

Jack gave a snort. 'Countermeasure? Where do you imagine we are? I think you've spent too long with people who lived through the Cold War,' he jeered. 'I'm not being tactical. I'm trying to save a life.'

'No one has to die,' Alannah declared. 'Except you, of course, Jack. I don't mind adding your name to my list immediately.'

'Then why haven't you? Why go through this process of taking pills? Am I important to keep alive? If you think I'm some sort of bargaining chip, think again. No one knows I'm here,' he lied. 'It's why I needed to record my thoughts.' *Keep talking, keep talking*, he urged himself. 'There's no cavalry riding towards me,' he assured her, surprised at how calm and confident he sounded. *Hurry, Matt!*

'I have my reasons.' She smiled. 'Now, I won't ask again. Swallow the pills. Let me see several at a time. Mark, here are your car keys.' She flung them the short distance and he caught them awkwardly.

'What do you want me to do?' he asked.

'Drive it back to where we came from! What else?'

Ah, so that's how I didn't see them arriving, Jack thought. He had been too focused on the beach to pay attention to the front of the house. They must have cruised down the road with no lights on and in first gear to be that quiet.

'Leave it in the driveway,' she snapped.

'What are you going to do?' Mark asked.

'I'm going to make sure this bastard doesn't bother us any more.'

Jack watched Mark slide a glance towards his wife, whose eyes blazed with both disappointment and unbridled fury at him. She'd worked off her gag.

'She speaks to you like a trained monkey,' Jem said. 'I've obviously been getting it wrong all these years talking to you as an equal and with respect. You weak bastard. Mark, you're embarrassing.'

Alannah began to laugh. 'I think she wishes you dead.'

'No, I wish *you* dead, you Russian bitch,' Jem said, rounding on her captor.

The blow from Alannah in response was fast and vicious and Jem landed sprawled on the floor, spraying blood. Her shock and pain as much as her anger was pumping that blood faster.

'I am not Russian,' Alannah spat.

'Yes, but you're still a bitch,' Jem said, heaving herself to a seated position and putting a palm to her face where she'd been hit.

Alannah didn't take her eyes off Jem. 'Mark, why are you still here?'

'Yeah, Mark, do as your Russian whore commands. Drown yourself on the way out too – I hope the kids and I never have to see you again.'

'You don't mean that,' he said, sounding shocked.

'Oh, I mean it. The best thing you can do for yourself right now is kill yourself or just leave. You'll find nothing waiting for you at home except the police. Now fuck off and do your monkey trainer's bidding!'

Jack would have cheered loudly if he dared, but Jem was only making it worse for herself. Perhaps that was her intention, to make Mark turn on Alannah, but Jack didn't think the guy had the balls.

Alannah apparently found only humour in the situation, laughing again before turning serious. 'Go!' she commanded the hesitating doctor. 'I mean it.'

Mark obediently left and Jack watched Jem's expression settle into one of defeat. He really did worry whether Jem would survive this crisis. But there was no time to ponder. Alannah's attention was firmly back on him. 'Now, Jack, I've asked you nicely, but I'll gladly stab her again if you don't begin to swallow those pills.'

Jack obliged, knowing that he somehow had to make something happen before the sedatives took full effect.

31

Matt had set in motion an opportunity to view the CCTV video from the docks that would indeed be helpful if it was working. He groaned to himself as he drove, thinking about how in all the best crime TV, that essential footage was somehow corrupted, lost, stolen or the camera had been switched off.

He checked the sat nav. Another ten minutes at most. His mind was swirling with the news of the DNA discovery. What a find. It could so easily have been missed, and now here was Nikki Lawson pointing them to her killer. He hoped he would bring justice to the embryologist, who by all accounts had been as good as someone could be in her profession. Talking with her colleagues, he'd learned that Nikki was a lone wolf. She didn't mingle much with the others, didn't have a boyfriend, and someone had posed the notion that Nikki might have been gay. No one was sure. Her parents lived in Queensland and, from what he was gathering, she didn't have a relationship with them. There were no siblings. She was an enigma, really good at her work but aloof.

'Never rude, no,' a junior lab technician had responded during
Matt's brief visit to MultiplyMed. 'Nikki was just . . . well, she
was blunt.'

Another agreed but had added, 'Yes, she had an economy with
words and her style was direct, that's for sure, and she didn't suffer
fools easily, but that's giving the wrong impression of her. She was
also kind; she was the one who would work the awkward hours
or the holidays so the rest of us could have the special times with
our families. She had great empathy for our clients and for all her
fellow workers, even when she was trying to hide it.'

Matt nodded. 'I can tell you cared about her. Did she ever
come to work hungover or high?'

Both looked back at him perplexed. It was the second
colleague, a little older than the first, who answered. 'Nikki,
hungover? I don't think she ever drank alcohol, never talked
about going out drinking like a lot of people. I don't know about
drugs, but if she did use them, I had no sense of it. She was always
first in and last out and she'd never complain about re-checking
something. She told me once she liked to dance. Not ballet or
ballroom, but in her own style, privately on the dancefloor. She'd
just "tune out", in her words.'

'I think she might have been a little depressed,' the first
colleague said. He was young and looked suddenly embarrassed
for speaking up.

'What makes you say that?' Matt frowned.

'Er . . .'

Matt now smiled encouragingly. 'Say it, please. I'm trying to
unravel the mysterious circumstances in which she died. Let's help
her,' he urged.

'Well, I was having some problems with my father and Nikki
told me that she'd walked out on her family and hadn't seen or
spoken to them in years. I got the impression, though I could be

wrong, that she'd been abused. I think her bright hair and wild way of dressing, the tattoos and even the attitude, was all part of Nikki trying to be in control.'

'John, you're a bit young to be drawing such sweeping conclusions about—'

'No, it's insightful, thank you.' Matt had nodded, smiling John's way. They didn't know that Nikki had taken ecstasy, had indeed drunk alcohol and had taken another drug that toxicology was double-checking but looked to be a hefty sedative. Given what he knew, he suspected Nikki had been somehow 'encouraged' to take all of them.

The pair nodded as Matt continued. 'We may need to check some other stuff, but for now we're grateful. Thanks to you both.'

If Nikki had been such an island, so determined to live life on her terms, and especially if she had been abused in childhood, Matt thought, it would also explain how hard she had fought to beat her attackers.

Matt returned to the present. If there really was an organised crime syndicate operating out of Adelaide, then Matt knew it would do his career no harm to be right at the heart of the investigation as the scam unravelled. He dialled Jack, but found himself listening to his voicemail recording, which was odd. Their calls had become increasingly regular and tense as the English detective's hunch seemed to be gaining weight, so why wasn't he picking up?

He didn't leave a message, but rang again for good measure and got the voicemail again. Ah well, Kadina was behind him now; it wouldn't be more than seven minutes before he eased into the small township of Wallaroo.

Mark had returned and was given the job of watching Jack. He'd probably approached again from the road so no torch was required, meaning he hadn't risked being seen by anyone who might be on the beach, Jack figured. At this time everyone was likely tucked away in their homes, anyway.

As soon as Mark walked back in, Alannah handed him a knife, winking at Jack and saying, 'I always carry two.' The women had left, Alannah pulling Jem behind her. Jem didn't struggle and although Jack wished she had, he knew the sensation of that blade punching into her body would be on repeat in her mind, the pain forcing its way through the shock. He remembered it all too well.

'Where has Alannah taken Jem?' Jack asked. He sensed the first vague blurring of his mind as the pills began to have an effect. How many had he taken? Six?

'Are you sleeping with my wife?' Mark asked.

Protect Jem. 'Tell me how that might have worked?' Jack asked, filling his voice with exasperation.

Mark didn't bother trying to shape the notion. 'She wouldn't anyway. Jem's not capable of being unfaithful.'

'You take her for granted,' Jack said.

'What's that supposed to mean?'

'Just some advice from a man who presumably won't see the morning. Someone with all that you have – especially Jem – should be content, that's all I'm saying.'

'Who's to say I'm not?'

'Oh, come on, Maddox. You're knee-deep in this shit. Stop kidding yourself that you're going to get away with this. My student died. So have others. And look at the way the Lithuanians treat you. Alex might be innocent, but he essentially pats you on the head and his wife treats you like an errand boy. I can't imagine that's a comfy partnership.'

'Errand boy?' Mark repeated, sounding incredulous. 'You're joking, right? Alex has no idea and I mean that. He thinks his wife is amusing herself by importing furniture, but he's clueless as to what she's truly capable of. But let me assure you, Alannah may be cunning and ruthless, but it's all down to my expertise, my planning.'

Jack shrugged at the boast; Mark was digging himself in deeper.

'She put up the money, found the other investors but without me there is no operation. No way in for the material we source, no way to find the clients to use it. The clinics are my invention and the jewel in the crown was my idea to use the legal couriers, legal transportation methods.'

Jack acknowledged this with a tilt of his head, expressing that he was not in the slightest impressed. 'As I said, knee-deep. So now she's using ships. I can't see it working as well.'

'It won't.'

'Why do it, then?'

Mark shook his head. 'I don't want to any more. It started small. I'd convinced myself it was just a sort of shadow service I could offer to couples who'd exhausted the normal avenues of help but who had the money and the determination to keep trying. Look,' he said, trying to rationalise it, 'we all know that success lies in the numbers. Every gambler knows that probability increases every time you roll the dice or spin the ball around the roulette wheel. Your number will come up eventually.'

Jack raised his brows. 'How does that justify death?'

'Death was never part of my plan. This was meant to be an Aussie operation. Pay fertile women for their eggs, sell them to those who are desperate for children. But I needed the money to set up the clinic and its team. Alannah was a client. Unsuccessful after five or six attempts . . . I can't tell you what that does to a woman. I've seen it enough to know that something breaks inside.'

'Am I supposed to feel sorry for her?'

'No, I'm just trying to explain how this all got so out of hand. She was so distraught at being unable to give Alex a child of her

own that it twisted her into something else. When MultiplyMed
wouldn't let her do another cycle a couple of years ago, she
actually said to me, "If I build you a clinic, will you put some
eggs into me?"' He gave a mirthless chuckle. 'I was so shocked
that I laughed it off, but she wouldn't let it go. I put all the
obstacles in front of her, hoping that she'd run out of steam.'
Mark shook his head. 'It only made her more determined, angrier.
She wanted control. She wanted a child and nothing was going
to get in her way, especially not Mother Nature or the Australian
government.'

'Why capitulate to her?'

'She wore me down. But she's smart enough to search out
someone's weaknesses. Mine was my family, believe it or not. My
desire to set up a bulletproof future for my children. I told her
once that I wanted to give them each a house when they turned
twenty-five. They could sell it, use it as an investment, start a
portfolio with it or simply live in it. I didn't care, I just wanted
each of my kids set up so they wouldn't have to worry about what
most twenty-somethings worry about.'

'What's wrong with working for it?'

'It's not that. I wanted them to be able to follow their dream
and have the freedom to work at what they want to do, not
because they had mouths to feed or rent to pay.' He shrugged.
'I also wanted a good life for us, for me and Jem. And I didn't
want to have to wait until I was creaky to enjoy life. Alannah
could see I was envious of her husband's wealth and her lifestyle.
She homed in on that,' he said, putting his hands up in surrender. 'And then she worked me over, using that as her whip.
I thought it would be some small Adelaide clinic that offered
black-market fertility – that's how she sold it to me. Small. Nice
income. Happy families all round. Me in control of all of it. I'd
do the collections, the transfers. That was the plan!' he spat.

'I could keep everyone safe and healthy because I'm bloody good at my job.'

'It takes two hands to clap,' Jack said and yawned. If Mark talked for much longer, he'd be asleep – or dead. He needed to make a move. He pushed himself off the wall where he'd been leaning. 'I'm not interested in your justification, Maddox. Your activities have led to the deaths of many, plus you have blood directly on your hands.'

'She threatened my family.'

Jack laughed bitterly. 'So you pushed Greg Payne off a hillside?'

'Rather him than me . . . or Jem.'

'Well, I'm interested to see how a court responds to that justification. Meanwhile your wife is bleeding, Mark, dragged off somewhere by a psychopath, and you don't seem to care.'

'Of course I care,' Mark pleaded. 'I love her!'

'You let your shonky partner stab her and you did nothing, you coward.'

To Jack's shock, Maddox's chin trembled. Was the man about to cry? Jack could take him while he was distracted, even with tranquillisers slowing him down.

Do it now! Jack rushed at him. It all felt like it was happening in the slowest of motions. As he moved he dropped a shoulder in a perfect rugby tackle stance from his schooldays and, despite the confined space, his full weight met the unprepared Mark square in the solar plexus. It felt like he'd run into a stone wall but the wall dropped nonetheless. Jack knew from his rugby days that even the biggest of men could go down, feel winded and disoriented. This was Mark Maddox's state in the moment: breathless, groaning, rolling from side to side and desperately trying to suck in air.

With some luck, he might have also banged his head. Jack hoped so. Anything to slow him down. Jack didn't linger, because his mind was feeling as though it wanted to float. He resisted it, but there was no doubting the fizzing sensation that had begun at the back and base of his neck.

It wouldn't be long now.

Jack burst drunkenly onto the deck, half falling, half stumbling onto the sand. He was astonished to note, even through the dense darkness, that he couldn't see the shoreline. He could hear the sea, taste the sea, even sense the sea, but he could not actually see it. Where was it?

What a daft thought, he told himself.

It was Kate's voice back in his mind. *Hurry up, Jack. She won't think twice about killing her.*

Where? Where has she taken her?

Best guess? The boat.

In his mind he thought his gaze whipped along the full length of the beach, looking towards Jem's house, but in his heart he knew he was moving at half his normal speed.

What was he looking for again? A boat?

The dinghy, stupid, Kate reminded him.

He began to run.

Mark had regained his breath and his wits. He hauled himself to his feet, shaking off the dull arrival of a headache. Reaching for the back of his head, he felt a small lump and remembered the scuffle now, berating himself for letting Hawksworth take him by surprise. It was his own fault for believing he could explain to the detective that none of this was intentional on his part. He had to agree; it had sounded pathetic to try and argue the case, even to his own ears.

But the way they had all spoken down to him was not something he could tolerate or forgive. How Jem had behaved was the real shock. Her contempt cut the deepest, hurt the most, bled the worst. He had given her everything; she had wanted for nothing. His patients, his staff, even their friends would likely give a limb for a chance at living her life, with all the money she needed and three beautiful children, along with a man who had never strayed. What more could she want? Her lack of gratitude and respect was contemptible. And going by the way her attention had been riveted on the policeman and his on her, Mark was now convinced that she was the unfaithful one.

He hated this place as intensely as his wife loved it. He'd like to burn her beach house down in the same way she was burning their life down. Right now they should be finalising where in Europe they might spend the Australian winter. Jem had wanted to see a leg of the Tour de France and he wanted to do centre court at Wimbledon for a quarter final at least. They had talked about combining both and he'd almost completed a rough itinerary for them to consider.

Instead, did he now have to go on the run?

Would it mean shifting countries?

Staying in hiding?

This was all Hawksworth's fault. He heard a car and could see headlights and slow movement, as though someone was looking for a house number. But he wasn't going to wait around to see where it was stopping. He suspected he knew exactly where this car would pull in.

He was out of the sliding doors and, despite his pounding head, moving at speed down the beach within seconds.

Jack thought he was running. The sand was damp, so he should have been able to cross it faster than he was, but the figures ahead seemed to be getting further away. He couldn't actually see them – was following the light of their torch – but the light was jerking around. He presumed that was because Alannah was all but dragging Jem alongside her, probably threatening her constantly.

Trip, Jem. Fake it, he cast out, hoping she would somehow sense what he needed.

The sea sounded like it was everywhere and yet felt like it was nowhere. He fell into a small pool that had been left behind in the sand and took the opportunity to drop to his knees and scoop up as much saltwater as he could cup in hands. He drank. It was heinous but it did the trick; within a moment or two he began to retch. Jack knew the journey back to full alertness was long, but this was an essential step, provided he didn't keel over where he knelt and not wake up. He forced himself to swallow more seawater, retching again and again, as burning, salty liquid came coughing back up. He had barely eaten dinner. Even so, that little bit of food would help the tablets to work. He took a final two scoops, checking for Alannah's torch in the distance. He could see the small tunnel of light dancing around and realised what must be happening. Jem was being forced to help drag the dinghy out to sea, which was no doubt increasing her blood loss. Alannah was obviously planning to go it alone, without husband or Maddox.

Jem was dispensable.

Jack heard a sound and looked back over his shoulder to see a figure, dimly lit against the house, running towards him. Maddox. *Bugger!* But Jem's husband had no torch and was running blindly in the dark, yelling for Alannah. He rushed past Jack without seeing him to his right, crouched in the night.

Jack hoped his belly would hold and a moment after Maddox had loped past, he retched for the final time, the sound carried away by the wind. He hoped he had held on long enough.

32

Alannah's glassy stare looked demonic in the glow bouncing off the torch's narrow column of light, Jem thought.

'Pull, you stupid bitch!' Alannah screeched.

The going had become harder, not just because Jem was bleeding, but because it was boggy underfoot now and the marsh-like sand wanted to suck her deep with each footstep.

Jem let go of the dinghy, her breathing laboured. 'I can't do this any more. I've got no strength.'

The wind was beginning to whip up, tearing at their raised voices.

'Shall I stab you again?' her captor threatened.

'That won't improve your chances,' Jem said, impressed that she could sound so dry in the circumstances.

'Maybe not, but it may bring a momentary pleasure.'

Jem's weariness fused with her despair to spill anger. 'Listen, you psychopath. I have three children who are—'

'Tell someone who cares. All you hateful women at school, always moaning about your children and your husbands.' Alannah began to mimic their groans. 'I just can't get Phoebe to knuckle down to homework; someone's head will roll if Millie isn't made captain this season; I'll be damned if I allow Ruby to miss out again at having Mrs Chapman for English.' She gave a sneer. 'You're all so shallow and pointless. Be grateful you have those daughters and your rich husband to provide for you.'

Jem stayed on the offensive. Her physical education teacher had drilled it into her to always remain on attack. 'What about *your* rich husband? Where does he fit in?'

'Because of you and your policeman friend, I've had to leave him behind. He'll get over it.'

Jem heard a familiar voice yelling. 'Oh, look, here comes my husband. Why don't you have him instead?' she spat.

Alannah laughed. 'I could if I wanted him.'

Mark arrived, out of breath and wild-eyed. 'Alannah, what the hell?' He doubled over to cough before looking up at Jem. 'How are you doing?'

'Thanks for thinking of me second, Mark. Why don't you pull the dinghy like the good little donkey you are for your boss.'

'She's not my—'

Jem felt herself swaying, as though life had become blurred around the edges. 'Mark, I don't care any more.' She meant it in every way. It suddenly felt easy to let go. Die? Perhaps. Her children would never forgive her, though. Her thin cardigan was thick with her blood. Was the world swaying or was she? 'I don't give a toss about what she is to you . . . except that she was clearly important enough that you've chosen her over your children, your wife, the life we've built.'

'Jem,' he began with appeal in his voice.

'No, you're not the man I thought you were. You're weak and you're cowardly and I think you and your Lithuanian make a great pair. So here, take the rope and both of you just fuck off, will you?' Jem dropped to her knees. Her world was narrowing but she hadn't lost all her senses yet, and she heard Alannah's question.

'Is Hawksworth dealt with?'

'He took the tablets,' Mark confirmed.

So Jack's dead, Jem thought, feeling instantly bereft. *Must be my turn.*

Alannah continued. 'Good. Well, you know we can't leave her alive.'

'Alannah, I will kill you before I allow you to hurt Jem any further. She's coming with us. I need to get her to a hospital.' Jem had not heard Mark speak so firmly to Alannah previously.

She heard Alannah sigh. 'Then you haul her into the dinghy. We haven't got too far to go.'

You poor, trusting fool, Mark, Jem thought. *Do you really think she plans to let either of us live?* But she was beyond caring; she suspected life was slipping away anyway. She felt Mark haul her up and flop her into the dinghy. After that she didn't know anything.

Jack had followed the torchlight, as Mark had a minute or so before him, angling slowly towards the water, which he'd estimated to be more than a kilometre out from its previous shoreline. He knew he was well behind the women but he was not ready to show himself yet, not until he'd worked out Alannah's intentions.

The sea was close now. The roar of its waves and the salt in his hair spoke of its powerful presence. They'd be able to launch the dinghy soon and they'd be lost to him. He looked back over his shoulder; he could see another torch in the far distance. It had to be Matt, but he couldn't risk yelling to his colleague. Matt would see the same light he could.

He must press on alone, hopefully take them by surprise. He figured all the fight had gone out of Mark anyway. It had surely not been in his plans to risk his wife's life or be forced to go on the run. That left only Alannah for him to deal with if she attacked.

He nearly stumbled right up to them, only realising how close he was just in time. Hidden in the shadows, he noted that Jem looked to be unconscious in the dinghy and Mark was shouldering the rope. He was right, they'd be gone in moments.

They all heard Matt yell at the same moment.

Alannah immediately snapped off the torch. 'Was that Hawksworth?' Jack heard her ask.

'Couldn't be,' Mark replied nervously. 'He was all but out cold when I left him.' Jack admired the lie.

'So who the hell is that, then?'

'Search me,' Mark said.

'You idiot. He's probably set dogs on us. Right, you're a spineless bastard, Mark, but frankly I need you to help me right now. Unless we get to water in the next few minutes, it's over. This damn tide!'

'I need to see,' Mark grumbled and she obliged, turning on the torch again but standing in front of it to reduce how much could be seen from the beach.

Jack was glad she had no idea that he was within striking range.

'Let's run,' he heard Mark say and was taken by surprise to see his prey suddenly lurch forward with a low growl of effort. Alannah, despite the sickness that had her in its grip, also managed a trot. Jack knew he couldn't take them both – he had to hope Matt was giving chase – but he also knew he couldn't lose them in the dark. He staggered after them, the sand sucking at his feet. Within a few heartbeats, the water was around his ankles and he could hear Alannah's soft cheer; she was evidently excited that they would soon be gliding towards the cruiser that would whisk her out to sea.

'Just a little further, Mark, and we can start the motor,' she said.

The water was quickly past knee height and halfway up his thighs before he could plan. His mind was swimming with all the various possibilities and scenarios, but he couldn't ignore the feeling that his vision was tunnelling. Whatever tranquillisers had got through were now busily at work, aiming to put him to sleep.

He had to make his move now, whatever it was to be.

In the end it could be nothing more than relying on surprise; Alannah might be vicious but she was compromised and he had to count on that infection affecting her agility and power. Maybe it was Mark he should aim to take out first, because he still had his strength and wits.

'Help me in, Mark, quick!' he heard Alannah instruct and Mark gave a groan as he toppled Alannah into the dinghy like a newly landed fish.

The water was rising. Now hip deep. *Move*, Jack told himself but it was Alannah who made the decisive move as she found her feet.

'By the way, Mark, I don't need you any more.'

Jack heard a strange, throaty yell and then a gurgle. He blinked in the darkness and could just make out Mark staggering backward, clutching at his neck.

She's slashed his throat! Jack thought.

Mark fell forward, making only guttural noises.

Jack watched in horror as Alannah kicked the kneeling Maddox overboard before heaving on the ripcord of the dinghy's motor. It sprung to life and then died. He heard her curse as she dragged it with all her strength again. If it started, he would lose Jem.

He threw himself in the direction of the dinghy and could no longer feel the sand; they were out to sea.

'You're kidding me,' Alannah yelled with exasperation as she realised someone else had arrived to make her life difficult. 'I knew not to believe him,' she told Jack, almost conversationally, straightening from her position over the motor. Either she didn't feel threatened by him, or her crazed mind had removed her ability to feel fear.

'Too late, Alannah,' he said, trying to scramble into the dinghy and not doing a very good job of it. 'It was the dead tide that spoiled your party. You should have read up on it.'

He'd managed to get a knee onto the side of the rubber craft, making it list, but he'd overestimated what strength he had left to haul himself up.

'I'll tell you what, Hawksworth,' she said. 'I'll give you a choice.'

'What choice?' Jack felt stupid clinging to the side, unable to do much more than that for now. His arms no longer felt as though they belonged to him.

'Me or her?'

'What?' He sounded dim.

Jack watched Alannah bend down and, with some sort of inhuman strength, drag a groaning Jem over the side of the dinghy, her head soon beneath the water. She began to struggle.

'Choose, Jack. Stay with me and take your chances, or try to save Jem. Her husband's already dead, bleeding out into the ocean, so imagine those poor children without either parent.' She cackled a laugh that seemed to come from the depths of her new madness and without hesitation she slipped Jem fully into the water. 'Choose!' she commanded, reaching for the ripcord.

The choice wasn't hard. He let go.

Alannah gave her trademark sneer. 'Bye, Jack. Hope you both die trying to save each other.'

'Don't ever feel comfortable, Alannah,' he yelled. 'I'm coming for you.'

She laughed and gunned the motor again; this time it caught.

Before she could take off, Jack dove away from the boat in search of Jem, who was likely sinking fast in the dark. From beneath the water he heard the motor roar and felt the vibrations of the dinghy leaving him behind.

But he couldn't think on that now. He was kicking away, angling to where Jem had disappeared. In his heart he knew the water wasn't that deep, so he had to trust himself and find her.

In the shadows above the beach, Alex Petras couldn't see much but he heard a wail that could have come from a man or a woman. He could certainly hear the attempts to start the dinghy's engine, which suggested to him that the yell had not been Alannah. Then came a pause; could he make out a voice? He tried to siphon it into his mind but he knew he might be making it up now that the wind was stirring and the tide was coming back in.

And then he heard the familiar sound of the dinghy's motor catching and then the revs that told him it was speeding off into the distance.

Alannah or Mark? He was going with Alannah. His wife was a cat; she knew how to reinvent new lives.

This was it.

She was deserting him. He didn't know what Alannah had been up to, but she was certainly doing something so underhanded that she was prepared to run away from her life, her home . . . and him. Suddenly Alex didn't care if she could explain it, if she pleaded on bended knee, promised that she would wait for him before leaving.

No. This Lithuanian didn't forgive. And she knew men like that; she had been raised by a man like that.

'You don't mock me, Alannah. You don't treat me as some lesser being, orbiting around you like a moon to a sun. I am the sun . . . and *you* orbit *me*,' he muttered, needing to hear himself reach his desperate decision.

He paused and listened for the distant death of the dinghy's motor, gave it a couple of minutes and pulled out his mobile phone.

It felt like a lifetime before Jack exploded at the surface and although he initially felt refreshed from the cold shock of ducking under the sea, he soon realised that the drug was still determined to make him lose consciousness.

He was staying awake on pure willpower.

But he had to keep Jem safe.

He must not surrender.

She was limp in his arms but he was reassured that she coughed as he sucked in his own lungful of air after emerging. She was groaning but not making sense. He needed her to remain lifeless a little longer because if she began to struggle in shock or fear, he didn't think he'd be able to hold her.

They'd drifted further out than he'd realised and he needed to get his bearings. He knew he must not sink and take Jem with him. He rolled onto his back, Jem's chin cupped in his left palm, her body sagging against his.

'Jem?' He floated, forcing himself to concentrate on breathing slowly and regularly. 'Jem?' he tried again.

'Mmm?' It was a whimper.

'It's Jack.'

'My Jack,' she moaned.

'You're okay, I've got you and I'm not going to let you go.'

He swallowed. 'We're going to slowly head back to the beach. Just float, Jem. I'll do the rest.'

'Floating with you,' she murmured as though slipping off to sleep.

He knew not to complicate this moment with any more information. Besides, he only had room in his mind for gently kicking
them back to where he hoped Matt waited. In the distance he
heard the buzzing sound of the outboard motor cut to silence.
Either she'd made it to the cruiser or Alannah's dinghy had
capsized. He didn't hold out hope for the latter, much as he
wished that might be the case.

No, Alannah had got away from him. She thought she'd won.
But all she was doing was holding off the inevitable.

He or someone like him would hunt her down.

He or someone like him would find her and make sure she paid
for all the lives she'd taken or ruined.

'Jack?'

'I'm here,' he said, soothing her as he paddled backwards, not
rushing, not exerting himself too much. He had no idea how much
further they yet had to swim.

'Where's Mark?'

'I don't know,' he answered as truthfully as he dared.

'Am I dying? I need to know Mark's there for the children. My
babies.'

Where was she finding the willpower to be this alert?

'I won't let you die. Help is nearby,' he said, not letting her
hear how much of that was simple hope rather than fact. 'Be still,
Jem, let me swim.'

Mercifully, she fell silent.

He paddled on in the dark until he felt a bump. They'd hit the
shore and he'd never been more grateful to feel land.

There was a shout, light bobbing around them and strong
hands suddenly under his arms, hauling him backwards. He felt
the scrape of the sand against his skin as his shirt rode up. It was the
most reassuring sensation he could imagine.

'Jack! Mate!'

He opened his eyes. 'Matt?'

'You're okay,' his friend said calmly, and Jack thought he may have inwardly smiled at Matt using the same reassuring words that he had used only minutes earlier himself.

'Look after Jem. Tell me she's breathing.'

Jem was dragged from between his legs. He felt her absence keenly.

'Jem! Jem!' Matt yelled, trying to win a response.

And then Jack heard the words he needed to hear.

'She's breathing,' Matt said. 'Let me get ambulances down here.'

'Matt. They made me swallow a lot of tranquillisers.'

'A lot of what, mate?' Matt asked as he waited for the emergency call to be answered.

It seemed Jack couldn't form his words very well any more. 'Sleeping tablets.' He wasn't sure that came out right either. 'Pump my stomach.' He sighed and let his head rest against the sand, turning to look towards the cruiser. As he let go completely, Jack saw an explosive flash on the horizon and a booming sound. He closed his eyes against the blinding light illuminating his surroundings.

Alex Petras had held off pressing the button when he suddenly noticed a man running towards the shoreline. Soon he was able to make out two other figures rolling up on the beach and then being hauled away from the water.

He didn't imagine the smaller of them was Alannah, and then he knew it couldn't be when he heard the newcomer yelling Jem's name.

'So be it,' he whispered and pressed the button he'd been told to press.

Alex Petras watched his beloved cruiser explode spectacularly against the horizon and with it, the wife he'd considered magnificent since the day he'd met her.

33

When he woke, Jack was in the now-familiar space of a hospital bed, wearing yet another hospital gown. All hospital wards seemed to look and smell the same. His first thought was that he should ask someone to take a photo for Joan, for her private amusement.

A nurse with shiny blonde hair and a warm smile came into view. 'Hello, Jack. I'm Margo.'

He grinned. 'Nice way to wake up.' His voice was croaky and his throat ached.

She chuckled. 'You'll probably need a drink. Here, let me help,' she said, lifting his shoulders so he could sip from a plastic beaker that had a straw. The water felt like a balm as he swallowed. 'You're at the Royal Adelaide, if you're wondering,' she said. 'And we performed a gastric suction, which might explain why your throat feels scratchy or painful.'

'As in stomach pump?'

She nodded. 'I'm not going to ask why you swallowed so many pills. Tranquillisers, apparently?'

'I promise you, I didn't choose to,' he replied.

'Oh?' she said, full of concern. 'The medical team believe they got most of it emptied in time. The rest simply relaxed your muscles and ultimately gave you a good night's sleep.'

Jack gave a painful laugh. 'I think the aim was to make it a permanent one.'

She frowned. 'That's awful. I'm so sorry. Don't say any more, but I think that explains why there's a detective waiting outside. Enough?'

He nodded. 'Thank you. Er, the woman I was with – how is she?'

There was a knock at the door and Matt walked in, beaming. 'There you are,' he said. 'Thought you'd never wake.'

The nurse helped Jack to sit up fully. 'I'll let you be. Call me if you need me.'

He nodded and looked to Matt expectantly. He knew he must look nervous. 'Jemima?'

Matt lifted a hand. 'She's going to be okay. Nasty bump on her head, concussed, and she lost a lot of blood but she's already been in surgery to repair the wound. The blade miraculously missed the artery and nerves, but it has led to partial lung collapse. She'll be in for a while recovering.'

'And Mark Maddox?'

'Not such good news, I'm afraid. He washed up an hour or so after you both.'

Jack nodded. He'd presumed as much. 'Drowning or . . .?'

Matt shrugged. 'He's with our good friend, Dr Alison Moore, who will confirm soon enough but I suspect the slash across his throat will tell its tale.'

'Good.'

'Good?' Matt frowned.

'I want to hang a murder charge around Alannah Petras's neck on top of everything else. I witnessed her do it. I know it was dark and I was compromised by the sedatives, but I saw her, Matt.

I watched Maddox stagger backwards in the shallows, clutching his neck, probably taking his last breath.'

'We haven't told his wife yet.'

'Are you leaving that to me?'

'Only if you want to. She'll be formally interviewed when she's well enough.'

Jack sighed. 'No, I'll tell her. What about the explosion?'

'The guys are out there now, looking for a body.'

'I'm only interested in one.'

'Put it this way: the cruiser's a wreck and there was no one to be rescued on board. And if she managed to get out first, they'll find her floating around if the treacherous seas out that way don't deal with her.' He shook his head. 'Did you know it was Alannah Petras running the syndicate?'

Jack sighed. 'Not at all. I was paying more attention to the husband. Where is he, by the way?'

'We're still looking for him. I wondered if we should be looking for two sets of remains from that cruiser.'

Jack shook his head. 'Unless he found another way to get to the boat, it's my understanding he wasn't on the cruiser. I also don't think he knew what his wife was up to. I think he's one of the casualties, like Jem. Innocent and yet their lives have been profoundly affected.' He shook his head sadly.

'We'll need a full debrief as soon as you're up for it.'

'Of course.' Jack nodded. 'Tomorrow for sure.'

'Looks like you'll get your joint op, Jack. Major Crimes wants this racket closed down, all the infrastructure and supply chain pinpointed and dealt with. Your boss is delighted, apparently.'

He found a smile. 'Thanks for everything, Matt.'

'I should have got to you earlier.'

'If you had, you'd have been given similar treatment. As it worked out, you were the cavalry arriving just at the right moment.'

Matt's look suggested that Jack was being generous and Jack wanted to assure him he was being genuine, but the detective was already lifting a hand in farewell.

'Rest up, mate. We'll catch up later today if you feel brighter. I've left some fresh clothes for you – hope you don't mind me ransacking your suitcase.'

Jack raised a hand in thanks. He still felt pathetically weak but as soon as Matt had gone, he called Margo again and asked if he might see Jem Maddox.

'She's awake but not breathing easily. Leave it a few hours. We need that lung re-inflated fully.'

Jack nodded in understanding, though he was disappointed.

That evening, Jack, now out of his gown and dressed in his own clothes again, was permitted to see Jem. He looked around her room's door before tapping gently on it.

She was awake, propped up in the hospital bed. She smiled. 'Jack,' she said, sounding weak, but her tone was warm and welcoming. 'I've been longing to see you. They said you were going to be fine.'

He moved to the bed. 'I am,' he reassured her. 'And you're going to fully recover too.'

'So they tell me.' She grinned. 'Not that they're telling me much. I hope you'll be more forthcoming.'

He took a silent breath. 'I'll tell you what I know. Do you remember much?'

'I remember that whore stabbing me,' she said.

He grinned. 'I see your colourful vocabulary when it comes to Alannah Petras is intact. *She* isn't though.'

'What do you mean?' Jem frowned.

'I watched her boat blow up while lying on that beach with you all but unconscious.'

Jem's mouth dropped opened in surprise. 'She's dead?'

Jack shrugged. 'I wish I could say for sure. But it's highly likely and, if not, then she'll be quickly found and taken into custody. I can't imagine what happened, though. They were bragging about how she was such a good sailor.'

There was a momentary silence as he watched Jem's forehead crinkle in thought before she cut him a sly look. 'I wouldn't put it past Alex Petras to be behind this.'

That surprised Jack. 'I didn't think he was involved. Do you know—'

'I don't believe he was either. But what I do know is that despite his sophistication, he's a proud Lithuanian man who came up the hard way. I got the firm impression he was not going to stand by and be humiliated by his wife without taking some action.'

Before Jack could say more, she lifted a hand and made him wait while she took some shallow breaths.

'I think it's plausible,' she continued, struggling slightly with her breathing now, 'that his suspicions could have led him to take certain steps.' The oxygen mask she wore kept filling with vapour.

He shouldn't allow her to exert herself but he needed to hear this. 'You think this was a husband's revenge?'

'Could be, even though for the wrong reason. He left me in no doubt that he would make her pay a price only her kind under-stood – whatever that meant.'

'I guess we'll find out soon enough. Alex is now on the Major Crimes radar between here and the UK, and there's probably a European team involved too.'

'I don't remember much else. I do remember drowning, or at least feeling as though I was. But you found me, didn't you?'

Jack nodded.

'In the dark, even full of sleeping tablets, you found me.'

'Well, I felt I must because you still owe me seven dollars.'

She burst into laughter and then had a coughing fit.

He waited, feeling guilty for causing it. Nurse Margo arrived.

'Really, Mr Hawksworth? I just told you she has a collapsed lung.' It was a mild admonishment, but her tone was warm. 'You have thirty seconds before you need to let her rest. You too.' Margo left.

Jack's gaze met Jem's and their expressions became more serious.

'Mark's dead, isn't he?'

Jack hesitated only for a heartbeat before he squeezed her hand and nodded. 'I intend to make sure she's held responsible for his murder.'

Jem's chin quivered and he watched her swallow hard for a couple of seconds. 'Of course, I'm sad, and I need some time to process it, but it's probably for the best.'

He waited, a query in his expression.

'I mean, imagine the circus we'd be facing. Mark was guilty, I think I've finally accepted that. I don't think he was a born killer or a bad man in his heart but he was weak and led by that woman down a path I would never have thought possible.'

'Yes. I've confirmed that he did participate directly in killing someone.'

Tears leaked over her ears and rolled around her oxygen mask. 'The Mark I married was all about preserving life. A doctor, for crying out loud. I think it's probably a good thing that he doesn't have to publicly answer for his sins, for his sake as much as mine and the children's.'

'That's very rational of you, Jem.'

'It's the drugs,' she quipped. 'Let's see how I am in a few days. Who knows how I'll adjust.'

Jack nodded. 'Well, there are three children to adjust for.'

'Yes, they are the loves of my life. We'll have to learn how to live without their dad. They worshipped him, you know. He was always the fun one.'

'You're fun too,' Jack said.

She smiled sadly. 'When do you leave?'

He was glad she didn't ask whether he was leaving. 'Er, I imagine in a couple of days. I have to report back to my chief at Scotland Yard. She holds the purse strings tight.'

'She?'

He gave a small gust of a laugh. 'Yep. Terrifying woman.'

Jem raised a brow. 'Sounds as though you like her.'

'I feel as though I'm answering to my mother.' Jack lifted his eyes to the ceiling.

That made her chuckle. 'I think you love women, Jack,' she said.

He held up his hands in surrender. 'Guilty.'

'Just not one in particular?'

'I'm not good for one in particular,' he answered quickly. 'I'd let them down. This job . . . it's a killer for relationships.'

Jem sighed. 'Well, if you ever need a home away from home down under, there's a beach house at Wallaroo that will always make you welcome.'

He smiled and placed a hand on top of hers. 'It was lovely, Jem.'

They both knew to what he referred.

'I still don't regret it,' she admitted with a warm smile, despite her panting breaths. 'But I need to put that to the back of my mind now. I think I'm going to need to put on some armour for the way ahead.'

'The police will do their best to shield you.'

She pulled her mask away from her face and covered his hand that was holding hers. 'Go, Jack. I'm awful at goodbyes and I just know there're a lot of tears ahead.'

He stood, bent down and cupped her face with his other hand.

'Thank you for saving my life in several ways,' she said.

'You're welcome,' he whispered and then kissed her gently.

When he drew back a little she murmured, 'You promised not to let me go.'

He didn't think she'd remember that. He covered his heart with his hand. 'You're safe in here.'

'Don't forget me.'

'I promise,' he whispered and kissed her once more, tasting her salty tears before he tiptoed gently out of the room and her life.

34

LONDON, MAY 2008

Jack found a small table for two, just slightly beyond the canopy of the café so that they could lap up the morning sunshine. The approach of summer seemed to have put a bounce in the step of most people out and about. Soon enough, his eye caught a flash of red and it was Kate hurrying towards him.

She arrived in a flurry of perfume, giving Jack a big hug and kisses to each of his cheeks. 'Jack, you look wonderfully tanned,' she said, looking around for somewhere to place her large handbag.

Jack smiled. 'And you're a sight for sore eyes. How are you?'

'Stressed,' she admitted, tucking the bag between her ankles. 'I came up from the tube and got lost in Waterloo Station and then went out the wrong entrance. Why are we here again?'

'I just thought we'd try somewhere different.'

'Lower Marsh?' Her tone was all puzzlement.

'I'm betting this area will be hot in the next decade. You know South Bank, once known as north Lambeth, was mostly marshland?'

She laughed. 'If you start giving me a history of the place, I'm going to spit in your face. I didn't come all this way for one of your boring lectures.'

'You know, a lot of women find my incredible knowledge quite fascinating,' he replied dryly.

'Well, not this one.' She reached for the menu.

'Anyway, Kate, I mean it, you look great,' he said. 'Life's taken a lovely turn, I hope?'

She shrugged. 'I'm still on a good roll at the moment,' she said. 'Teacher treats me too well. I worry I'm going to let him down.'

'You won't,' Jack assured her. 'Because you're aware of how toxic this job can be sometimes, so you're going to do everything in your power to put him at the top of the list regularly.'

Her smile warmed him.

'So, breakfast?' he asked.

'Why not in the middle of this strange little street?' She laughed.

'Do you know, in Australia there are loads of fabulous street cafés and everyone's out and drinking, eating – even mid-morning – having coffee and cakes.'

'Yes, Jack, quite obviously because it's sunny.'

'It's sunny here.'

'I'm betting it's the same temperature right now as we go into summer as it is there, going into winter.' She shivered slightly into her pillar-box-coloured coat.

'That's true. Mark my words though, Kate, this road will be teeming with people in years to come, which is why I think I'm going to buy a shop here.'

Her mouth opened as she took in his words. 'What?'

'You heard me.'

'But what are you selling?'

He laughed at her. 'Not me. I'm going to rent it to a café and it's going to serve brilliant coffee for starters, and fabulous fresh food. I think this little street is going to become a magnet at lunchtimes in particular, but I can also see bars booming on summery nights.'

She looked at him in that affectionate way she sometimes did that unnerved him, and he was glad to be interrupted by the arrival of a waitress with a pierced nose, wearing Doc Martens.

He gestured for Kate to go first. She ordered shakshuka and then he gave the waitress a bright smile. 'I can't resist the simple poached eggs on toast, please. And I'll have a flat white too.'

The young woman gave him a grin. 'Nice tan.'

'I've been on an Australian beach.'

'Oh, I'm going to Australia next year. Saving up now.'

'Good for you. First time?'

She nodded.

'You'll never want to return.' He winked.

'Hope so! Let me get your orders in.'

Kate refocused on Jack. 'So where do you plan to live now you're back?'

He sighed. 'Not sure yet. But I'm all right at Lauren's flat for three months while I find somewhere.'

Kate's expression darkened. 'Does that not bring back bad memories, of you know—?'

'Well, I think when I finally venture out onto that rooftop – and I will – then I'll confront whatever darkness awaits then. Luckily the flat itself has only good memories for me.'

'Jack.' Kate reached to hold his hand and he didn't pull away. Her gaze held his with affection. 'Let me be with you when you do.'

He nodded. 'Okay. We'll wait for a summery evening in June and we'll share a bottle of something delicious. I'll cook. Bring the teacher.'

'No, just us, I think. We need to deal with and banish those demons.'

He gave a nod to say she was right.

She changed the subject. 'What did Rowland say?'

Jack smiled. 'Oh, she's happy at how it all went down, and we got what we needed to initiate a joint op. The clinics in Vilnius and Belgrade will be shut down, and the courier service will face a lot of hard questions and the equivalent of an enema by the time they're finished with.' He nodded. 'I can certainly sleep better at night knowing we got some justice for Amelia Peters.'

Kate nodded. 'You did well, Jack. What's next, workwise?'

'Back to the grind. I'm returning full time. Rowland says she'll brief me next week on a couple of potential ops that might have international threads. She's sounding pretty upbeat after our first outing together.'

Their breakfasts arrived.

'Well, I suppose she can slap you on the back and say at least this time you didn't have an affair while on your Australian case.'

He raised his flat white. 'What does she know?' he remarked, keeping his tone dry.

Kate laughed, frowning slightly as she tried to work out whether his remark had another meaning.

'Here's cheers, Kate,' Jack said, and at her grin added, 'That's how they say it down under.'

'Cheers, Jack.'

They clinked cups. 'Nice to be back,' he said, already regretting that it wasn't an Aussie coffee. *Here's to you, Jem,* he cast out silently.

ACKNOWLEDGEMENTS

The idea for this story came out of my own experience with IVF back in 1990, which delivered twin sons into our lives. (They're turning 32 as this book comes out!) What an amazing area of science it is . . . when it works. We were fortunate on our second try but I saw the desperation of other women who had experienced so many disappointing rounds of this technology without the happy news we received. It was heartbreaking to be in that waiting room sometimes, because the tension we all brought formed a third presence around each couple. As a woman wanting to be a mother, with that ticking clock sounding loudly and feeling like you may never hold your own child – well, it can create such sorrow. I handled myself calmly and kept my fears private and still my closest friend didn't want to tell me she was pregnant for the second time – obviously picking up on the angst – and people began to stop talking about babies around me. Any form of trying for a baby can add strain but IVF, which is expensive and invasive, with lots of tests and frankly humiliating situations, can take an enormous toll on a couple. I wanted to bring all that emotional darkness into this story.

Bringing Jack Hawksworth to Australia has been a project that required a lot of help. So many people have allowed me to rummage through their expertise and send out messages for help with how to get around a particular situation or storytelling obstacle. They've each been brilliantly patient and generous.

I'll start with a nod to former detectives Mick Symons in Australia and Mike Warburton from the UK, who both became involved early and made it possible for Jack to arrive in Australia in a credible way. Also early to the story was the lovely Verity Bell, an embryologist at one of the leading fertility clinics in Australia who gave birth to Archer during the course of researching this book. She didn't blink once with surprise at my crazy questions or the black-market storyline, and she patiently taught me how a lab would work behind the scenes and about working with human material.

Dr Karen Heath, Senior Specialist Forensic Pathologist at the SA Forensic Science Centre, was such a blessing to meet. Her delight at showing me the ropes in the pathology lab was infectious and I'm sure I created the pathologist in this tale with Karen's lovely sense of humour and steady presence in mind. Having already written *The Orphans*, I was no stranger to the mortuary and so we could talk and roam freely. I am so grateful for her brilliant guidance and generosity, including her recollection of a real case she had worked on from which she permitted me to dissect the bit I needed. Hearing her recount it was like a firework going off in my mind for how to take my story forward.

Busy author and masterclasser Tricia Stringer (whose top-selling books many of you will have enjoyed) took time out from her manuscript to spend a day with me at Wallaroo. She couldn't resist it, I don't think, as Wallaroo is her hometown and she wanted to be sure I got the setting just right, including the public holiday beach-goers and the storm.

Michael Simms from Flinders Ports was a great help at just the right time, as I had no understanding of how the port works and the comings and goings of the grain ships. Thank you also to all the fishing people who chimed in to help explain a dead tide – or slack/dodge tide as we call it here – including another master-classer, Anne Cavalieros.

Thanks also to Phil Rogers, one of the founders of Wendy's Supa Sundaes who I worked with in the early 1980s and learned plenty from about franchising and BOGOFs!

The gorgeous little Mediterranean cottage where Jack stays is real. It's owned by artist Rosie Begg and is called Athelney Cottage. The day she kindly showed me around and served me fresh lemonade in her 'opinion garden', I met Percy the parrot, every bit as colourful and chatty as described.

I'm grateful to Pip Klimentou, who is always quietly in the background of my books, giving me a valuable opinion as a reader as to how the story is ticking along.

Thanks to the Penguin Random House team, all so eager to get another 'Jack' onto the shelves, and a special mention to the wonderful duo in Melbourne who take good care of me through the whole editorial process – my publisher, Ali Watts, and my editor, Amanda Martin. I have taken a couple of editorial liberties: the World Egg Bank came online in 2007 but I held it off a year or so because it suited my purposes, and the reference to Café Mia at Wallaroo is out by a couple of years.

Thanks to my patient, affectionate Ian, who puts up with me in so many ways, especially my never-want-to-go-to-sleep attitude. Will and Jack, thanks for the endless laughter; here's another one you'll never read because it doesn't have swords and guns or screaming warriors on horseback.

Fx

BOOK CLUB NOTES

1. It doesn't take long for Jack to be drawn in to a new case. What personal attributes of his make him an ideal detective?
2. Why do you think the Yorke Peninsula is the perfect setting for the crime syndicate to conduct their illegal activities?
3. Do you think doctors have an obligation to assist patients desperate to conceive at all costs?
4. Issues of infertility and assisted pregnancy affect a huge number of people worldwide. Do you agree with Jem that if there's a black-market demand for reproductive material, it's reasonable for someone to fill that gap?
5. Jack is warned against getting romantically involved with another woman linked to his cases. Why do you think he always seems to be drawn into these relationships?
6. Jack tells Jem that desperate people are often willing to break the law. Do you think these people are to blame for the consequences of their actions?
7. If you're helping someone to achieve a lifelong dream, it's hardly a crime. Discuss.

8. Did Nikki and Greg get what they 'deserved'?
9. Do you think Jem's infidelity was understandable and justifiable under the circumstances? Discuss.
10. Do your feelings about the criminal acts in *Dead Tide* change when you consider them from the perspective of the women selling their eggs versus Alannah's perspective?

ALSO BY FIONA McINTOSH

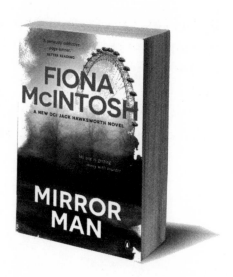

'A seriously addictive page-turner.'
Better Reading

Police are baffled by several deaths, each unique and bizarre in their own way – and shockingly brutal. Scotland Yard sends in its crack DCI, the enigmatic Jack Hawksworth, who wastes no time in setting up Operation Mirror. His chief wants him to dismiss any plausibility of a serial killer before the media gets on the trail.

With his best investigative team around him, Jack resorts to some unconventional methods to disprove or find a link between the gruesome deaths. One involves a notorious serial killer from his past, and the other, a smart and seductive young journalist who'll do anything to catch her big break.

Discovering he's following the footsteps of a vigilante and in a race against time, Jack will do everything it takes to stop another killing – but at what personal cost for those he holds nearest and dearest?

A heart-stopping new thriller that questions whether one life is worth more than another.

Want more DCI Jack Hawksworth?

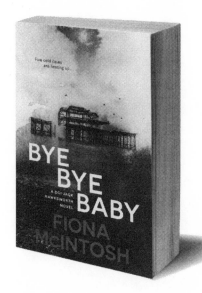 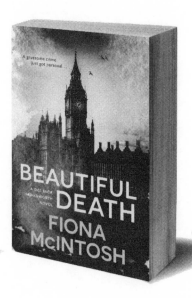

Two heart-stopping thrillers from a powerhouse Australian author

Discover a
new favourite

Visit **penguin.com.au/readmore**